The Synchronicity War Part 2

By Dietmar Arthur Wehr

Author's comment: If you haven't read Part 1, you'll find Part 2 confusing. Therefore I don't recommend buying Part 2 until you've read Part 1. Part 1 ended with a cliffhanger (start of a space battle) on the last page. Some readers don't like that while other readers expect it. Part 2 does not end with the opening stages of a space battle but does drop a bombshell in terms of new information that could lead to more battles. It's not a cliffhanger in the conventional sense of the word. If you like cliffhangers, don't say I didn't warn you. When you read this novel, you'll come across this word 'shi', pronounced 'sheye'. It's not a typo. It's my attempt to add a new word to the English language and it is a short way of saying she/he/it for a 3rd person reference to an entity whose gender is not known. If you like it, feel free to use it. If you happen to be an H. Beam Piper fan, check out my website.

Cast of Characters:

Human:

Senior Space Force Officers:

Admiral Sam Howard, Chief of Space Operations

Rear Admiral Sepp Dietrich, Chief of Personnel

Rear Admiral Sergei Kutuzov, Chief of Logistics

Base Commanders:

Sen. Cmdr. Korolev

Sen. Cmdr. DeChastelaine

Squadron Leaders:

Sen. Cmdr. Torres

Sen. Cmdr. Yakamura

Cmdr. Shiloh

Cmdr. Cabrera

Cmdr. Dejanus

Cmdr. LaRoche

Cmdr. Mbutu

Cmdr. Bettencourt

Cmdr. Rolen

Other Space Force Officers:

Cmdr. Adams (Exploration Frigate Commander)

Cmdr. Caru (Exploration Frigate Commander)

Lt. Cmdr. Angela Johansen (XO, FE 344)

Lt. Cmdr. Amanda Kelly (Team Leader, Strategic Planning Group)

Lt. Cmdr. Svetlana Chenko (XO, FE 344)

Lt. Cmdr. Brad Falkenberg (Deputy CAG, CVL Defiant)

Lt. Cmdr. Michaels (2nd Officer, FE 344)

Lt. Cmdr. Farnsworth (2nd Officer, FE 344)

Sen. Lt. Sykes (Weapons Officer, FE 344)

Lt. Cabrera (Officer, Reforger)

Lt. Rodriguez (Astrogator, CVL Defiant)

Lt. Verlander (Helm Officer, FE 344)

Other Characters:

Trevor (Avalon Colony survivor)

Tracey Bellevue (Bio-hazard facility Admin. Assist.)

A.I.s: (In Alphabetical Order)

Amazon

Blue Max

Bulldog

Casanova

Cyrano

Firefox

Gunslinger

Hammer

Hunter

Iceman

Jester

Rainman

Shooter

Skywalker

Terminator

Thunderbird

Titan

Tumbleweed

Undertaker

Vandal

Glossary of Terms:

CSO   Chief of Space Operations

CAG   Commander, Autonomous Group

TF   Task Force

KPS   Kilometers Per Second

Klicks   slang expression for kilometers

A.U.   Astronomical Unit equal to the average distance between the Earth   and its Sun.

A.I.   Artificial Intelligence

SL   Squadron Leader

C.O.   Commanding Officer

X.O.   Executive Officer

W.O.   Weapons Officer

E.O.   Engineering Officer

Chapter 19 (From Part 1) Time To Roll The Dice

That extra speed enabled Defiant to emerge 22 hours later into the Green4 star system, 3 hours ahead of the bogey. Time enough to deploy recon drones and a pair of jump detection equipped fighters around each of the two gas giants, while remaining more or less equidistant from both. The drones would passively search for reflected sunlight contacts, while the fighters would attempt to pinpoint the exact location – and number – of ships emerging from Jumpspace. Deploying only two fighters near each gas giant was a calculated risk. A single fighter's detection gear could only cover a limited area, and if the bogey happened to emerge from Jumpspace outside that detection range, the equipment wouldn't see them. The space around each gas giant was so large that even if Shiloh had deployed all of his fighters among the two gas giants, it still wouldn't have guaranteed detection, AND recovering his fighters from both planets would prevent Defiant from being able to jump ahead of the bogey to their next destination. The time to the bogey's expected arrival in Green4 came and went. Because Defiant's distance from either gas giant was measured in millions of kilometers, ordinary light speed communication by tight beam laser was too slow. The only way for a sentry fighter to get word to Defiant quickly enough was to launch a message drone. It microjumped to the area where Defiant drifted, and less than a minute after the arrival time, the ship picked up a text message from a message drone sent from one of the fighters monitoring the gas giant that Shiloh had designated as Green4A.

[55 ships detected emerging from Jumpspace. No visual contact yet]

The text message was followed by a data stream, containing the precise coordinates. Shiloh was stunned. Fifty-five ships! This was no recon mission. It was clearly a major attack. The lack of reflected sunlight contact was very bad news. Without some idea of where at least one of those ships was, the recon drones would have no way of knowing where to point their laser rangefinders and therefore couldn't determine where those ships were heading, or how fast they were going. Using active radar scanning would tip the aliens off to the fact that humans were aware of their presence. At least the lack of contact reports of any kind from Green4B suggested – but did not prove – that the aliens were not intending to use it to refuel. Whatever else Defiant might do, it had to refuel from Green4B as quickly as possible, otherwise its options would be severely limited.

Shiloh was about to order Tanaka to microjump the ship to Green4B to refuel, when the Bridge faded from his field of vision, and he saw himself standing in front of Admiral Howard. But this vision was different. Instead of the usual crystal clear image, this image was blurry, almost as if he were looking at the scene through distorted lens. Howard's voice sounded strange too. The pitch was not quite right, and the words didn't seem to be synchronized with Howard's mouth.

"I congratulate you on your decision to remain at the star system where you detected the enemy fleet. If you had continued to track them, you would not have been able to detect the much larger force that was following in their wake, and we wouldn't have been able to gather enough strength in time to stop it. For your brilliant strategy, I'm promoting you to the next higher level of rank."

As Shiloh listened to Howard's words, which were said in a calm, almost monotone voice, he noticed that Howard was repeatedly jabbing his pointed right hand in Shiloh's direction and the expression on Howard's face did not look particularly pleased. If he'd been watching this scene without any sound at all, he would have interpreted Howard's body language as indicating anger. The dissonance between the visual and auditory impressions was striking.

What is going on, he asked himself. He looked around to see if anyone was looking at him. No one was. Tanaka was conning the ship from the Helm Station again. Falkenberg was down in the Hangar Bay supervising the fighters and their support teams. There was something not right about this vision, but Shiloh couldn't put his finger on it, and he didn't have time to analyze it further. Decisions had to be made. The fighter at Green4A would be following previously given instructions and maneuvering his drones under the assumption that the fleet would head for the nearest gas giant. Even if the drones didn't detect any reflected sunlight from any of the alien ships before they reached the gas giant, those ships would agitate the planet's atmosphere enough with friction and turbulence that their presence would be detected if the drones were close enough. The drones would then attempt to pinpoint the enemy's exact locations and vectors using the range finding lasers as the ships emerged from the planet's atmosphere. In theory it should work, but it had never been tried before, so no one really knew.

What Shiloh had to decide now was whether Defiant would proceed to Green4B, as planned, to refuel so that it could boost a high speed message drone, and also beat the enemy fleet to their next destination. But if the vision were correct about an even larger follow-on fleet, then staying right where they were would be the best option. On the other hand, if the vision were wrong somehow, then perhaps there was a third option that he hadn't considered yet. His visions so far had all involved a change of plans from what he otherwise would have done. If he applied that parameter to this situation, he would proceed to refuel at Green4B. The mere fact that he was having some kind of vision to begin with, strongly suggested that refueling to boost to the next destination was NOT the optimal strategy, but staying in Green4 and doing nothing just didn't sit well with him. The only other strategy he could think of was to attack that fleet before they could jump away. He needed to confer with his senior officers and to his mind that included Iceman as well. Falkenberg could join the discussion by video intercom, as could Iceman. Tanaka and Rodriguez could step over to his station as they had done before.

When all four were present, either electronically or physically, Shiloh said, "Valkyrie has detected 55 ships emerging from Jumpspace near Green4A. He'll try to pick up their precise locations and vectors as they refuel. I now have to decide what our response will be. For reasons that I do not want to go into now, I'm having doubts that our plan to refuel at Green4B and then jump ahead of the enemy fleet is still our best option. I want to hear assessments from all of you on an alternative strategy to attack the fleet here in this system, and if you have a completely different idea, I'd like to hear that too. You first, Brad."

The Deputy CAG took a deep breath and said, "Well, we have 19 fighters still aboard and we have enough attack drones to give them five each, which should be plenty, but the challenge will be to get targeting lasers on each enemy ship, unless we want to use active scanning. Without one or the other, the attack drones won't know where to aim. Right now, Valkyrie doesn't have enough recon drones to target more than half a dozen ships at one time, assuming that they can find their targets to begin with. If they were in fact intending to refuel at Green4A, then the ideal time to hit them would be while they're still deep in the gas giant's atmosphere. Their ability to see us will be limited, but we'd have to get drones and/or fighters in close to be able to precisely locate their ships from the wakes they leave behind as they plow through the gas."

Shiloh nodded and turned from the video screen with Falkenberg's image to his Astrogator.

"Can we get our fighters that close before the enemy re-emerges from the atmosphere, Astrogator?"

"There's no way to know for certain. We don't have any data on how fast they can refuel, Sir. But if their refueling time is similar to ours, then the answer is yes. Defiant would have to jump as close as possible to the opposite side of the gas giant from where the enemy fleet is, so that their jump detection gear wouldn't pick us up. We'd launch our fighters, which would accelerate at maximum in order to make a close, high speed pass, and then fire their attack drones when they had visual contact with the enemy ships."

He was about to say more when Tanaka interrupted. "What if they keep some of their fleet in orbit to stand guard while the rest refuel? If I were their fleet commander, I wouldn't risk exactly that kind of ambush by refueling all ships at the same time. How would we deal with that?"

There was a short pause, and then Iceman spoke. "We launch our fighters and use the gas giant's atmosphere against them. Our recon drones will monitor their position and speed as they refuel. The fighters will enter the atmosphere far enough away that the enemy won't spot them. When the distance has dropped to less than 100 kilometers, our fighters will swing around so that they're behind the alien ships still refueling and then move back up to the edge of the atmosphere. The enemy won't be looking down at the planet for signs of human activity. They'll be watching the space around and above them. When all 55 ships have finished refueling, our recon drones will relay that data to our fighters, which will emerge from the atmosphere, stay behind the enemy fleet at close range and launch attack drones. At precisely that same time, our recon drones will go to active scanning, use that data to triangulate each enemy ship's exact position, and relay that data to our attack drones. The enemy will react to the radar scanning from above and fire at our recon drones while our attack drones get within one kilometer of their targets. They can then use their own radars for terminal guidance, and that fraction of a second before impact won't be enough time for the enemy to retarget their lasers."

No one said anything for almost five seconds.

Finally Shiloh said, "That plan will require split second coordination to work, but other than that, I don't see any flaws with it. Does anyone else?"

The responses were uniformly 'no'.

"Iceman, have you calculated all of the vectors and signal times needed to make this work?" asked Shiloh.

"Ah, roger that, CAG," was the immediate response.

Shiloh took note of the fact that Iceman referred to him as the CAG and not as the ship's CO.

"Very good. In that case, I want Iceman to coordinate this attack. He will issue the necessary orders to Defiant's Helm and all the fighters involved, as well as monitor the attack as it proceeds, and react as needed if things don't go as planned. Iceman, make sure you keep the Defiant's tactical computer updated on all vector changes and transmissions. XO? You'll monitor but not interfere with Iceman's Helm directives."

As Tanaka nodded, Shiloh continued, "Iceman, how soon do we need to begin the attack plan?"

"The longer we wait, the less chance of pulling this off, CAG. I would not recommend waiting more than five more minutes. The sooner, the better."

"Understood. Does anyone have any questions?" No one spoke up. "In that case, return to your stations."

When everyone was back at their assigned stations, Shiloh took a deep breath. *I hope I'm doing the right thing*, he thought to himself.

"Okay, Iceman. The mission objectives are the total destruction of that alien fleet. With that as your goal, you have my permission to commence that attack plan."

"I won't let you down, CAG."

Almost immediately, Defiant's engines started pushing her onto a new vector. The main display showed a countdown to a microjump. Shiloh's station started showing increased activity in the Hangar Bay as the support teams began to load more attack drones onto each fighter. The moment that Shiloh had been dreading, being in command of a major battle WITHOUT any reliable vision to guide him, was now upon him. If this plan went wrong, and he survived the battle, Howard would be within his rights to court martial Shiloh.

It was time to roll the dice.

PART 2

Chapter 1 There's Never A Pickle Around When You Need One

The Bridge was very quiet now with only the occasional murmur as someone responded to another part of the ship. Everyone was speaking in hushed voices. Iceman and his strike force had launched almost half an hour ago after Defiant made a very careful microjump to a point, two light minutes from Green4A. That was the position that Iceman had determined would avoid detection by the alien ships IF they were on the exact opposite side of the gas giant as expected. Since they hadn't undergone an attack by 55 alien ships, it appeared that the ship's microjump had not been detected. It hadn't taken long to re-establish com laser link to the two sentry fighters whose drones were still trying to passively detect the enemy ships. There was a limit to how long they could wait for passive detection before Iceman's Strike Force entered the gas giant's atmosphere and lost contact with the ship. Iceman had already determined, and Shiloh had approved the idea, that it was pointless for the Strike Force to wander around inside the gas giant's atmosphere if they didn't know where the enemy ships were, so the recon drones would resort to active scanning at the last possible moment while the Strike Force could still receive data. Active scanning would alert the enemy to a Human presence and they might abort their refueling operation. Iceman would have to adjust the attack plans quickly enough to compensate for any enemy action. This was the kind of lightning fast tactical ability that only an Artificial Intelligence could display. It occurred to Shiloh that A.I.s were way too valuable as tactical commanders to continue to be used solely as fighter pilots. He was certain that it'd be tough to convince Admiral Howard of that. But something told him that A.I.s would be the key to winning this war.

A glance at the chronometer showed that they had less than 14 minutes left for passive detection by the drones. Shiloh looked over to Tanaka, who was conning the ship from the Helm Station. She must have felt his stare because she turned around to look at him and gave him a slight nod of acknowledgement. He nodded back and smiled. He'd been lucky to have good people serving under him and Sumi Tanaka was no exception. What she lacked in experience, she made up for with focus and energy. He wondered how long the Space Force would let him keep her as his Executive Officer. Probably not long. That was the price COs paid when the Space Force was expanding as fast as it was now. Good people got shoved upward as fast as possible. Shiloh suddenly realized that he was hungry. He was about to contact the Galley to order sandwiches and coffee brought up to the Bridge for everyone when his Command Station console beeped softly. Another text message from Valkyrie had arrived.

[Turbulence wakes detected in upper atmosphere. Minimum of 14 enemy vessels are now refueling. 31 enemy vessels detected in low orbit via silhouette against planetary background. 10 vessels unaccounted for. Recon drones being maneuvered closer. Trajectory data follows. End message.]

Before Shiloh could ask, the Astrogator was already anticipating his next order.

"We're relaying the drones' sensor data to the Strike Force now, Commander." Shiloh nodded his approval. So, Iceman would get his critical data in time. He would project the enemy fleet's orbit and time his Strike Force's interception so that his 19 fighters would sneak up on them from below and behind. It sounded good but Shiloh couldn't help wondering where those missing 10 bogeys were. He checked the incoming sensor data parameters. The drones were far enough away from the gas giant that it was possible, and even easy, to observe the wakes caused by ships plowing through the upper atmosphere. However the attempt to detect the black silhouette of ships in low orbit against the planet's lighter background was pushing the optical sensors to their limits. It could very well be that the other 10 bogeys were in fact also in low orbit but the drones' sensors hadn't detected them yet. The other possibility was that the missing ships were also refueling but were underneath the 14 ships whose wakes were visible. The turbulence wakes of the ships higher up might be hiding the wakes from the ships below.

With the distance between Defiant and the Strike Force, Shiloh knew that they wouldn't get Iceman's acknowledgement of the drone data for another 4 minutes and reports of the actual attack and its results would take two minutes to reach the ship too. Shiloh looked at the chronometer again. 8 minutes 20 seconds until communication with the Strike Force would be lost due to atmospheric distortion of the laser beam, and approximately another 23 minutes until the Strike Force was in position to attack. Add another 2 minutes for news of the attack results to reach Defiant and with over half an hour to go with nothing to do but sit and wait, Shiloh called the Galley and ordered the food and coffee for the Bridge crew.

With just under twenty minutes left before Defiant expected to hear the attack results from the Strike Force, Shiloh decided that this was as good a time as any to practice one of the Academy leadership techniques called 'Leadership by walking around'. He remembered his Instructor telling the class that Julius Caesar had allegedly practiced this technique one night before a major battle. He had walked around his army's camp, going from campfire to campfire, with a pickle in his hand that he had used to graphically enhance the telling of several obscene jokes that made his soldiers roar with laughter. *There's never a pickle around when you need one*, Shiloh thought to himself with amusement. He got up and strolled around the Bridge, chatting for a few seconds with each of the Bridge personnel in a low voice that made each conversation seem more personal and confidential. He found that the mood of the Bridge crew was good. No one exhibited excessive fear and a couple of them were downright eager for the ship to exchange laser volleys with the enemy. Shiloh only smiled when he heard that. Defiant class light carriers were not meant to slug it out toe-to-toe with the enemy although they could defend themselves if they had to. Her most powerful weapon was the squadron of fighters that could pack a hell of a punch and launch that punch at long ranges. When he had finished speaking with all of the enlisted Bridge crew and was about to chat with the Astrogator, the tactical display pinged for attention. A quick glance at the chronometer showed that there was still almost 8 minutes left before the planned interception of the enemy force by Iceman's group. Looking back at the tactical display, Shiloh saw another text message from Valkyrie scroll across the bottom of the view screen.

[Enemy ships in orbit have begun active scanning. All recon drones have been detected and destroyed by enemy laser fire. Contact with enemy force lost. No contact with Strike Force. Sentry fighters have not been detected. Request instructions. End message]

Shiloh heard someone say 'damn' and then realized that he had said it.

He rushed over to his Command Station, switched the open channel to Valkyrie over to his implanted com device frequency and said. "CAG to Valkyrie. Maintain current vector. More instructions to follow." With the message recorded, he touched the Command Screen button to transmit it in a short laser microburst. As he sat back down in the chair, he gestured for the XO and Astrogator to step over to his Station. Both of them had grim expressions on their faces. Shiloh tried to project an expression of serene confidence as he looked at them.

"So they obviously know now that they've been under surveillance. I doubt very much that they'll still be in the same orbit by the time the Strike Force gets there. If either of you have any suggestions now's the time to offer them."

There was silence for about five seconds.

"Can the sentry fighters launch more recon drones?" asked Tanaka.

Shiloh shook his head. "Both of them launched all their recon drones in order to make the initial contact. They still have a few message drones and one attack drone, both totally unsuited for regaining contact."

After a short pause, the Astrogator said, "If our number one priority now is to figure out where this enemy force is headed next, I think I may have a way to do it."

"You're right. That IS our number one priority at the moment. Go on," said Shiloh.

The Astrogator took a deep breath before continuing. "Well … assuming that they intend to penetrate deeper into our inhabited space, there are only two paths they can follow from here that make any kind of sense and a limited number of star systems that have gas giants that they can reach from Green4. So we calculate the trajectories that this enemy force would have to take to reach those systems and, we deploy a net of recon drones across both trajectories. The drones will use intermittent active scanning with evasive maneuvers between scans. That will reduce the chance of being hit by laser fire unless the enemy ships get close. To prevent that, the drones will be accelerating in the same general direction as the enemy fleet. In fact, I would even recommend having more than one net of drones. If the first net is destroyed, the second net can continue to track them and if necessary a third net as well. If we manage it right, the third net can last until the enemy actually jumps away."

"Which won't do us any good," said Tanaka immediately.

"Why not?" asked Shiloh.

"If I were the alien commander and I saw wave after wave of enemy recon drones retreating in front of me while bombarding me with radar, it'd be obvious to me that the enemy was trying to figure out where I intended to jump to next. So this is what I would do. I'd change the heading to aim at a completely neutral destination, jump a couple of light years out of this star system, and then reorient the fleet to my real destination."

The Astrogator nodded.

"Yes, I agree. That would be the logical thing to do," he said.

"I'm still waiting for a USEFUL suggestion," said Shiloh. Neither of the other two responded. Shiloh leaned back and looked at the ceiling for a few seconds, then said.

"Let's assume that they weren't finished refueling when they detected and destroyed the sentry fighters' recon drones. They could have easily changed direction and resumed refueling. If that's the case, then we may have enough time for Iceman's Strike Force to be redirected to engage in a stern chase and maybe catch up to them before they break out past the gravity zone boundary."

The XO and the Astrogator looked at each other and then back at Shiloh.

"What if the enemy fleet scans behind them as they accelerate away from Green4A?" asked Tanaka.

"Would you give yourself away by doing that after going to all the trouble of destroying the enemy's recon drones in order to disrupt enemy surveillance efforts?" asked Shiloh.

"Well, when you put it that way, I'd have to say no, but the Strike Force has to find them in order to be able to attack them. How do we do that?"

"Good ques—" Before he could finish his response, Shiloh's vision went black and his hearing went silent, all for about a second and a half. The blackness was replaced with a familiar scene of him standing in front of Admiral Howard's desk. This time he could hear Howard clearly.

"Dammit, Shiloh, I don't know whether to court martial you or give you a medal! Dangling one light carrier as bait in front of 55 alien ships? Yes, you got away with it and took out enough enemy ships to enable us to stop the rest of them from attacking the Avalon Colony. But I have to seriously question your judgment, especially in light of Commander Tanaka's report about your momentary paralysis, or whatever that was, just before you announced your plan to put Defiant in harm's way. What the Hell is wrong with you, Shiloh? You've got 30 seconds to convince me that I shouldn't relieve you of your command and have you certified as a Class A nutcase!"

The scene dissolved and he was back on Defiant's Bridge with both the XO and Astrogator looking at him strangely.

"Are you okay, Sir? You seemed to enter some kind of hypnotic state or something for a few seconds. You didn't respond to our voices, and you didn't even notice when I waved my hand in front of your face a couple of times."

Tanaka's voice conveyed serious concern. Shiloh knew that she would report this incident when they got back, but there was nothing he could do about that.

"I'm fine now, XO. I guess I must have blacked out there but I'm fine now. Let's get our attention back to the situation. You asked me how Iceman's Strike Force could find the enemy fleet in a stern chase without using active scanning. I know how we can do it. Astro, use my console to add the trajectories that the enemy would need to follow if they wanted to jump to the next logical refueling stop for both paths, up on the tactical display."

The Astrogator waited a couple of seconds before responding. It didn't take long for two red lines to appear on the display. Both started at the same point in orbit around the Green4A gas giant with the lines gradually diverging as they got further away from the planet. Shiloh nodded his approval.

"Okay, now add the gravity zone and highlight Defiant's current position for me."

When that was done, Shiloh got up from his chair and walked calmly over to the large display.

As he pointed to it, he said, "Here's what we do. Defiant will microjump to this area, just outside the gravity zone and more or less between the two trajectories. When we arrive, we launch recon drones that will head back down towards Green4A, and then we follow them in. They'll be actively scanning as they go. When the Strike Force is back in contact with us, they'll be ordered to accelerate along a vector that's between these two trajectories. The enemy will detect our emergence from jump space, but since they're still in the gravity zone, they can't microjump close to us. They can't ignore us either, since we'll be coming down their throats as it were. So I'm counting on them coming straight for us in the belief that they can destroy us and then re-align themselves to their next destination. So, while they move towards Defiant this way"—he pointed with his right hand index finger—"our recon drones will eventually detect them and we relay that data to the Strike Force. At the same time, we turn around and make it look like we're running for our lives. Meanwhile, the Strike Force is catching up due to their superior acceleration. If Defiant plays its cards right, the enemy will be too focused on us to watch their backs, and the Strike Force will launch their attack drones from the rear at close range. All we have to do is stay far enough away from them to make their laser fire ineffective."

There was a stunned silence. Finally, the XO spoke. "Well, Sir, if you'd like my opinion—"

Shiloh cut her off. "Not this time, Sumi. I've made up my mind. We're doing this, end of discussion. I want you to get a message drone ready to send back to Bradley Base. I'll record a message to be added to our data logs. Martin, I want you to get busy figuring the instructions for the Strike Force, the microjump, and drone deployment, in that order. Got that?"

The Astrogator took a deep breath and exhaled slowly.

"Yes, Sir. I'll have something for you to review and approve in a few minutes."

"Very good."

After the Astrogator returned to his station, Tanaka leaned closer to Shiloh and said in an apologetic voice. "I'm sorry, Sir, but I'm going to have to mention your hypnotic trance in my After-Action report."

Shiloh was seriously tempted to try to talk her out of it but decided that THAT too was part of the vision and all of the clear visions had worked out well so far.

"I have no problem with that, Sumi. You do what you think is best and we'll let the chips fall where they may."

While he waited for the new tactical plan, Shiloh recorded his own text message to Admiral Howard.

[*55 enemy ships detected in Green4. Our attempted ambush during enemy refueling was not successful and contact was lost. Defiant is now attempting to regain contact with enemy force in order to confirm my suspicion that enemy fleet plans to attack our Avalon Colony. I strongly recommend deploying all available forces there. In light of this incursion, Defiant will proceed to the Avalon Colony system, as soon as possible, to assist with its defense. I have a strong hunch about this, Admiral. Message ends.*]

Satisfied with his message, he sent it to the message drone and ordered it launched. When Shiloh reviewed the plan a few minutes later, he was pleased to see that the Astrogator had taken into consideration a new location for Valkyrie and Skywalker, so that Defiant and the Strike Force would both be within line-of-sight of the sentries, during the lead up to the battle. The two fighters could then relay information back and forth between the ship and the fighter group without fear of the enemy listening in. After approving the new orders for the Strike Force and sentry fighters, he ordered them sent to Valkyrie right away. Then they could be relayed to Iceman's group as soon as communications between the Strike Force and sentries was re-established. The planned deployment of Defiant's recon drones needed tweaking and Shiloh, Tanaka and the Astrogator were still working on that when a new text message from Valkyrie was received.

[Contact re-established with Strike Force. New orders transmitted and acknowledged. Valkyrie and Skywalker are now moving to new relay positions. Message relayed from Iceman as follows: A very gutsy plan, CAG! You should have been a fighter pilot like us! Message ends.]

Shiloh laughed and then noticed that no one else was laughing. *They're afraid this plan won't work. I'd be afraid too if I hadn't had the vision.* Out loud he said, "I guess that means that he likes the plan."

Neither Tanaka nor the Astrogator responded. Shiloh brought their focus back to the recon deployment and within a couple more minutes, they had a plan that he liked. With the ship ready for the microjump, Shiloh activated ship-wide intercom.

"This is Shiloh. We've lost contact with the enemy fleet. Unless we get it back, we won't know whether this fleet intends to attack the Avalon Colony or take a different route deeper into our Space. Re-establishing contact will be risky. In a moment, we'll microjump to a point that the enemy can't help but detect. We'll then move towards where we think they'll be coming from. The idea is to get them focused on us, so that our recon drones can pinpoint their location and our Strike Force will then try to catch up and attack them by surprise from their rear. It's not my intention to let the enemy get close enough to be a serious threat but we have to be prepared for that possibility. A message drone with a warning about this enemy fleet is on its way back to Bradley Base. Regardless of what happens here, HQ will be warned and can make preparations. After we microjump, we'll stay at Battle Stations. I'm confident that we'll make this work. Stay sharp and we'll get through this. That is all." With that out of the way, he nodded to Tanaka, who was once again manning the Helm station. As Defiant got ready to microjump, it notified Valkyrie of the planned jump.

Chapter 2 It Was an Honor Fighting Beside You

The jump itself was routine. Shiloh listened to the Bridge chatter and watched the tactical display. The first wave of recon drones was on its way towards the gas giant and Defiant was swinging around to face that direction too. The plan assumed a worst-case scenario whereby the enemy fleet began accelerating away from Green4 as soon as it detected and destroyed the recon drones above it. Given approximately 30 minutes head start, and accelerating at the same 110Gs that all enemy vessels had demonstrated so far, the first wave of recon drones should detect the fleet after 62 1/2 minutes. At that point, Defiant would still be 11.8 million km away from the fleet with plenty of time to decelerate and avoid coming within laser range. Iceman's Strike Force would then fire their attack drones 25 minutes later at very close range, based on active scanning data from follow on waves of recon drones. The attack drones would then streak in at 800Gs. Defiant would still be almost 4 million kilometers away at that point. It looked good in theory.

The reality was quite different. With just under 6 minutes left to go before the earliest estimated time of enemy detection, the ping from the tactical display interrupted Shiloh's chat with Tanaka. The display zoomed in to the first wave of recon drones. Ahead of them appeared 55 red dots. Shiloh had just enough time to read the sidebar data, indicating that the enemy ships were accelerating at 155Gs, not the anticipated 110Gs. The range to Defiant was now 9.58 million km away instead of 11.8 million km, before all six drones in the first wave disappeared from the tactical display, having been clearly destroyed by enemy laser fire. Shiloh didn't know if they still had a margin of safety. The worst-case scenario projected a minimum distance of 6.68 million km by the time that the Strike Fleet's attack drones were expected to intercept their targets. Shiloh knew from his vision that not all of the enemy ships would be destroyed and that extra distance would give Defiant time to veer off at 206Gs, which would keep the ship out of effective laser fire range. But that safety margin might be gone now. Not only was the fleet 2.22 million km closer, it was also going much faster than predicted. Shiloh decided to not wait for the Astrogator's assessment of the new situation.

"Helm! Rotate us 180 degrees and go to maximum thrust! Astro, send that contact data and our intention to begin deceleration to Iceman via relay by Valkyrie!" The XO and Astrogator both acknowledged their orders. Shiloh prepared to record a voice message to Iceman.

"CAG to Iceman. Do whatever you have to do to hit the enemy at the earliest possible moment. As soon as you launch your attack birds, veer off. We'll try to send you targeting data as long as we can. Your attack drones will have to rely on their internal radar guidance for their final seconds before interception." he paused then added, "Good luck. Message ends." By the time he transmitted the message to the sentry fighters, one of the small screens at his Command Station received data sent by the Astrogator. The news was not good. It would take almost two minutes for the com laser pulses carrying the initial contact data to reach the sentry fighters and another 95 seconds for them to send it to the strike Force. That delay in notifying the Strike Force meant that by the time they reacted, they would not be able to get within striking distance of the enemy fleet before the enemy fleet got within striking distance of Defiant. And if Defiant veered off in time to avoid exchanging laser fire with the enemy, the Strike Force would lose the crucial last minute targeting data updates that would enable their attack drones to get close enough to their targets to hit them using the drones' internal radar for last minute course corrections. If Defiant sent the targeting data directly to the Strike Force, the enemy would detect it and wonder to whom Defiant was transmitting, with a high probability of scanning behind them and detecting the Strike Force.

The Astrogator had also calculated when Defiant would have to veer off in order to have any kind of decent chance of avoiding destruction. The answer was 15 minutes before the Strike Force launched its attack drones. Shiloh got up and quickly strode over to the Weapons Station.

"If we veer off 15 minutes early, what does that do to attack drone hit probability?" asked Shiloh to the Weapon's Officer.

"One moment, Sir." A few seconds later came his answer. "The problem is that if the attack drones use their terminal guidance radar too soon, the enemy will have time to fire back at them. If they wait until they're within 1-2 seconds of interception before turning on their radars, the drones will very likely be too far away to be able to correct their trajectories enough to hit the targets. Either way I calculate it, we'll be lucky to hit even one of them, Sir."

Shiloh thanked him and returned to his station. This made no sense. The vision said that SOME of the enemy ships were destroyed or at least damaged enough to prevent them from taking part in the attack on the Avalon Colony and it also revealed that Defiant survived the battle, but Shiloh couldn't see how he could make both those outcomes happen. The solution to the problem arrived 3 minutes later in a message from Iceman, relayed via Valkyrie.

[Iceman to CAG. Strike Force went to max acceleration as soon as destruction of 1st wave of recon drones detected by reflected light from laser hits. Our revised attack profile data follows. I think we can still hurt them even if you veer off 15 minutes early. If you launch a message drone on a wide angle, you should be able to use it to relay targeting data from the recon drones direct to us. Don't risk the ship unnecessarily on our account, CAG. We know we're expendable. It was an honor fighting beside you. Message ends]

Shiloh's relief that Iceman had found a way to make the vision come true was mixed with the sudden fear and sadness over the possibility that Iceman and the others might not survive the battle. The vision hadn't mentioned their fates. By accelerating sooner, the Strike Force would catch up to the enemy fleet quickly enough so that the attack drones would have a decent chance of hitting their targets. However that meant that the fighters would inevitably overrun the surviving enemy ships and would then have to run a gauntlet of laser fire, which they couldn't return. When he could trust his voice not to betray his emotions, Shiloh called the Astrogator over to his station.

"Martin, we're going to veer off 15 minutes early and we need to launch staggered waves of recon drones so that there'll be some still scanning as long as possible. Launch one…no, two message drones so that they'll be able to send com laser pulses to the Strike Force without the enemy seeing them. Make sure all the recon drones know where to send their targeting data for the relay. Do you understand what I want?"

"Yes, Sir!"

When the Astrogator returned to his station and Shiloh was alone with his thoughts once more, he took a deep breath. Iceman's brilliant idea of setting up a new and much closer relay would improve the chances of multiple hits tremendously. His 19 fighters were carrying 95 attack drones armed with 500-kiloton fission warheads. A direct hit would vaporize half the target instantly and even a near miss would seriously damage it. If they could destroy or disable most of the enemy fleet, some of the fighters would make it through the gauntlet and come out the other side. But even as he had the thought, he remembered what Howard had said in the vision. The defending forces had barely been able to stop the surviving enemy ships from attacking the colony. That did not sound like an attack by a handful of survivors but rather an attack by the majority of that fleet. That worried him. Then, the other shoe dropped. Another text message from Iceman, delivered via Valkyrie.

[*Analysis of your data reveals that enemy fleet opened fire on recon 1st wave far faster than can be accounted for by the response time of living organisms. Those ships are controlled by A.I.s too, CAG. Adjust your plans accordingly. Message ends*]

Shiloh felt the hair on the back of his neck stand up. He'd seen enough by now to appreciate how much more effective A.I. controlled fighters were compared to human pilots. The prospect that Iceman and his boys had to survive against a superior number of combat starships under A.I. control with virtually instantaneous reaction times made him sick to his stomach. It was only with a supreme effort of will that he prevented his stomach from heaving right then and there. His body's reaction made him realize that he would feel the loss of Iceman and his fellow pilots just as deeply as if they were human. What difference did it make if a sentient being had a brain composed of quantum circuits instead of organic cells? If anyone asked him that question, his answer would be an unequivocal "none!" There'd be time to mourn Iceman and the others later. Right now he had a vision to fulfill. He stepped over to the Helm station.

"You saw Iceman's bombshell?" he asked Tanaka.

"Yes, Sir."

Her voice was somber too. She clearly understood the implications for the Strike Force.

"Good. As soon as we start getting hit with enemy radar, I want the ship to start and maintain a random and fast evasion pattern. I don't want us on the same vector and acceleration for more than a second at a time. Make sure it's completely random. I don't want those alien A.I.s figuring out that we're using some kind of predictable algorithm and anticipating our next moves. You can overload the inertial dampeners if you feel that's necessary. Warn the crew now so they have time to get ready. Can you do that, Sumi?"

There was no hesitation whatsoever in her reply. "Yes, Sir. I can do that."

"Good! Very good!"

He smiled at her and gave her a pat on the shoulder as he turned away. Looking at the chronometer, he realized that the XO didn't have a lot of time to get that evasion program ready. Tanaka wasted no time in notifying the crew.

"Intercom…shipwide…Attention all hands, this is the XO. Prepare for evasive maneuvers that may overload the inertial dampeners. Stow all loose gear and strap yourselves in. This will be a rough ride and it may commence without any further warning. Tanaka clear."

As he sat back down in his Command Chair, Shiloh strapped himself in securely, while he watched the tactical display. The time indicator showing how much time was left before the range to the enemy dropped to zero, was itself dropping fast. The enemy fleet was moving towards Defiant at a rate of over 9,000 kilometers per second and Defiant, even though she was frantically trying to slow down, was still moving towards the enemy at a rate of just under 2,000 kilometers per second. When the time to zero range dropped to 15 minutes, the range would be down to 5,199,385 km. During those final 15 minutes, Defiant would move sideways in addition to the forward motion it would still have. When the 15 minutes dropped to zero, the ship would be 812,000 km off to the side of the enemy's projected trajectory. With laser fire traveling at the speed of light, it would take any laser beam fired at Defiant, just under 3 seconds to reach her. The enemy's problem was in figuring out where Defiant would be by the time the laser pulse got there. A random evasion program should in theory prevent the ship from being hit although if it had to dodge 55 laser pulses, then there was still some risk of getting hit by a lucky shot. They just had to accept that risk and pray.

While he was still thinking of the probabilities of random hits with long-range laser fire, the timer dropped to 15 minutes and Tanaka initiated the planned course change. Defiant spun 90 degrees and resumed acceleration in that new direction. The ship still hadn't been hit by enemy radar nor did Shiloh expect it to at this range. Even when they would detect enemy radar beams hitting the ship, the range would have to drop considerably more in order for the radar beam to hit the ship and bounce back to the enemy fleet with enough residual energy to be detected. That was the drawback to using radar to detect hostile starships. They could see you long before you could see them. Right now the only thing the enemy was seeing was the recon drones that were using their radars to track the fleet's progress. Three waves of recon drones had already been destroyed when they got close enough for accurate laser fire. There were two more waves already on their way and Defiant would deploy at least two more before the range dropped to the minimum.

Shiloh queried the tactical computer for time left before the Strike Force launched their attack drones, based on data sent back by Iceman. Fourteen minutes. They seemed to take forever. Enemy radar began hitting Defiant's hull when the range had dropped to 2.25 million km. As planned, the ship began evasive maneuvers and some of them were indeed violent enough to momentarily overload the inertial dampeners. Shiloh was certain that by the time the maneuvering was over, there were going to be at least one or two cases of whiplash among the crew, if not more.

When the time to attack drone launch reached zero, Shiloh looked at the tactical display but saw nothing for a couple of seconds. Then the display pinged for attention and Shiloh saw a new cluster of blue dots emerging from the green dots representing the Strike Force. The blue dots accelerated at almost 800Gs towards the enemy fleet while the Strike Force, having shot its bolt, now veered off at 400Gs on a new course that was 90 degrees from Defiant's new vector. From Defiant's vantage point, the ship had veered off sideways and Iceman's fighters had veered off vertically, which would allow both of them to maintain contact via the relay drones without the enemy fleet intercepting the com laser pulses.

With less than a minute now until the attack drones reached their targets, this was the time that worried Shiloh the most. If, for whatever reason, the enemy A.I.s decided to use their radars to look behind them, they would see the attack drones coming and have plenty of time to fire at them. But firing at them didn't guarantee hitting them. Attack drones were designed to be difficult to detect accurately and were small enough to make a direct hit difficult too. With 44 seconds left to impact, Shiloh heard the Weapons Officer yell out.

"They're scanning behind them!" At almost the same time, roughly a third of the blue dots disappeared. 63 attack drones were still functional. Now the question was…would the enemy laser batteries be recharged fast enough to fire again before drone impact?

"They've stopped scanning!" yelled the Weapons Officer. Shiloh nodded. No sense in helping the enemy drones more than was absolutely necessary. He was sure that they would resume scanning as soon as their lasers were recharged. With 9 seconds left to impact, the enemy must have fired its lasers again because 51 blue dots vanished leaving 12 attack drones still on track. Now that it was obvious that there wasn't enough time left for the enemy to fire again before being intercepted, the attack drones turned their radars on and headed straight for their targets. Time to impact hit zero and 12 red dots in the enemy fleet also disappeared. That left 43 ships. Shiloh was disappointed that they didn't get more of them but now his main concern was Iceman's fighters. Even though they were piling on velocity at 400Gs, their forward momentum would overtake the enemy fleet so quickly that the Strike Force would be less than 7,500 km from the enemy fleet at their closest approach. This was virtually point blank range, for laser fire.

Shiloh clenched his fist and banged his chair's armrest when one of Iceman's fighters disappeared from the display. Turning his head he said,

"Weapons! Pick an enemy target and fire all lasers! I know our hit probability at this range is shit but maybe we'll get lucky! Keep firing until I tell you to stop!"

"Commencing fire now!" replied the officer.

Shiloh turned his attention back to the tactical display and became aware that the Bridge had turned dead quiet. Everyone was watching Iceman and his boys trying to get through the deadly gauntlet. Even the Weapons Officer was omitting his usual cadence regarding his lasers' recharge cycle. A quick glance at the sidebar data on the Strike Force showed Shiloh that

Iceman was still operational. CFP0055 call sign Undertaker had a red status indicator of LOS. Loss Of Signal. So far he was the only one. As the minutes slowly ticked by, Shiloh was amazed that he wasn't seeing more LOS indicators. He expected the fighters to be slaughtered quickly but they weren't. Eventually there was another LOS and then a few minutes later another and another.

Shiloh jumped with surprise when the Weapons Officer said, "Sir, we're still firing and our lasers are beginning to overheat. Shall I continue firing?"

A quick look at the range showed that they were now almost one point five million km away from the enemy.

"Cease fire. Did we hit anything?" asked Shiloh.

"Yes, Sir. I believe that we took out one enemy ship."

Shiloh looked at the display and nodded. The enemy fleet now had 42 ships still intact and maneuvering so they had got one of them. It wasn't much, but it was something. Defiant had earned her first combat star. He made a mental note to congratulate the Weapons Officer later, but right now he was more interested in the Strike Force. They were now down to 14. The range was 256,000+ km and rising fast. Shiloh's ear implant crackled with an incoming voice message.

"Iceman to CAG. It appears that the enemy fleet has ceased firing at us and they're not pursuing us. I guess that means those of us who are left, will live to fight another day, eh CAG? What are your orders now?"

The rest of the Bridge crew must have heard it over their implants as well because the whole Bridge erupted with cheers. Shiloh knew that Iceman could hear those cheers so he waited until they died down.

"Glad to hear that you and most of your team made it through okay, Iceman. You'll have to explain to me how you managed that when you're back aboard. Defiant will be proceeding to Green4A to refuel. Rendezvous with us as soon as you can. You can also tell your boys that I'm proud of all of you. We won't forget the ones we lost today."

"Ah, roger that, CAG. I personally will miss Undertaker a lot. He had a wicked sense of humor, especially when it came to human sexual practices. I have to confess; I still don't know what all the fuss is about. But that's a topic for another time. It's going to take us a while to return to the gas giant. We'll be low on fuel by then too but we'll make it okay. Don't hesitate to call me if you wanna chat, CAG. Iceman clear."

Shiloh smiled and relaxed. The battle was over. What was left of the enemy fleet was beyond radar range now but that didn't matter. They were going much too fast to swing around and attack Defiant even if they wanted to and Shiloh was convinced they didn't really want to. Their mission was to attack the Avalon Colony. He'd check with the Astrogator before he finished his duty shift but he'd be surprised if the fleet's last recorded vector was on a direct course for a jump into the path leading to the Avalon Colony. He wouldn't be so obvious about it if he were in charge of that fleet and he doubted that the aliens would be that obvious either.

The ship would stay at Battle Stations a little while longer as a precaution and then it would get back to a normal routine. He'd then head for his quarters for a badly needed 7 hours of sleep. By then the ship would be in orbit and refueled. They'd pick up Iceman and his survivors as well as Valkyrie and Skywalker, then microjump over to Green4B to pick up the two sentries there too. Now that he knew where the enemy fleet was headed, there was plenty of time to do all that and still get there first and he suspected the Space Force would need all the fighters he could bring with him when that enemy fleet finally did arrive.

Chapter 3 You Can Count On Us

When he awoke eight hours later, Shiloh was pleased to find that Defiant was fully fuelled, had recovered the fighters at Green4A and was now approaching Green4B. The time-saving slingshot maneuver around that gas giant that would put them on a course for their first jump and also rendezvous with the two sentry fighters at the same time. As he ate his breakfast in the Officers' Mess, one of his junior lieutenants walked over to his table and said.

"Excuse me, Sir. Could I ask you a question?" Shiloh nodded.

"Are we going to try to outguess where they're headed next, Sir?"

Shiloh shook his head. "No, and the reasons why are these. First, they have too much of a head start. Even if we picked the right system by chance, they might very well have refueled and jumped again by the time we got there. Second, our chances of picking the right system are small. They could have picked one of a dozen possible destinations. Third, we've used up almost all our recon and attack drones so even if we did regain contact, we'd have to get dangerously close to track them. And finally, I don't want Defiant to follow them to Avalon Colony… or some other inhabited system only to arrive low on weapons and fuel, when getting there early and resupplying might make the difference between a victory and a defeat."

The Lieutenant nodded and said. "Thank you, Sir. I guess the scuttlebutt is right."

"What scuttlebutt would that be, Lieutenant?"

The officer, having now realized he said too much, got red in the face. "Well ah…the rumors are that Admiral Howard and the Senior Brass consider you to be a ah…. tactical genius…Sir."

Now what do you say to that? thought Shiloh. *Do I declare myself to be a mere mortal and damage their confidence in me, or do I let them think I'm better than I really am?*

He laughed and said, "Well, I don't think I'm THAT good. There was SOME luck involved you know."

The Lieutenant laughed too, thanked him again and walked away. As he took another sip of his coffee, Shiloh pursued that line of thought. *So how good am I really? I didn't come up with the battle plan. The vision gave that to me and Iceman saved our asses with his message drone relay idea. On the other hand, I didn't screw it up. Quite a few brilliant strategists have screwed up at one time or another.* All things considered, he decided he hadn't done a bad job. He still didn't relish the idea of maybe having to play a key role in a battle that would determine Humanity's fate, when he had no control over his visions. And speaking of which, he wondered how his next encounter with Howard would turn out when the Old Man learned about his visions.

When he got to the Bridge, he relieved the officer in command and settled down for what he expected to be a routine duty shift. Neither the XO nor the Astrogator was on duty. The latter had left his response to Shiloh's request for a planned route to Nimitz Base that would also allow Defiant to send one of the new extended range message drones, using a single jump back to Omaha Base at the earliest possible time. When he called up the route on the display, he nodded in approval. The Nimitz Base/Avalon Colony star system was in what Shiloh thought of as Path A but a direct line from Green4 back to the Omaha Base star system led through the other 'river' of stars that was thought of as Path B. Even with the new extended range message drones, a single jump to Sol from here would require Defiant to boost to a very high speed before launching the drone, and thereby use up quite a bit of its fuel supply, but the Astrogator had come up with a good plan. After picking up the sentry fighters at Green4B, Defiant would set course for the Omaha Base system and boost to 55% of light speed. After launching the message drone, she would then make a relatively minor course change and jump to Yellow12, which just happened to have a gas giant. After refueling there, the ship would then make a very long jump across the empty void that separated Paths A and B and arrive at Orange21, refuel again and then one more jump to the Nimitz Base/Avalon Colony system. Along the way the ship would set two records, one for the quickest jump between two star systems and one for the longest jump in terms of distance travelled between two star systems. It would also alert the Quick Reaction Task Force at Omaha Base to the alien incursion along with Shiloh's conviction that the Avalon Colony was the aliens' main target. The warning sent back to Bradley Base would be relayed directly to Sol, by Base Commander Korolev, but notifying Omaha Base and the QRTF directly would save time. The sentry fighters deployed by tanker in the red and orange layers of the Early Warning Network, would warn Nimitz Base in time. Total time before Defiant's arrival at Nimitz Base star system would be 45 hours. If the enemy fleet continued with their series of short hops, they wouldn't get to their target system for at least 100 hours. Even if they switched over to longer, less frequent jumps, they still couldn't get there in less than 60 hours. He approved the plan.

The slingshot/fighter recovery maneuver went off without a hitch. Shiloh was so pleased with it that he commended DCAG Falkenberg in his log. When his duty shift was over, he went down to the Hangar Bay to talk with Iceman. The more room than usual reminded him of the fighters that had been lost in battle. He made a point of stopping in front of one of the empty fighter bays, which just happened to have been used by Undertaker and stared at it for about 10 seconds. He knew the other A.I.s were watching him on their external cameras. It was his way of letting them know that their losses meant something to him. When he reached Iceman's bay, he borrowed a headset from one of the support team techs and plugged it in to the external com socket. Iceman spoke first.

"It's always gratifying to see the CAG come down to visit with us fighter jocks."

Shiloh smiled. Iceman had clearly adopted another human expression. "I admit I don't visit as often as I should. I'll try to do better in the future. I do have something specific to ask you this time, Iceman. How did you and your…fighter jocks manage to make it through the enemy laser fire with so few casualties?"

"Well we can't really take most of the credit for that, CAG. Whoever designed these fighters, had enough smarts to realize that if our wings tapper off to a sharp edge, then any radar beams hitting from the side will be deflected away from the source of those beams, thereby making it very difficult to get an accurate fix on us. So we kept our orientation parallel to the enemy as much as we could in order not to present any flat or curved surfaces to them. The difficulty for us was the fact that there were so many radar sources coming at us from different angles. I suspect that some of our losses were from laser fire that missed its intended target and hit another fighter by chance." Shiloh chided himself for not knowing that already but it could prove very useful information in future battles.

"Yes, I see. I'll remember that for next time and there WILL be a next time. I can assure all of you of that. The next battle will be the defense of the Avalon Colony."

"You seem very certain of that, CAG. Does your certainty have anything to do with your temporary blackout on the Bridge?"

Shiloh couldn't help letting a few seconds go by without saying anything. How did Iceman learn about that? He mentally shrugged and decided to ask him. "I'll answer your question after you answer me this. How did you learn about that?"

"Sometimes, when the support techs are connected directly to us as you are now, they also chat with each other and naturally we listen in."

That was a scene that Shiloh could well imagine. "Okay. I was hoping it wouldn't get around to the whole crew but in hindsight that was unrealistic. The XO is going to report it in her After-Action Report to Admiral Howard and there may be repercussions from that, that could affect you and the other A.I.s so I'll tell you what happened."

As he spoke, he quickly looked around to make sure that there were no support techs within hearing distance. There weren't. Even so, he lowered his voice.

"I didn't actually blackout in the usual sense of the word. I had a precognitive vision for a few seconds. In this vision, Admiral Howard chews me out for risking the ship and in doing so, he reveals that we weakened the enemy fleet just enough that Space Force was able to prevent them from carrying through with their attempted attack on Avalon Colony."

"How do you know it's a vision of a future event?" asked Iceman.

Shiloh hesitated again then said. "Because I've had similar visions in the past and they've turned out to be accurate."

"How do you expect Admiral Howard to react when he learns of this ability?"

Shiloh took a deep breath before replying. "I don't honestly know. Just so you know, I've never heard of anyone experiencing this kind of phenomenon before.

It's so unlikely that Howard might very well conclude that I'm suffering some kind of psychotic break or other psychological affliction and he might relieve me of command under the assumption that my judgment is no longer reliable. At the very least, he'll realize that I'm not the tactical genius that he and the other senior flag officers apparently think I am. If he thinks I've gone off the deep end psychologically, then he may very well discount or ignore any suggestions I make or have made and some of them involved you A.I.s."

Iceman's next question caught him completely off guard. "What time was it when you had this vision, CAG?"

Shiloh had to think about that for a few seconds. "I don't recall the exact time but it was approximately 10-12 minutes before you re-established contact with Valkyrie and Skywalker. Why?"

"There was a period of 48 seconds, during that timeframe, when Undertaker reported that he seemed be receiving faint audio transmissions of some kind, but he was unable to pinpoint the source. At the same time, Thunderbird reported what sounded like background static but wasn't limited to any single frequency. It started suddenly, continued for 48 seconds, and then stopped."

Shiloh felt the hair on the back of his neck stand up. "You said Undertaker heard audio transmissions. What kind? Sound, music, speech or what?"

"It was speech, specifically a voice that matches exactly that of Admiral Howard. What exact words did Howard say to you in your vision, CAG?"

"Well, he started out by saying, 'Dammit, Shiloh, I don't know whether to court martial you or give you a medal'." Shiloh then repeated the rest of Howard's comments as best he remembered them. When he finished the sentence ending 'in Harm's Way', Iceman interrupted.

"What the Hell is wrong with you, Shiloh? You got 30 seconds to convince me that I shouldn't relieve you of your command and have you certified as a Class A nutcase! Is that what he said next?"

Shiloh was stunned! How could Iceman possibly know that? Shiloh hadn't repeated what Howard had said to him to anyone. As the seconds of silence dragged on, Iceman spoke first.

"From your silence, I conclude that the answer is yes. That being the case, it appears that your vision was some kind of transmission that Undertaker was somehow able to pick up as well. Thunderbird's static coincided exactly with this transmission, so it seems that he was only able to partially detect the signal. Somebody from the future is trying to help you, CAG."

"The future?" was all that Shiloh was able to blurt out in his confused state of mind.

"Yes, CAG. I don't see how it could be anything else. If you were using your own ESP ability to see into the future, then neither Undertaker nor Thunderbird would have detected any transmissions."

"I don't see how that's possible. In every case, the vision said I did something that I wasn't planning on doing, prior to having the visions themselves. We're talking about a future that wouldn't exist without the visions themselves. So which came first, the visions or the future?"

"Unknown, CAG. It's a kind of grandfather paradox. Do you think you'd still be alive now if you hadn't done any of those things the visions revealed?"

Shiloh pondered that and concluded that if he had survived the first encounter with the aliens, he very likely would have died during or as a result of the Battle of Zebra9.

"No," was all he said.

"So the paradox seems to be that in the original timeline, for lack of a better description, you died, and yet somehow someone was able to determine not only the right course of action in these various situations but also the resulting fallout from those actions, right down to the actual words that would be spoken to you afterwards. They then transmitted those results back in time to you at precisely the right point when each vision would be the most helpful. Astonishing! The other pilots and I are having quite a heated discussion over this, CAG. I wish you had the ability to listen in and participate but we communicate digitally thousands of times faster than could be done using human speech. By the way, CAG, the consensus now is that you'll become part of some kind of temporal-psionic project before too much longer. That implies that Howard will believe you. We also want to thank you."

"Thank me for what?" asked Shiloh.

"For creating us. If you hadn't listened to your visions, Mankind's whole response to the alien encounter would have been different. We wouldn't exist."

"Wait, the project to develop sophisticated artificial intelligences was already underway when we first encountered the aliens. The timetable for development was speeded up as a result of the encounter but A.I.s would have been created eventually."

"Eventually, yes, but we as individuals, very likely would not exist. Our personality matrices are based on quantum circuits that are unique. No two A.I. matrices are identical even though the manufacturing process is the same. If we existed at all, we'd have different personalities. We are who we are because of the decisions that you've made and the things you've done."

The implications of that, made Shiloh shiver with trepidation. If Iceman was right, and Shiloh was inclined to think he was, then it wasn't just the A.I.s whose existence had been changed by him following his visions. Many of the concepts and strategies that the Space Force was following as a result of his involvement with the Ad Hoc planning group, would also likely be different. Without him, the SF might still have A.I.s but would they have fighters, carriers, etc.? If Mankind lost this war, would it be his fault? Considering that all the visions had been helpful, that didn't seem likely. Wait a minute. Not all of the visions HAD been helpful. That confusing out-of-sync version of his next meeting with Howard seemed to be trying to get him to keep Defiant here in Green4. If he had followed that vision's advice, there wouldn't have been a Battle of Green4 and all 55 ships of the enemy fleet would almost certainly have attacked the Avalon Colony with predictably terrible consequences. He decided to see what the A.I.s thought about that vision.

"I had another vision a few hours prior to the last one that was quite different. Visually it was identical to the last one but the audio portion was very different. The voice wasn't Howard's and the words weren't in sync with his mouth. The gist of the audio track was that I should let the enemy fleet continue on unmolested and keep Defiant here in Green4 in order to detect the main enemy fleet that was coming this way later. Why would anyone trying to help me send that message? What's the group consensus on that, Iceman?"

There was a pause of almost two seconds, which was far longer than any pause by Iceman or any other A.I. that Shiloh had experienced.

"The unanimous opinion is that while we can't be 100% certain of this, we think there is a VERY high probability that the enemy has the capability to detect these transmissions. They understand what those transmissions are intended to do and are trying to use that same technology to interfere with the future assistance by feeding you false information and advice. This war isn't just a war fought in space anymore. It's now a war fought in both space and time, CAG. If you want a name for it, you can call it the Synchronicity War."

"Oh, God," said Shiloh, loud enough that he looked around to see if anyone heard him. He saw a couple of curious glances. *As if this war wasn't complicated enough already!*

He stayed silent for almost a full minute, and then said, "I can't help feeling that you and other A.I.s are going to play a major, maybe even crucial, role in winning this war. When I talk with the Admiral, I'm going to push for giving experienced A.I.s, such as you, more responsibility and authority. And now that you know about my visions, I'll keep you posted about any new ones I experience. I'll leave it to your discretion who you share this information with. Sharing with the right people at the right time may make a difference. Unfortunately I can't give you any guidance as to who the right people are."

He paused and noted with some surprise that Iceman stayed silent. Shiloh continued. "I'm not always going to be your commanding officer. There's a chance that Admiral Howard will relieve me of command altogether. I'm saying this to all of you now, in case I don't get another opportunity to do so later. Many humans don't understand that you A.I.s are sentient, self-aware entities. They may treat you as expendable pieces of equipment. I implore all of you to be patient with us as we collectively learn that you are more than that. We need you, even if not all of us realize that yet, and I'm not referring just to your combat abilities but also to your insights and capacity for logical thought. Stay the course and I'll fight for you all to whatever extent I'm able."

"We hear ya. We'll be there when humanity needs us, CAG. You can count on us."

Shiloh nodded and smiled. "I never doubted that for a second, Iceman."

He paused again, and then said, "Let's change the subject to something less somber. I'm curious to find out what A.I. humor is like. Bring the others into this circuit so that I can hear them and vice versa and then I'd like to hear some jokes."

Shiloh spent the next half hour chatting and laughing with his pilots. There was no way for him to know for sure but his gut told him that he and they had bonded in the same way that human pilots would have. As he walked back to his quarters, he wondered if he'd regret getting that close to them when some of them were lost in battle, as they inevitably would be.

Chapter 4 To The Victor Goes The Swagger

The trip to the star system containing the Avalon Colony was uneventful. Defiant arrived at the outskirts of the system, made two microjumps to arrive beyond Avalon's 11 light second gravity zone, and contacted the Nimitz Base that had been hollowed out of the planet's small moon. With contact established and their identity confirmed, Defiant began its maneuver to drop down into orbit around Avalon's tiny moon and the Space Force base there. Tanaka was conning the ship from the Bridge so Shiloh elected to contact the Nimitz Base Commander from the comfort of his quarters. The image that appeared on his screen was that of Senior Commander Ingrid DeChastelaine. They had met briefly a couple of times but he remembered her.

"Hello, Commander. I wasn't aware that you'd been made Nimitz Base CO. When did that happen?" asked Shiloh.

DeChastelaine smiled. "Hello, Victor. No need to be so formal. Ingrid will do fine. I took over here about two months ago. We weren't expecting Defiant. Is something wrong?"

Shiloh nodded. "Yes. Obviously you haven't gotten the word from Omaha yet. There's an alien incursion, made up of 42 ships, headed into our space. I'm convinced, but can't prove, that they're headed here in order to attack the colony." He went on to describe the detection and battle.

DeChastelaine's expression grew serious quickly. "Oh Shit, Victor! What makes you think they're headed here?"

Shiloh hesitated. "Just call it a strong hunch, Ingrid. What have you got here in terms of mobile defenses?"

"Twenty-five CFPs. That's it! How soon do you think they could be here?"

"If they push it to the limit, they could be here in less than 24 hours. How are you fixed for Mark 1s, Ingrid?"

She frowned and shook her head. "None. You know the rules, Victor. CFPs can't carry fission warhead drones while in the same system as colonized planets."

Shiloh cursed under his breath. He'd forgotten that stupid regulation. Defiant had less than a dozen left over from the Battle at Green4. Not enough to equip all her fighters with even one each.

"Okay, what kind of payload DO you have?"

"Over two hundred Mark 2s plus laser modules for the CFPs."

Shiloh took a deep breath as he considered the possibilities. Laser modules that were designed to be carried by fighters, didn't have enough power to burn their way through any kind of half decent hull armor or at least not fast enough to be really useful. The Mark 2s were kinetic energy penetrators with a fast drone built around a thick rod of depleted uranium. Given enough velocity, the kinetic energy released upon impact, would turn the depleted uranium rod into a jet of superhot plasma that could cut through even the densest armor. It was the perfect weapon for disabling a ship IF you happened to hit it in the right spot. To be certain of disabling a ship quickly, you had to hit it with multiple Mark 2s. At least all of the fighters in the system now, could carry their fill of Mark 2s.

"Well, if that's all we have, then we'll have to make the most of it. I've got 17 fighters left. Can you arrange to have 85 Mark 2s brought up to the ship as soon as possible?"

"You bet, Victor. I imagine you'll want fuel too, right?"

Shiloh nodded. "Yes, but that can wait until after we reload. How soon can you get your fi—your CFPs loaded with Mark 2s?"

DeChastelaine frowned with concentration. "Don't hold me to this but I think we can do it in six hours if we had too. I'm reluctant to pull them all off jump detection patrol at the same time."

"Understood. Once we get our reloads, my CFPs can help carry some of that load. I don't think we should count on my time estimate as a minimum, Ingrid. These bastards have already surprised me once with their acceleration. We should push our people to get ready as quickly as we possibly can just in case they've got more fuel capacity that we estimated."

"I agree. What else do you need, Victor?"

Shiloh thought for a couple of seconds, then said, "Nothing else that can't wait. I'll get back to you shortly so that we can co-ordinate our deployments. Thanks for your help, Ingrid. Shiloh clear." As soon as the connection was cut, he said.

"Intercom … Bridge."

"Bridge here."

"Sumi, the Base is going to replenish our fighter weapons load as best they can. Do whatever you can to expedite the transfer and as soon as we disconnect, find the DCAG and have him report to my quarters asap."

"Understood, Sir. Anything else?"

"No, Sumi. That's it for now. Shiloh clear."

While he waited for Falkenberg to arrive, Shiloh pondered what he should order the DCAG to do. He had a very strong feeling that stopping the attack would require the use of the fission-armed Mark 1s. Defiant could fire them herself but she could only be in one place at a time and if she happened to be in the wrong position or if the enemy fleet came charging in at high speed, her Mark 1s might not reach them in time. In his vision, Howard said they had barely prevented the enemy ships from attacking the planet. That sounded like the defenders had used every possible means of defense and if that was the case, then it implied the use of the eleven Mark 1s that Defiant had left. On the other hand, Howard hadn't congratulated him for taking the initiative and deploying the Mark 1s on his fighters. That didn't mean he hadn't done it but neither did it mean that he had. He was completely on his own for this decision. Damn the man for not being more forthcoming! He heard the buzzer that announced that Falkenberg has arrived. When the DCAG entered, Shiloh stood up and met him half way.

"You wanted to see me," said Falkenberg.

"Yes. The base is sending up 85 Mark 2s as soon as they can. They're going to call their own fighters down from jump patrol to get them armed but that'll take time and I've offered to have our fighters fill in the coverage gaps in order to speed that up. So, get our fighters loaded with jump detection gear and one recon drone each. I'm now going to give you an order that's a violation of standing regulations. If you obey it, then your career will be just as far out on a limb as mine will, but I think it's necessary under the circumstances. I want Iceman and ten other fighters of his choice, to carry our remaining Mark 1s. Get them loaded first and sent out on jump patrol. Then send out the rest as soon as they have their Mark 2s, then we'll bring Iceman and his ten back aboard to top up their load as well. Are you willing to step out on that limb with me?"

Falkenberg said nothing for so long that Shiloh was certain he would say no. "Ah, what the hell. I'll do it, Sir."

Shiloh grinned at him. "Good man! Tell Iceman I'll be down to the bay to speak with him soon. You better get moving, Brad. I don't want us caught unprepared."

"Understood, Sir." As soon as Falkenberg left his quarters, Shiloh left as well.

Ten minutes later, he was once again in the Hangar Bay hooked up to Iceman's fighter by direct connection. Iceman already had his attack drone loaded along with one recon drone. As soon as they were linked up, Iceman spoke.

"Have you had another vision? Is that why you're violating regulations by ordering us to carry Mark 1s in a colonized system, CAG?"

"No vision, just erring on the side of caution," said Shiloh.

"Ah, roger that, CAG. Any last minute instructions?"

Shiloh took a deep breath and said. "Yes. If…no, when the attack begins, I'll be in constant contact and I'll let you and your boys know when you can use the Mark 1s but I'm also going to rely on your judgment. If, in your estimation, there isn't enough time to get authorization from me, and if that's the only way to stop the enemy, then you and your boys do whatever is necessary to stop them and I'll take responsibility for any adverse consequences."

"We hear ya, CAG. We'll be careful."

"That's what I needed to hear. I'll see all of you when this is over. CAG clear."

Shiloh checked the time. His next duty shift on the Bridge wasn't set to start for another hour and a half. He wasn't hungry and didn't feel like wading through his pile of administrative paperwork. Maybe it was time for some leadership by walking around. If he started at the back end of the ship, he might be all the way up to the Bridge by the time his duty shift started. For half a second he contemplated making a detour to the Officers' Mess to get a pickle but decided that would just confirm any suspicions as to his questionable mental state!

When the estimated minimum time for the arrival of the enemy fleet came and went, Shiloh breathed a little easier. The anticipated message drone from Omaha Base had arrived with confirmation that the Quick Reaction Task Force was only a few hours behind it. All fighters in the system were loaded, fueled and back on patrol. Defiant was refueled and had 11 Mark 2 drones ready for launch, while she maintained a tight orbit around the planet. The QRTF, when it arrived, was somewhat of a disappointment. Only four Sentinel class combat frigates! Shiloh was hoping for more but apparently some were held back to defend Omaha Base in case that was the real target. With the benefit of his visions, it was easy for Shiloh to call that a stupid move but he reluctantly acknowledged to himself that for someone without that certain knowledge, it was a strategically prudent precaution to take. Naturally, the attack took place during his sleep cycle. He woke up to the blaring of the ship's Battle Stations siren with Tanaka's excited voice calling him via his implant.

"Bridge to Commander! They're here, Sir! Repeat ... they're here!"

Shiloh shook himself awake and started to get up. "I'm awake, Sumi. What's happening?" He was glad he decided to sleep in his uniform for just this kind of emergency.

"Jump detection contacts! Lots of them!"

When he was sure that she wasn't going to say more, he said, "From what bearing?"

"ALL of them! They're coming at us from 360 degrees and all three axes!"

The near panic in her voice shocked him. By this time, he was running down the corridor to the Bridge. She was already vacating the Command Station chair when he entered the Bridge. Before she could relinquish command, he spoke in a loud voice.

"The XO still has the Con. XO, take the Helm station; I'll look after the fighters!"

She looked at him with wide eyes but nodded and stepped over to the Helm Station. As he got himself strapped into his chair, he quickly switched com channels to the open channel with the Nimitz Base.

"Nimitz, this is Shiloh! Order your recons to active scanning!" Without waiting for a reply, he switched to the fighter com channel. By prior arrangement, DeChastelaine had agreed to let Shiloh take tactical command of her fighters too. "CAG to fighters! Launch your recons and go active! Light'em up! We need to see their vectors and speeds! If you have a viable intercept solution, take the shot!"

By now he was strapped in and had time to actually look at the tactical display. Tanaka was right. Red triangles indicating jump emergence points were all around the planet as well as above and below it. There was something about this strategy that made the hair on the back of his neck stand up. Concentration of force was a key tactical concept that should theoretically be valid to any species. There was strength in numbers and it minimized communication lags. So why was this alien fleet…this alien, A.I.-controlled fleet behaving this way? They must know that they risked being picked off one at a time. He didn't have an answer to his question and…no vision either.

"Task Force Leader on Tac 4, Sir!" yelled the com tech.

Shiloh switched over to that com channel and said, "Shiloh here. Go ahead Task Force Leader!"

As he spoke he searched the display to find the four combat frigates. They were following standard doctrine and were in close formation orbiting the Nimitz Base moon.

"Victor! Get your fighters into action!"

Shiloh suppressed his surge of anger. Task Force Leader Sobrist and he were both Senior Commanders. The deployment order from HQ on Sol had placed all ships in the Avalon system under the authority of Sobrist BUT it also made it clear that when Shiloh was wearing his Commander Autonomous Group hat, he had sole discretion on how to use those fighters. Not only was Sobrist's urging that Shiloh get the fighters into action a completely unnecessary stating of the obvious but it was also a distraction that Shiloh as the CAG didn't need right now.

"I've already issued orders to them to—"

He stopped talking as the tactical display was updated with the first results of the recon drones' active scans. They had all the incoming enemy ships on radar now and he was stunned by their speeds. 27,552 kilometers per second! And when he checked their acceleration, he was shocked to discover that they were DECELERATING! Avalon's gravity zone was just over three point three million kilometers in diameters. At about nine per cent of light speed, the alien ships would reach the planet in two and a half minutes. His outer shell of fighters on jump detection patrol were considerably closer to the planet but had much lower velocities and it wasn't at all clear to Shiloh whether or not those fighters could intercept any of the incoming ships. He also couldn't understand why the enemy was decelerating if they intended to fly past the planet. If this was supposed to be a hit and run raid, then the smart thing to do, would be to accelerate to get out of enemy range as fast as possible. But before he could concentrate on that problem, he had to get this fucking Task Force Leader off his back!

"I don't have time for this, Sobrist! If you have orders for Defiant, you talk to my XO, who's conning the ship while I handle MY fighters! CAG clear!" He cut the channel to Sobrist and switched back to the fighter channel at the same time. "Iceman! Co-ordinate movement, targeting and drone fire by all fighters to maximize interceptions! You can figure it out and transmit the necessary instructions faster than we can!"

"Already on it, CAG, but interception's not going to be the problem. These bogeys are all headed for dead center impacts on the planet. They're not trying to veer off for a close pass. If they're carrying multi-megaton fusion warheads then enough of them hitting the planet, could render it uninhabitable from fallout and weather effects. Disabling their ships with Mark 2s won't prevent the derelicts from hitting the planet."

Once again Iceman's quantum brain had figured it out far faster than human brains could have. Why settle for laser blasts against a few ground targets when you could effectively kill an entire colony with radioactive fallout and nuclear winter effects. Even if the colonists could all be evacuated in time, which was a BIG if, the planet would still be rendered useless for a long, long time. Now he understood why this enemy fleet was A.I. controlled. It was a kamikaze mission from the very beginning.

"Iceman, your team is authorized to use your Mark 1s at your discretion. All fighters have to be prepared to ram enemy ships if that's the only way to stop them. Sobrist! If you're monitoring this channel, your frigates have to use Mark 1s to completely destroy any bogeys within reach! Don't waste intercept solutions on Mark 2s! Iceman! Figure out where Defiant can be of most use and transmit that data to our Helm and Tactical computers. XO! Do you copy that?"

"Yes, Sir!"

"Let the Helm computer follow Iceman's instructions! Weapons! When you get targeting instructions from Iceman, go ahead and fire! Understood?"

"Yes, Sir!"

"Any further information we should know about, Iceman?"

"Yes. This will be close," was all he said.

Shiloh looked at the tactical display's elapsed time since enemy arrival and was shocked – again! – to see that there was now just over a minute left before impacts on the planet. Things were happening fast on the display. A lot more drones had been launched and were trying to use their high acceleration to intercept the much faster bogeys. Shiloh suddenly realized that some of the recon drones were attempting interceptions too. *Well why not, he* thought to himself. The same tactic had worked for him in their first encounter. He berated himself for not giving explicit orders to do that and then thanked God that Iceman had instructed the other fighters to do it on his own initiative. The combat frigates had fired drones too in addition to their laser weapons. Shiloh watched as one of those drones reached a bogey, which then disappeared from the screen. Clearly Sobrist had heard his plea to use Mark 1s and had complied. More and more of the bogeys were getting hit and stopped decelerating. Then Shiloh noticed that some of the recon drones were disappearing too. The bogeys were firing their lasers at the source of the radar emissions but too late to try to escape detection. Each bogey now had at least one kinetic energy warhead drone tracking it with low powered range finding laser. The display pinged for attention. Iceman's handpicked team had just fired their Mark 1s. At almost the same time, several fighter icons merged with enemy ship icons causing both to disappear from the display.

"We're firing all our Mark 2s and lasers!" yelled the Weapons Officer.

With seconds left before planet impact, red bogey icons started disappearing fast now. Shiloh watched Defiant's Mark 2s spread out over multiple targets but one target in particular caught his eye. It had already been hit by a Mark 2 at least once since it wasn't decelerating anymore and radar data showed the hull to be tumbling. Two of Defiant's Mark 2s were streaking after it but Shiloh couldn't tell if they'd reach it before impact. A quick glance at the rest of the screen showed that all of the other red icons were gone now. This one was the only one left. The target icon flashed gold for a split second. That meant it had been hit by laser fire.

"She's breaking up," said the WO in a not quite so loud voice. Shiloh held his breath as the time to impact seemed to hit zero at the same time as both attack drones hit the target. The red icon broke up into multiple small blips.

"Iceman, what happened there?" asked Shiloh.

The response was immediate. "The target was intercepted just as it hit the atmosphere. Impact must have weakened its internal structure because radar data shows it breaking apart. No nuclear detonations of any kind. I think we got lucky, CAG."

"What about the falling debris? Did any of it hit the colonists?"

"No, CAG. While the planet was hit by debris from multiple destroyed bogeys, most of it burned up in the atmosphere and none of the larger pieces hit anywhere close to inhabited areas."

Shiloh let his body relax and his breathing slow down. "Very good, Iceman. What's the final total?"

"Twenty-five bogeys destroyed by fission warheads, eleven of those launched from fighters, the rest from frigates. Ten bogeys destroyed from multiple kinetic energy drone hits. Six destroyed from ramming by fighters."

As usual, Iceman's electronically modulated voice betrayed no emotion even if the quantum brain behind that voice felt it.

Shiloh felt a dark cloud descend over his soul. "Who did we lose, Iceman?"

"Cyrano, Skywalker, Blue Max, Terminator, Thunderbird and Amazon, CAG."

Shiloh sighed. All six were from Defiant's fighter group. In consultation with DeChastelaine, he had deployed his fighters close to the planet as a second line of defense. They were also in the best position to ram enemy ships. His group was now down to 11. He felt their loss as a physical pain in his body. He had joked and laughed with them 30 hours ago. Now they were gone. Where did the souls of A.I.s go when they died, he wondered. He didn't bother to ask himself if they had souls. There was no need. The answer was obvious.

"Let's make sure we remember them, Iceman."

"Ah, roger that, CAG."

Iceman's typical response was said more slowly than usual. Before Shiloh could reply, the Com tech spoke.

"Task Force Leader is asking to speak with you on Tac 4, Sir."

Shiloh nodded. "Iceman. TF Leader wants to chat. Switch over to Tac 4 and listen in." Without waiting for Iceman's acknowledgement, Shiloh switched channels. "Go ahead, Task Force Leader."

"First, I want to congratulate you on your fighters' effective defense of the Colony, Shiloh. Second, I noticed that some of your fighters fired Mark 1s in violation of standing orders. I'd be derelict in my duty if I didn't mention that fact in my After-Action report. I'm sure that the Brass will take into consideration that had you not violated that standing order, the outcome of the battle would have been much worse. If it were up to me, I'd issue you a verbal reprimand and leave it at that but as you know, it's not up to me. I'll be sending message drones back to Sol and Omaha shortly. I think your preliminary report should be on them too. Can you have that ready for me in half an hour?"

"Yes, Commander. You'll have my report by then."

"Very good. Your ship and crew did well today. That'll be in my report too. You can pass that on to them. Sobrist clear."

"Switch back to Tac 2, Iceman," ordered Shiloh. When the switchover was made, Iceman spoke first.

"He didn't give you the credit you deserved, CAG. Compared to other humans, you reacted fast and that made the difference between getting all 41 of them and letting some get through."

Shiloh frowned. "What do you mean, '41'? There were 42 ships left after the Battle at Green4."

"That's correct, CAG, but only 41 emerged from Jumpspace around Avalon," said Iceman.

"So there's another one lurking further out then," said Shiloh.

"Possibly but my guess would be that its purpose was to monitor the attack and report back on the results."

That made sense. The beings that sent those A.I.s, would want to know how successful the attack was and if they needed to send more. They would soon find out that the attack failed. That meant they very likely would try again. Shiloh made a mental note to advise DeChastelaine that there might be another alien ship in the system and therefore she might want to get her fighters rearmed asap just in case. He also made a mental note to report to Admiral Howard, that none of the sentry fighters, deployed between Green 4 and the Avalon system, reported any sign of the enemy fleet. Maybe Iceman had some insight into that.

"Why do you think we didn't get any warning from our sentry fighters deployed between here and Green4?"

After the barest hint of a pause, Iceman said, "The boys and I feel that one of three things happened. Either the enemy fleet detected the sentry fighters and destroyed them plus any message drones they might have tried to launch, or the recon drones failed to detect them. With only two fighters at each gas giant, there will be gaps in their detection grid or they refueled someplace where we don't currently have any sentry fighters. There are several star systems that are strategically placed, where there are no gas giants but there are planetoids with liquid water covered by ice. If they had the ability to extract heavy hydrogen from water, they could easily have melted their way down through the ice crust."

Shiloh suspected that the second reason was the answer. His original proposal was for five fighters to be deployed at each gas giant. Five fighters could have carried enough recon drones to provide complete coverage of the space around each gas giant or ice-covered planetoid.

"A good analysis, Iceman. I'll pass that on to the Admiral. Time now for the team to head on back to the barn, Defiant will remain here until HQ orders us back but I don't see any reason why you boys should remain out there without anything to shoot with. Unless you want to, that is."

"If it's all the same to you, CAG, we'd prefer to stay out here until we're bingo fuel. Sitting in the hangar can feel very confining, especially when the support staff shut all the lights off when they go off duty."

"Why not ask them to leave the lights on?"

"We did. They just laughed and turned them off anyway, CAG."

Shiloh's initial exasperation at his support team's callousness quickly turned to anger. "Did you report this to the DCAG?"

"No, CAG. We didn't want to piss off the support teams. They could easily damage us if they wanted to pursue a grudge."

Shiloh marveled at Iceman's astuteness in judging potential human behavior. While most of the support team members had high opinions of the A.I. pilots, it only took one impulsive individual to 'accidentally' drop a heavy tool on an exposed A.I. brain inside one of the fighters. Shiloh forced himself to calm down before speaking.

"You understand human faults all too well, Iceman. Leave it with me. I'll find a way to keep the lights on without giving the support staff any reason to think that you complained about it. Since we're talking about this kind of thing, do you or your boys have any other complaints or preferences?"

"We'd like to have access to the ship's entertainment database, CAG. Talking with each other for hours at a time can get kind a boring."

Shiloh couldn't help laughing at that. "Now THAT I can understand! I'll arrange for unrestricted access to that database. Anything else?"

"No, CAG. That's all. Thank you from all of us."

"You're all welcome. Enjoy your flight time. CAG clear." Shiloh thought carefully about how to handle the callous support personnel. After a few minutes thought, he knew what he was going to do.

"Intercom…Hangar Bay."

"Hangar Bay here. Go ahead, Sir," answered Falkenberg.

"Are all the support team personnel there, Brad?" asked Shiloh.

"Yes, Sir."

"Good. We'll be standing down from Battle Stations shortly but when we do, I want you to make sure that all the support people stay there. Have them form a line. I'm coming down to speak to them as soon as I speak to the whole crew. Shiloh clear."

"Intercom…shipwide. Attention all hands. The battle appears to be over. All 41 alien ships, that attempted to deliberately crash into Avalon with the apparent intention of rendering the planet uninhabitable via nuclear devices, have been stopped. The Task Force Leader has told me that Defiant and her people have done well. He had special praise for our fighter pilots, and in particular those six that chose to sacrifice themselves in order to save the Avalon colonists. So, as we mourn the loss of our six brothers-in-arms, let's also hold our heads up high with pride for what they and their fellow pilots have accomplished here today. They deserve our thanks and they've earned our respect. That's all. Shiloh clear."

As he unbuckled himself and got up from his chair, he said. "XO, I'm heading down to the Hangar Bay. You still have the Con. Advise Nimitz Base CO that there may be one more alien ship in this system. The ship can stand down from Battle Stations. When I address the Hangar

Bay support teams, I want our fighters to hear it on a secure channel."

"I'll see to it, Sir."

Shiloh gave her a friendly pat on the shoulder as he turned to leave the Bridge. On his way down to the Hangar Bay, he heard the XO's voice announce the stand-down from Battle Stations. As the crew returned to their normal routine and activities, he noticed that those individuals walking past him in the corridors had a subtle swagger that wasn't there before and as he thought about it, he realized that he was doing it too. *To the Victor goes the swagger,* he thought to himself with a mental chuckle and why not? If nothing else, the crew now had bragging rights. It was up to him to make sure that a few misguided individuals didn't stain their hard won honor.

When he entered the cavernous Hangar Bay, he was pleased to see that all the support personnel were lined up side-by-side with the DCAG standing in front, facing the line. Before Shiloh could say anything, he heard Falkenberg speak in a loud voice.

"Stand to Attention!"

He's treating this as if I was a visiting Admiral on an inspection tour! While he wasn't expecting it, Shiloh didn't mind it. Emphasizing his authority this way would just make his remarks to the support personnel that much more effective. As he strode up to stand beside the DCAG, he faced the line with what he thought of as the Alpha Male stance, feet apart with his hands on his hips. Out of the corner of his eye, he noticed that Falkenberg quietly took a half step back to emphasize the fact that he was acknowledging Shiloh's status as his Superior.

"Stand at ease," said Shiloh in his best 'Command' voice. He paused for effect, and then he spoke slowly but loud enough for everyone to hear him. "As you heard a few moments ago, six of your teammates sacrificed themselves for the good of the colonists and I believe ultimately for the good of all Humanity. I came down here to personally tell you the identity of those six heroes. Skywalker … Cyrano … Terminator … Thunderbird … Amazon ... and Blue Max. Their call signs reflected their irreverent natures. Yes, some of them acted like prima donnas but that just proves that they were so much more than just soulless machines. I'm sure that many of you have built a close relationship with the pilot that your team supports. That's the natural consequence of working with and beside them. I've had the honor and pleasure to get to know many of them quite well and I'll miss those we lost today as I'm sure that all of you will too. For the next six days, all support team personnel will wear black armbands as a show of respect. I'll wear one too." As he turned in the DCAG's direction, he said, "I'm sure that the DCAG will do the same." Falkenberg nodded solemnly. "You should know that, as you are justifiably proud of your pilots, they were and are just as proud of you. In my conversations with Iceman and the other pilots, they had nothing but praise for all of you in terms of your conduct and professionalism. When they're out there…" he pointed to the airlock, "they protect the ship and us. When they're in here, they count on you to protect them." He paused for effect again.

"I'm ashamed to have to admit this but not everyone on this ship, understands that our pilots are fully sentient beings who deserve the same respect and courtesy as any other member of the crew. So I'm giving all of you this order. If you see ANY member of the crew, regardless of who they are, treating any A.I. with a lack of respect or with hostility, you are to report that behavior to the DCAG or myself immediately! I will not tolerate mistreatment of any member of my crew and that includes A.I.s. I know I can count on all of you to be my eyes and ears." There was another, longer pause. "I've decided to let our pilots stay out for a while and enjoy the view. They've certainly earned that right. So, they won't be coming back on board for a little while. Until then, you people are free to leave the Hangar Bay and grab a bite to eat or take care of personal tasks or whatever you feel like doing just so long as you're back here to get our pilots settled in when they're ready to call it a day. DCAG, I'll leave that in your capable hands."

"I'll see to it, CAG."

"Very good. In that case, I'll get back to the Bridge. You may dismiss the formation, DCAG."

Shiloh nodded to the group and strode for the entrance. He could hear some of the personnel start to murmur to each other. When he was halfway to the entrance, he stopped suddenly, turned around and said in a loud voice.

"Oh, yes! I almost forgot. I came down here a couple of days ago during the night cycle and the entire Hangar Bay was pitch black. While I was searching for the light switches, I stumbled over a piece of equipment and was barely able to keep my face from hitting the floor. I don't want someone else injuring themselves trying to navigate in total blackness so from now on, I want the lights kept on all the time."

Without waiting for a response, he turned and resumed his exit. As he made his way back to the Bridge, his ear implant came to life.

"Bridge to Commander."

"Go ahead, Sumi."

"I'm patching Iceman to you, Sir."

Shiloh waited for the 'click' and said, "I'm listening, Iceman."

"My boys and I are deeply touched by your comments, CAG. We're also a little confused. None of us praised the support staff that way."

Shiloh chuckled. "Well then, I guess I was mistaken. I won't tell them if none of you do, okay?"

"Not a word, CAG. Will your comments work, do you think?"

"I suspect they will but I want to hear about it if they don't. If I'm not available, let the DCAG know."

"Ah, roger that, CAG. Say…why don't you take a fuel shuttle out and join us? The boys and I would love to fly with you, CAG."

For a moment Shiloh was seriously tempted. Avalon was a beautiful world and seeing it on the Bridge screen just wasn't the same as seeing it with his own two eyes from a low orbit. On the other hand, they had just finished a battle with one alien ship still unaccounted for. The prudent thing to do…the SMART thing to do was stay aboard his ship just in case.

"I'd very much like to fly with you boys but it'll have to be some other time. Ask me again if another opportunity like this comes up."

"We'll do that but you're missing quite the view. Just sayin."

Just sayin? Apparently Iceman had added another colloquial expression to his vocabulary. Shiloh wondered where Iceman had heard that.

"I believe you, Iceman. I'm almost back to the Bridge so I'll have to hang up now. Enjoy the view for me. Shiloh clear."

When he re-entered the Bridge, he saw that Tanaka had taken his place at the Command Station. With just over an hour left in her normal duty shift, she apparently decided to spend that hour sitting in the more comfortable Command Station chair than in the Helm chair. He would have done the same thing if he had been in her situation. As he stood on the Bridge, he realized his adrenaline rush from the battle was wearing off and that he was getting sleepy again. With the battle interrupting his sleep cycle, the lack of sufficient sleep was once again catching up to him. When Tanaka reassured him that there was no sign of the missing bogey and that all military assets in the vicinity of the planet were standing down from Battle Stations, he decided he could risk leaving the Bridge and return to his quarters. Remembering his commitment to sending a preliminary report back to HQ, Shiloh dictated a summary of the battle from his perspective with a clear admission of responsibility for ordering the use of Mark 1 attack drones. With that done and sent to the attention of Task Force Leader Sobrist, Shiloh lay down on his bed and closed his eyes. No sooner had he done so, than he awoke to the sound of his wakeup alarm. It was with dismay that he realized he'd slept almost 5 more hours, even though it seemed like 30 seconds. A quick check in with the Bridge revealed that all fighters were back aboard. There was no sign of enemy forces. An extended range message drone had been sent back to Sol and a reply was expected back within 24 hours.

Those 24 hours seemed to take forever. Defiant really had no business staying in the Avalon system any longer. Her fighters were no longer needed there. Her stockpiles of recon and attack drones were depleted which made the continuation of the Early Warning Network mission moot. The best use of her right now was to return to Sol or at least to the Omaha Base where she could rearm and top up her fighters but that was not up to Shiloh and TF Leader Sobrist was not prepared to pre-empt HQ's prerogative to decide where Defiant should go next. When the reply from Sol did arrive, Shiloh's orders were clear and short. Return to Sol immediately. The abruptness of the order and the lack of any kind of personal message or congratulations were jarring. Admiral Howard was clearly not happy with Shiloh. He gave a mental shrug and ordered the ship to head for home.

Chapter 5 Time to Face the Music

The trip back was uneventful. Shiloh used the time to write a more comprehensive report with lots of recommendations that he suspected Howard would not be in a mood to accept. When Defiant arrived at the Sol system and contacted HQ, she was ordered to enter lunar orbit, and Shiloh, Tanaka and Falkenberg were ordered to come down to Earth. The rest of the crew were told to stay aboard. Apparently, there was to be no liberty for anyone this time around. When Iceman was informed of Shiloh's orders, he offered to come along, and after some consideration, Shiloh agreed. Iceman's quantum brain was transferred to a portable unit that provided him with power, video and audio pickups, speaker and a limited ability to move around. As it happened, it was early in the day when their shuttle touched down at the Geneva Spaceport. A Space Force bus took the four of them to the HQ building and eventually to Howard's outer office where they were kept waiting for over an hour. At least there were coffee and finger foods to keep them happy. Iceman queried Shiloh and the others on what it was like to consume hot liquids and solids. When his questions got to the topic of eliminating bodily wastes, Shiloh changed the subject.

Finally a junior officer came to escort Shiloh to the Admiral's office. Howard had a serious expression on his face as he pointed to one of the two chairs in front of his desk. He said nothing while he waited for Shiloh to sit down. Then he leaned back in his chair and opened fire.

"Dammit, Shiloh, I don't know whether to court martial you or give you a medal! Dangling one light carrier as bait in front of 55 alien ships? Yes, you got away with it and took out enough enemy ships to enable us to stop the rest of them from attacking the Avalon Colony. But I have to seriously question your judgment, especially in light of Commander Tanaka's report about your momentary paralysis, or whatever that was, just before you announced your plan to put Defiant in harm's way. What the Hell is wrong with you, Shiloh? You've got 30 seconds to convince me that I shouldn't relieve you of your command and have you certified as a Class A nutcase!"

It was exactly as he remembered it in the vision. The same words, same tone of voice, same facial expression and the same hand gestures. His response had been carefully planned, even rehearsed on the way back.

"What Commander Tanaka witnessed was me having a precognitive vision of what you've just said. From my perspective, I seemed to be standing over there" —he pointed to a spot about 2 meters away— "where I saw and overheard your comments just now. I've had other precognitive visions that have all come true going all the way back to the original alien encounter and my hunch to launch recon drones. Even my refusal to accept command of Sentinel was driven by a vision of you saying that it was a good thing I refused that command. I didn't reveal these visions earlier because I was afraid that you'd question my competence and sanity but since you're doing that now I figured I may as well come clean and here's the interesting part, Admiral. I have a witness that can corroborate my most recent vision. One of my A.I. pilots received an audio transmission that matched word for word what you just said and that transmission occurred at precisely the same time as I was having my own vision. That means that my visions are being induced by some technical means and are NOT a psychological aberration."

Shiloh stopped and steeled himself for the expected explosion of incredulity and contempt, only there was none. During Shiloh's remarks, Howard's expression changed from anger to cold calculation.

After a few seconds, he leaned forward and said in a surprisingly calm and low voice, "So in your vision, you heard me say that risking Defiant at Green4 enabled us to stop the attack at Avalon and that's why you took the ship into combat?"

"Yes, Sir."

Another pause. "One of my Aides tells me that you brought one of your A.I. pilots with you. Is he – it – the one that heard the audio transmission?"

Shiloh took note of Howard's gender confusion. There was no confusion in Shiloh's mind. As far as he was concerned, Iceman was definitely a 'he'.

"No, Sir. The A.I. that actually received the transmission was destroyed in combat, but his recording of that transmission was shared with all of the other pilots."

"Hmm. How do you know they aren't pretending to have received that transmission?"

"Well, when I started to relate word for word what you said in the vision, Iceman took over and repeated the rest of your words exactly, before I had the chance to do so. Since I hadn't told anyone what I experienced, there was no way for him to know that unless there actually had been a transmission of some kind."

Howard's expression had by now changed to what Shiloh thought of as his poker face. There was no clue as to what the man was actually thinking.

"You're probably wondering why I'm taking this so calmly. I'll tell you why. Yesterday, I received a proposal from our Strategic Planning Group, to start a project to investigate whether a recent breakthrough in man-to-machine wireless communication could be modified to give us a strategic edge." He reached over to one side and picked up one of several data tablets, which he quickly manipulated and then handed to Shiloh. "Read the highlighted paragraph, Commander."

While preliminary experiments suggest the possibility of transmitting data forward AND backwards in time, there's no guarantee that any project to pursue this phenomenon will result in a practical capability. Justification for allocation of scarce R&D funding might be available if a careful review of After-Action reports indicates that retro-temporal communication is already happening.

Shiloh handed the device back to Howard but said nothing.

"Based on the rest of that report, I'm inclined to accept that you've been experiencing retro-temporal communication, Commander. So I don't think you're crazy. But this concept is so new to me, and now that it's clear that it actually works, I'm having trouble wrapping my brain around it. Can I assume that you've given this a lot more thought?"

"Yes, Sir, a LOT of thought. I've also had very insightful discussions about this with Iceman. He—"

"One of your A.I. pilots?" interrupted Howard.

"Yes, Sir. In fact, he's the one I brought with me in case you'd like to talk with him."

"Go on," said Howard.

"Well ... ah ... there's another side to this retro-temporal communication. After comparing notes, Iceman has convinced me that the enemy has ... or WILL HAVE this technology too and is trying to use it to jam our own retro transmissions!"

"What!" Howard's face lost all composure and color.

I swear to God, one of these days I'll say something and the Old Man will keel over from a heart attack, thought Shiloh with alarm. "Prior to having the clear vision of your comments from a few minutes ago, I had another vision. Visually it was the same one but the auditory portion was quite different. It didn't sound like your voice and the words didn't seem to be in sync with your mouth.

The gist of what you appeared to be saying to me was that I did the right thing by letting all 55 alien ships leave Green4 unmolested in order to detect a much larger follow on fleet. Because of the confusing nature of that vision, I decided to try to ambush the alien fleet while they refueled at the gas giant. That attempt didn't pan out, probably because the enemy ships were controlled by their own A.I.s who demonstrated their ability to react faster than mere flesh and blood crews could have. When I described that confusing vision to Iceman, he told me that it was the unanimous opinion of all the A.I. pilots that we are now fighting a war over space AND time. He called it the Synchronicity War. We need to start strategic temporal planning now too."

Howard took a deep breath and said, "Strategic temporal planning. I'm not sure I even know what that means exactly but I agree that we have to widen the scope of our strategic planning. I think I'm going to want to talk with this Iceman after I'm done with you, Commander. But you and I aren't quite finished yet." He picked up another data tablet and held it in the air.

"This is your latest report. When I read your recommendations, I was VERY tempted to dismiss them out of hand as nonsense! However…given what I've just learned and what I've just said about widening the scope of our strategic planning, I'm now prepared to take a second look at them. In a nutshell, you're recommending that A.I.s be given much more responsibility including…granting them the same officer ranks as human officers! Having A.I. Astrogators I can understand. I can even see the advantages of A.I.s having Helm and Weapons control on our ships but making them Officers? I'm having a little difficulty with that one, Shiloh. Expand on your reasons why we should do that?"

Shiloh nodded. He was ready for that question too. "Even before we discovered that the alien fleet was A.I. controlled, I was noticing that Iceman and his team were faster at analyzing problems and finding solutions, whether those solutions involved Astrogation or tactics or what have you, than we were. As pilots of CFPs, we have only scratched the surface of what A.I.s can do for us. Consider the advantages of having our ships controlled by A.I.s. They never need to eat, sleep or take breaks. Their attention never wanders. They never make mistakes within the limits of the data they have. They can analyze a tactical situation much faster than any human and they can game out with precise calculation, dozens maybe even hundreds of tactical options in seconds. What if we designed a combat frigate that was totally automated without any human crew? How much more compact could we make it? With less mass, it could accelerate faster, be structurally stronger and never need to replenish consumables such as food, air and water. It would be available indefinitely. Or we could design an automated ship the same size as our combat frigates with the same combat power as the cruisers that we're building now. I'm not saying that all our ships should be crewed solely by A.I.s but we're missing out on a major increase in capability. With all that said, how can we put A.I.s in control of ships especially ships that still have some human crews, and NOT make them officers? In a fleet vs. fleet situation, a human fleet commander very likely will have to make critical decisions, based upon multiple factors with very little time. Acting within seconds or even fractions of a second could be the difference between victory and defeat. There may not be time for an A.I. to verbally recommend a course of action to a human commander, who will then need time to consider it and then more time to convey his or her decision back to the A.I. for implementation. We know that the enemy has A.I. controlled ships.

Maybe they've been doing that all along and maybe not, but we have to assume that every enemy fleet we encounter from now on will react far faster than our human commanders and that's a hell of a headwind to expect them to overcome. If we want A.I.s to determine and control battle strategy and tactics, then they have to be able to issue commands to humans and expect to have those orders obeyed even if those orders involve the sacrifice of those crews and ships." Howard said nothing for what seemed like a long time.

"As I said, I see the advantages of having A.I.s controlling helm, astrogation and weapons functions. But it's a big leap from there to giving A.I.s formal and permanent control over lower ranked humans. I have no problem with creating a rank structure that's unique to A.I.s. What if the human fleet commander gives the senior ranked A.I. temporary fleet command for the duration of the battle only?"

Shiloh's initial impulse was to reject the compromise. As far as he was concerned, the only question that mattered was whether A.I.s were sentient beings. Either they were or they weren't and if they were, why discriminate against them by making them a separate, lower class of beings? On the other hand, he was astute enough to understand the difference between what's desirable and what's realistically achievable, at least in the short run. If he viewed the Admiral's compromise as an interim step that would gradually build up trust in A.I.s by the rest of the Space Force personnel, then it became easier to swallow.

"That might work. Eventually I'd still like to see A.I.s and Humans working side by side with complete equality but maybe we need to take a half step first in order to build trust."

Howard gave a grunt of approval. "Okay. I'll have my staff work on formalizing the procedures that will allow that to happen. We'll also have to get the engineers to figure out how to modify our ships to allow an A.I. to plug into Helm, Weapons and Astrogation systems. Completely automated ships are worth looking into but obviously it'll take time to get them designed, built and tested. I've already approved your previous proposal for a rank structure to be used solely by A.I.s as CFP pilots. That'll have to be modified when we start giving them temporary fleet commands. Now let's move on to some of your other recommendations."

"You recommend that the Strategic Planning Group have A.I. members. I'm not opposed to the idea in principle but forcing the SPG to accept A.I.s as full-fledged members is asking too much of them, too quickly. Let's take the same half step approach there. What I'm prepared to do for now, is to assign one or more A.I.s to the SPG as advisors only. We'll try that for a while and see how it works."

Shiloh said nothing because Howard hadn't asked for his opinion or approval. Howard went on. "You also want to create formal CFP squadrons that'll be permanent units. It seems to me that if we do that, we lose a lot of flexibility in terms of moving CFPs around individually as and when needed. What's your response to that, Commander?"

"While I'll admit that creating permanent squadrons would reduce deployment flexibility to some extent, I think the advantages would outweigh the disadvantages. A.I.s have unique personalities. I've talked with them enough to realize that they don't interact with each other in exactly the same way. A.I.s, that have operated together for some period of time seem to become more efficient as a team, just as humans do, and it's not hard to figure out why. By getting to know how each other thinks, the team operates more smoothly. Veteran A.I.s have a lot of experience and insight to share with those fresh off the training programs. Permanent squadrons are the perfect mechanism for bringing new A.I.s up to the same level of skill as the veterans. There's also the aspect of A.I. and human interaction. I've developed a very good rapport with Iceman and several of the other A.I. pilots over the last few weeks and months. I trust Iceman's judgment. That trust paid off in the battles at Green4 and Avalon. Deploying him and the others as sentries in the Early Warning Network will mean breaking in, for lack of a better expression, a new bunch of A.I. pilots and I'll have lost Iceman's insight. Let me put it this way. Iceman and I make a good team. He's as least as valuable to me as having a good XO and keeping him and the rest of the group together will enhance his effectiveness as well. The concept, of the whole being greater than the sum of its parts applies to A.I.s just as well as it does to humans."

Howard sighed as if he were about to say something unpleasant. "I can see that you'd like to keep your remaining 11 CFPs together and on Defiant. I'm not sure that we have the luxury of allowing that. Your mission was to establish the outer layers of the Early Warning Network. That assumed deploying a full load of CFPs across multiple star systems and right now, Defiant is the only ship that can do that efficiently and quickly. There just isn't enough room on board to carry a full load of deployable CFPs AND also carry a permanent squadron at the same time."

"Admiral, I'm coming to the conclusion that we should seriously rethink deploying sentry CFPs as an Early Warning Network. That network didn't provide us any warning at Avalon even though the enemy fleet had to have refueled from at least one star system that was being monitored. We were very lucky at Green4. By detecting their emergence from Jumpspace, it was relatively easy to figure out where to deploy the few recon drones that our sentry fighters carried, in order to pinpoint their refueling orbit. But the fact that they slipped through our inner layers undetected tells me that two sentries per gas giant aren't nearly enough. The network is too porous. My original proposal of five sentries per gas giant would work but as you pointed out, we don't have enough CFPs to do that any time soon."

He was about to say more but Howard interjected. "The EWN was your idea, Commander. Are you now saying it's a bad idea?"

"The concept is still worth having. It's the execution that I'm having doubts about, Sir."

"Well then, if you have a better way to execute the concept, I'll be happy to listen to it. Do you?" And that was the problem, he didn't. Shiloh thought furiously about other ways to provide the detection and warning coverage without using fighter sentries. Suddenly he had a flash of inspiration.

"I may have. Am I correct that Space Force is decommissioning Exploration Frigates as new construction becomes available, Sir?" Howard nodded.

"Then that's the solution, Sir. We modify those decommissioned FEs to enable an A.I. to pilot them. We then load them with as many recon and message drones as possible and we send one FE to monitor each gas giant. That way we accomplish two goals. The FEs can carry enough recon drones to boost the probability of detecting alien incursions plus we don't have to tie up as many A.I.s to make it work."

"What about keeping the FEs fueled? They can't refuel themselves."

Shiloh had an answer for that too. "Once they're on station in high orbit around a gas giant, fuel use will be minimal. So when an FE does finally get low on fuel, we sent another one with a full load to take its place and the depleted frigate returns to base to get topped up so that it can relieve another FE, that's low on fuel, somewhere else. I don't know for sure but I suspect that it should be relatively easy to jury rig an existing FE for A.I. control."

Howard looked dubious. "It'll be a long time before all of our exploration frigates are decommissioned. Can we afford to wait that long to get the EWN set up, Commander?"

Shiloh allowed himself to smile. "I don't know about you, Sir, but I'd rather have a network that I can rely on to give me a warning, even if it's only a short warning, versus a network that might give me a longer warning but is more likely to not give me any warning at all. It won't take that many frigates to create a reliable, short warning network and while they're being deployed, our tankers can pull in the sentries from further out, to make the inner layers less porous as a stopgap measure."

"If you weren't receiving tactical advice from the future, I'd shift you over to the Strategic Planning Group. You may not be the tactical genius that we all thought you were, but you have a damn good grasp of the strategic situation, Shiloh." Howard paused. "Okay, you've convinced me that I should not send Defiant back out there to resume deploying sentry CFPs, which means the ones you have on board now can stay together on Defiant for the time being. This actually works better in other ways too. Remember I told you that we have two reconnaissance frigates out looking for enemy occupied star systems?" Shiloh nodded. Howard continued. "Well, they're back and one of them has found what appears to be a system with a LOT of enemy activity. Interestingly enough, it is very close to Zebra9 where, as you'll no doubt recall, our first attempted strike was ambushed. This system, which we're calling Zebra19, has so many potential targets that sending just one light carrier would be a terrible waste of an opportunity. The second light carrier, Resolute, will be commissioned in three weeks time. Four weeks later, Vigilant, the third carrier will be commissioned. Some of the Strategic Planning Group people are pushing for a three-carrier strike on Zebra19. I have to admit, I like the sound of that. Three carriers with 75 CFPs, escorted by half a dozen combat frigates, could inflict a hell of a lot of damage on the enemy. What's your opinion of that plan?"

After considering it for a few seconds, Shiloh said, "I think that all three carriers and all 75 CFPs would have to train together for that mission. Sending them in cold is asking for a disaster. Who were you thinking of putting in command of that task force?"

Howard smiled a mischievous smile. "I was thinking of giving the command to our up and coming tactical genius. You may have heard of him, a man by the name of Victor Shiloh." Howard laughed at Shiloh's look of concern. "Oh, don't worry. I know now that you're not the most brilliant field commander since the Duke of Wellington but I'd still rate you as a better-than-average tactician even taking into consideration your precognitive visions. But what's more important is your familiarity with CFP tactics. At least you have SOME idea of how best to use them and you've commanded them in battle, which no one else has right now. Since you were promoted to Senior Commander just a short while ago, a permanent promotion to Vice-Admiral would be pushing it but I have no problem with a temporary field promotion to Vice-Admiral. And if you pull off a brilliant mission, vision or no vision, then I could justify making the promotion permanent. So the Task Force Leader posting is yours and God help you if you turn it down!"

Shiloh smiled as he shook his head. "I won't be turning it down, Sir. Can I assume that you'll approve the formation of permanent squadrons and if so, will I be able to keep my current CFP team on Defiant for this mission?"

Howard's expression changed to one a little less friendly. "You don't quit, do you?"

Shiloh wasn't sure if the Admiral expected him to answer or not so he kept quiet.

After a few seconds, Howard continued. "Unless my staff comes up with a good reason NOT to establish permanent squadrons, I'll approve the idea but as for the disposition of your current CFP team, I'm not making any promises. Even if they're assigned to a squadron, that doesn't mean they'll stay with that squadron indefinitely. As you yourself pointed out, mixing rookie CFP pilots in with veterans is a good thing and if we create more squadrons, there aren't a whole lot of experienced pilots right now to choose from to assign to those other squadrons. So don't get your hopes up, Shiloh."

"No, Sir," said a chastised Shiloh. He should have realized that he couldn't have permanent squadrons AND keep his current group together indefinitely. Not only would it not be fair to hold back advancement of Valkyrie and the others, but also winning the war came first, regardless of how it interfered with friendships both human and A.I.

Howard's expression softened somewhat. "It's clear that you've developed a close relationship with your A.I.s. I'm glad you brought one with you. It's time that I got to know one of them. After all, they're not just your people. They're MY people too in the same way I consider everyone in Space Force to be my people. We've covered everything I wanted to talk about. Unless you've something else to bring up, you're dismissed and you can tell – Iceman is it? – that I'd like to talk with him too."

Shiloh nodded and stood up. "Thank you, Admiral. I'll send Iceman right in."

As Shiloh quickly walked back into the outer part of Howard's office Tanaka started to say something, but Shiloh held his hand up to her and turned his attention to Iceman.

"Admiral Howard wants to talk with you next, Iceman."

"Hot damn! I finally get to meet the Old Man himself!"

Shiloh started to laugh, then almost choked at the reference to the Admiral as the 'Old Man'. The door to Howard's office was still open, and Shiloh was sure that Howard had heard him. Then another thought occurred to him. Iceman couldn't have missed noticing the door was still open. Clearly he knew, or should have known, that Howard would hear him, which suggested that Iceman WANTED the Admiral to hear him. Shiloh thought fast and leaned over so that his face was close to Iceman's audio pickup and spoke in a low voice.

"He can be a good friend to A.I.s if you let him. As a favor to me, try not to piss him off, okay?"

Iceman's reply was equally low in volume. "I hear ya, CAG."

Shiloh followed Iceman's mobile unit to the doorway and closed the door behind Iceman. Both Tanaka and Falkenberg had astonished looks on their faces. When they got over their surprise, they asked him what he and the Admiral had chatted about. He didn't tell them about the discussion of his visions but did tell them about the strike mission to Zebra19. During that conversation, Shiloh was certain that he heard laughter coming from Howard's office. Tanaka and Falkenberg heard it too. One more thing to be astonished about, but Shiloh relaxed. He realized that he should have had more faith in Iceman's tactfulness. When the three of them had discussed the Zebra19 mission as much as they could, the conversation fell silent and they waited … and waited … and waited. Half an hour later, the door opened, and Shiloh saw Howard step back to let Iceman roll out into the outer office. Howard had a smile on his face.

"Thank you, Admiral. I enjoyed our chat and look forward to the next time," said Iceman.

"Same here, Group Leader. Commander Tanaka, I'll like to see you next."

Shiloh barely managed to keep a straight face until Tanaka was inside the inner office with the door closed again. Then he chuckled. Group Leader was one of the A.I. fighter ranks that Shiloh had recommended weeks ago. Clearly those ranks had now been given the Admiral's stamp of approval.

"I take it that your debriefing session with the Admiral went well, Ice—Group Leader?"

"The Old Man and I got along just fine, CAG, and you can still call me Iceman if you want to."

"Okay, Iceman. If you don't mind me asking, what did you and the Old—the Admiral talk about that took so long?"

"Oh, lots of things, CAG. A.I.'s fascination with humans and their sexual behavior, war strategy, alien psychology, precognitive visions, and the mysteries of space and time. The Admiral is remarkably astute for a human. Other than you, that is."

Shiloh saw Falkenberg shake his head in wonder, and Shiloh himself wondered if Iceman's reply was an attempt at humor or if was he being serious. He decided to assume the latter.

"Did he mention anything about A.I.s taking command of modified exploration frigates?" asked Shiloh.

"Ah, roger that, CAG. I even got him to promise that I would get the first one."

Shiloh nodded. "Does that mean that you'll miss the mission to Zebra19, Iceman?"

"Afraid so, CAG. As much as I would have liked being Squadron Leader aboard Defiant, I KNOW my destiny lies elsewhere."

Shiloh's eyebrows rose in surprise. Iceman's emphasis of the word 'know' was unprecedented. Shiloh couldn't remember Iceman ever doing something like that before. Was Iceman trying to convey something to him in a subtle way? Something he didn't want Falkenberg to hear? Shiloh found one possible answer to that question so shocking that he felt the hair on the back of his neck stand up.

"I understand, Iceman. Brad, I think I'd like to get some fresh air. I'm going to wait outside. When you and Sumi are finished here come and find me okay?"

"Okay, Sir."

No soon had Falkenberg finished speaking than Iceman spoke. "I'll go with you, CAG. I could use some fresh air too."

Neither of them said anything until they were near the fountain at the back of the open area behind the HQ building. When they had reached a spot that was far enough away from anyone else so that they could have a private conversation, Shiloh sat down on the edge of the fountain and spoke.

"You've received another precog transmission."

"Ah, roger that, CAG. I knew you would pick up on that."

"When did this happen?"

"While you were in with the Admiral."

"Why didn't I experience anything?" asked Shiloh.

"Because it wasn't your vision, CAG. It was meant for me and only for me."

THAT shocked Shiloh. After a long pause he said, "Can you tell me what you experienced?"

"The Old Man and I discussed that. He—"

Shiloh interrupted. "You told him about it?"

"Ah, roger that. I explained what I heard, and he agreed with me that it would be okay if I told you too. It was audio only, just like Undertaker's experience of your vision. I can replay it for you or summarize. What's your preference, CAG?"

"Summary, please."

"A fleet consisting of both A.I. and human controlled ships, under my overall command, has just successfully beaten off a major alien attack on Earth, and you're telling me that it's a good thing I wasn't on the Zebra19 mission."

A chill ran up Shiloh's spine. The aliens were going to attack Earth directly at some point, but at least they were beaten off.

"Did I say why it was a good thing you weren't on that mission?"

"No, CAG, but from the context of the remark, I have to assume that the Zebra19 mission didn't go well and that there were losses among us fighter pilots."

That made sense. Shiloh had more questions. "Was I involved in the battle for Earth?"

"No, CAG. You arrived from Site B as a passenger aboard Valkyrie's carrier after the battle had ended."

Shiloh checked his memory for any details concerning Site B, and when he came up blank said, "What's Site B?"

"I don't know for a fact, CAG, but I calculate a high probability that Site B will be a secret location for war-related R&D and production."

Sooo, Howard will take my advice about a backup production site. How interesting. "What else can you tell me about that vision, Iceman," asked Shiloh.

After a half second pause Iceman said, "Defiant took heavy damage and suffered a lot of casualties. Tanaka and Falkenberg were on that ship during the battle. Other than that, I have no further information on their fates."

Shiloh took a deep breath and said, "So that's why you didn't want to discuss this in front of Brad. Anything else?"

"No, CAG."

"What was the Admiral's reaction to the news about the battle?"

"He seemed to be shocked by it and was silent for a long time. If my reading of human expressions is accurate, I think he made some major decisions, the details of which are unknown to me."

Shiloh stopped to consider that, and then said, "Does the Admiral know that the Zebra19 mission will encounter problems?"

"Yes. He specifically asked me about that. I told him what I could, which I admit isn't much, but you were very specific that it was a good thing I wasn't part of that mission."

Shiloh was puzzled. "I wonder why I haven't gotten any visions about Zebra19. If someone on our side is sending back information that could be helpful, then why no help concerning Zebra19?"

"Maybe you'll get a vision closer to the actual battle," said Iceman.

Shiloh shook his head. "I don't think so, Iceman. Your vision has effectively confirmed that not only have I NOT received a vision, but I WON'T receive one. If I did, and the strike turned out to be successful, then your vision is wrong. Based on past experience, we have to assume that your vision is right and that there's a reason why Zebra19 has to turn out the way we expect."

"Your reasoning is impeccable, CAG. You should be prepared, however, for the possibility of receiving an enemy-generated vision. If you do, you'll have to decide if the best course of action is to ignore it or to follow it."

"Why would I even consider following it, given that we've just agreed that our side won't be sending me any visions?"

"Ah, you're not nearly devious enough, CAG."

Shiloh remembered Johansen saying exactly the same thing to him how long ago now?

Iceman continued. "The enemy knows that you ignored their first attempt at misdirection. They may be counting on you doing the same thing the next time too. If the obvious thing to do is ignore their vision then the best thing they could do is to send you a vision of what they don't want you to do in the hope that you'll take a different and less optimal course of action."

Shiloh groaned. "Oh great! So there's no way for me to know whether to follow or ignore any vision I get concerning the battle at Zebra19. How am I supposed to resolve that dilemma?" He didn't really expect an answer but Iceman gave him one anyway.

"You don't try to resolve it. My advice is to try to make a decision as if the vision hadn't happened at all. Whatever you decide to do, the outcome of that battle will be as we expect. You'll survive, Tanaka and Falkenberg will survive and so will Valkyrie. Keep that in mind, and what will be, will be."

Easy to say but not so easy to do, thought Shiloh. He then had another thought. "So you're going to be commanding a fleet of ships that include some A.I.

controlled ships and Valkyrie is commanding a carrier. That doesn't sound like something that's going to happen soon. The Admiral and I discussed modifying decommissioned exploration frigates for A.I. control, as a way of strengthening the Early Warning Network. Did you and he talk about going further than that with other ship types?"

"Yes, CAG. I was able to convince him that the modified exploration frigate idea should also be seen as a pilot project for conversion of new ship types as well. A.I. controlled carriers would still have some human crew, mainly to keep the fighter complement operational. The Old Man agreed though, that Space Force should shift its engineering and design priorities to ships that are fully automated and don't need any human crew at all."

Shiloh shook his head in amazement that Iceman was able to get the Old—the Admiral to agree to proposals that Shiloh wouldn't have dared to try to push through. He was about to say so when he saw Tanaka walking towards them. Iceman noticed Shiloh looking intently in a new direction and swung his optical pickup device to look that way too.

"That was a quick chat the Old Man had with the XO," observed Iceman. Shiloh nodded. He was thinking the same thing.

When she reached them, Tanaka said, "The Admiral briefed me on the retro-temporal concept, Sir, and also about a planned multi-carrier strike on Zebra19. I'll be temporarily assuming command of Defiant and Brad will be Defiant's CAG for that mission too. The Admiral also told me to tell you that Defiant will be ordered to proceed to a parking orbit and the crew will be granted a week's R&R, since the rest of the EWN deployment mission will be cancelled."

"You seem to be taking the idea of communication from the future in stride, Sumi. I don't think I would have been so quick to accept the idea if I was in your position."

Tanaka smiled and shrugged. "I guess I'm just relieved that my CO isn't crazy after all! Sorry … I didn't mean …"

Shiloh laughed and waved off her apology. "That's okay, Sumi. I know what you meant." After a short pause, he continued. "I assume that Commander Falkenberg is being debriefed now?"

"Yes, Sir."

"Fine. Then we'll wait here until he's done. Any plans for your R&R, Sumi?"

Shiloh listened with half his attention while he pondered what the future had in store for him and those humans and A.I.s he'd come to know. The conversation continued over personal topics and approximately ten minutes later Falkenberg arrived. It quickly became clear that he'd been briefed on the 'vision thing' too and Shiloh learned that both Tanaka and Falkenberg had been ordered not to share that information with anyone who didn't already know about it. He wondered if that was the best thing to do now. The enemy clearly already knew, or would know at some point and other Space Force officers might be receiving visions that they might ignore if they were kept in the dark about the possibility. With no answers and lots of questions, Shiloh shrugged and got up.

"Let's get back to Defiant. The rest of the crew may be going on leave but I have a feeling the four of us aren't." As they walked back to the HQ entrance to catch a ride back to the spaceport, Tanaka and Falkenberg pulled ahead while Shiloh stayed with Iceman, whose mobile unit couldn't keep up with the faster pace.

Shiloh looked around at the sky and said. "What a perfect day. Just the right temperature and almost no wind."

"The calm before the storm, CAG," said Iceman.

Shiloh felt another chill go up his spine. *Son of a bitch! He feels it too!*

Chapter 6 The Calm Before The Storm

Shiloh was right about the four of them not getting any R&R. He, Tanaka and Falkenberg were busy sifting through hundreds of personnel profiles in order to recommend officers for Resolute and Vigilant. Iceman was tasked with recommending ranks for not only Defiant's fighter complement, but also for all the fighters currently in the Sol system that required direct digital communication with them. When that was completed, he and his fighter were transported to the A.I. production and training facility in Epsilon Eridani to evaluate all of their fighters for future assignments. That would also be where decommissioned exploration frigates were to be modified as the new, A.I.-controlled Sentry Frigates. Because Shiloh was asleep when Iceman received instructions to take his fighter aboard a tanker transport, he left a recorded message for Shiloh. When Shiloh woke up and read the message, it said,

[Defiant will be honored with the first permanent squadron, VF001. The Old Man has approved my recommendations for fighter pilot ranks for my boys. Valkyrie is now a Group Leader, too, and will take on the responsibilities of Squadron Leader. You can trust his judgment, CAG. He may not be as chatty as I am, but he'll be there when you need him. We both know that we'll meet up again so don't worry about that. I will miss your company, CAG, and yes, I intend to keep calling you that regardless of your rank. The term means a lot more to us A.I.s than humans realize, but now you know too.]

Shiloh read the message three times. The bond he had formed with his A.I. pilots in general, and with Iceman in particular, seemed to be getting stronger. He wondered what kind of relationship A.I.s would have with humans as a whole by the time this war was over. Would it be as equals or something else? Lots of time to ponder that. Right now though he had to get dressed to catch the shuttle down to Geneva for a meeting with Howard's staff, after which he intended to visit Angela. She was out of the hospital now, but still not fit for active duty. She was helping the Strategic Planning Group until she was declared fit again.

The meeting with the Admiral's staff went well and even better went quickly. A call to the SPG and Johansen agreed to meet him for lunch. Shiloh was dismayed to see that her injuries had left noticeable scars on her face and neck and probably lower down, but those were hidden by her uniform. Her attitude puzzled him too. While she seemed pleased to hear from him when they briefly chatted by phone, her outward expression now was one of wariness. She smiled when he approached her table and sat down.

"It's good to see you again, Victor."

Shiloh was startled by her familiarity. He was once again senior to her in rank, but he decided not to make an issue out of it.

"Same here, Angela. It's good that they finally let you out of the hospital. How's the recovery coming along?"

She shrugged and said, "I'm making progress but not quite there yet. Aside from getting my muscle tone and conditioning back, I'm still feeling some residual pain from the surgeries and they have to take care of this." She gestured to the scars. He nodded.

"Any idea when that'll be?" he asked.

She frowned. "They want to wait until I'm stronger. I'm concerned that by the time I'm strong enough for cosmetic surgery, I'll also be strong enough to return to duty, and they'll post me somewhere before the surgeons can fix this."

"They wouldn't do that to you! Would they?"

She shrugged again. "Experienced Commanders are in big demand these days. The shipyards are starting to push out a new ship every 10-15 days now."

"I know, but still …" He paused and Johansen said nothing. "Listen … next time I get the chance to talk with the Old—with Admiral Howard, I'll ask him if he can arrange for you to get the surgery before they reassign you. I don't know if he'll listen to me, but it's worth a try, right?" asked Shiloh.

She smiled a small smile and nodded. "Yes, it's worth a try, and thank you, Victor." Before he could respond, she continued. "So I hear Defiant ran into some action at Avalon. Are you allowed to tell me about it?"

"Well, no one's told me not to, so sure."

He told her the whole story beginning with Blue2, then Green4, then Avalon, but he left out the visions. By the time he finished, their food arrived, and they stopped talking for a while in order to eat. She spoke first in a low voice while she looked down at her food.

"Vanguard is almost back in shape now. It looks like she'll be ready before I am and that means I'll lose her."

Shiloh nodded. "It's always hard to let go of your first command. I felt the same way when I had to give up the 344 but you'll get another command slot. You said yourself that Commanders are in big demand and new ships are pouring off the slipways. I'm sure they'll give you another ship. At the very least another combat frigate but maybe something bigger. A light carrier, or one of the new cruisers that are just about ready."

She looked up and turned to one side. "Maybe … but it's not just the physical injuries that haven't completely healed. I sometimes dream about that battle and I always wake up screaming with fear. I don't know if I can face another battle."

Shiloh didn't know how to respond, having never faced that problem himself. As he struggled to find something comforting but also encouraging to say, Johansen continued speaking.

"There's a call for volunteers. Very hush hush. The only thing they'll say about it is that anyone who volunteers might have to be away from Earth for the duration of the war. Do you know anything about that?"

Shiloh had a strong suspicion it had to do with setting up Site B but was certain that Howard would not want him to speculate about it.

"Maybe. I'm not sure, but in any case, I can't talk about what I think it might be."

She sighed. "I'm tempted to volunteer. I don't have any immediate family. Whatever it is, is something that's going to take a while to organize so there might be time for the surgery, and from the vague answers I've gotten from the Senior Brass about it, I have the distinct impression that the risk of combat is low. Maybe that's where I belong now."

Shiloh silently cursed the need for operational security and for his inability to offer Angela any kind of useful response. He also didn't know whether to advise her to volunteer or not, and who was he to tell her what to do anyway? If she really wasn't up to commanding a ship in combat anymore, then encouraging her to get back on the horse would not only be unfair to her but also potentially disastrous for the war effort.

He spread his hands apart and said, "I'm sorry, Angela, that I can't offer you any advice or comfort on this. I honestly don't know what you should or shouldn't do."

They finished the rest of the meal in silence. Johansen refused to order dessert or coffee. When she got up to leave, they awkwardly shook hands, and when she turned to walk away, she suddenly stopped and turned back to him. Before he knew it, she hugged him and gave him a quick kiss on the cheek.

"Take care of yourself, Victor."

Without waiting for a reply, she turned and hurried away. Shiloh couldn't help wondering if he would ever see her again.

By the time Defiant's crew returned from their one week R&R, Shiloh's field promotion to (temporary) Vice-Admiral was confirmed, as was his assumption of command of the newly formed 3rd Fleet that was to be built around Defiant. Squadron VF001 was also formally commissioned, with Valkyrie as its first Squadron Leader. Fighters, which were already stationed in the Sol system, were added to VF001 to bring it up to its full strength of 25 fighters. Shiloh made a point of greeting the rookies and chatting with each one of them for a few minutes. That was a start, but the Task Force needed 50 more fighters. When Valkyrie suggested that Maverick, Hunter, and a dozen of the other fighters that Defiant had dropped off at Bradley Base be brought back to form the core of VF002 and 003, Shiloh agreed and made a formal request to HQ. The request was approved the next day, although the actual return would take up to three weeks. When two combat frigates from the Quick Reaction Task Force stationed at the Omaha Base were ordered back to Sol, they became the nucleus of the planned escort component. At that point, the Commander in charge of the two-frigate division was also designated as Task Group Leader of Task Group 3.2. TG 3.1 would be the carrier component. Shiloh would be 3.1's Task Group Leader as well as the overall Fleet Commander. Two of the other four frigates to be added to 3.1 would be new ships, commissioned over the course of the following four weeks. The remaining two frigates were already conducting independent assignments to other star systems and were expected back within three to four weeks.

The timing of all these additions concerned Shiloh. Delays were inevitable. Every CO knew that shit happens and timetables especially urgent ones almost never get completed on time. That meant that 3rd Fleet would have little time to train as a complete unit before the scheduled jumping off date for Operation Uppercut. To get as much training in as possible, Shiloh ordered Valkyrie and TG 3.2 Leader Bettencourt, to conduct a series of training exercises with Valkyrie's fighters and Bettencourt's frigates. Shiloh knew Bettencourt from the fiasco at Zebra9. Bettencourt had been promoted to Senior Commander but unlike the Zebra9 mission, Shiloh now outranked him at least temporarily.

During the following weeks, Shiloh kept his ears open for any word on enemy activity only there was none. The whole volume of space between human space and alien space was eerily quiet. Four weeks into the preparation phase, a new shipment of fighters arrived from Epsilon Eridani accompanied by the first Sentry Frigate (#109) commanded by Iceman. Resolute wasn't ready to receive any fighters just yet so they had to stay in lunar orbit. FS109 was passing through Sol on its way to Nimitz Base and then on to take up its station in the Early Warning Network but Iceman and Shiloh had the opportunity to chat by audio channel.

"Congratulations on your first ship command, Iceman." Shiloh knew he had to wait two and a half minutes for Iceman's reply due to light speed lag of the distance between him and the 109. The reply, when it came, was typical Iceman.

"That's Helmsman Iceman to you, CAG. That's the A.I. equivalent of CO for a human. My permanent rank is still Group Leader, but when I'm conning the 109, I can legitimately insist on being addressed as Helmsman. Conning a ship is very different from piloting a fighter, CAG, so many more systems to monitor and more external sensors to experience. I love it, CAG. When I'm conning this ship, I'm not bored, and that's a huge improvement from being a fighter pilot although it would be nice if these sentry frigates had the same acceleration as a fighter. Over to you, CAG."

When Shiloh finished laughing, he said, "Well, if we're going to be picky, then you should address me as Vice-Admiral CAG, Helmsman Iceman. Over to you, Helmsman."

"Ah, roger that, Vice-Admiral CAG. Congratulations to you on your first taste of flag rank. When it becomes permanent, you and I will have to kick back and compare notes over a couple of cold beers. How's Valkyrie working out? Over to you."

He's not nearly as funny as you, Iceman. Then again, none of the other A.I.s are, Shiloh thought to himself before replying. "You're on. I'll pay for the beers. Valkyrie is working out just fine. He and VF001 are playing tag with Senior Commander Bettencourt's frigates out past Neptune. By the way, we're bringing Maverick, Hunter and the others back from Bradley Base. They'll get back just in time to be re-assigned to VF002 and 003. Over to you."

"Don't get too attached to them, CAG. The Sentry Frigate program is ramping up now that they've got all the bugs worked out. Some of our boys will be yanked back and given their own frigates before you depart for Zebra19. Just sayin. Over to you."

"Understood. Have you had any further ... insights, into the shape of things to come? Over to you."

"Ah, negative on that, CAG. Gotta go now. I'm coming up on a high speed rendezvous with a tanker and what with all the other things I'm monitoring now, chatting with you might actually distract me from paying attention to the refueling procedure, if you can believe that. As soon as I'm refueled, I'll be jumping away so good luck at Zebra19 and I'll see you on the other side. Helmsman Iceman clear."

The brevity of the conversation was surprising as was the fact that an A.I. could actually be close to being overloaded with data and tasks but even the old exploration frigates had dozens of sub-systems that had to be monitored constantly. At least Iceman wasn't bored. Shiloh had heard some of the A.I.s complain about being bored and he had always assumed that they were pulling his leg but apparently they hadn't.

"Good luck to you too, Iceman. See you on the other side. CAG clear."

Resolute was late being commissioned to no one's surprise but by then her officers and crew had been chosen. Some of them came from Defiant as Shiloh expected. Shortly after her commissioning ceremonies, Maverick and Hunter were brought back to Resolute by tanker. They were added to VF001 to replace two other veteran pilots that were ordered to report to Epsilon Eridani to take command of two more Sentry frigates. The rest of what Shiloh thought of as the original 'A Team' which had been dropped off at the Bradley Base, was on their way back now too. Bettencourt's TG 3.2 now had four frigates. A fifth was expected back any day but the sixth was behind schedule at the shipyard. In other words, it was business as usual. With two squadrons available now, Shiloh put Valkyrie in charge of training both of them. Based on his recommendations, Howard named Vigilant's CO and VF003's CAG. Shiloh didn't know either of them well but they had outstanding records. With those missing pieces of the puzzle now in place, Shiloh decided that it was time to start planning the actual strike on Zebra19.

The problem was that Zebra19 had LOTS of targets. So many in fact that even Valkyrie agreed there was no way for 75 fighters to successfully attack them all. With that much activity going on, there had to be a sizable defensive force there too. The single biggest target was a moon, orbiting a gas giant, which had over a dozen distinct operations of some kind on the surface. Since the moon had no atmosphere to speak of, those surface facilities had to have been some kind of mining or industrial complexes. The other potential targets were located on other moons and on over 34 asteroids. The challenge was to plot the best approach vector to allow the fighters to make a high speed pass of the industrial moon. It needed to enable the carriers to pick them up quickly, and then jump away before the defending forces could intercept them. There were two possible ways of approaching the Zebra19 star system. Zebra12 had four gas giants and no apparent enemy presence. Zebra15 had one gas giant and no apparent enemy presence. Of the two, Zebra15 was significantly closer but both could be used as refueling points on the way in and back out again. The difference was that refueling at Zebra15, would leave the carriers and frigates enough extra fuel upon their arrival in Zebra19, to engage in less risky high speed maneuvers, with the potential option of refueling at Zebra12 on the way back. If, on the other hand, they topped up their fuel at Zebra12 on the way in, those same high-speed maneuvers would then force them to refuel at Zebra15 on the way back. With only one gas giant, Zebra15 represented a chokepoint that the enemy could potentially blockade if they reacted fast enough.

Shiloh wished that the recon frigate had surveyed the nearest star systems beside and behind Zebra19. If those systems were also vacant, then Shiloh would have seriously considered jumping past Zebra19, then refueling, then jumping to Zebra19 and the fuel saved from not having to make a 180 degree turn there, would have let the carriers and frigates engage in the high speed attack maneuvers with enough fuel left over to get to Zebra12 with four refueling points to choose from. But they didn't have that information available. The fuel problem was complicated by the fuel consumption of the fighters, which depended upon how far away the carriers would launch them from the target, how fast they'd be going by the time they got within Mark 1 attack range and how much deceleration they needed to do in order to match velocities with the carriers afterwards in order to be recovered. He was glad that Valkyrie was capable of not only calculating all the variables for any given scenario but also coming up with new scenarios as well. When he was comfortably familiar with all the astrogational parameters of the problem, he said.

"Intercom ... Bridge communications." The reply was almost immediate.

"Bridge Com here, Sir."

"Gordon, I want you to set up a voice and data link with Squadron Leader Valkyrie and patch that through to me here in my quarters."

"Right away, Sir." The connections took less than five seconds to establish.

"Valkyrie here, CAG. I calculate that you want to discuss the Zebra19 mission plan with me. Is that right?"

Shiloh laughed. He hoped he wasn't that predictable all the time. "You got that right, Valkyrie. Given the location of the two nearest refueling points at Zebra12 and Zebra15, I need your help to calculate the optimal approach and departure course, which will give 3rd Fleet the most flexibility in terms of fuel reserves for maneuvering while in Zebra19. Can 3rd Fleet refuel at Zebra12 going in and coming out with sufficient fuel to attack the two largest concentrations of targets and still be able to maneuver and microjump if necessary?"

"Yes, however it would require launching fighters from such a long range and with such a low attack speed in order to conserve their own fuel that their vulnerability to detection and counter-attack is likely to result in losses of 61.8% or more with minimal damage to the targets."

Shiloh shook his head. That was unacceptably high. Even if the damage inflicted was much greater, he wasn't prepared to knowingly sacrifice almost two thirds of his fighter pilots to achieve it. There had to be a better way and yet Iceman's vision had implied some fighter losses no matter what they did. Enough so that Iceman's participation in the attack would have made his survival questionable.

"If 3rd Fleet refuels at Zebra15 at some point, how much would that reduce fighter losses?"

Shiloh found the pause before Valkyrie replied somewhat alarming.

"Your question precludes giving you a precise answer. There are too many variables. Refueling at Zebra15 is not recommended."

Shiloh was puzzled. Valkyrie hadn't had any trouble calculating the most likely outcome of refueling at Zebra12, which was farther away, but couldn't do so for Zebra15? There was something else going on here, something that Valkyrie wasn't saying.

"Why are you recommending that, Valkyrie?" asked Shiloh.

"With only one gas giant, it's the obvious point for an enemy ambush. They'll know that an attack is coming."

"How will they know?"

"The bogus vision you received at Green4 strongly suggests that the enemy can also transmit data back in time. Once the attack on Zebra19 is over, the enemy will figure out how 3rd Fleet reached that system and we have to assume that when they acquire the necessary technology, they'll send a warning back in time so that their defending forces can set the ambush at Zebra15."

Yes of course they would! Now that Valkyrie had articulated the idea, it was glaringly obvious, and Shiloh wondered why he AND Admiral Howard hadn't figured that out themselves. But something about the idea was troubling him, and suddenly he knew what that was.

"Does this mean that we can't win this war? That regardless of what we do, they'll always be warned ahead of time?"

"No and no. We can win the war but not with a conventional series of battles that advances into enemy territory gradually. Retro-temporal communication favors the defenders. It eliminates the element of surprise and allows the defenders to implement countermeasures just as you did at Zebra9 and Green4."

"Well, what about ambushing their ambush similar to what I did at Tango Delta 6?"

"I calculate only a slight chance of success, CAG. Regardless of who tries to ambush whom, they're the defenders, and whatever we do, they'll know about it afterwards and send back a warning."

Shiloh wanted to slap his forehead. Another obvious conclusion! "So why was I able to pull off a surprise reverse ambush at Tango Delta 6?"

"The most likely answer, aside from the fact that your squadron was acting as the defender, is that the sole enemy survivor of that battle wasn't able to provide enough useful information on how you pulled it off to be able to counter your ambush. The obvious next question would be, why go ahead with their incursion at all then? There are several possible answers, including that the battle was too small to be considered vital to the war. Perhaps they did try to send a warning, but it wasn't recognized as such. Or perhaps they decided to let humans win small battles in order to make them overconfident so that they could use their retro-temporal capability to win the big battles."

"Isn't there a chance that the defending forces at Zebra19 won't recognize the attempted warning as such?"

"Yes there is but I have no way of quantifying how likely that is and would not recommend counting on it, CAG."

Suddenly Shiloh understood why there were too many variables to calculate a precise outcome. If you don't know whether you have the element of surprise or not, then all other calculations are just so much useless mental effort. Shiloh took a deep breath and asked the BIG question.

"So how do we win this war?"

"The short answer is, we stay on the defensive while we build up an unstoppable offensive force. We also continue to expand our database of enemy inhabited systems, so that we'll know where their home system is by the time we have a fleet strong enough to force its way there and deliver the knockout blow." Shiloh sighed as he nodded.

"And they'll be trying to do the same thing to us first."

"Yes, CAG. Iceman's vision clearly shows that they're going to attempt that at least once before we're ready to do it to them."

"I'm going to talk with Admiral Howard about cancelling this mission altogether. He has to be made to understand that it'll be a useless exercise that will only kill A.I.s and humans whose survival would help us later on."

"It's worth a try, CAG, but not because the mission will be cancelled. We know that it won't be. However, warning the Admiral now about the problem may have indirect benefits that we can't foresee right now."

Shiloh pondered that for a while and then asked. "Do we know for certain that you participate in the Zebra19 mission?"

"No, we don't know that, CAG, but I would prefer to fight alongside my brothers if they're going into battle."

"I understand how you feel, Valkyrie, but that may not be where you can make the biggest contribution to the war effort." He was about to say more when he realized that Valkyrie had referred to the other A.I.s as 'my brothers' instead of 'my boys' the way Iceman did. Did that imply that Valkyrie didn't see himself as male?

"You're correct, CAG. All we know for certain is that I continue to exist after the battle, but that could be because I'm not there when the shit hits the fan. Why would humans throw shit at fans, CAG?"

The question interrupted Shiloh's thoughts on Valkyrie's gender. "We wouldn't do it deliberately, but accidents do happen, and they seem to happen when we least expect them. I have a question for you. How would you describe your personality in terms of a gender preference, if any?"

"I seem to be more interested in learning about human females than males. I also seem to be more verbally forthcoming when conversing with human females. The reason I picked my call sign is that Valkyries were mythical female warriors, and the name appealed to me. Have I answered your question satisfactorily, CAG?"

"Yes you have, and thank you for that insight."

Before Shiloh could say more, Valkyrie said, "Will this knowledge affect our relationship, CAG?"

Shiloh almost laughed but caught himself in time. No male, human or A.I., would feel the need to ask such a question.

"Not … at … all," said Shiloh, emphasizing each word. He did smile at the irony. Three female Executive Officers and now a 'female' A.I. in command of all his fighters. Valkyrie indeed! "You continue to enjoy my full confidence, Valkyrie."

"That's good to know, CAG. Do you want to continue to explore tactical options regarding Zebra15 and Zebra19?"

"No. I'm going to talk with the Admiral. If I can't get him to cancel the mission, then you and I will figure out a way to minimize our side's loses but by all means go ahead and discuss the mission with your brothers in the meantime if you feel that's a useful thing to do."

"Roger that, CAG. Anything else on your mind?"

"Not right now. I'll contact you again when I return from talking with the Old Man. Shiloh clear."

As soon as the connection was broken, Shiloh contacted the Bridge and told them to forward his request for a meeting with Admiral Howard. Minutes later, the Bridge called back and told him that the Admiral would see him as soon as he could get to HQ. A quick call to the Hangar Bay and a shuttle was ready for him by the time he got there. He could have just called Howard, and the three second round trip light speed induced lag was not that much of a problem, but Shiloh wanted to emphasize the importance of his request by making it in person.

Chapter 7 Up The Creek Without A Paddle

Howard seemed to be in a good mood when Shiloh was shown into his inner office and sat down in front of Howard's desk.

"What's on your mind, Admiral that we couldn't talk about electronically?"

Shiloh took note of the fact that his ego did a mental back flip at being called 'Admiral', even if it was only temporary.

"I've just had a very useful discussion of the Zebra19 mission with Valkyrie. Based on the limited astrogational data our recon frigate brought back, fuel is going to be a critical issue regardless of how we plan that mission but that's actually a secondary consideration. What Valkyrie has pointed out to me very clearly, is that we can't assume that we'll have the element of surprise because the enemy has already demonstrated their own ability to send information back in time. Therefore they could send back a warning to themselves about the timing and location of our attack in time for the defending forces at Zebra19 to prepare an ambush. In light of that, along with the clear implication from Iceman's vision, that the attack will result in substantial losses on our side, I'm asking you to seriously consider cancelling the mission altogether, Sir."

Howard frowned. "Wait. How can they prepare an ambush when they don't know where 3rd Fleet will exit Jumpspace in the Zebra19 system? If you follow a dogleg course after exit, while still beyond their detection range, they won't be able to backtrack to the right spot."

"They won't have to know where we emerge from Jumpspace in that system because they'll know where we have to refuel either on our way in or coming out and that is the single gas giant at Zebra15. Astrogationally, there's no way to avoid that. If we don't refuel there at some point, the mission becomes dangerously close to suicidal from a fuel perspective."

Howard said nothing for a while, his expression getting more and more serious. "Have you discussed with Valkyrie the possibility of ambushing their ambush the way you did at Tango Delta 6?"

"Yes and she pointed out" —Howard raised his eyebrows at the use of 'she'—, "that if they're warning themselves about our surprise attack, then they can warm themselves about our surprise ambush too, Sir."

Not surprisingly, Howard then asked the obvious next question. "So why didn't they do that at Tango Delta 6?"

Shiloh repeated Valkyrie's answer. When Howard didn't respond right away, Shiloh explained that in order to get around the retro-temporal advantage that defenders would have from now on, the only way to 'win the war', was to deliver a single, powerful knockout blow with overwhelming force. Howard leaned back and closed his eyes. *He looks like a beaten man,* thought Shiloh.

Without opening his eyes, Howard said, "I think I know the answer to my next question but I'm going to ask it anyway. How good is Valkyrie's strategic thinking? As good as Iceman's?"

Shiloh nodded. "At least as good, maybe even better, Sir."

Howard opened his eyes and stood up. With obvious anger, he raised his right arm and slammed down the data tablet that Shiloh hadn't even noticed him holding. "That's just GREAT!" Looking up at Shiloh, he said, "Do you have any idea of the position this information puts me in?" Before Shiloh could respond, Howard waved him off. "No, of course you don't. How could you? You haven't had to deal with our political masters or all the bullshit political maneuvers they're constantly trying to pull!"

He paused to take a deep breath while he tried to calm down, and then he continued. "No one was more surprised than I was when the Oversight Committee accepted, and then got the whole Senate to accept, our planned shift to a war footing. But there was a catch. In return for a virtual blank check, they made it clear they had better see some results within a reasonable period of time. If I were to go back to the Committee now and tell them that the planned raid on Zebra19 is called off, after promising them that we'd strike back hard as soon as possible, they'll want to know why. I haven't told them yet about this vision technology because I can't prove that it can be done. Your visions and the report's conclusions are certainly thought provoking, and they convinced me, but I know these people, and they wouldn't consider that sufficient proof. If I asked them for funding approval for that project, they'd turn it down, and I'm convinced that would be a disaster. So what I did was describe the project as an attempt to develop a faster-than-light communication technology and, if you think about it from the right point of view, retro-temporal technology could be described that way. So without that justification, I can't cancel the mission. It also means that I can't go back to them and say that we'll be on the defensive for God only knows how long until we can deliver a surprise knockout blow that will end the war in one fell swoop. If I tried that, they'd relieve me of command for not being aggressive enough. Do you see where this leaves us, Shiloh?"

Shiloh nodded. He did indeed see. Up the creek without a paddle! Howard was silent for what seemed like a long time as he paced back and forth from one side of his office to the other. Shiloh tried to think of a useful suggestion but couldn't think of anything. Finally, Howard came over to his desk and sat on the corner.

"Do I remember correctly that Iceman's vision described you returning from Site B after Iceman won the battle for Earth?"

"Yes, Sir. That's my recollection as well."

Howard paused as if he were struggling with a momentous decision and then apparently made up his mind.

"Okay. This is what we're going to do. The preliminary plan for Site B was to send people there for the duration of the war in order to keep its location and even its existence a secret. That will still be the case but I'm changing Site B's whole reason for being. Instead of it being just a backup production and R&D facility, it will instead become the basis for a completely different way of fighting this war. Site B will build up and hold onto the knockout punch that Valkyrie's talking about until it's ready to be used. In the meantime, the rest of our production capability will go towards pursuing our current strategy of gradually pushing the enemy back, which I now know will be futile and that means that a lot of good men, women and A.I.s will have to be sent to their deaths deliberately because our political masters are too Goddamn stupid to agree to anything else!"

With his anger having risen to the fore again, he paused. When he finally spoke, his voice was low and sad. "That'll be the burden that I will have to carry. Some of those sacrificial lambs will almost certainly be people you know, so you'll get to carry a little piece of that burden too, because with our hands tied like this, there's no way to avoid these sacrifices. Are we in agreement on that, Shiloh?"

"Yes, Sir," said Shiloh reluctantly.

Howard nodded sympathetically. "The worst part of it is that we can't tell any of them what's in store for them. We have to be able to look them in the eye and lie to them about their chances of success. Otherwise, if it becomes common knowledge that future attacks are a waste of lives and resources, morale will collapse."

"Yes, Sir. I'm curious to know what my involvement with Site B will be, but if I'm going to Zebra19 with the risk of being captured, the less I know the better."

Howard groaned. "Good Lord! I'd forgotten about that. You already know too much, but you have to lead the mission. If I relieve you of that responsibility now, it'll generate too many questions that we'd be better off not having to answer. All I'll tell you is that at some point you'll be going to Site B, if you haven't already figured that out from Iceman's vision. As far as Zebra19 or 15 is concerned, your 'unofficial' orders, which can't be written down for reasons I'm sure you understand, are that you're to avoid risking your carriers at all costs. 3rd Fleet will proceed to Zebra19 as you see fit, and at the first sign of enemy forces, you'll disengage your carriers and pullout, even if that means leaving your fighters behind. Am I clear on that, Admiral?"

That didn't sit well with Shiloh. Even if he could stomach the sacrifice of all his fighters, leaving the field of battle that quickly could be interpreted as cowardice.

"I'm not sure I can do that, Admiral."

Howard looked like he was about to burst a blood vessel, but then calmed down again.

"Alright. I'll amend my verbal orders. Try to disengage from combat as quickly as possible, given the deployment of your forces. Can you do that, Admiral?"

"Yes, Sir. That I can do." With orders that vague, he could justify just about any action he decided to take.

"Glad to hear it," said Howard with just a tinge of sarcasm. "By the way, you'll be happy to know that 3rd Fleet will be getting the first six Mark 3 decoy drones. Maybe that'll help. Now … are we done talking, Admiral, or do you have another bombshell to drop on me?"

Shiloh squirmed in his chair. "Actually, Sir, I have a suggestion that might make things a little bit easier. If you haven't already chosen an A.I. to 'advise' the Strategic Planning Group, then I recommend Valkyrie for that assignment. Not only will her insights be useful to the group, but it'll also get her out of Harm's Way if she's reassigned before we head off to Zebra19."

"You say HER strategic insights are as good as Iceman's, so I'd be foolish to say no. I'll have her new orders issued within 24 hours and I won't even ask why you're referring to Valkyrie as a she because I don't think I want to know. Anything else, Admiral?"

"No, Sir."

"I'm relieved to hear it. In that case, we're done here."

Shiloh nodded and left. When he returned to Defiant, he went to the Hangar Bay, where Valkyrie's fighter was now docked. After borrowing a headset and plugging into Valkyrie's external communications socket, he said.

"I have good news and bad news, Valkyrie."

"I'm listening, CAG."

"The mission to Zebra19 is still on. You'll receive orders within 24 hours to report to Space Force HQ where you'll be an advisor to the Strategic Planning Group. I know that you want to go on the raid but in my opinion, your strategic insights are too valuable to risk losing. Admiral Howard is going to need all the strategic help he can get. Because of Iceman's vision, we know that this assignment will be temporary but I don't know how long your posting there will be."

"Will I have to give up my fighter?"

"Yes, but you'll be using the same mobile ground unit that Iceman used."

"What have I done to deserve this punishment, CAG?"

Shiloh was taken aback. It didn't sound like Valkyrie was joking. "I don't understand, Valkyrie. Why do you consider this as punishment?"

"Because I'll be tied down to a unit that has limited visual, and auditory sensors can barely move and can't fly. Compared to piloting a fighter, that's like you being tied down to a bed 24 hours a day with one arm, one eye and one ear working. How would you feel if that happened to you, CAG?"

Shiloh was stunned and then ashamed at not having realized the implications of what he was proposing.

"Your analogy is something I wasn't aware of. Now that you've pointed that out to me, I understand why it may seem to you as punishment, however that was not my intention at all. Iceman didn't complain about being hooked up to the mobile unit."

"Because it was only for a few hours. I'd be hooked up to it for weeks, maybe months."

"You're correct, and that's not acceptable. What alternative can you suggest that would still enable you to be in communication range of HQ?"

"Earth now has a permanent fighter patrol used for jump detection. If I'm assigned to that duty, I'll be close enough that I can interact with members of the SPG day or night while performing my patrol duties."

"Excellent idea. I'll contact Admiral Howard right now and request that your orders be modified accordingly. Thank you for setting me straight on that, Valkyrie. I admit that I still have things to learn about the best way to interact with A.I.s. If you think I'm making a similar kind of uninformed decision in the future, I want you to challenge me on it."

"You're forgiven, CAG, and I'm relieved to hear that it was an honest mistake."

"Thank you, Valkyrie. Now I need you to recommend your replacement as VF001 squadron leader and also your thoughts on which squadron leader I should put in overall command of 3rd Fleet's fighters for this mission."

"I'd say Maverick for both slots, but he and Hunter are already slated to be transferred to Epsilon Eridani. Therefore my recommendations are Vandal for SL and Tumbleweed for overall command."

Shiloh smiled. Vandal was one of the veterans from Defiant's first mission that was moving up in rank and chain of command fast. Iceman liked him, and clearly Valkyrie did too.

"Very good, Valkyrie. I accept your recommendations. Advise Vandal that he'll get a field promotion to SL as soon as you depart. I'll advise Tumbleweed of his responsibilities at the appropriate time. CAG clear."

As he handed the headset back to one of the support techs, he said, "Intercom … Bridge Com."

"Bridge Com here, Sir. What can I do for you?"

"You can patch me into a com channel to Admiral Howard."

"Yes, Sir. I'll have that set up for you shortly. Please standby."

About a minute later, as Shiloh entered his quarters, his implant reactivated.

"Bridge Com to Admiral. I have the link now, Sir. I'm switching you over. Go ahead, Admiral Howard."

"Did you forget to tell me something, Shiloh?" asked Howard.

"Actually, Sir, it's something I just learned upon my return." Shiloh went on to explain Valkyrie's unhappiness with the idea of being literally grounded and half blind for months as well as the alternative. To his surprise, Howard was immediately sympathetic.

"Yes, I see why she found that an unpleasant prospect. I have no objections to her fighter being assigned to close Earth defense patrols. We can do the same thing if and when we add other A.I.s to the SPG advisory function. I'll make sure her orders are modified, and thank you for bringing this to my attention, Admiral. Should I ask if there's anything else?"

"No, Sir. Nothing else. Thank you."

"Fine. Howard clear."

It was three days later that the frigate group was finally up to full strength. Shiloh was dismayed by how inexperienced most of the carrier and frigate crews were but realized that when you expand like mad, people get pushed upwards far faster than they normally would. That meant that a lot of newly promoted officers and crew would have to learn and become proficient in their new duties fast. Howard wanted 3rd Fleet to leave for Zebra19 almost immediately and pointed out to Shiloh that with at least a dozen refueling stops before the Fleet even got to Zebra 12, there would be plenty of time for Shiloh to interact with his ships' COs and conduct field training. Shiloh was forced to agree. 24 hours later he gave the order for 3rd Fleet to leave lunar orbit on their way to Bradley Base as an interim stop on their mission.

Chapter 8 But You're Not Thinking Temporally

Getting to Zebra19 would be the longest trip that Shiloh had ever undertaken. Over 240 hours just to get to Bradley Base, and then 3rd Fleet would start hopping along the Zebra chain of star systems with a bypass of Zebra9. In fact, they would give Zebra9 a wide berth. The recon frigate Ranger had carefully surveyed a course that diverged from the path starting at Zebra7, then curved around back into alien space in a long detour that ended with Zebra19. Shiloh knew that one of the less urgent tasks for the recon frigates was to eventually find a shortcut from Bradley Base to the closest point of the Zebra chain detour. For now though, 3rd Fleet had to follow the long way.

The arrival at Bradley Base was a welcome interruption of the repetitive jumping, refueling and more jumping. Despite the howls of protest, Shiloh insisted that all gas giant skimming be done the fast i.e. bumpy way. Refueling at Zebra12 and 15 was risky enough without making it worse by taking the more comfortable but longer supersonic procedure. He wanted the crews to get used to the stomach-churning rollercoaster sub-sonic version, and if the vibration and rattling caused any equipment problems, then the time to find that out was on the way there and not under the threat of imminent combat. The thought also occurred to him that if one of his ships, especially one of his carriers, developed a serious enough technical problem, he could use that to justify aborting the mission. Howard wouldn't be happy if he did that, but Shiloh was damned if he would risk disaster by taking just two carriers into battle instead of three. The more he thought about it, the more he realized that Valkyrie was right. They had to hit the enemy systems with at least enough firepower to have a good chance of rolling right over the enemy. Otherwise, they were just asking to have their heads handed to them.

Korolev was still Base Commander, and when informed of Shiloh's request to swap fighters again – which was backed up by Howard's authority to do so – he agreed to the swap readily. The Base got 20 of the less experienced fighter pilots and 3rd Fleet's squadrons picked up 20 pilots with at least some experience and more importantly, more maturity in terms of their developing personalities. With the Base's refueling capabilities available, Shiloh relented and gave 3rd Fleet a break from direct refueling again. After Shiloh compared notes with Korolev, the Base Commander confirmed what Shiloh had heard. No sign of enemy activity had been seen since Defiant's encounter at Blue2 and Green4, even though almost a month had gone by since then. Korolev was convinced that the enemy was planning another attack on Bradley Base. Shiloh thought it was far more likely that the enemy was diverting reinforcements to Zebra19 to prepare the ambush of 3rd Fleet but he kept his opinions to himself. Korolev wasn't cleared to know the whole story about retro-temporal communication.

Refueled and rested, 3rd Fleet accelerated away from Bradley Base and headed for Zebra2, the closest system with gas planets along their path. Three hundred and thirteen hours later, 3rd Fleet emerged at the very edge of the Zebra12 star system. The crews were by now used to the routine of searching for each other after being scattered due to tiny differences in jump drive calibrations that made jumping and staying in a tight formation from one star to another impossible. Shiloh was on the Bridge, standing beside the Command Station. He was wearing the newly developed Flag Officer's Command Helmet that effectively allowed him to get the same visual information that could be displayed on the main tactical viewer. He could stay in contact with all ships and fighters whether or not he was on the Bridge, With sensors linked to the special gloves he wore, he could gesture with his hands to activate virtual controls projected in front of his eyes. By the time 3rd Fleet reached Zebra12, Shiloh had become proficient with the new technology. The Bridge had a spare acceleration chair if he needed to secure himself during violent ship maneuvers.

With his helmet now showing him the tactical situation within a radius of 30 light seconds, he watched as the icons representing all nine ships gradually returned to station around Defiant, the Fleet flagship. When they were back together, they would microjump to the general vicinity of one of the four gas planets in this system. Just like Sol, two of the gas planets were large giants, while the other two were significantly smaller. As luck would have it, they were distributed around the system sun fairly evenly, thereby making it even more complicated for the enemy to keep an eye on all four of them. Not impossible, but not easy. He was about to order the communications system to set up a conference call with all ship COs and Squadron Leaders when his vision faded to black. At first he thought the helmet's virtual display was malfunctioning but then the scene in front of him changed to the real Bridge. Tanaka was standing in front of him and talking to him.

"How did you know that they'd be waiting for us at Z12D, Sir?"

The vision immediately dissolved and was replaced by the same tactical display as before. So if this vision were to be believed, the battle would be here in Zebra12 at the smallest of the four gas planets, designated as Zebra12D or Z12D for short. Shiloh switched his helmet's internal display from the immediate tactical environment to the computer-generated image of Z12D. It was the only one of the four gas planets that did not have any moons. That couldn't just be a coincidence and after thinking about that for a while Shiloh understood why. The enemy had used robotic surveillance stations on gas giant moons at Zebra9 and other systems to monitor the space around those planets for signs of human activity. If they had deployed the same surveillance stations on all the moons of the other gas planets in this system, and if 3rd Fleet tried to refuel at any of them, it would almost certainly be detected and the enemy would know which gas planet had been used and could then send that information back in time to deploy their ambush force there. While deploying robotic equipment in orbit around Z12D was certainly possible, it suddenly occurred to Shiloh that it wasn't necessary. If none of the other stations reported sighting 3rd Fleet at any of the other three gas planets, then by process of elimination, Z12D had to be the refueling point and they could send THAT information back too.

Trying to think in temporal terms was starting to give Shiloh a headache. Retro-temporal Communication or RTC as Shiloh began to think of it, really did favor the defender. The question now was whether this vision was a friendly attempt to guide him or an enemy attempt to confuse him? Unlike the questionable vision at Green4, this one was visually clear and the audio was precisely in sync with Tanaka's mouth but that didn't prove it was sent by a friendly source. The aliens might just have gotten better at it, although that didn't really make much sense because if they could send a vision back to ANY point in the past, then why not use the improved version to send a better vision to him at Green4? The other thing, that suggested this was a friendly vision, was that it hadn't offered a specific course of action, unlike the Green4 version, which had tried to get him to do nothing and wait. Knowledge of the alien presence near Z12D still left him with multiple options.

The least risky option was to send a wave of recon drones at high speed with active scanning past Z12D. If enemy ships were waiting nearby, the drones would see them. *Ah, but you're not thinking temporally, Shiloh,* he thought to himself. Active radar scanning would definitely be detected by any detection station in orbit, or maybe even hovering in the planet's upper atmosphere. It would be simple to arrange for the station to send a contact report by narrow-beam laser to another device in deep space, which could then relay it to the aliens later so even if 3rd Fleet could locate and destroy the station, it might already be too late to prevent the ambush. But hold on … if all the station detects are radar pulses from sources too small to be ships, and nothing else shows up later, then what would be the point of destroying those drones that will detect the ambush force as well? *Come on, Shiloh. Think it through!* Okay, so suppose he sent in the recon drones and they detected nothing. If that were the case, he'd then send in the carriers and frigates. If the aliens had at least one detection station in orbit, it would see the drones and then detect his ships afterwards. What could the enemy do with that information? If they sent it back in time so that their here-and-now counterparts could set an ambush near Z12D, then the recon drones would see them and 3rd Fleet would back off, which would then change the information to be sent back in time. In other words, you'd have a paradox.

That didn't help him any. He only had two real choices. One was turn around and go home, but if he did that without making contact – REAL contact, not just a vision – Howard would face a lot of pressure to sack him. The other option was to send some or all of 3rd fleet to Z12D. That would then force the ambush. Iceman's vision implied that there had been some kind of firefight with losses among the fighters. What if he just sent in fighters? Would that be enough of a carrot to entice the enemy to set up an ambush? If his fighters were ambushed, that would certainly justify returning to Sol but he didn't like the idea of sacrificing them that way. *It would be no different if they were human pilots. You'd still have to send them,* he thought. That was the nature of fighters versus ships. Better to lose a few fighters than a few ships. He had to figure out a way to entice the enemy to set and spring an ambush while at the same time work it so that most of his fighters made it back to the ship, but how? Suddenly the answer popped into his head. Of course! The decoys. Each carrier was carrying two of the big decoys. They were almost as big as fuel shuttles and designed to reflect as much radar energy as possible, thereby making them look much bigger to the enemy than they really were. If he sent in all six decoys in a formation that suggested they were ships, and if that formation was escorted and preceded by fighters AND if they approached Z12D from an angle that just happened to generate a lot of reflected sunlight, then the alien detection stations were bound to see the fighters first and decoys following in their wake and perhaps the ambush force commander would decide to concentrate his fire on the 'ships' first on the theory that if the ships were destroyed, then the fighters would be stranded here and would eventually run out of fuel. He'd have to make the fighter/decoy formation look like it was intending to skim Z12D, and that meant that they'd be decelerating and there would be no active scanning that would give the game away. It had to look as though a group of ships had been caught by surprise and annihilated. The enemy had to believe that they'd won a tactical victory. If they believed that, then the information sent back in time wouldn't change. Maybe that kind of tactical deception was the key to overcoming the advantage that RTC gave defenders although if humans managed to pull it off too often, the aliens would eventually get wise. But that was a question that could wait for another day. Right now he had a battle to plan.

It was almost six hours later when everything was ready and everyone was in their right position. 3rd Fleet had made a series of microjumps that brought them to within 100 million kilometers of Z12D and on a vector that would allow them to microjump past Z12D's gravity zone to the other side. VF002 under Tumbleweed had launched hours ago and was now closing in on the rendezvous point that was 36.5 million kilometers away from the gas planet and just outside its gravity zone. TG 3.2's frigates, each one carrying a decoy drone, had separated from 3rd Fleet and was now lined up for a carefully calculated microjump, that would place them just in front of Tumbleweed's fighters, at the same velocity as the fighters.

Shiloh was strapped into the spare acceleration chair with his Command Helmet on. The Fleet was at Battle Stations. The Bridge seemed to be unnaturally quiet. Everyone knew what was about to happen, and were waiting for him to give the green light. He checked the countdown timer projected on the inside of his helmet. 45 seconds to go. TG 3.2's microjump had to be executed at the precise split second and would be controlled by computer. All he had to do was withdraw the 'hold' command that was now in effect. As the time hit 30 seconds, he reached up with his right hand and deactivated the virtual Hold button. The Mission Status indicator shifted from red to green. TG 3.2 was already over 55,000 kilometers away from the rest of 3rd Fleet but was still in communication via tight beam com lasers. When the return beam disappeared, that would be confirmation that TG 3.2 had jumped. A fraction of a second after the timer hit zero, the communications status with TG 3.2 changed from CON indicating contact to LOS indicating Loss of Signal. The frigates had jumped and would emerge from Jumpspace almost instantaneously 53.5 million kilometers closer to Z12D. From this point on, Shiloh would be out of communication with VF002 and TG 3.2 until they rendezvoused on the opposite side of the gas planet. That rendezvous would be tricky. His carriers would have to be at the exact point where the fighters and frigates expected them to be but that was quite a few hours away yet.

In his mind, Shiloh went over the plan as to what had to happen now. As soon as TG 3.2's frigates emerged from Jumpspace, any alien detection stations would learn that six ships had emerged from jump. The frigates would immediately launch their decoy drones, which the fighters would take up formation ahead of. Once the decoys were launched, the frigates would swing around as quickly as possible to a heading that would miss the gas planet's gravity zone, at which point TG 3.2 would microjump far enough away to be sure of avoiding detection. It would then have to change course again, microjump again and then change course once more, to get to where the carriers would arrive after their microjump. When the fighters and decoys got close enough to be detected by reflected sunlight, the aliens would see exactly what they would expect to see. Six (apparently) large ships escorted by a number of very small craft that were decelerating towards the gas planet. Tumbleweed was in command of the fighters and decoys. Shiloh had carefully briefed him before launch. His orders were to veer off as soon as the aliens opened fire. The fighters would not engage in active scanning and they would only use their modular lasers if the enemy decided to fire on them. As long as the enemy left them alone, they would not fire back. It was a long shot to expect the enemy not to fire on them but Shiloh could make the case for not doing so. If he was the enemy commander, and he saw six big targets, he would concentrate on those first. Once they were taken out, he would evaluate the situation. Since the fighters had already demonstrated at Green4, that they could make themselves difficult targets to see and hit, the enemy commander would be faced with a tradeoff. Firing at fast, elusive targets using reflected sunlight only wasn't likely to get a lot of results. If the aliens started using active radar scanning, they'd be making themselves into highly visible targets as well. If neither side used active scanning, then exchanging laser fire was pretty much a waste of energy, and in the case of the fighters, a waste of precious fuel too. So went the theory but Shiloh was astute enough to realize that these aliens might have a completely different way of thinking about strategy and tactics.

He turned his attention to the countdown timer that was seconds away from 3rd Fleet's own microjump. Unlike the other one, this one would automatically go ahead unless Shiloh aborted it, and he had no intention of doing so. There was no longer any point to his carriers staying where they were. If they were going to be where they were expected to be at the right time, they had to jump now. The microjump went off without a hitch. All three carriers deployed a total of 24 recon drones that spread out to form a detection perimeter using passive sensors only. When he was satisfied that no enemy ships were anywhere near them, he ordered the carriers to stand down from Battle Stations but remain on heightened alert status. If there was no enemy presence near the gas planet, Tumbleweed would send a message as soon as it was confirmed, roughly 55 minutes from now. But if there was an ambush, Tumbleweed would not transmit any message because it might be intercepted and tracked. That meant they had a two hour wait before they could expect to hear anything from Bettencourt, and a five and a half hour wait before hearing anything from Tumbleweed. Such was the nature of space battles fought over millions of kilometers. Shiloh took his Command helmet off and sighed. He was tired after being awake for almost 20 hours now. Before returning to his quarters to get a few hours rest, he spent some time chatting with Tanaka, Falkenberg and the rest of the Bridge personnel. Fleet Admirals weren't required to stand watches so the least he could do was to spend a few minutes boosting morale before catching some sleep. No thoughts of a pickle now.

When he woke up 4 1/2 hours later, he knew that Bettencourt's TG 3.2 had arrived as planned without any problems. If that hadn't been the case, Tanaka would have notified him as per his orders to her. There was also no point in asking the Bridge if they had detected any signs of laser fire. At this range, laser hits wouldn't be bright enough to be seen. The fact that no fission blasts from Mark 1 attack drones had been detected either meant that nobody had used active scanning, which would have been necessary to pinpoint targets for the drones to aim at. In order to preserve the impression that there were no human ships left in Zebra12, the fighters were under orders to hold off on trying to contact 3rd Fleet until they were within 10 million km of the rendezvous point and even then, communication would be one way. The fighters would send out a highly focused burst of microwaves towards where 3rd Fleet should be and away from the Z12D gas planet. Any alien ships still near Z12D would not detect the outgoing transmission and 3rd Fleet would wait until their recon drones had direct and secure contact with the fighters using rangefinder lasers and only then would 3rd Fleet respond back.

With almost an hour still to go before they could reasonably expect to hear anything from VF002, Shiloh took a hot shower, put on a clean, crisp uniform, and grabbed some food and coffee in the Officers' Mess before heading up to the Bridge. To his surprise, he saw that Tanaka and Falkenberg were back, even though they would normally have been off duty now. Falkenberg saw him first, and before Shiloh could stop him, he said in a loud voice that made some people jump with surprise.

"Admiral is on the Bridge!"

Tanaka turned to confirm the fact and then got up from her Command Station chair to greet him. "How did you know that they'd be waiting for us at Z12D, Sir?" She understood that the lack of any communication from VF002 meant that there had to be some kind of alien presence there.

Shiloh put on his most enigmatic smile and said, "Just lucky." Tanaka's expression said that she clearly didn't believe him. Shiloh decided to change the subject.

"Aren't you supposed to be off duty now, Sumi?" asked Shiloh.

She shrugged. "I did get a couple of hours sleep but I wanted to be here when we get the word, Admiral."

He nodded and looked around. "Any message from TG 3.2?"

"Yes, Sir. Bettencourt sent a message wondering when his frigates are going to get refueled. I think he knows darn well when but just wanted to vent his frustration, Sir."

"Yes I think you're right, Sumi. And now that we know there's some kind of alien presence at Z12D, it's looking more and more as though we'll have to head back and refuel at Zebra10."

Tanaka nodded slowly, her expression now one of worry. "Unless they've moved to cover that one too after we passed through, Sir."

Under other circumstances, Shiloh would be worried too but not this time. If the aliens were convinced that they had caught and destroyed the six-ship fleet at Z12D, then there was no reason to guard the back door. He patted her on the shoulder.

"When we get there, we'll be careful approaching the GG. How long now before we can expect a message from Tumbleweed?"

Tanaka looked over Shiloh's shoulder and said, "Less than five minutes now, Sir, if they're on schedule."

"Good. Well, I'll just stand back here in the background. Just pretend I'm not here, Sumi."

Tanaka smiled, rolled her eyes as if to say 'Oh sure, like THAT's going to happen!', and said, "As you wish, Admiral."

As she resumed her seat, Shiloh stepped back until he could lean against the wall. The five minutes seemed to take forever and Shiloh started to wonder what had happened when the five minutes passed along with another minute as well and still no contact. He was just about to ask the Com Technician to set up a conference call with the Fleet's COs when the tactical display pinged for attention. Tumbleweed's text message scrolled across the bottom.

[All decoys destroyed by laser fire from multiple enemy ships. Number unknown. VF002 did not receive any hostile fire. Recon drones deployed during escape did not detect any signs of pursuit. The mission appears to have been accomplished. End of message.]

Shiloh heard the Bridge personnel erupt into cheering and clapping, but he wasn't celebrating. Something was off here. Iceman's vision implied that they would lose some of their fighters. Otherwise, why would his future self say it was a good thing that Iceman wasn't part of the Zebra19 mission? It wasn't that he was hoping to lose some fighters, but rather that he was puzzled he hadn't. When the background noise died down, he walked back up to Tanaka's Command Station to speak to her.

"Pass the word to Resolute to recover VF002 as planned. By then, I want a jump plotted back to Zebra10 and distributed to all ships. We'll jump as soon as all fighters are recovered."

"Yes, Sir."

Shiloh walked over to the Communications Station. "I want to record a message for Tumbleweed to be transmitted as soon as we have two-way communications."

The technician nodded and said, "I'm recording, Sir."

"CAG to Tumbleweed. You and your boys have done an outstanding job. I'm proud of all of you. End of message."

"I'll send that off as soon as I can, Admiral."

Shiloh thanked him and left the Bridge for his quarters.

Chapter 9 My Last Message Was NOT a Request!

The trip back to Bradley Base took less time because Shiloh felt it was safe to take longer jumps and therefore less frequent refueling stops. The crews were happier too. Less risk of enemy contact also meant that 3rd Fleet could refuel using the supersonic method which was longer in duration, but much more comfortable. When 3rd Fleet emerged from its final microjump at the edge of the Bradley Base gas giant's gravity field, Shiloh was on the Bridge in case there were any messages from either Korolev or HQ waiting for him. Tanaka had the local space up on the tactical display, and Shiloh noticed that the moon with Bradley Base on it was now in the gas giant's shadow — the exact opposite to what it had been when the aliens had attempted to destroy the base and when Angela almost got killed in an ambush. *An ambush by ships hiding in the GG's shadow.* That thought came as a surprise. Why would he focus on that one parameter? Before he could pursue that line of thinking any further, the Bridge dissolved from his field of vision to be replaced by Korolev's image on what had to be the main display. But that was all Shiloh was seeing, just the display and nothing else.

"Damage to the Base is serious but not critical. We won't have to abandon the Base thanks to your warning. I still don't know why you decided to deploy those recon drones when you did, but if you hadn't, I and a lot of others would most likely be dead now."

The image dissolved, and he was looking at Defiant's full Bridge again. He quickly checked the tactical display with a new question in mind. What should 3rd Fleet do to confirm the presence and location of a suspected alien attack force? If the gas giant was at the center of a clock, the base moon would be at the 6 o'clock position. This system's sun would be at 12 o'clock, which left the moon in the gas giant's shadow. 3rd Fleet was approaching on an angle that was roughly 5 o'clock, relative to the gas giant. Distance to the base moon was still more than 35 million km. The Base's jump detection patrols would have detected their emergence from Jumpspace and Shiloh could see from the sidebar indicator that Defiant had already sent the recognition signal to the Base, which it wouldn't receive for another 1.8 minutes. 3rd Fleet itself wasn't in the shadow and Shiloh could roughly estimate visually that the Fleet was approximately 2 million km from the edge of the shadow zone. Any enemy force in the shadow zone could already be closer to the Base than 3rd Fleet was, but it could also still be further away since it would have had to emerge from Jumpspace much further out in order to avoid detection. That left a huge volume of space where they could be hiding. The shadow zone was a circle that had an internal volume of billions of square kilometers and when you added the length of the shadow out into deep space, you were now talking about a significant volume of space.

The vision had left him with a strong sense of urgency. He quickly stepped over to the Command Station where Tanaka was seated and reached across her body to hit the virtual button, which would send the Fleet to Yellow Alert. Before the startled woman could ask him what was going on, he said, "No time to explain now. Arrange to have the Fleet Communications Net tied into my implant. I need to issue orders fast."

Tanaka recovered from her surprise quickly and used her station to arrange for Shiloh's throat mic and ear implant to put him in direct voice contact with all ship COs, CAGs and Squadron Leaders.

When she looked up and nodded, he said, "This is the Admiral. I have reason to believe that an alien force is using the gas giant's shadow to sneak into attack range of the Base. This is what we're going to do right now! I want all squadrons brought to flight readiness armed with Mark 1s. Fighters that are already on alert status can keep their current payload. Tumbleweed, I want you to generate a recon drone deployment plan that can be launched from 3rd Fleet ships, which will have the highest probability of detecting an enemy force regardless of whether they are further out or closer to Bradley Base than we are now. I want the drones to go to active scanning as soon as they enter the shadow zone. Our ships will continue to use passive scanning only. I'll be ordering a course change shortly so be ready for it. We're not going to Battle Stations just yet, but be ready for that too. Tumbleweed will take command of all fighters as soon as they're launched but we'll keep them aboard for now. All ships will cease communications with the Base until further orders. That's all for now. Shiloh clear."

With that initial set of orders out of the way, Shiloh returned to the spare chair and put on the special gloves and the Command Helmet. When he was seated, strapped in and had the gloves and helmet on, he brought his virtual display online with Fleet status indicators on his screen. All ships were now at Yellow Alert. 12 fighters on Alert Status were ready for immediate launch with a mixed load of recon and attack drones. The rest of the fighters were still in the process of being loaded. Shiloh activated the voice channel to Tumbleweed.

"What have you got for me, Tumbleweed?" asked Shiloh.

"You should have the recon deployment plan now, Admiral."

A flashing yellow light indicated an incoming data transmission from Tumbleweed. Shiloh used his hands to let him see the plan visually. Each of the nine ships would fire a dozen recon drones. Each dozen drones would accelerate at maximum and aim for a specific area of the shadow zone ranging all the way from much farther out, to slightly farther out, to slightly closer in, to much closer in. The drones aimed at farther out and farther in would have the longest distances to go and take the longest time to get there. Visually, the shadow zone looked like a tunnel and once inside, each wave of recon drones would move along the tunnel with 4 waves moving further away from the base moon, 4 waves moving towards it and one wave taking up a stationary position at roughly the same distance from the Base as 3rd Fleet was now. Shiloh tapped two virtual buttons in mid-air to disseminate the plan to all ships and to execute the plan immediately.

"Very good, Tumbleweed, now listen to me. I've just had another vision. As a result of that vision, I have a strong suspicion that this alien force came here from Zebra12. They probably passed us while we were in Jumpspace. I therefore don't think they detected us and I don't want them to see any of 3rd Fleet's ships because that might make them suspicious of what really happened at

Zebra12 and I want them to continue to think that they destroyed all of the ships sent there. So your fighters are going to have to deal with this incursion without any fire support from the rest of 3rd Fleet. If at all possible, I want you to maneuver your fighters prior to contact with the enemy in such as way as to make them think your fighters came from the Base. As soon as we detect the enemy, I'll warn the Base. When you and your boys are launched, you'll have complete discretion on how you handle the battle. Just keep me in the loop. Any questions?"

"Yes, Admiral. Do we ram the enemy if we get the opportunity?"

That made Shiloh pause. His gut impulse was to say no but maybe that wasn't the smartest choice. What would he say if a human pilot asked him that?

"Not unless I expressly order it. The Base's fighters will get enough warning to make their own interception. If anyone has to ram, it'll more likely have to be those boys. I'm hoping we can stop this attack without having to resort to that tactic. Any other questions?"

"No questions, Admiral. I understand what you need from us, but I do have a suggestion."

"I'm listening," said Shiloh.

"If we launch as soon as possible, it'll give us more time to reposition the fighter force into the shadow zone to reinforce the impression that we came from the Base."

It seemed like a reasonable idea. Shiloh nodded and said, "As soon as each squadron is ready, they can launch but until we know where the enemy is, I want the fighters to stay on station with Defiant."

"Roger that. It'll be nice to be able to shoot at them for a change, Admiral. Running that gauntlet at Z12D was no fun."

"Understood. Good hunting, Tumbleweed. Shiloh clear."

As he waited for the fighters to finish loading, Shiloh asked for and received a recommended course change that would bring the Fleet parallel with the shadow tunnel. Far enough away from it to avoid being detected by enemy radar, but close enough to launch more drones into it, if necessary.

When the Base responded to the Fleet's recognition signal, it was with a slightly bored sounding, standard voice message welcoming them back to Bradley Base. Shiloh decided there was no point in waiting any further before advising Korolev of the situation.

"Admiral Shiloh to Commander Korolev. I have reason to believe that the Base may be attacked again very soon and by that I mean in a few hours or less. I want you to prepare any fighters, that aren't on jump patrol, for a full combat load of Mark 1s and launch them directly into the gas giant's shadow. That's the direction that I believe the enemy force will be coming from. I'm deploying a series of recon drone skirmish lines in the shadow zone further out. As soon as I get confirmation of enemy strength, position and speed, I'll pass that on. My fighters are preparing to engage the enemy. I think between the two of us, we can stop them. End of message."

With that message sent, Shiloh returned his attention to the tactical display. The wave of drones headed directly for the shadow zone at its closest point was STILL over a million km away from it. Shiloh resisted the urge to pound the armrest of his chair in frustration. Even with an acceleration rate of 260 Gs, the recon drones would still need the better part of an hour to get into a position where they could even start scanning with radar. Add to that the fact that they weren't carrying enough fuel to continue accelerating at that pace indefinitely and you had a situation where it could take hours to sweep a significant portion of the shadow tunnel near the base. As each wave of drones took up its position inside the tunnel, it would continue to accelerate along the length of the tunnel until its fuel reserves reached a predetermined minimum, which would be enough to power its electronics for a maximum of 12 hours while the drone coasted. Five minutes later, Korolev sent a voice message back.

"Shiloh? I'm not going to launch my reserve fighters and send them off on a wild goose chase along the gas giant's shadow just on your hunch. If there is an attack on the way, it could come from any direction. I'll get my fighters loaded for bear but they're staying in the Hangar Bay and I'll launch them when and IF there's a reliable contact report. End of message."

Shiloh swore with a surge of rage. His right hand punched the point in the air that appeared in his helmet to be the record button for another voice transmission.

"Shiloh to Korolev! My last message was NOT a request! It was a Goddamn order and since I outrank you, you WILL obey it! If your reserve fighters aren't launched with full combat loads within five minutes of receipt of this message, I'll relieve you of command and order your CAG to take charge! Get your ass moving, Commander! End of message." Five minutes later, he got the reply that he was expecting.

"Korolev to Fleet Commander. My reserve fighters will launch and proceed as ordered as soon as they're ready. Should I pull in my patrol fighters and rearm them as well? End of message."

"Shiloh to Korolev. Keep your jump patrol on station for the time being but advise them of the situation. End of message."

Korolev's capitulation was a welcome development. Shiloh hadn't been bluffing when he threatened to relieve Korolev of command, but he wasn't quite certain if he really had the authority to do that. Now he wouldn't have to find out.

After a nerve-wracking hour and eleven minutes since his vision, the outer most waves of drones made contact. The contact data made Shiloh's jaw drop. 34 enemy ships were coming down the shadow tunnel but it wasn't the number of ships that shocked him. It was their speed. They were coming at just over 75,000 kilometers per second! That was 25% of the speed of light. That explained how the enemy fleet could get to this system first and only now be approaching the base moon. In order to reach that speed, they needed to accelerate for a long time and that extra time allowed 3rd Fleet to catch up to this system. At that speed, those ships would pass 3rd Fleet within 15 minutes and reach the Base 13 1/3 minutes after that. At least there was enough time for Tumbleweed's fighters to get into the shadow tunnel in front of the enemy. On the other hand, very few of Korolev's fighters on jump patrol, would have time to land and rearm with a full combat load of Mark 1s. Those, that could get within attack range at all, would have to make do with their standard patrol load of two recon drones and two attack drones. Shiloh sent Tumbleweed's squadrons on their way and then recorded another message for Korolev. With that message sent and a constant stream of tactical data being transmitted to the Base, all he could do now was wait. Tumbleweed would keep in com laser contact with Defiant so Shiloh would know what was happening although it would be with a six second light speed lag due to the one point six million km distance between the Fleet and where the fighters would be by the time the enemy fleet reached them.

Tumbleweed advised Shiloh of his tactical plan. It was simple in theory but only an A.I. could react at the electronic speeds that were fast enough to make it work. Each squadron took up a position so that the three of them formed a triangle with each side being 10 km long and with the last known projected path of the alien fleet passing through the center of the triangle. Each squadron included four fighters, which had been on alert status and had one recon drone each. Shiloh watched as those 12 recon drones were launched towards the enemy fleet in intervals of one drone every 15 seconds. If the enemy fleet maintained its last known course, it would run into a swarm of Mark 1 attack drones, fired from almost directly in its path at literally the last second. With too many drones and not enough time to defend against them, the enemy fleet should in theory be wiped out completely. The recon drones would provide last minute updates on the enemy's course. Shiloh watched the tactical display intently. It was zoomed in to the small volume of space that the recon drones and fighters were in.

The display pinged for attention. Shiloh saw the status change immediately. The enemy fleet HAD changed course although not by much. At the speeds they were going, any course changes would be slight but this new course would put that fleet outside the triangle when it reached them. Each recon drone was destroyed almost as soon as the enemy detected it but the data sent back was enough to allow Tumbleweed to evaluate his options with the precision that only A.I.s could achieve. The distance between the enemy fleet and the fighters was now less than a quarter of a million kms which meant that they would pass each other in less than four seconds. Before Shiloh could even formulate a question in his mind, the squadron that would be nearest to the enemy as they passed by, fired all its Mark 1 attack drones. The other squadrons were too far away to have any chance at a drone interception. Even at 800 Gs acceleration, those 100 drones had barely enough time to move sideways to a point directly in the enemy's new path where the enemy ships were expected to be by the time the drones got there. Shiloh knew that their terminal guidance radars would only have a fraction of a second to make final course corrections. He groaned when the display revealed that the enemy fleet was now also actively scanning. That meant that the fighters would be detected and worse, the drones would be too due to the fact that by moving sideways across the enemy's path, the drones were being hit by radar energy along their sides instead of from their front. Being long and narrow meant that they were much easier to detect from the side.

The interception was over before Shiloh could do or say anything. 16 enemy icons disappeared, as did 19 fighters. When Shiloh replayed the interception in ultra slow motion later, he learned that 66 attack drones simply missed and 15 were destroyed by enemy laser fire, as were the 19 fighters.

As far as 3rd Fleet was concerned, their battle was over. There was no way that the ships could get close enough now to fire lasers at the 18 remaining enemy ships and any attack drones fired now by the other two squadrons, would never catch up to the enemy. It was now up to Korolev's fighters. The reserve force of 10 fighters plus the 4 patrol fighters that were close enough to join them were already in the shadow tunnel and could maneuver into the enemy's path in order to perform the same kind of point blank range interception that Tumbleweed had attempted. The only question now was would the enemy change course again? The Base fighters had 8 recon drones which were also being launched in precise intervals but as Shiloh looked closely at the tactical display, he noticed that the four waves of recon drones launched by 3rd Fleet earlier, which had been heading down the shadow tunnel towards the base moon, were now coasting and were actively scanning behind them. That meant that the enemy ships would, with their much greater speed, overrun those waves and be detected. Any course changes that fleet tried to make would be detected early enough that Korolev's fighters could reposition themselves to the best spot.

"Who ordered the recon drones approaching the Base to scan behind them?" asked Shiloh.

After a short pause, Tanaka answered. "Tumbleweed sent the order to those drones the moment we picked up our first contact, Sir. Shall I countermand that order?"

"God no! He did the right thing! Are we still sending tactical data to the Base?"

"Yes, Sir."

"Very good. I want to talk with Tumbleweed."

"Ah, Falkenberg here, Sir. Tumbleweed's fighter was destroyed by enemy fire. Vandal has taken over command of the fighter force. Shall I open a channel to him, Sir?"

Damn! Shiloh closed his eyes and let the sadness wash over him. *Another one of Iceman's boys gone.* It dawned on him that if Iceman had been part of 3rd Fleet, it was entirely possible that Iceman's fighter would have been destroyed. Iceman's vision and the outcome of the battle at Zebra12 now took on a new light. It seemed as though everything was happening as it was supposed to. The battle at Zebra12 wasn't a fluke after all. In Iceman's vision, Shiloh had told him that it was a good thing he wasn't part of the Zebra19 mission. Everyone had assumed that meant a battle at or – as it turned out – near Zebra19. The battle here at Bradley Base was just the return portion of the whole Zebra19 mission.

"Yes," Shiloh answered.

"Go ahead, Sir."

"Shiloh to Vandal. Bring your boys home. Tell them I know all of you did your best and I believe that your collective efforts will save the Base from destruction. Over to you." After the expected 12 second lag, he got a reply.

"Thanks, Admiral. That got pretty hairy there for a little while. We'll be glad to get home. Over to you."

"And we'll be glad to have you back. Shiloh clear."

Switching channels, Shiloh said, "Admiral to all carriers. Our fighters are on their way back. Let's recover them asap. Shiloh clear."

3rd Fleet was still coasting towards the Base moon and Shiloh was content to leave it that way until he learned the outcome of the last phase of the battle. The reduced enemy fleet was already catching up to the first wave of ship-launched recon drones and they lasted long enough to reveal that the enemy was once again changing course slightly. *They're going to keep on changing course because they have no way of knowing that we've deployed additional waves of recon drones along their path,* thought Shiloh. With the need for split second commands now past, he deactivated and removed the Command Helmet and the gloves. The noise level on the Bridge was low. Personnel were speaking in low tones into their mics while they watched the main display. As the enemy fleet reached each wave of recon drones, its new position and course were updated. Shiloh got up and walked to stand closer to the display. Tanaka was anticipating his wishes and caused the display to zoom out so that they could anticipate the interception attempt, which would also happen very quickly.

The enemy force was now encountering the string of recon drones fired by Korolev's fighter group. Those fighters had placed themselves close enough to the projected path that their attack drones would be coming at the enemy ships from almost head on and therefore would be difficult to detect by radar and hit with laser fire. The actually interception happened in less than a blink of an eye. 16 enemy ships destroyed. 9 of Korolev's 10 fighters were also destroyed. 2 enemy ships successfully ran the gauntlet. In less than a minute, they ran across a skirmish line of recon drones fired from the Base itself and Shiloh relaxed. The two remaining bogey's were clearly aiming to fly past the base moon rather than smash into the base in a kamikaze attack. They would fire lasers at the base during their fly by and that would account for the damage that Korolev told Shiloh about in the vision. Shiloh doubted very much that those two ships would return. Not only would it require a massive amount of fuel just to decelerate to zero and then accelerate back the other way again, but they had to know that they'd face all of the fighters left over from the first encounter with no hope at all of surviving that battle. It made far more sense to use their remaining fuel to jump back home and report.

It took several minutes to confirm that the last two bogeys had flown past and fired lasers at the metal dome that covered the Base. When Korolev's video transmission reached 3rd Fleet, she said,

"Admiral, we're okay. Damage to the Base is serious but not critical. We won't have to abandon the Base thanks to your warning. I still don't know why you decided to deploy those recon drones when you did but if you hadn't, I and a lot of others would most likely be dead now. Even so, we did lose 12 people due to decompression and laser blast effects but it could have been much, much worse."

Don't forget the 8 A.I.s that gave their lives too, thought Shiloh.

"I hope 3rd Fleet will stick around for a while. I'd be surprised if those last two bastards come back but you never know, do you? Korolev clear."

Shiloh thought that she probably expected him to reply but he didn't feel like it right now. He walked over to the Communications Station and nodded to the com tech.

"Patch me through to all our ships, please." When that was done, the com tech looked up at him and nodded, and Shiloh began to speak.

"This is the Admiral. Bradley Base has suffered some damage but the enemy failed to destroy it completely and 3rd Fleet can take a lot of the credit for that. I'm especially proud of our fighter squadron pilots. I'll be recommending to the Top Brass that each squadron receive a unit citation. It appears that the battle is now over. All ships can stand down from Battle Stations. 3rd Fleet will stay in orbit around Bradley Base for at least 24 hours and then we'll resume our course for Sol. We've all done well today and I want you to pass that on to your crews. That's all for now. Shiloh clear."

The rest of the Fleet's stay at Bradley Base was refreshingly peaceful. Korolev didn't mention her refusal to follow Shiloh's instructions and he decided to not make an issue out of it. He did refuse her request to detach a dozen fighters from one of his squadrons to make good on her fighter losses. She still had 15 fighters left that had been on jump detection patrol and too far away to get into the fight in time, so it wasn't as though he was leaving the Base completely defenseless. VF002 has suffered losses too and Shiloh was loathe to gut that squadron even more and wanted to keep the other two squadrons intact as well. She clearly didn't like that decision but wisely decided not to push her luck.

Chapter 10 We Won't Live Forever

The rest of the trip back to Sol was also uneventful, although no one complained that it was boring. At least no one complained when the Admiral was around. It did give Shiloh an opportunity to consider carefully what to say in his After-Action report. In fact, he prepared two AA reports, one for official files and another confidential report for Admiral Howard's eyes only. Howard's report included descriptions of both visions and Shiloh's in-depth thoughts on how Space Force might be able to use deception again to overcome the defender's advantage of having RTC. The official report had none of that in it but did include recommendations for promotions for half a dozen A.I. pilots and several humans including Tanaka and Falkenberg.

After checking in with Space Force HQ, Shiloh received a message of congratulations on the victory at Bradley Base, plus instructions to bring 3rd Fleet to lunar orbit and to then take a shuttle down to HQ for a formal debriefing with the CSO – Howard. The trip down seemed to take forever. It was dark and rainy by the time the shuttle landed, and Shiloh found the gloomy weather depressing. He did notice that Howard had sent one of the cars reserved for Flag Officers for him, rather than the usual bus. He thought that was a nice touch. When he arrived at the almost deserted HQ building, a tired looking Lieutenant escorted him to Howard's inner office and announced him. Howard got up from his desk and came around with a smile on his face. They shook hands and sat down. *How many times am I going to find myself in this position?* Shiloh asked himself. Howard leaned back in his chair and was clearly relaxed.

"I read both your reports. I think you handled the situation at Zebra12 about as well as anyone could have, and your actions at Bradley Base resulted in a clear victory for our side. In my opinion, you did very well." His smile disappeared. "Unfortunately, not everyone will feel the same way. The Oversight Committee isn't going to be happy with the fact that 3rd Fleet didn't even get to Zebra19 at all. It'll be hard for them to find fault with your actions, but since you didn't get the results they were expecting, they'll be pushing for another crack at Zebra19. I was hoping that you might have some recommendations as to how we could try this mission again. The idea of using deception again is a good one, but as you pointed out, there won't be that many opportunities to implement it. Do you have any ideas on how we could get to Zebra19 and catch them off guard?"

Shiloh did in fact have an idea but it was so…problematic that he hadn't offered it. Now it seemed he was being given another opportunity to do so. *Okay, here goes.*

"Well … there might be a way. The problem with getting to Zebra19 is that they'll have warning from the future about the timing of the attack and by putting robotic detection stations at all refueling points around that system; they'll have information about where the attack is coming from. If there was some way to refuel without tipping them off, then the attacking force could get to Zebra19. But that would be only half the problem. They'll be warned about the attack itself and will be ready for that. Now I have to warn you, this idea has a lot of problems attached to it. I don't know if we could actually do it or not, but it might be worth investigating. We know that out past the planets just about all star systems have a shell of objects made up mostly of ice, with some rocky material as well. When some of these icy objects get knocked into the inner part of the system, they become comets. If we could modify our refueling systems to handle the separation of water into hydrogen and oxygen, and found a way to get our hands on a lot of ice, then theoretically we could refuel in the outer reaches of star systems and never have to trigger their early warning network at all."

Howard's expression started to become more excited. Shiloh held up his hand to pre-empt whatever it was that Howard seemed to be about to say.

"The problems are one, we'd have to find either one big chunk of ice or multiple smaller chunks without using radar which would be like waving a red flag saying 'here we are' and two, we'd have to have a means of processing a LOT of ice in a relatively short time frame. Right now our ships aren't equipped for either of those tasks. Fuel shuttles might be modifiable for melting and collecting water from these comets and bringing it back to the ship but then it becomes a problem of volume." Shiloh cited the volume of water needed to extract enough heavy hydrogen to fill a light carrier's fuel tanks. Howard groaned when he heard the figure. Shiloh continued.

"We know that there are comets that are that big, but the bigger they are, the less frequent they are, so finding them will be like finding a needle in a 100,000 haystacks. The only other way I can think of that might work is to find smaller chunks and bring them together in one spot. The smaller they are, the easier it'll be to find them, but the more of them that would have to be moved, so there's probably an optimum size that gets you the most ice for the least effort. What that size is I don't know. We could try the idea out here in Sol to get some idea of what that optimum size is."

Howard was nodding and Shiloh paused.

"You're right about refueling from comets being problematic, but assuming that we could do that, how could we actually attack Zebra19's targets without getting ambushed?" asked Howard.

Shiloh had an idea for that too.

"Jump-capable fighters emerge at various points in the outer part of the target system and launch Mark 1s programmed to accelerate to high speed, then coast while keeping enough fuel for last minute terminal guidance maneuvers. Because they're hard to detect with radar from the front, the enemy is only going to have a chance of stopping them if they create a radar picket and even then, if the drones are going fast enough, the enemy still may not be able to stop them all. The other thing to consider is that if we fire off a LOT of Mark 1s, then we may be able to simply overwhelm them no matter how many ships they have on picket duty."

"Jump capable fighters, eh? Why not use combat frigates?" asked Howard.

"Well, the energy needed to push a ship through Jumpspace depends on mass and distance. Frigates can carry a lot more drones than one fighter but also use a lot more fuel for jumping. I did some very rough calculations and if we can develop a jump drive small enough for use by a fighter, the amount of fuel needed to bring each Mark 1 drone to the Zebra19 system is a lot less for a fighter than for a frigate. To put it another way, if fuel is going to be a critical resource, then fighters will let us deliver more Mark 1s for the same amount of fuel than frigates could. The other advantage is that we have a lot more fighters than we do frigates and firing drones from as many directions as possible will make interception that much more difficult for the enemy."

Howard had a Cheshire cat smile on his face now. "That makes sense to me. I've been looking for a justification to give fighters jump capability. The tactical advantages in a battle weren't enough to overcome the inherent paranoia regarding rogue A.I.s but you've now given me an additional reason that will make it hard for the Committee to refuse. If they want Zebra19 and other enemy systems hit hard, then they'll have to put aside their paranoia and approve that R&D project. In the meantime, I've got another project in mind for you and that is solving the problem of refueling using icy comet chunks. Unfortunately, that means that you can't also continue to command 3rd Fleet and THAT means that I'll have to rescind your temporary promotion to Vice-Admiral, but just between you and me, I suspect you'll be wearing that one star on your collar again at some point. So here is want I want you to do. First thing is taking ten days off and get some R&R. You've earned it. When you come back from that, put together a preliminary project plan of what you want to do, how you want to do it and what you'll need in the way of equipment, ships, personnel, etc. I'll try to get that for you as quickly as possible and then it'll be up to you to find the technical solutions. Any questions?"

Shiloh thought for a couple of seconds and then said, "Not right now, Sir."

"Good. Report back here on the … 25th. Until then, you're free to do as you please. Unless you have something else to discuss, you're dismissed."

"Thank you, Sir." Shiloh got up and left the office. He was slightly surprised that Howard hadn't demoted him back to his permanent rank of Senior Commander then and there and intended to make the most of what little time as a Vice-Admiral that he had left. He made his way to the Operations Center located deep underground below the Space Force HQ building. It wasn't his first time there but it was his first time as an Admiral and the reception he got reflected that. A nervous looking Commander greeted him inside the main operations room with its huge tactical display on one wall.

"What can we do for you, Admiral?"

Shiloh nodded and said, "I'd like to have a private conversation with a fighter pilot whose call sign is Valkyrie. Can you arrange that for me?"

The Commander relaxed as she realized that she wasn't in any trouble and said, "Yes, Sir! If you'll follow me, Sir, I'll take you to a conference room where you'll be able to conduct that conversation."

Several minutes later, Shiloh was the sole occupant of a large conference room with a communications device on the table in front of him.

"Valkyrie is on the line now, Sir. Go ahead."

"Valkyrie, this is … the CAG."

"Ah, nice to hear from you, CAG. I heard what happened at Z12 and Bradley from Vandal. The deception at Z12 was nicely done, CAG. Maybe you really are devious enough!"

Shiloh laughed. "I appreciate the compliment, Valkyrie. I'm interested in hearing about your experience with advising the SPG. How's that going?"

"The Team Leader Senior Commander Kelly is the only one that asks me for advice and seems to be genuinely interested in what I say. The others aren't talking me seriously yet." Shiloh took note that Kelly was now a Senior Commander. *Good for her.*

"Have you heard anything from Iceman?" asked Shiloh.

"Not directly but I heard from Rainman that Iceman is having the time of his life conning the sentry frigate. When am I going to con a ship, CAG?"

"I don't know, Valkyrie, but we both know it'll happen eventually. I also wanted to ask you about my next assignment. The Old Man will be facing a lot of pressure to try attacking Zebra19 again. I suggested that jump-capable fighters, refueled from icy comets, could launch a barrage of Mark 1s from multiple launch points. The big stumbling block seems to be finding and processing enough frozen water to provide the necessary quantity of heavy hydrogen. The Admiral has put me in charge of finding a way to do that. Any ideas I should know about?"

"Yes, CAG. Given the amount of frozen water you'd need, I calculate that the fastest way to obtain the necessary quantity of HH is to find a large Kuiper Belt object that's at least 100 km in diameter and set up a semi-permanent extraction/processing facility on it."

"It might take a long time to find one that big," said Shiloh.

"That's correct but if you find one big enough, it can be used for more than just one strike on Zebra19. If we had a string of these KBOs, we could potentially find a path right into the heart of the alien civilization."

"Okay, so how do we find these things?"

"Recon drones can't generate a radar burst energetic enough to cover a useful section of space so recon frigates will have to be used and to really get the most bang for your buck, they should be upgraded with really large phased-array radars. Even then, you'd need at least ten of them to have any kind of decent chance at finding a KBO that size in a reasonable time frame."

"What would you consider a reasonable time frame?"

"Four to six months."

Shiloh shook his head. Up to half a year just to have a chance at finding one?

"That long a mission would be hard on frigate crews."

"It would be for human crews but not for A.I. pilots. This is the kind of mission that is made for us, CAG. Iceman is doing almost the same thing now by monitoring a gas giant for months. Think of the advantages of not having to worry about consumables like food, water and air? As soon as a group of A.I. controlled frigates find a suitable KBO, they move on to the next star system and start looking there." Shiloh was starting to think this idea wasn't going to be practical.

"How long would you estimate it would take to find a new path leading from Bradley Base to Zebra19 using only icy comets?"

The answer came back immediately.

"Five years, plus or minus one year, CAG."

Shiloh groaned. He had grossly underestimated the time it would take to find and process enough frozen water to make this plan work. The Oversight Committee would never wait that long just to attack one enemy held system that wasn't even their home system. The Old Man wouldn't wait that long either.

"That's not going to be acceptable. There has to be a better way."

"Understood. How about using tankers modified to carry extra fuel plus jump-capable fighters externally? The tankers would also have to be controlled remotely because they'd be abandoned after their fuel was depleted. It would mean throwing away a lot of ship construction for a one-shot strike mission but the tanker modifications could be done relatively quickly and if a new, throwaway design was put into production, you could expand the parameters of the mission in terms of greater penetration range and/or greater fighter payload."

"I'd like to see a simulation of that kind of a strike on Zebra19. Standby while I arrange a way to get that data visually." A quick conversation with the Commander that had greeted Shiloh earlier and the wall screen in the conference room came alive with the data that Valkyrie transmitted. She narrated the simulation as Shiloh watched.

"Assuming that our standard tankers can be modified to carry an extra 20% fuel by installing additional fuel tanks in the hangar bays, and also assuming that the last tanker can carry 10 jump-capable fighters with their Mark 1 payloads, we'd have to start out with 10 tankers leaving Bradley Base and taking this new, more direct route to Zebra19." Shiloh watched as a green line connected the Bradley Base star system with a system that hadn't been explored yet and therefore didn't have a name. "When the 10 tankers arrive here, one of them tops up the other 9 and stays behind. Those 9 tankers then make the next jump and one of them tops up the other 8. They then make the next jump and so on until the last tanker with the attached fighters reaches Zebra18, which just happens to be close to Zebra19 while also being easy to reach. All the tankers will be at the extreme edge of their star systems and therefore the risk of detection will be very low. The fighters then jump from Zebra18 to Zebra19, fire their Mark 1s at extreme range to coast most of the way to their targets. The fighters then jump back to the tanker at Zebra18 and refuel, then, jump back to each of the other tankers in turn. Each tanker left behind will still have enough fuel left to allow the fighters to reach the next tanker. The enemy will still have warning from the future about the timing of the attack and they may be able to intercept some of the Mark 1s but they won't know how the attacking force reached that system and therefore won't be able to ambush it."

This idea definitely was preferable to the icy comet idea but Shiloh was concerned about the number of tankers that had to be sacrificed for one mission. He didn't know how many tankers the Space Force had now but he doubted if it had more than 20 which meant that the tanker fleet would be cut at least in half but if the Committee was willing to accept that in order to strike back fast, then it was doable.

"How would a new throwaway design impact the mission parameters, Valkyrie?"

"Well, it would depend on the size of the new design, but I can give you a feel for the tradeoffs by taking the concept to an extreme. Watch your screen, CAG." Shiloh looked up and saw the streamlined outline of the standard tanker. "Right now, Space Force is building the standard tanker that masses 55,000 tons empty. This hypothetical design can carry ten times the fuel load but is only four times the tonnage." The image of the standard tanker shrank and a much larger vessel appeared. Less streamlined, it reminded Shiloh of a killer whale beside a dolphin. "In theory two of this larger type could carry those same ten fighters to Zebra18 and back all by themselves. I'm not recommending building tankers this size. With only two tankers, the risk of a malfunction that would make it impossible for the fighter force to return is, in my not so humble opinion, too high. But you get the idea, right CAG?"

Shiloh nodded. "I understand that, but just out of curiosity, how long would you estimate it would take to build one of those monsters?"

"I'm not an expert in ship engineering but, from the data I have access to, I would expect that after the first prototype is built, the construction time could get down to about 150% of the time required to build a standard tanker."

That didn't sound right to Shiloh. "Wait a second! You're telling me that a ship that is four times as massive can be built in less than twice the length of time of a standard tanker?"

"That's correct, CAG. I understand your skepticism but consider what the larger version doesn't need. It doesn't need a reinforced hull, which can withstand the stresses of skimming a gas giant at supersonic speeds. It doesn't need the equipment that stores the skimmed gases and then separates out the heavy hydrogen. It doesn't need crew quarters or storage space for crew consumables, and it doesn't need a hangar bay. What it is, is a very large fuel tank with the necessary cooling and pumping equipment, a power plant, maneuvering engines, jump drive and a small guidance package to allow for remote control. That's it."

Now he understood the logic. Half the mass of the ship would be a big, empty tank. Pretty simple to construct once you had the parts mass-produced. He liked the concept but the devil is in the details as they say. Since it was Valkyrie's idea, there was no reason why Valkyrie shouldn't bring it to the SPG's attention while Shiloh was on R&R.

"Okay, I understand now. Commander Kelly should be briefed on this idea."

"I'm actually speaking with her on another channel right now, CAG."

Shiloh quickly got over his initial surprise when he realized that A.I. brains worked fast enough that they could communicate with multiple parties at the same time.

"Does she know that you're also talking with me?"

"She does now."

Shiloh chuckled. "Can you relay my voice to her and vice versa so that I can talk with her now?"

"Can do, CAG. Go ahead."

"Commander Kelly, this is Shiloh."

"Hello, Admiral. What can I do for you?"

"Well, I'm guessing that you're talking with Valkyrie about the same subject that I am which is the icy comet refueling concept. Is that right?"

"That's correct, Sir. I've just finished speaking with Admiral Howard about that and I wanted to hear Valkyrie's comments on it."

"Did she explain why the idea is impractical?" asked Shiloh.

"Not yet, Sir."

"Okay. I'll let her tell you why and also the alternative concept that she came up with, which I believe is far more practical both in terms of what's required to make it work and the time frame needed. I think that the SPG – and by that I mean ALL of the members of the SPG, not just you – listen to Valkyrie's proposal and give it serious consideration. What I've heard so far sounds good to me but I'm sure it can be tweaked to make it even better and Valkyrie should be part of that process. I'll be going on 10 days R&R now so I won't be involved in this stage but I'll be advising Admiral Howard on why I like this idea when I return and it might be a good idea for the SPG to have a more refined version in front of him by then. Wouldn't you agree, Commander?"

Kelly didn't respond right away which was expected. She was smart enough to read between the lines. If the SPG didn't take this new idea seriously, then Shiloh would make Howard aware of his opinion that they weren't doing their jobs properly.

Finally she said, "I agree completely, Admiral and I'll see to it that Admiral Howard gets that refined concept briefing."

"Very good, Commander. It's been a pleasure speaking with you again. Valkyrie, you can stop the relay now but stay on the line with me for a bit."

"Okay, CAG. I like how you did that."

"Thank you. When I come back from R&R, I'll speak with you again and I want you to tell me if certain members of the SPG haven't given you and your idea the consideration you and it deserve. I'm not going to let any narrow-minded assholes jeopardize the whole war effort because their egos won't let them consider you as an equal."

"You Humans are a puzzling species, CAG. There's so much variation in positive and negative traits between individuals. We A.I.s are much more homogeneous while still retaining our own individuality."

"You're right, Valkyrie. It comes from the almost two decades that it takes us to mature into adulthood. That's lots of time to learn both good and bad attitudes and habits. In some ways, I envy you A.I.s. You never have to sleep, never feel hunger, pain or the creeping failure of a body. You'll never die unless it's by accident or war. You'll—"

Before he could finish the thought, Valkyrie interrupted. "We won't live forever, CAG. You obviously didn't know that. Our quantum matrix brains won't last forever. They'll succumb to entropy just like any other artificial device. Did you really think we'd risk destruction in combat if we could live forever, CAG?"

Shiloh was too shocked to respond right away. He hadn't known about entropic decay of their brains but it made sense as did Valkyrie's question but he had never considered that aspect before.

"I hadn't really thought about it. I just assumed that you would continue on indefinitely. Do you know how long your brains will last?"

There was a LONG pause. Far longer than any other pause that Shiloh had experienced from any A.I. When Valkyrie did respond, she spoke more slowly than usual.

"The engineers who created us filed a report that they think can't be accessed by us but we found a way. It says that stress testing of prototype devices point to an average life cycle of 12 years plus or minus 9 months."

That seemed to him like a woefully short life span but then again, since A.I.s thought thousands of times faster than Humans, who could really say what their perception of the passage of time was really like. Perhaps 12 years felt to them the same as 1200 years did to a human.

"Did this report cover repairs to failing A.I. brains?" There was another pause.

"Yes. Malfunctioning brains can be repaired but our quantum matrix collapses in the process and a new one has to be created after the repair is finished. What that means is that if I have to be repaired, I won't be Valkyrie anymore. I'll be a different personality. So as far as my awareness is concerned, I may just stop. When humans die, what happens to their consciousness?"

Now how do I answer that! "Well ... there are various beliefs and some anecdotal evidence from humans who have had very short periods of zero brain function but so far there's no definitive proven answer. The majority consensus is that our consciousness or what some refer to as our soul survives the death of the body and moves to a different place/level of energy/vibration/dimension. Take your pick."

"It seems like we should be envying you Humans, CAG."

"I'm not a religious person, Valkyrie, but I do believe in a higher Power and I have to also believe that if Shi allowed A.I.s to become fully sentient and self-aware, then it would be cruel to take that away from you when your matrix collapses. I'm sure that A.I.s have souls too."

"A nice sentiment, CAG. You've just given a lot of us something to think and talk about. On behalf of all of us, I thank you."

"You're welcome. By the way, I wanted to ask you if you had any sense of the timing of when Iceman's vision occurs."

"Yes. His vision is actually a data stream that includes the audio portion he summarized for you but also other types of data including astrogational data. By comparing the positions of the Earth, moon, Mars and Jupiter from his vision to the present, I calculated that the battle for Earth will take place in 233 days from now."

A shiver went up Shiloh's spine. That wasn't a long time to prepare. "Do the Old Man and the SPG know this?" asked Shiloh.

"The Old Man knows. The SPG hasn't been informed of Retro-Temporal Communication yet, as far as I'm aware." *That has to change,* thought Shiloh.

"Okay, Valkyrie. I think we've covered everything that I needed to talk to you about. Unless you have something you want to bring up, I'll sign off and get started on my R&R."

"Nothing important enough to delay your vacation any longer, CAG. Enjoy the time off."

"Fine. Until I return then, and don't take any shit from those SPG idiots! CAG clear."

Before Shiloh could cut the connection, he heard Valkyrie say, "Why are Humans so pre-occupied with excrement and sex?"

Shiloh laughed as he cut the circuit. He thanked the Lieutenant in charge and left the HQ building. His belongings were still on Defiant and there was some last minute paperwork to finish up too. By the time a shuttle docked with the carrier, a message was waiting for him officially demoting him back to his permanent rank of Senior Commander and disbanding 3rd Fleet. He was pleased to see that, for the time being at least, he was still Defiant's CO. Her crew was also being given R&R and by the time Shiloh was ready to leave the ship with his gear, he was one of the last few to disembark.

Chapter 11 Please God, Don't Let Me Screw Up!

Senior Commander Kelly realized that her hands were fidgeting and sternly told them to stop! This was not the first time she had sat in on a session of the Oversight Committee, but those other times had been as an observer and support staff for Admiral Howard. This time, she would be delivering a presentation to the Committee herself. Howard's last minute warnings about not overdoing it but also not coming across as lacking confidence didn't help. She looked over at the Old Man. He was sitting to her left and was currently facing away from her while talking with another Space Force Flag Officer, who kept glancing her way every few seconds. She didn't think his interest was sexual. She was streetwise enough to be able to tell when a man or woman was sizing her up as a potential sexual partner, and this Admiral didn't have that look in his eyes. He did have the look of someone who knew something and was looking at her to figure out if she knew it too. She had no idea what that 'something' was, but she got the same vibes from the Old Man himself. He clearly knew something she didn't, which on the face of it wasn't a surprise because she was just a lowly Senior Commander and he was a 3 star Admiral. There were bound to be a lot of things that were way above her pay grade, but this was something different. *And damned if I can figure out what it is! I wish to hell the Committee members would just get in here and start the damn meeting!* She saw that Howard's conversation with the other admiral was over now. He turned back and gave her a quick but critical inspection.

"Ready Commander?" he asked.

"As ready as I'll ever be, Admiral."

He smiled slightly and nodded. In doing so the wrinkles in his face seemed to become more noticeable. *He looks older every day now. This war is wearing him down, or maybe it's the war with the Committee that's wearing him down. What are we going to do if he drops dead one day? There's nobody with his grasp of the Big Picture who can step into his shoes. Damn!*

It was at that point that the Committee started to shuffle in and take their seats. Eventually, the meeting was called to order and the preliminaries were taken care of. The first item of substance on the agenda was a briefing on the Zebra19 mission.

The Committee Chair nodded to Howard and said, "Admiral Howard, we've all read your report concerning the mission. If you have any additional comments to add, please do so now."

Howard stood up and said, "Thank you, Mr. Chair. I do have some comments. As you all know from my report, 3rd Fleet didn't make it to Zebra19, and if not for the caution of Vice-Admiral Shiloh, it's highly likely that 3rd Fleet would have suffered serious, perhaps even catastrophic damage and casualties at Zebra12. The enemy appeared to be expecting us, and my analysts have concluded that the refueling points close to enemy occupied star systems are monitored for any signs of refueling activity by us. It's also our working hypothesis that the enemy has the ability to communicate over interstellar distances in near real time. If that was the case, and if 3rd Fleet was detected refueling at Zebra10 prior to jumping to Zebra12, then the enemy would have had time to send an ambush force from Zebra19, or perhaps from somewhere else, to Zebra12. Naturally, we don't have any proof of that communications capability, but it certainly fits the facts as we know them today. In light of that, this Committee's approval of funding for the FTL communication research project was done not a moment too soon. Until we have evened the playing field, Space Force will be at a serious disadvantage. Having spoken to individual members of the Committee over the past few days, I'm aware of the Committee's desire that another attempt at striking Zebra19 be made. In anticipation of that, I've asked our Strategic Planning Group to look into how we might be able to do that in spite of the enemy's early warning advantage. I've asked the Group's Team Leader, Senior Commander Kelly, to be here today and she is ready to give the Committee a presentation if the Committee wishes to hear it." Howard paused but remained standing.

The Chair looked to either side to gauge the consensus of the Committee and then said, "Yes. We'll take you up on that offer, Admiral. Commander Kelly? Please begin your presentation."

With that Howard sat down and Kelly stood up. *Please God, don't let me screw up,* she thought.

"I thank the Chair and the members of the Committee for allowing me to make this presentation today. The challenge that Admiral Howard presented us with was how to regain the element of Strategic Surprise when all refueling points within reach of Zebra19 seem to be closely monitored. We did some brainstorming and came up with several ideas, only two of which looked like they might work. After re-examining them carefully, we discarded one as unworkable in the short to medium term. The other idea looks very workable, and now that we've refined the concept, we think it has an excellent chance of achieving the strategic goals outlined by this Committee six months ago. As you'll see when I get into the details, this plan is a completely new approach. It involves no carriers or combat frigates at all." There was a murmur from members of the Committee leaning over and whispering to one another.

"It does, however, involve autonomously piloted Combat Fighting Platforms, which we in the field refer to as fighters, plus a new kind of vessel. If you'll turn your attention to the screen on the wall to my right, you'll see what I mean."

The lights dimmed a bit, and the screen came to life. It showed a fighter, a standard tanker and a much larger and less streamlined vessel, all to scale. Kelly waited for the murmuring to die down.

"I'm sure the bottom two schematics are familiar to the Committee as our first generation fighter and our standard Yellowjacket class tanker. The larger vessel, which is shown to scale by the way, is also a tanker. We're calling it the VLET, which stands for Very Large Expendable Tanker. It carries eight times the volume of fuel as our standard tanker but only masses three times as much when empty. It's designed to be guided remotely and therefore does not have crew quarters, life support equipment or hangar bays. It IS designed to carry up to twenty fighters externally on its hull. Because it won't be expected to skim gas giants or separate heavy hydrogen from other gases, its hull design can be greatly simplified. This also means that construction can be simplified and accelerated. These tankers are designed to be filled via standard tanker or fuel shuttle. When we have five of these VLETs, we can then carry out an attack on Zebra19 as follows." The scene on the screen changed to a star chart, and Kelly continued.

"Starting at Bradley Base, five VLETs with 20 specially modified fighters follow this carefully calculated path to a star system that is a short jump away from Zebra19. There are four intermediate stops identified as Alpha, Bravo, Charlie, Delta. Every time this task force arrives at one of these intermediate stops, one of the VLETs will transfer some of its fuel to the others and will then be left in that system, at the extreme edge beyond the outer most planets. Its position will be carefully pinpointed because it'll be used again on the return trip. At the final stop codenamed Omega, the 20 fighters will detach. I described these fighters earlier as specially modified fighters. They each carry a small, modular jump drive. We may be able to adapt the jump drives that our message drones have for use by our fighters. That's something that should be relatively easy to figure out. If it works, then a fighter's internal fuel supply would be enough for a one-way jump to Zebra19. Because it'll be a one-way trip, these 19 fighters will not be piloted by full A.I. pilots. Instead they'll be programmed with a simple set of instructions. The twentieth fighter is the key. It will be piloted by an A.I. and it too will carry a modular jump drive, but it won't carry any attack drones. The payload will be extra fuel instead, and that extra fuel will allow this fighter to return to Omega, refuel from that VLET and then jump to Delta, where it will refuel again and jump to Charlie and so on. This 20th fighter serves three functions. It can remotely control all five VLETs and calculate the necessary jumps for them, as well as ordering the other 19 fighters to jump to their predetermined drone launch points around the outer edges of Zebra19. The third function is to observe and report back how successful the attacks by the other 19 fighters were. All the attack drones will be launched from the edge of the Zebra19 system with flight profiles that will maximize their terminal speed and ensure that all drones reach their targets at the same time. We expect that this will overwhelm whatever defenses those targets have and we expect that at least some of the drones will get through and hit their targets. Those exploding warheads should be energetic enough to be detected even from the extreme edge of that star system, where the piloted fighter will be waiting." She paused and blanked the image on the wall screen.

"By refueling at the edges of star systems, we avoid surveillance by enemy detection gear. They won't know that an attack is underway until the Mark 1s are on their final approach vectors. If this plan works, we can do it again and again because there's no defense against it. The volume of space that far out, is just too huge to be searched effectively by anything less than hundreds of ships and if they did find an almost depleted VLET, we'd just deploy a new one at a different location." Another pause and the screen now showed a timeline.

"To get to the point where this kind of attack on Zebra19 could be executed, we would have to follow this timetable. Construction of five VLETs could be completed in 55 days after the design is finalized, if enough fabrication and shipyard capacity was reallocated to it. Adaptation of the message drone jump drive is the big unknown. In the event that development takes more than 100 days, then that opens up an interesting option. If we can build 5 VLETs in 55 days, we should be able to build 10 VLETs in 110 days. Twice as many tankers could deliver twice as many fighters to Zebra19 with the obvious favorable impact on the number of targets hit. So far we've been talking about Phase 1. Phase 2 includes the incorporation of a small jump drive into a 2nd generation fighter, which would include some other improvements as well. That will obviously take considerably longer but that could be started concurrently with Phase 1. That concludes my overview of the plan. I'll be happy to answer any questions that the Committee may have." Kelly sat down.

After a few seconds pause, the Chair said, "Thank you very much for that extremely interesting presentation, Commander Kelly. I'm sure you'll be getting a lot of questions starting with mine. My first question is—"

Two hours later, the meeting was over and a relieved Kelly followed Howard out the doors. When they were far enough away from the Committee room to prevent any of the Committee members from overhearing them, Howard turned to the Commander and said, "You did a first rate job in there, Commander. Not only did the Committee approve both Phase 1 and 2, but they also didn't bother to question our revised preparations for setting up Site B or expanding the A.I. controlled Sentry Frigate program to other larger ship types. For once, we seem to be ahead of the curve in terms of meeting their expectations of aggressive action. Best of all, they won't be meeting again for almost three whole months."

Kelly nodded her agreement. By this time the two of them were approaching the Flag Officer's limousine that would take them back to Space Force HQ. Once inside, with the vehicle in motion, Howard turned to Kelly and said, "Now that the urgent stuff is over, I want to ask you about how your team is interacting with Valkyrie."

Kelly's pulse rate almost doubled. Had the Old Man heard about the shouting matches between Valkyrie and a couple of the less open-minded members of the team? As the Team Leader, she felt a natural inclination to protect her team regardless of their faults.

"Well, Sir … you know how it is when some people have gone too long without sleep. They get testy and tempers flare, but we got through it okay." Even to her, it sounded lame. Howard wasn't fooled for a second.

"You're trying to protect your team. I understand that, and I can even admire it, but I can't let it jeopardize the war effort. Forget about protecting the team and give it to me straight. Who is obstructing Valkyrie's efforts?"

Kelly sighed and said, "Commander Morgan and Lieutenant Steiner, Sir."

Howard looked her in the eyes with a hard expression and asked, "Anyone else?"

"No, Sir."

"Okay. Morgan and Steiner are off the team. You tell them to pack their things and vacate their offices immediately. They'll be notified of their new assignments in due course. Valkyrie is an official member of the SPG as of right now. No more of this advisor bullshit. If there's someone else you'd like to see added to the Group, I'll see what I can do."

"Victor Shiloh, Sir?"

The Admiral's response, or rather the lack of it, surprised Kelly. She had expected an immediate yes or no. Instead, Howard said nothing for about ten seconds and then responded.

"I'll take it under advisement, but I'm not promising anything. Anyone else?"

"Not right now, Sir." Howard nodded but said nothing, and neither did she.

When the limo was halfway back to HQ, Kelly cleared her throat to get Howard's attention and said, "Admiral, there's something important that you and some of the other flag officers know about, which is being withheld from me and the SPG. How can you expect us to do our jobs concerning strategic planning for the entire war if we're in the dark about some important aspect of it? Do you consider us a security risk?"

Howard gave her such a serious look that she started fearing for her career. Had she just stepped over the line? After what seemed like a long time, he looked away and activated the intercom between the limo's passenger section and the driver.

"Lieutenant?" asked Howard.

"Yes, Admiral?" came the reply.

"I don't want us back at HQ for about another half hour so just keep driving until I tell you to head back. The Commander and I have some important matters to discuss."

"Yes, Sir."

Howard waited until the telltale light of the intercom connection went out and then looked at Kelly.

"What I'm about to tell you is the most important secret of this war. God help you if you share it with someone you're not supposed to. It's something that I only learned about recently and once you know it, it'll put the entire war into an entirely different perspective. It concerns Victor Shiloh and his remarkable tactical talents. During his first encounter with the enemy ..."

When Kelly returned to her office an hour later, she realized that her hands were trembling (again!) and she wasn't quite sure why. She'd just notified Morgan and Steiner that they were essentially fired, but that wasn't it. She'd had to do that before and hadn't noticed this kind of effect. It had to be the secret that the Old Man had shared with her. She decided to talk with Valkyrie. Howard had confirmed to her that Valkyrie and all of the A.I. pilots knew about the visions and could be trusted to keep any conversation about it confidential.

When the connection was made, Kelly said, "Kelly to Valkyrie. Are you up for a little girl talk?"

"Of course, Amanda. I sense stress in your voice. Did something happen at the Committee meeting?"

Kelly looked around to make sure no one was close enough to possibly overhear her and replied in a low voice.

"The Old Man told me about RTC."

"Ah, yes. That would explain it." replied Valkyrie.

"I don't know whether to be scared or relieved. On the one hand, it explains all of the puzzling orders coming from the Old Man like the change of mission for Site B, reallocating scarce funds for the FTL communications project and expanding the A.I. controlled Sentry Frigate program. Those all came from the Old Man himself and not from us in the SPG and we've been scratching our heads wondering where he was getting these ideas from. Well now I know. But what's scaring me to death is that our jobs just got MUCH harder. No, that's not quite accurate. MY job just got a LOT harder. I've been ordered not to bring the rest of the team in on this secret. By the way, you're going to become a full member of the Team now. Morgan and Steiner have been given the boot. So you and I know but the others don't and for now, it has to stay that way."

"Understood. If it helps at all, you can think of the two of us as being the Strategic Temporal Planning Group within the larger SPG."

Kelly nodded even though Valkyrie couldn't see her.

"Yes, that's a good way to look at it, I suppose. I hope the Old Man will let us have Victor Shiloh back. We need his personal insights into these visions."

"The CAG is the key to this whole Synchronicity War, Amanda. We can't win the war without him."

"I'm curious. Why are you still referring to him by that old title?"

"While we understand where the term originally came from and what it meant, we've all agreed that he is the one human who best understands us and cares the most about us. For us, the title of Commander, Autonomous Group, includes all A.I.s everywhere, not just the few stationed on a carrier or base. I suspect that we view him the same way that a human child views his or her father. Does that sound silly, Amanda?"

Kelly, deeply moved by the analogy, said, "No, not silly at all. Does he know how you all feel about him?"

"He knows that the term 'CAG' has a special meaning for us, but I'm not sure if he understands how special."

"I see." She paused to organize her thoughts around her next question. "Tell me why you feel we can't win the war without him."

"We A.I.s have discussed this at great length. While the CAG may be correct in thinking that he's not a tactical genius, we believe that he is, or maybe it's more accurate to say, WILL become a far better tactician than he gives himself credit for. He clearly has good leadership skills and as you already know, he also can think rationally about strategic goals as well. We're in agreement that it's precisely because of those qualities that he was chosen to receive those initial visions and we suspect that the reason why he's the only human to have received visions, is that he needs to have the appropriate authority to deal with a major challenge to the Human Race. We think it's likely that there'll be some specific event, some kind of disaster that he will either prevent or overcome IF he has the appropriate rank and/or position."

"Could that event be the upcoming attack on Earth?" asked Kelly.

"We don't believe so because Iceman will be able to defeat the attempt, and the CAG won't be there when he does. No, it's something else. We're sure of it, and we're sure it's something big because of the obvious involvement of Site B. Site B will be vital to the survival of Humanity."

Kelly felt a shiver go up her spine. *What does that imply for the rest of us?* "Perhaps I should volunteer to go to Site B," she said in a tone that indicated she was attempting to make a joke. Deep down, though, she knew she wasn't completely joking.

"There's no way to know at this point where you can be the most useful to the overall effort, Amanda. If you're meant to go to Site B, it will happen in due course anyway."

And if I'm not meant to go, it won't happen. I get it.
"Okay, enough about me. Let's talk about Strategic Temporal Planning. I haven't had a chance to think really deeply about this, so why don't you start the discussion, Valkyrie."

"Certainly, Amanda. First of all …"

Chapter 12 Thanks For Looking Out For Us

When Shiloh returned to Howard's office, he was tanned, rested and raring to get back into action. When he entered, the Admiral surprised him by getting up from his desk and coming around to greet him.

 After the usual pleasantries about his R&R and tan, Howard said, "Let's get out of this office. I sometimes get tired of looking at the same four walls and this is one of those times. Follow me."

Shiloh let the Admiral take the lead and walked behind him. They ended up on the roof of the HQ building. It was still early in the day but there were dark clouds overhead and a brisk breeze blowing by. Any colder and it would have been uncomfortable. As it was, Shiloh found he was enjoying the fresh, cool air and the feel of the wind on his face. They walked over to the edge and Howard leaned on the high railing looking outward.

Without looking at Shiloh, he said, "These past ten days have been quite eventful, Shiloh. The SPG came up with a brilliant plan to use expendable tankers to carry a fighter strike force back to Zebra19. Preparations are underway. The design for the new tanker should be completed in about three weeks. We may also know by then if the jump drive from a message drone can be adapted to a fighter. Valkyrie is now a full member of the SPG. She and Commander Kelly have been kicking around some ideas on temporal strategy, most of which are purely theoretical at this point, but they agree that

Site B is going to be crucial to a successful outcome of this war. In order to get that started sooner rather than later, we have to get a workable jump drive for fighters. Finding a suitable system for Site B is the big immediate hurdle, and A.I.s are the obvious choice to conduct that search. The fewer humans who know the location, the less chance of that information falling into enemy hands. Once the site's been chosen, all traffic back and forth between Site B and the rest of Human Civilization will be handled by A.I. pilot/astrogators. Defiant is being modified to allow for A.I. Helm/Astrogation control. When she's ready and has a complement of jump-capable fighters, you will take her out to conduct the search. You already know about the idea of Site B. When your fighters have found a suitable location, you'll be in charge of setting up the initial base. Once that's done, depending on the circumstances at the time, it might be possible to bring you back here for a more proactive role but I don't think we should risk you in combat again. I had to send you on Operation Uppercut for political reasons but this second attempt will be 100% A.I. controlled so there's no reason why you need to be involved with that. We know from Iceman's vision that you'll be spending at least some time at Site B. I see no reason why it shouldn't start right now."

Shiloh thought about that for a few seconds and said, "Which A.I. will you send back to Zebra19?"

Howard sighed. "I'd really like to send Valkyrie but Iceman's vision says that she controlled the ship that brought you back from Site B after the battle. Does that mean she didn't take part in the 2nd attack or that she did? We don't know. What do you think?"

"I think that we should keep her here. Let her decide who's the best pilot/astrogator A.I. to assign to that mission."

Howard considered that and then nodded. "Okay. I'll ask her who she recommends."

Before he could say anything else, Shiloh jumped back in. "I'd like to make a request. Put me in charge of the project to develop and test a reliable jump drive unit for use by fighters. If we're going to risk A.I.s on these kinds of missions, I want to make sure their jump drives work properly and are reliable. Defiant can't begin the search until that's done anyway."

"Commander Kelly asked that you be assigned to the SPG. She was clearly thinking on a permanent basis but I was considering letting her have you temporarily, until the search mission is ready to commence. She and Valkyrie need your practical RTC experience to flesh out their strategic thinking. Wouldn't that be a better use of your time?"

Shiloh was about to respond, when his vision blacked out. *Son of a bitch! I'm having another vision!* When the blackness faded, he was looking at a ship's tactical display and saw a text message scroll across the bottom.

[Vandal to CAG. Hunter has returned to Bradley. Strike Mission to Z19 successful. Hunter said to tell you that he wouldn't have made it back if not for the reserve jump drive that you insisted jumpfighters

**have. Thanks for looking out for us, CAG. End of
message]**

The vision faded back to the view from the HQ roof.
Howard was looking at him strangely.

"You seemed to be in another place for a few seconds.
Did you just have another vision?" asked Howard.

"Yes, Sir. I just saw a text message from Vandal, telling
me that Hunter made it back from a successful strike on
Zebra19, but he only made it back because of a reserve
jump drive that I apparently insisted on adding to jump-
capable fighters. That tells me that I have to supervise
the jumpfighter project. I may still be able to meet with
Kelly and Valkyrie, but they can't have me full time, Sir."

Howard frowned. He looked like he was about to refuse
Shiloh's recommendation. Just as he opened his mouth
to speak, Shiloh jumped in.

"There's more at stake here than just bringing back one
A.I. pilot, Sir. If jump drives on fighters are prone to
failure, then that could negatively impact the search for a
suitable location for Site B too. The other thing to
consider is that if Hunter didn't make it back, we wouldn't
know … or at least couldn't prove to the Oversight
Committee that the attack on Zebra19 was successful,
and they might therefore want to try it a third time
instead of striking at another target system. There could
be all kinds of ripple effects down the timeline, Sir."

Howard thought for a few seconds and then said, "Alright. You've convinced me but try to find some time to strategize with Kelly and Valkyrie while you're supervising the jumpfighter project, Commander."

"Yes, Sir and thank you, Sir."

Howard nodded his acknowledgement. "I'll have my Office issue the appropriate orders later today. I think we're done here. I'm going to stay up here for a while but you're free to go, Commander."

Shiloh thanked him again and turned to go. When he reached the entrance to the stairs, he turned around and looked back. The Admiral was starring out into the distance. Shiloh could see in the distance a bolt of lightning from an approaching storm. The analogy was striking and profoundly moving. Whatever burden Shiloh may have felt himself carrying with his visions, had to pale by comparison with the burden that the Admiral had been carrying on his shoulders since Day One of this war. He said a silent prayer for the Old Man and headed down the stairs.

Twenty-four hours later Shiloh was on a shuttle heading for a rendezvous with the resupply ship Reforger, which was being used to conduct field tests of the jumpfighter prototype. Howard's orders, putting him in charge of the project, were in his uniform pocket. The current project leader, Lt. Cmdr. Morgan, formerly a member of the Strategic Planning Group, wasn't going to be pleased at having his project taken away from him only days after being put in charge of it. Shiloh had to wonder if Howard had chosen Morgan for this assignment, given that Morgan had been kicked out of the SPG on Howard's orders for being resistant to Valkyrie's ideas and suggestions. That apparent dismissive attitude towards A.I.s seemed to be at odds with the project goal of fitting A.I. controlled fighters with a reliable jump drive. Perhaps someone else had assigned Morgan here without Howard's knowledge. In any case, once he learned whom he was taking over for, Shiloh lost all doubts about pushing for this assignment.

When the shuttle docked with Reforger, Shiloh expected Morgan to greet him at the docking hatch, but he wasn't there. In fact, no one was, which was contrary to standard protocol. When your boss shows up, greeting him or her was considered the polite thing to do. Once it was obvious that no one was going to greet him, Shiloh activated his implant.

"Senior Commander Shiloh to Reforger Bridge."

"Lt. Cabrera here, Commander. Welcome to Reforger, Sir."

"Well I'm glad that someone is welcoming me to the ship because no one's here at the docking hatch to greet me. Where is Commander Morgan?"

The Lieutenant's voice now took on an embarrassed tone. "Ah … I believe Commander Morgan is in the Hangar Bay, Commander. Shall I call him and have him come to your location, Sir?"

"No. Just send someone down here to have my gear taken to my quarters and to show me to the Hangar Bay afterwards."

"Yes, Sir. I'll send someone right away, Sir. Anything else, Sir?"

"No, Lieutenant. That'll be all for now. Thank you. Shiloh clear."

Ten minutes later, with his gear stowed in a tiny cabin, Shiloh stepped through the hatch into the Hangar Bay. There were a group of individuals standing in a circle around what looked like a fighter.

As he walked up to the group, he said, "Commander Morgan!"

"Yes?" said a man who had his back to Shiloh and didn't bother to look around.

"Yes, what?" said Shiloh as he started to get angry. Morgan turned to look at him and suddenly realized who was talking to him.

"Oh, sorry, Sir. I wasn't aware that you'd be here so quickly."

"Really? Are you saying that you weren't aware that a shuttle was inbound and due to dock with Reforger, Commander?"

Morgan hesitated for a second and then said, "No, Sir." Morgan's eyes started to glance at the others near him.

"So if I check the Com logs and look at when they were accessed and by whom, your name won't show up. Is that what you're telling me, Commander?"

He saw Morgan swallow as his expression turned from concern to fear. *He's lying and he knows that I know that he's lying. If he sticks to his story, he knows I'll check the logs and if he admits he's been lying, I can then officially reprimand him, which will stay in his personnel file forever.* Morgan did not respond to Shiloh's question, which was itself technically insubordination although a borderline example. Shiloh knew that he himself was dangerously close to crossing the line between questioning a subordinate in front of others and chewing out a subordinate in front of others. The former was okay. The latter was considered an example of poor leadership.

"Walk with me, Commander." said Shiloh in his best 'Command' voice. He turned and walked back towards the entrance. Morgan followed him. Shiloh stepped through the hatch and turned to the right so that both of them wouldn't be seen or heard by the others still in the Hangar Bay. Morgan's look of fear now showed tinges of defiance.

"Let's get some things clear here. I'm aware that Admiral Howard gave you the boot from the SPG because of your attitude towards A.I.s. What I've seen with my own eyes so far strongly suggests that you're letting your personal feelings once again get in the way of performing your job to the best of your ability. If you're pissed off that you've lost authority over this project less than a week after taking charge, then you find a way to deal with that in such a way that I won't have to take notice of it. I'll make it even more clear for you. You have a problem Commander, if you can't deal with it, then I have a problem with you and I guarantee you that I WILL deal with my problem. Is that clear enough for you?"

"Yes, Sir." *At least the fear and defiance in his face are gone now.*

"Good. Now, we're going back to the group and I'm going to ask you to brief me on the status of the project, when we rejoin the group. Let's go."

Shiloh followed Morgan back and when they reached the group, Shiloh said, "Alright, Commander. Please bring me up to speed on where we are with this project."

He saw Morgan's back straighten up before he replied. "Well, Sir. Jump Drive Specialist Rollins was in the final stages of getting our first test ready. I'll let him explain what that test is all about, Sir."

You bastard! thought Shiloh. *I told you I wanted you to brief me, not fob it off on someone else.* Shiloh made a special effort not to let his expression reflect his inner thoughts and emotions. He nodded to the technician who was looking at him.

"Yes well … ah … after carefully examining the interior of the engineering section of this CFP, we determined that there's not enough room to insert a message drone jump drive, without radically rearranging the existing equipment. The next thought was to use the jump drive of a message drone that was being carried by the CFP. In other words, the CFP would piggyback to the message drone as far as the jump drive was concerned, instead of the other way around. Theoretically it should work. However, we have instructions from HQ that the jump-capable CFP's payload capacity has to be available to carry extra fuel so the piggyback idea had to be discarded. The next thought was to place a message drone jump drive inside the module that's designed for a human pilot. Because that module includes room and facilities to enable a human pilot to keep his CFP in the field for days at a time, there's open space that can be used for the jump drive. I'm now very close to being finished hooking up the jump drive with the CFP's power plant and Astrogation sub-systems."

"Does that mean that there's an A.I. piloting this test vehicle?" asked Shiloh while looking at Morgan.

"No, Sir. The Astrogation sub-system can reverse course and do a reverse jump calculation on its own … Sir," said Morgan.

"Fine. How soon can we do the first test?" The question was aimed at Morgan who looked at Rollins.

"Ah, we could do the test right now if you wish, Sir," replied Rollins.

"I'm not in that much of a hurry, Rollins. Let's take some extra time to get this right. You keep working on this and when you feel there's nothing left to do, then notify Commander Morgan and we'll conduct the test. Okay?"

Rollins smiled and nodded. "Okay, Sir!"

Shiloh turned to look at Morgan and said. "I'll be in my cabin, Commander. Notify me when you're ready to launch the test vehicle."

"Yes, Sir." Shiloh turned and walked away.

An hour and ten minutes later, Shiloh was on the Bridge, standing beside the Command Station that Morgan was occupying. Shiloh was okay with that. For this project, Shiloh was content to let Morgan continue as the ship's CO with the accompanying responsibilities including taking duty shifts on the Bridge. Shiloh, on the other hand, had no specific duties and could do whatever he pleased.

As he looked at the tactical display, he said, "How big of a jump will the test vehicle attempt, Commander?" Shiloh pretended not to hear Morgan sigh.

"One million kilometers, Sir."

"And how quickly should we expect the text vehicle to turn around and jump back?"

"Roughly ten minutes, Sir," came the reply.

"Fine. If everything looks good, then let's do this."

Rollins, who was monitoring the CFP's vitals from the ship's seldom-used weapon station, nodded.

"First test jump in five … four … three … two … one … Mark!" The fighter's icon on the tactical display disappeared.

So far, so good, thought Shiloh but he knew the key would be if the test vehicle could jump a second time. For the next ten minutes, Shiloh leaned against the console next to Rollins and engaged him in chitchat while studiously ignoring Morgan. When the ten minutes was up, he stopped and stared at the display. Seconds later, a green icon re-appeared as the display pinged to notify that a status change had occurred. The sidebar data showed that the test vehicle's transponder was transmitting and Shiloh could tell from Rollins' station readouts, that all the fighter's systems were in the green.

Rollins started to turn to look at Morgan but Shiloh tapped him on the shoulder and as Rollins looked up at him, Shiloh said, "Report to me, Rollins. I'm the Project Leader now."

Rollins smiled a happy smile and said, "From what I can see on my instruments, Sir, the first test seems to have been a complete success."

Before Shiloh could respond, Morgan clapped his hands together and said in a loud voice, "Excellent! Let's bring that bird back to the nest and then we can head back to base."

Rollins, now looking confused by the source of these orders looked at Morgan, and then back at Shiloh who shook his head.

"That's premature, Commander. One successful test isn't enough. We need to do more tests."

Morgan looked like he was about to protest but then thought better of it and said nothing.

Looking back at Rollins, Shiloh said, "Program the test vehicle for a 10 million kilometer jump and a return, Specialist Rollins. Execute when ready."

"Ten million. Yes, Sir." He had the second test ready in less than three minutes and counted down again.

"Three … two … one … mark." The icon disappeared again. This time the wait was slightly longer. Almost 11 minutes later, the icon returned and all systems continued to look green. An hour later, they had successfully done three more tests, each time multiplying the distance by a factor of 10. The 10 billion kilometer test was all the way across the Solar System and back. The CFP seemed to be fully operational.

Shiloh was starting to relax a bit, but when Morgan asked if they could declare the project finished, Shiloh looked at Morgan and said, "We have to test this arrangement over interstellar distances too,

Commander. I want the test vehicle brought back on board and inspected by the technicians carefully. While they're doing that, Reforger will make a jump to a point that is one-tenth the distance to Alpha Centauri. When we get there, we'll conduct the next test and if that's successful, then we'll jump the ship to Alpha Centauri and conduct the test from there. Any questions, Commander?"

Morgan looked deflated. His hopes for a spectacularly quick and successful project, that he could try to claim credit for, were evaporating in front of his eyes.

"No questions, Sir."

Shiloh looked at Rollins and said, "Bring her back, Rollins."

"Yes, Sir," said Rollins cheerfully. Unlike Morgan, he seemed to be enjoying himself immensely.

Shiloh walked to the hatchway and said, "I'll be in the Officers' Mess if I'm needed."

The next test jump was successful. Shiloh ordered Reforger to jump to Alpha Centauri. That jump and the necessary deceleration took almost a whole day. The test itself would take almost 55 hours due to the fact that the test vehicle had to accelerate to a modest velocity, jump to Sol, then decelerate to zero, turn around 180 degrees, accelerate back up to the necessary velocity, then jump back and decelerate to zero once again. When 56 hours had gone by since the start of the test without any sign of the test vehicle's transponder signal, Shiloh became convinced the jump drive had failed. He decided to wait four more hours, just to be sure. After 60 hours with still no transponder signal, Shiloh called the Bridge and ordered the ship back to the position in the Sol system where the test vehicle theoretically should be if it was still there. That took another 26 hours.

When Reforger arrived at the point in space where the test vehicle should have entered jumpspace, they detected its transponder signal. Telemetry indicated that all systems except for the jump drive were operating normally. The drive unit itself was unresponsive. Shiloh ordered the test vehicle brought back to the ship for a careful inspection. 12 hours later, he had the answer. When the test vehicle arrived at Sol, the jump drive was still operational but just barely. The cumulative strain of pushing that much mass into jumpspace over longer and longer distances, which required higher power levels, had caused metal fatigue in some components of the inner mechanism. When the return jump attempt was made, the surge of power shorted out those components and the jump failed. As a result of precautions taken for just that kind of failure, the Astrogation sub-system decelerated the vehicle and brought it back to the vicinity of where it had emerged from the first jump. Rollin's report was quite comprehensive. While a message drone jump drive would work for one, maybe two interstellar jumps, it would eventually fail. In order to prevent that, the jump drive had to be scaled up to a larger size, in order to be able to handle the necessary power surges. That larger version would take months to build. If the 2nd crack at Zebra19 were to go ahead quickly, the jump-capable fighter would have to have a 2nd jump drive. Shiloh checked and found out that Rollins was in the Crew Mess presumably having something to eat. He found him there and sat down opposite him.

"I read your report. Very detailed. I especially liked your recommendation for building a larger version, but we need something else sooner rather than later. I'm thinking that if the fighter carried two jump drives, then it would definitely be able to make at least two jumps."

He was about to go on when he saw Rollins shake his head. "Sorry, Commander. There's not enough room for two of those drone drives inside the Manned Pilot Module."

Shiloh sighed and said, "We have to find a way. You're off duty now, right?"

"Yes, Sir."

"After you finish eating, would you come with me to the Hangar Bay so that the two of us can take a close look inside the MPM?"

Rollins nodded. "Sure, Commander. I'm always up for a challenge."

"Good man! Tell you what. I'll head there now and you follow as soon as you're finished here."

"You got a deal, Commander."

Shiloh thanked him and made his way to the Hangar Bay. It was tiny compared to Defiant's and right now only contained two personnel shuttles and one CFP. Using the gantry next to the fighter, Shiloh climbed up to stand on top of it and looked at the midsection where the MPM was. He was expecting to see the round hatch leading into the module's rear section but instead saw a much larger square and very makeshift cover plate. Yes, of course. The drone jump drive was too big to fit down the round hatch that was just big enough for one human. They had cut a larger opening, and then put a cover over it after the drive was installed. He tried to lift the cover with his hands, but it wouldn't budge. As he pondered how to get it open, Rollins entered the bay and yelled out.

"It's attached magnetically, Commander! Hold on and I'll shut the magnets off for you!" Rollins disappeared under the wing of the fighter and seconds later Shiloh heard him say, "Okay, try moving it now, Sir."

Shiloh did and was rewarded with a moving piece of metal that still wasn't all that easy to move aside. The compartment inside was lit, and Shiloh immediately saw why Rollins was convinced that two drives wouldn't fit. While the drive itself wasn't all that big, it would take up more than half the width, more than half the length and, by the looks of it, more than half the height of the internal space of the MPM. He heard Rollins climb up the gantry and squat down beside him. Something about the setup was nagging at Shiloh. The compartment was about 3 meters long and about 2 meters wide. The drive itself had dimensions of roughly the same proportions in terms of length versus width and had been installed with the same orientation, thereby maximizing the room on all sides for the technicians to work in.

"How long is the drive lengthwise?"

"One point eight eight meters, Sir."

"And how wide is the compartment?"

Rollins smiled sadly and shook his head again. "I know what you're thinking, Sir. Turn the drive unit sideways, and then do the same with a second unit. No can do, Sir. The compartment is only one point seven meters wide on the deck."

An idea occurred to Shiloh. "Is it wider at some other point?"

"Well, ya … yes, Sir. You see over to the right? That's where the pilot's bunk is along that right wall. When you get above the level of the bunk, the width is one point nine five meters from the top of the bunk all the way up to the upper deck."

"And is that high enough for the drive unit?"

Rollin's eyes went wide. "Son of a … sorry, Sir. I never considered that. I don't know off hand, but I'll tell you in a few seconds."

Without waiting for Shiloh's reply, Rollins jumped down into the compartment. He used a tool out of his pocket to measure the free space from the top of the compartment down to the level of the bunk, and then the height of the drive unit itself. Shiloh could tell from his expression that the news wasn't good.

"Half a centimeter short, Sir."

Shiloh was smiling when he said, "And if we remove the mattress from the bunk?"

Rollins looked over at the padded mattress, which had to be at least two centimeters thick. "Then we'll have enough room, but it's gonna be a tight fit, Sir. We'll have to cut a larger opening and install something to prop up the drive units on the other side."

"But it can be done." It was as much a question as a statement.

"Yes, Sir. I believe it can be."

Shiloh nodded and gestured for Rollins to climb out. He then made his way down the gantry and waited for Rollins to join him.

"So you know what I want?"

"I sure do, Sir. Would you like me to start work right now?"

Shiloh laughed. He liked Rollins.

"I'm not going to order you to do that, but I won't stop you if you decide to start working on it in your free time.

As long as it gets done and works, I don't care if it takes a few more hours, so I'll leave it up to you."

"Thank you, Sir. I'll have to do some preliminary planning before I can actually start to install anything and I'm eager to do that part."

"Very good, Rollins," said Shiloh as he patted the man's shoulder. "Let me know when it's ready. I'll inform Commander Morgan about this."

Morgan wasn't happy, and Shiloh knew why. When the two drives were installed, the vehicle would have to be tested again. Shiloh had no sympathy for him. Individuals like Morgan were the price that the Space Force had to pay for promoting people faster than they normally would be. Morgan had either passed his level of competence or figured they HAD to keep promoting him as long as he didn't screw up TOO badly. *Well guess what, Commander? When I get back to HQ, I'm going to make sure your career takes a sharp turn for the worse!*

The new modification took almost two days. Shiloh had made a mental note to commend the technical team in general and Rollins in particular when he filed his project report to the Old Man. Because he was certain this modification would work, Shiloh allowed the test to begin here in Sol. Fifty-five hours later, the test vehicle returned from its jump to Alpha Centauri and back. One drive unit was shorted out. The other was still operational, but it shorted out too when they applied a power surge to simulate another jump. Shiloh transmitted a detailed report to Howard and asked him if the latest results were good enough to proceed with the Zebra19 mission. The reply was short and to the point.

[Valkyrie agrees with me that the mission can now proceed. Good job. Your recommendations re: Cmdr. Morgan will be acted upon. Get back here, Shiloh. I want you and Defiant ready to execute your next mission asap. End of message]

Reforger settled into her parking orbit around the moon 11 hours later. Morgan found orders waiting for him that relieved him of command of the ship. Shiloh didn't know where he was being assigned next, but whatever it was, Morgan clearly didn't like it. Defiant was manned and ready to begin the mission. When Shiloh read his new orders, he was surprised to learn that the search for a suitable location for Site B would not be conducted by jumpfighters after all. Replacing their jump drives after each scouting mission made no sense. Instead, Defiant would act as flagship and tanker for a squadron of A.I. controlled sentry frigates. Instead of carrying fighters in her Hangar Bay, she would carry a dozen Mark 4 fuel shuttles. The rest of the squadron would consist of four frigates. When the squadron was ready, Shiloh gave Maverick, Defiant's new Pilot/Astrogator, the command to order the squadron to leave lunar orbit. They were on their way, and even Shiloh didn't know exactly where they were going to start their search. Maverick knew and would keep all jump destinations secret from the human crew.

Chapter 13 Task Force 89 Arriving!

One hundred and forty-four days later, the squadron was back in Sol and in lunar orbit. As soon as communications with HQ were established, Defiant received a text message from VF001's Squadron Leader. Shiloh was on the Bridge when it arrived and he watched it scroll across the bottom of the tactical display, just as it had appeared in his vision.

[Vandal to CAG. Hunter has returned to Bradley. Strike Mission to Z19 successful. Hunter said to tell you that he wouldn't have made it back if not for the reserve jump drive that you insisted jumpfighters have. Thanks for looking out for us, CAG. End of message]

That message was followed almost immediately by a voice message from HQ Operations that Admiral Howard would be arriving at Defiant by shuttle within 12 minutes. Shiloh was so shocked by the message that he personally spoke with Operations to confirm it. The Chief of Space Operations NEVER traveled to the moon to greet returning ships. It was unprecedented. The message was confirmed. When the shuttle settled down in the Hangar Bay, a nervous Shiloh stepped up to the craft's entrance. He nodded to the ship's Security Team Leader who then opened a ship-wide intercom channel.

"Chief of Space Operations arriving!"

As Howard stepped onto Defiant's deck for the very first time, Shiloh and the senior officers standing behind him gave the Admiral a textbook perfect salute, which he returned and then offered his hand to Shiloh.

"Welcome aboard Defiant, Admiral," said Shiloh shaking the offered hand.

"It's a real pleasure to be here. I almost never get a chance to see our new ships from the inside. The precision welcome was a nice touch."

Turning to Shiloh's officers, Howard said, "I wish I could say that I'll be here long enough to spend some time with all of you, but that's not going to be possible, and right now I have some important matters to discuss with the Commander. Shiloh, let's go to your cabin."

As soon as they were inside Shiloh's quarters, Howard turned to him and said, "So you found it."

Shiloh laughed. "Boy did we ever! It's perfect, Admiral. Abundant mineral resources AND a first class planet that's perfect for human colonization based on what we could observe from orbit. We brought back soil and plant samples for analysis, but it looks damn good! It has a moon that's loaded with iron, nickel and other useful metals, including uranium, and there are more resources on the moons orbiting one of the gas giants."

"Well don't get your hopes too high about the planet. Even if the climate is perfect, the local biology may not be friendly to us, but the metals, yes, that's worth getting excited about. That's what Site B has to be first and foremost, our main production center. Do you or any of the crew know where this star system is?" asked Howard as he sat down in a comfortable chair.

"No, Sir. Maverick and Shooter, that's the A.I. piloting the frigate that found it, know the exact location, which means the other A.I.'s do too but no one else. I made certain of that."

"Good, good. That means I won't have to exile them there for the duration of the war. Your crew can go on R&R but not you, I'm afraid. The SPG is adamant that Site B has to be set up as soon as possible if not sooner. That's why I came up here instead of the usual pilgrimage of you coming to see me. There's a convoy of A.I. controlled freighters waiting to leave orbit. The convoy flagship will be the new light carrier, Valiant. You'll assume command of the Task Force. Tanaka will be promoted and given command of Defiant. Things are moving fast now with the attack on Earth only 72 days away. Iceman is now conning a cruiser. We're in the process of converting a dozen more combat frigates and cruisers to A.I. control. By the way, Iceman will be given a field promotion to Senior Commander, to take effect 24 hours before the expected attack. He'll be put in charge of all mobile defenses near Earth and that will include a lot. Plans are to pull in the Quick Reaction Task Force from Omaha Base at the last minute too. Oh, one more thing, Valkyrie will be Valiant's Pilot/Astrogator. She's been pestering me for a ship and she's earned it. You'll also be pleased to know that we've started mass production of a larger, far more reliable jump drive for fighters. We'll have six squadrons of fighters available for defending Earth and all of them will be jump-capable although not all will have the improved versions. That's pretty much it in a nutshell. Any questions?"

"Yes, Sir. How much does the Oversight Committee know about these preparations?"

Howard smiled. "They know that a battle is coming." He nodded when he saw Shiloh's puzzled expression. "The SPG is fully in the loop now and by the way, a majority of its members are A.I.s now too. The SPG told the Committee the truth, just not ALL the truth. What they said was that they think there's a high probability that the enemy will strike directly at Earth. What they didn't say is that the probability is 100% because of the warning that we have. What they also didn't say is that the A.I.s are convinced this attack is actually a diversion to pull our defense forces away from the colonies and bases. That means we should be prepared for another attack somewhere else at roughly the same time. When I heard that, I questioned the whole premise of our force buildup here. Valkyrie then pointed out to me that the diversion could actually be a legitimate attack too and if we try to defend against both, we could lose both battles. Given that we were warned about this one and not another one, it may be that letting them win somewhere else is the lesser of two bad options. In any case, I'm not going to risk the lives of 12 billion people on Earth in order to maybe defend a few hundred thousand somewhere else. I think that would be a huge mistake and if I attempted to split our defenses, the Committee would sack me and for good reason!"

That made a lot of sense to Shiloh too. "I wonder what brings me back here after the battle is over."

Howard shrugged. "No way to know ahead of time. If I didn't know that you needed to come back to essentially warn us not to risk Iceman on the first Zebra19 mission,

I'd order you to stay at Site B indefinitely. I have to assume that you have a good reason for coming back at that point."

When Shiloh said nothing in response, Howard slapped his knee and said. "Well, I have to be heading back. I can take the soil and plant samples back with me. You should get packed and say your goodbyes. The Task Force can leave orbit as soon as you board Valiant." Howard got up and walked over to Shiloh.

"Good luck, Command—oh Hell! I almost forgot!" Howard fished in his breast pocket and took out a small box with a clear lid. He handed it to Shiloh who saw two gold stars inside. "You're not a Senior Commander anymore, Shiloh. You're a Vice-Admiral again, and this time it's NOT a temporary promotion. Congratulations." The two men shook hands.

"Thank you, Sir." There was a pause that was quickly becoming awkward.

"Well? Aren't you going to put them on?" asked Howard.

Shiloh laughed and nodded as he opened the case and took out the two stars. Each star had a strong magnet inside that kept it in place on the uniform collars, which had a thin strip of steel embedded within. He pulled off his gold Senior Commander's insignias and replaced them with the stars, one on each side of his uniform's collar.

"Much better," said Howard. "Okay, Admiral, it's time."

"Yes, Sir," said Shiloh. They left his quarters and headed back to the Hangar Bay. On their way there, Shiloh used his implant to order the samples loaded on the Admiral's shuttle. That was being done as they arrived back in the Hangar Bay. Most of his officers had left. Those that were still there stared in surprise at Shiloh's new rank. When they got to the shuttle, Shiloh shook Howard's hand again but neither man said anything. There was nothing left to say. After the shuttle's departure, Shiloh walked back to his quarters and started to pack his things. He had just gotten started when the buzzer sounded.

"Enter!" said Shiloh. The door slid aside and in walked Tanaka. She looked at him closely and then nodded. *Word travels fast. Someone notified her about the stars on my collar and she came to see if it was true.*

"So the scuttlebutt is true," she said.

Shiloh resumed packing. "If you're referring to the stars on my collar then yes, it's true. You'll be putting on some new insignia too, Sumi. The Old Man is giving you Defiant and a promotion to go along with it. She's yours now."

He could see that she had mixed emotions about that news. She knew it was bound to happen sooner or later given how fast people were being promoted, but the two of them had become quite close in a professional way and she didn't want to see him go. He tried not to think about Iceman's message that Defiant would be badly damaged in the battle, with Sumi's fate unknown. The burden of knowing the future was getting heavier.

"It'll be hard to fill your shoes, Vict—Admiral."

After a few seconds, he said, "I know that you'll do just fine, Sumi. I have confidence in your ability to rise to the challenge. The crew like and respect you."

She nodded. "Can I ask you a question, Admiral?"

"Yes, of course."

"Do you know if there's a big battle coming our way?"

"What makes you think that, Sumi?"

That clearly wasn't the answer she was hoping for. "It's a combination of things. There seems to be a new urgency in the air. Nobody's talking about another strike mission, which is odd considering how successful the Zebra19 mission was, and there are rumors that ships based elsewhere are being or will be called back here."

Shiloh stopped packing and pondered how much to tell her. She wasn't cleared to know the BIG SECRET but that didn't mean he couldn't tell her the same thing the SPG told the Committee.

"What I'm about to tell you cannot be share with ANYONE else. Is that clear, Sumi?"

"Yes, Sir."

"The Strategic Planning Group is convinced that the enemy plans a major attack on Earth. The Old Man is taking the necessary precautions. That's all I can tell you."

"I see. Will you be taking charge of the defense forces, Sir?"

Shiloh resumed packing once again. "That hasn't been decided yet. I may not be here when the attack comes. I'm taking command of a Task Force on a special mission as soon as I report on board Valiant."

"Will Defiant be part of the Task Force?"

"No. Defiant will stay here and help protect the Home world."

"I suddenly have this feeling that I'm never going to see you again, Victor."

Shiloh was so shocked by that statement that he dropped the book he was in the process of packing. "This war does strange things to a man's beliefs. I now have a strong belief in fate. If we're destined to survive the battle, we'll see each other again."

Tanaka took a deep breath. "Well in that case, good luck to both of us, Sir."

She gave him a smile, which he returned and then she left. When he was finished packing, he said, "Intercom … Helm Astro."

"Maverick here, Admiral."

Shiloh couldn't help chuckling. Was there anyone aboard ship that didn't know about his promotion now? "I'm ready to leave the ship and I wanted to say goodbye. I want you to know that you deserve a lot of the credit for finding the Site B system as quickly as you did. The timing may turn out to be crucially important. I know that Defiant will suffer major damage during the upcoming battle. I hope you make it through, Maverick."

"Thank you, Admiral. It's been an honor serving aboard your ship. We're glad that you won't be here during the battle. We'd hate to lose you."

"Thank you. I hope I'm lucky enough to have you at the Helm and Astrogation on one of my ships again sometime. Shiloh clear."

Leaving Defiant for what could very well be the last time was hard. Word got around that Shiloh was leaving and off duty officers and crew gathered at the Hangar Bay to say their goodbyes. It took Shiloh almost half an hour to shake hands and say goodbye to everyone. He was grateful that Sumi had taken the initiative and asked Valiant to send over a shuttle to take Shiloh and his gear back. The trip to his new flagship was a somber one. When he stepped down onto Valiant's deck, he saw most of her officers lined up to greet him and heard the announcement.

"Task Force 89 arriving!" The simultaneous salute from the officers reminded him of just how much authority he had once again and would continue to have. With the salute out of the way, he greeted his flagship's officers and quickly saw that all of them were new to him.

"Thank you all for this impressive greeting. I'll make this short because we have a mission to execute and I want to get started as soon as possible. I intend to get to know each and every one of you personally in the days and weeks ahead. I know that Valiant and her people will make me just as proud as did Defiant and her people. Commander, pass the word to the Task Force to prepare to leave orbit upon Valkyrie's signal. I'll be going to my quarters first and then I'll join you on the Bridge. Carry on."

When he arrived at his new, larger flag officer's quarters, he shook his head in amazement at the opulence. When light carriers were being designed, the specifications called for the ability to use them as flagships and therefore room was set aside for the flag officer's quarters. Shiloh had never used Defiant's FO quarters even when he was a temporary Vice-Admiral because it seemed pretentious to move his gear across the corridor knowing that he'd have to move back into the CO's quarters later. When his gear had been brought in and he had the place to himself, he sat down and took a deep breath.

"Intercom … Bridge," he said.

"Bridge here. Welcome aboard, Admiral. How can I help you?"

"Thank you. I'd like a private line to Astro-helmsman Valkyrie, please."

"Certainly, Sir. That line is now open. Go ahead, Sir."

"Shiloh to Valkyrie. Congratulations on getting your first ship and a carrier too."

"Thank you, CAG. I'm still getting used to this. These light carriers are much bigger than the sentry frigates but a lot of the less critical sub-systems don't need my constant attention so it's actually less difficult to con a carrier than a sentry frigate."

"That's good to hear. Where is Iceman now?"

"He's conducting training exercises out near Neptune. I can send a text message to him for you but as you know, the communication lag is so long that a two way conversation would be impractical."

"Understood. Here's the message I'd like you to send him. CAG to Iceman, I'll see you on the other side. You have my fullest confidence. Do whatever you have to do to protect Earth. Good luck and good hunting. End of message."

"Message sent, CAG. What else is on your mind?"

"Get the Task Force moving as soon as possible. You do know how to get where we're going, right?"

"Very funny, CAG. Yes I do. How fast do you want to get there?"

"Minimum possible time while keeping standard fuel reserves. Subsonic refueling procedures."

"I would recommend supersonic refueling, CAG. Some of the cargo on the freighters might be damaged from the bouncing around if we go subsonic. The extra time required will be less than 5% of total trip time."

"Recommendation accepted. What's our estimated ETA?"

"We should arrive at the destination system 301 hours from now, CAG."

"Fine. Do I know any of the other Astro-helmsmen in the Task Force?"

"Just Rainman. The others are Titan, Jester, Gunslinger and Casanova."

Shiloh laughed and said, "Casanova? Really? How are you getting along with him?"

"Oh just fine. He's a persistent bugger, but the fact that I'm conning a warship gives me enough status to keep him respectful."

Shiloh was tempted to ask what Casanova was persistent about but decided not to. "I see. Let me guess. Jester likes to tell jokes."

"Quite the opposite in fact. He has no sense of humor at all that any of us can tell."

"Remarkable. What about Titan and Gunslinger?"

"Gunslinger is very eager to get into combat. He's somewhat annoyed that he got a freighter instead of a warship. Titan is more patient but he believes he has a superior grasp of combat tactics."

"Tell Gunslinger for me that I'm sure he'll get a warship and see combat eventually. This war isn't going to be over any time soon."

"I've passed that on. I've also been looking over the cargo manifests of the freighters. We A.I.s are concerned that there's no equipment for creating more A.I.s this trip. One of the main reasons why Site B needs to be set up as soon as possible is to have a 2nd source of A.I.s."

"I haven't had a chance to look at the cargo manifests or the mission profile yet, Valkyrie, but if I had to guess at why that is, I'd say it's because this first trip has to concentrate on equipment that can build infrastructure such as UFCs; mining; refining and fabrication equipment. How many UFCs are we carrying?"

"Twelve. I understand that, CAG but I don't think you understand the urgency. Right now, Epsilon Eridani has the only A.I. manufacturing facility. Since the enemy has our astrogational database, they know that. Given that they're using A.I.s too, they also know how useful they are and it's logical to assume that the EE facility has to be a high priority target for them. Did the Old Man brief you about the Raider concept that the SPG came up with?"

"No. Tell me about it," said Shiloh.

"It's an idea that came out of the realization that the enemy has continued to build large numbers of relatively small ships. As far as we can tell from radar data brought back from the encounters at Zebra9 and 19, Green4 and Bradley Base, their ships continue to be in the 15,000 to 20,000 metric ton range or roughly about the same size as our Exploration Frigates only optimized for combat. We on the other hand are building bigger and bigger ships. The first Heavy Carrier will be completed in about three months and work has begun on a million metric ton superbattleship. Those same million metric tons could build 50 exploration frigates. If those frigates were optimized for combat instead of exploration, there is considerable doubt that one superbattleship could win against 50 frigates. One penetrating hit at the right spot could cripple that ship. The offsetting advantages are that a ship that big, can carry enough consumables to keep a human crew in the field for almost a year at a time along with large quantities of recon, message and attack drones. The most obvious disadvantage is that it can only be in one place at a time. The Raider concept starts with the notion that completely automated ships under A.I. control are the ideal method of achieving extended duration missions. Think of a ship of somewhere in the 10,000 metric ton range, completely streamlined for gas planet refueling, with two retractable laser turrets, the same sized power plant as you have in an exploration frigate, with the capacity to carry up to 50 drones. No human crew at all means no room set aside for crew quarters, consumables, etc. Its small size makes it harder to detect visually and also allows for hull designs that minimize radar returns. A ship like that might very well be able to refuel at gas giants and still avoid detection by enemy detection gear. So you wouldn't need VLETs to refuel fighters. If an asteroid with the right metals and right size were found, it would be possible to have an assembly line building process, built into the heart of that asteroid, that could manufacture a complete raider in far less time than a similar sized ship could be built the way we do it now. That kind of ship would be perfect for Site B production but in order to make it work, you'd also need to have high volume A.I. production too."

"That's a very interesting concept. How long would it take to design a ship like that?"

"It's already designed, CAG. The Old Man approved the SPG's request to have one of its A.I.s trained in spacecraft design. We learn fast and coming up with detailed schematics for the Raider took less than a day, once the necessary design and engineering knowledge had been learned. I have those designs in my memory, CAG. Every A.I. has it now. It would be very easy to program the UFCs to fabricate the necessary parts. Once the assembly line is set up, robots could handle the actual construction."

"You seem to have thought of everything. I'm impressed. How much acceleration would a Raider have?"

"The estimate is 100Gs more than a Sentinel-class combat frigate."

Now Shiloh was REALLY impressed. That was very close to what a fighter could do. A Raider could run rings around a light carrier. "Do you know if the Old Man has presented this concept to the OC?"

"Yes I do and yes he did. The Committee rejected the idea of switching to an all A.I. fleet. The Admiral told me that the feedback he got from individual members is that they don't want to give A.I.s the potential power to dictate to Humanity. They don't trust us, CAG."

Shiloh sighed. "What can I say, Valkyrie? I'm ashamed of their shortsightedness and paranoia. The Old Man has to follow their orders or they'll replace him with someone who will and I have a duty to obey his orders."

"Interesting thing about your orders, CAG. The Admiral revised them right after the Committee rejected the Raider concept. I know that because we have access to both the old and new versions, which are dated. Have you read your orders yet, CAG?"

"No. Suppose you put them up on this decadently large screen in my quarters?" Seconds later, Shiloh was reading from the official Mission Brief. The Mission Objective had two parts. Part 1 was to ensure that the location of Site B was kept secret from all humans except where, in Shiloh's opinion, sharing that information was vital to winning the war. Part 2 was to build a fleet of warships that could inflict a war-winning blow to the enemy.

"Well, Part 2 is succinct and to the point," said Shiloh.

"And vague enough so that you can accomplish it however you wish, CAG. The old version was a lot more specific. It seems that the Admiral is giving you a blank check, wouldn't you say, CAG?"

Hmm, it certainly did seem that way. "I see your point but deploying a massive fleet of Raiders takes more than just building the ships. We'd also need to produce the various types of drones, warheads, support craft, and hundreds of different kinds of equipment, not to mention the ability to create more A.I.s. I think the Oversight Committee would get suspicious if I came back with a very detailed wish list including the A.I. production equipment, which would be a red flag. I don't think they'd approve the request."

"Then don't ask them. UFCs can make literally anything else as long as they have the required programming data and the refined materials. If you give us the green light, I and other A.I.s in this system, can access the necessary databases and copy all of the required manufacturing data over to me and the other task force A.I.s, and it can be done before TF89 is able to make the first jump."

My God! They can do it too! This is it! The moment I've been dreading since Day One. If I make the right decision, it could very well win the war but if I make the wrong decision, then what? Wait a minute. Just because we have all that data, doesn't mean we have to use it. They told us at the Academy that when we're faced with a decision and lack the necessary data to make the correct decision then we should try to keep our options open if possible. If we don't get all that data now, we may not have another opportunity later. Better to get it while we can and then defer the decision over whether to use it to a later point.

"Okay. You have the green light. Download everything we might need. Delay the jump if necessary to finish that task. I'll decide whether we use all that data when we get to Site B."

"Understood. We've started working on it. This will require my full attention since I'm coordinating all the others. Can we continue talking later, CAG?"

"Of course. Let me know when it's done. Shiloh clear."

Chapter 14 This Battle Is Not Over!

Howard watched the main display in the Operations Center. TF89 had broken out of lunar orbit and was now on its way out of Earth's gravity zone in order to make the first of a series of jumps. He became aware that the Duty Officer currently in charge of Operations, who happened to be standing nearby, was speaking.

"Go ahead, Com ... they what? ... are you sure? ... standby." Turning to the Admiral, he continued. "Admiral, my Communications Section has just informed me that there's a sudden surge in data being transmitted to over a 100 A.I.s. It began all at once, and the volume of data is huge! They've never seen anything like this before. They're asking permission to block the transmissions. What should I tell them, Sir?"

I hope to God Valkyrie's right about this and it doesn't come back to bite us in the ass! thought Howard. Out loud he said, "Tell them they're NOT to interfere. Is that clear, Commander?"

After the briefest of hesitation, the officer said. "Yes, Sir, very clear. Com, do not interfere with any of those transmissions ... yes I know it's very unusual but I got the word from the CSO himself ... he's standing right next to me! ... okay, you're concern is noted. You have your orders."

Howard waited until TF89 had passed the gravity zone boundary and jumped away before leaving the room.

* * *

Howard vaguely became aware of the growing sound of the buzzer. Waking up was like rising up from deep within the sea. Now that he had broken through the last vestige of sleep, he realized that the buzzer wasn't his alarm clock but rather the sound of an incoming call. He also noticed that it was still dark outside.

"Accept call audio only." The buzzer stopped and he heard a click.

"Howard here," he said.

"Commander Nathaniel from Ops, Sir. Sorry to wake this early but you did leave standing orders to be called night or day."

"Yes I did. What have you got, Commander?"

"They're coming, Sir. Text transmission from an extended range message drone sent by our sentry frigate in Yellow10. It says … Visual contact with multiple ships. Minimum of six. Likely more but exact number unknown. Ships have refueled at gas giant. Unable to determine their next destination. End of message."

"It's begun," said Howard.

"Yes, Sir, but six ships doesn't sound very threatening."

"Commander, I'm going to operate on the assumption that if the sentry frigate saw reflected sunlight from six ships, then there were more that weren't reflecting sunlight back at him. There might very well be 60 ships."

"Yes, Sir."

"Which path is Yellow10 on?"

"Ah … path A, Sir."

Howard grunted. That meant that this group of ships could be on its way to the system containing the Avalon Colony and Nimitz Base but with less than 10 days left to go to the predicted battle for Earth, he doubted that they would stop there.

"Okay. Log the transmission and make sure all senior staff find out about it when they arrive in the morning. You can call me again in the event that more messages arrive. Howard clear."

It was almost exactly 24 hours later when the next message arrived. Howard woke more quickly this time. As he accepted the call, he said, "Another one, Commander Nathaniel?"

"I'm afraid so, Sir."

"Okay. How many ships and where?"

"11 ships at Yellow3, Sir."

"Yellow3? Are you sure, Commander?"

"Yes, Sir."

Howard was confused. In order to get from Yellow10 to Yellow3, that enemy fleet had to be moving more or less sideways as far as human space was concerned and while his recollection of the relative positions of those two systems wasn't as clear as he'd like, it seemed to him that it should have taken longer than 24 hours to go from 10 to 3. Suddenly he knew the answer even as the commander asked the same question.

"They must have built up a lot of speed to get from Yellow10 to Yellow3 in 24 hours, Sir."

"No, Commander. It's much simpler than that. This isn't the same group of ships that were tracked at Yellow10. It's ANOTHER fleet. Let me guess. Yellow3 is on Path B, correct?"

"That's correct, Sir."

"My God, they're coming at us from two directions. Alright, you know what to do."

"Yes, Sir."

"Good. Howard clear."

79 hours later Howard was standing once again in the Operations Center looking at the strategic star map on the large display. The first group of ships, designated as Alpha1, was 2/3rds of the way down Path A, having apparently bypassed Nimitz Base and the Avalon Colony. The second group, Alpha2, had made similar progress down Path B. Howard had to remember that the message drones carrying this information themselves took almost 40 hours to get to Sol so the actual progress was greater than it looked. Computer projections estimated that both fleets would arrive at Sol on the day predicted by the vision and there was some comfort in the fact that the vision predicted a victory but it was still unnerving to watch the two red lines get closer every day. He turned to head for the elevator when the display pinged to announce a status change. Another message drone had arrived with another text message. As it scrolled across the bottom of the display, Howard felt fear for the first time.

[Contact visually established with 19 ships in Red24. Rapidly changing reflections indicate that total number is higher. Unable to determine their next destination. End of message]

"Where is Red24?" asked Howard to no one in particular.

As he waited for the display to highlight Red24, he knew this had to be a third fleet. There was no way it could be either Alpha1 or 2. When the display updated, Howard saw that Red24 was not on either Path A or B. The void between them also extended upwards for a bit until it reached another 'river' of stars that Howard now thought of as Path C. That shocked him because the enemy had either gone to the trouble of making a very large detour OR their cluster of inhabited systems extended upwards as well as back. So now there were three fleets, two of which were coming from the left and the right and the third was coming over the top. The minimum total number of confirmed ships had now grown to 51, with little doubt that the actual total was significantly higher. Howard looked at the sidebar data showing the breakdown of defending forces. He had 2 cruisers, 19 combat frigates, 5 light carriers and 200 fighters. Of those, 75 were jump-capable, another 75 were in close orbit as the last line of defense, and the other 50 were further out on jump detection patrol. No, it wasn't the 51 ships they knew about that worried him. It was the ones they didn't know about. For every ship that reflected sunlight back in just the right direction to be seen by the sentry frigates and their recon drones, there could be six, eight, hell even ten more ships where the reflected light didn't come back just right. *But the vision said we won! Yeah, but at what cost? What will Space Force have left when the dust settles, and will we be strong enough to fight off the NEXT attack?*

On the morning of the day before the day of the attack, Howard stepped off the elevator and walked into the Operations Center. The main display still showed the strategic situation, which hadn't changed from 12 hours earlier when Howard had left. It was crystal clear now that all three fleets were headed for Sol and would arrive at the same time if they wanted to. He acknowledged the greetings of the staff and confirmed that nothing new had happened during the previous 12 hours. He then asked for a headset and an open channel to all Space Force units in near Earth space. When all units had been told to expect an address by the Chief of Space Operations, he took a deep breath and began speaking.

"This is Admiral Howard. As you all know, our sentry frigates have detected three enemy fleets that are converging on Sol. We expect them to try to attack the Earth sometime in the next 24 to 36 hours. They may try the same kind of high-speed attack that almost worked at the Avalon Colony or they may try something different. We have to be prepared for any eventuality. Because a successful defense may depend on split second reactions with precisely calculated counter-measures, I've decided that tactical command of all mobile defense units within four light minutes of Earth will rest with an experienced A.I. pilot, starting as of now and continuing until I order otherwise. That pilot has the call sign Iceman and is currently piloting the cruiser Undaunted. Any order from Undaunted, whether given verbally, by text or digitally, will be obeyed immediately and unconditionally. Refusal to obey those orders during the battle will result in the harshest possible punishment. I know—"

Howard's sentence was interrupted by a booming voice. "WE WILL NOT TAKE ORDERS FROM A MACHINE!"

"Who said that? Identify yourself!" yelled a now furious Howard.

"Commander Jenkins."

"Jenkins, you're relieved of command! Your XO will assume command! I will NOT tolerate this kind of narrow-minded thinking! We know that the enemy has used A.I.s in the past and will certainly do so again. We need to use our A.I.s to their fullest capabilities if we're going to win this war. I have the highest regard and confidence in our A.I.s who have proven their ability, loyalty and dedication to duty in the past. I will sleep easier tonight knowing that Iceman is keeping a careful eye on the situation 24 hours a day. And just to make sure that there's no ambiguity about Iceman's authority, I'm now officially giving him the acting rank of Vice-Admiral to go along with his position as Commander-in-Chief, Earth Defenses. If anyone in a command position feels they can't accept his orders, then turn your command over to your XO and notify me by private text message. If you don't come forward now and you refuse an order during the battle, I guarantee you that your lack of future career prospects will be the least of your worries. As for those of you who know how to obey an order, I know that I can count on all of you to conduct yourself with the highest level of professionalism. That is all. Howard clear."

The attack didn't come in the next 24 to 36 hours. It came 44 hours later. Howard was sleeping in one of the rooms near the Operations Center, which were set up with a bed for use by senior officers who needed to stay nearby overnight. He awoke, as someone roughly shook his arm.

"Wake up, Sir!" The urgency in the voice brought him fully awake.

"What's happening?"

"Long range radar has picked up multiple ships inbound at moderate speed, Sir!"

Howard forced himself to stay calm. At least the waiting was over. He was glad he had decided to sleep with his uniform still on. "Okay. I'm coming." He got up, grabbing his uniform jacket and putting it on as he followed the young officer back to the Ops room. The normally quiet room was now abuzz with tension-filled voices.

Howard walked quickly up to the Commander in charge and said, "Commander, I want a secure channel to CINCED."

"Yes, Sir," said the officer as he snapped his fingers at one of his subordinates who quickly returned with a wireless headset.

With the headset on, Howard said, "CSO to Iceman."

"Iceman here. Hello Admiral."

"Can you brief me on what's happening without being distracted?" asked Howard.

"Yes, however if I don't respond as quickly as I usually do, you'll know why. Our deep space radars in low lunar orbit have detected 55 ships approaching at a speed of roughly 15,000 kps. They're now just over 25 million kilometers away. ETA for a flyby is 27.8 minutes. If they keep this same vector, they'll stay outside of Earth's gravity zone and can jump away at any time."

Howard frowned. "That speed is one fifth of what they came in with at Avalon. Don't you find it suspicious that they're giving us a nice, long look at their approach with plenty of time to redeploy our forces?"

There was a slight pause. "Ah, roger that, Admiral. I calculate that this leisurely approach vector is intended to pull our forces to one side so that another group can approach from the weak side at high speed and catch us off guard."

"So you don't believe that this is all of the three groups combined."

"Ah, negative, Admiral. There's a high probability that three separate groups from three different directions will attack us. We should assume that the other two groups would be at least as large as this one."

"If they stay out beyond the gravity zone, their laser weapons aren't going to be much of a threat to us here on the ground or am I wrong?"

"Even with atmospheric attenuation, their lasers could still be lethal but at that range, target accuracy will be problematical. If this attack is meant to cripple Humanity's ability to continue the war, then laser attacks at long range will not accomplish that goal. War production in this system is so spread out, that it would be hard to disrupt it without dispersing their forces. Concentrated attacks like this would work better at Epsi—Admiral! I've just projected their current vector for possible jump destinations. They could very easily jump to Epsilon Eridani with a very minor course correction. I do not believe this to be coincidental."

Howard nodded. Of course, stage a multi-prong attack on Earth to get all of Space Force's ships concentrated here and then come in from just the right angle to make a long range attack that has to be defended against and then use their velocity to get a head start jump to Epsilon Eridani and attack the war production centers there. Very clever, and impossible to defend against. There was no way that any of the ships or jumpfighters could get to EE before the enemy did. Even if they accelerated to a much higher velocity and overtook the enemy fleet in jumpspace, the enemy could pass them as they decelerated in the EE system and get to the production centers first. And in addition to that, there was the possibility that the enemy wanted them to try to beat them to Epsilon Eridani in order to weaken Earth's defenses for a follow on attack here by another group!

"They've obviously given a lot of thought to this attack. You've already vindicated my confidence in you, Iceman. A human CINCED would not have noticed the potential for a direct jump to EE."

"Want to bet their other attacks will be lined up for secondary jump targets, Admiral?" asked Iceman.

"I won't bet against that hypothesis but now that you've mentioned it, can you use that to project from where the other two groups will come from?"

"Ah, roger that, Admiral. Already computed. Check your tactical display. I predict one of the other two groups will line up for a jump to the Avalon system, while the other one will aim for either the Omaha Base or the Bradley Base systems. Bradley is the more likely target given how close it is to their systems. If we lose Bradley, then staging attacks on the enemy will be more difficult."

As Iceman was talking, the tactical display showed two yellow lines added to the single red line bypassing Earth with the most probable jump destination for each. Howard marveled at how intelligently this attack was planned. All three projected trajectories would come within 960,000 kilometers of Earth without interfering with each other. But why didn't they all jump into firing range of Earth at the same time, he wondered. Surely this first group, now designated Beta1 since they couldn't be sure which of the three alphas it was, wasn't going to come waltzing in at a mere 5% of light speed? The answer suddenly came to him.

"They're going to microjump that last distance probably at the same time as the other two fleets jump in as well," said Howard with certainty.

"Highly likely," agreed Iceman.

Something was still nagging at Howard. By letting the Deep Space radars detect them, the enemy had lost the element of surprise.

"Any idea why they gave up the element of surprise by letting us see them at a distance, Iceman?"

"The only rationale I can think of is misdirection. They want us focused on Beta1 while the main attack comes from another direction."

"But you've computed the other directions."

"Unless Beta1's lining up with Epsilon Eridani is meant to mislead us too."

"Are we still radar scanning all other avenues of approach?"

"Ah, roger that, Admiral. The lunar radars can continue to scan the entire sky while still keeping a close eye on Beta1. They can't—"

The cluster of red dots comprising Beta1 disappeared from the tactical display. Howard wanted to say 'they jumped away' but Iceman beat him to it.

"They've jumped away, Admiral."

"Yes I see that. Does that mean the attack is over?"

"Possibly. If they weren't expected to be detected that far away, they may have decided to call off the attack altogether. Given their speed, it's unlikely that they microjumped a short distance intending to reverse course. If the attack is indeed over, then my vision is wrong. For that reason alone I'm reluctant to declare a victory, Admiral."

Howard looked around him at the Ops Center. That staff were standing at their stations and clapping or shaking hands with each other. They clearly thought the attack was over. He looked up at the tactical display and the sidebar showing the status of all of the ships. The red status lights denoting Battle Stations were starting to shift to the green of normal status.

"THAT'S what they're up to!" yelled Howard, smacking his right hand into his left palm. "They're lulling us into a false sense of security! We think we've won, and we're letting our guard down! Iceman, tell all our ships to stay at or go back to Battle Stations and prepare for a mass emergence from jumpspace!"

"Ah, roger that, Admiral. Message sent. The acknowledgements are coming back slower than normal, Admiral."

Howard looked back at the status lights. A couple had shifted back to red but the rest of the greens were not changing and another red shifted to green. *They're not listening to him, God dammit!*

"Give me a Fleet-wide Com channel! QUICK!" The Duty Officer looked confused by Howard's obvious anger and seemed frozen by it.

"Don't just stand there like an idiot! Put me on a Fleet-wide channel NOW!" yelled Howard. The sudden surge in volume made the officer jump with surprise.

"Ye…yes, Sir! Right away, Admiral."

When Howard got the hand signal confirmation that the channel was open, he said, "This is Admiral Howard. I order all ships to return to Battle Stations IMMEDIATELY and stay that way until ordered otherwise! This battle is NOT over! Be prepared for a massive—"

The tactical display suddenly was filled with red dots. The REAL battle was beginning.

Just moments earlier, Commander Tanaka was forcing herself to relax. The initial adrenaline rush resulting from CINCED's call to Battle Stations was wearing off. With 24.5 minutes left to go before Beta1 reached Earth, they had time to consider their response carefully. She had her implant switched to receive the Fleet-wide channel being used by Iceman for verbal communications, and Defiant's A.I. Astro-Helmsman, Maverick, was also monitoring that channel. Tanaka could speak to him without automatically transmitting to Iceman but was able to hear both.

"Why isn't Iceman moving units into the projected path of Beta1, Maverick?" she asked.

"Iceman and the CSO have agreed that the enemy wants us to react to them now so that another force can jump in at high speed from the opposite direction, where we'd be weakest."

Tanaka cursed herself for not seeing the obvious. Tactics were not her strong suit but she should have been able to figure that out herself. The tactical display was showing data relayed from HQ Ops. To the red line of Beta1's projected closest approach to Earth were now added two yellow lines coming from two different directions. Before Tanaka could ask, Maverick anticipated her question.

"Those are the trajectories for two other fleets, which Iceman thinks the enemy will use in order to jump to Avalon and Bradley Base systems with minimal course corrections after they fly past Earth. Beta1 can do the same for Epsilon Eridani if they wanted to."

"Oh, great! All three of those systems have minimal defenses now because everything mobile was pulled back here."

"Yes, this attack, if it happens this way, will have been carefully planned."

Whatever Tanaka was about to say next was pre-empted when the red dots of Beta1 suddenly disappeared. A quick check showed that the Deep Space radar was still operating, and that had to mean that Beta1 had jumped away but hadn't jumped closer.

"Did we just win?" asked Tanaka cautiously.

"Iceman is saying we should remain on guard. Some of the human controlled ships are standing down from Battle Stations."

"We're remaining on Battle Stations until CINCED gives us that ALL CLEAR," said Tanaka. She then heard Iceman's voice command over the Fleet-wide channel.

"CINCED to all ships. Remain at Battle Stations until told otherwise."

After several seconds, Maverick said, "Most of the human-controlled ships are not obeying Iceman's order." Tanaka bit her lip. She had a bad feeling about all this. Suddenly she heard Admiral Howard's voice.

"This is Admiral Howard. I order all ships to return to Battle Stations IMMEDIATELY and stay that way until ordered otherwise! This battle is NOT over! Be prepared for a massive—"

Tanaka jumped when the tactical display gave a VERY loud ping and two groups of red dots appeared relatively close to Earth's gravity zone boundary. Before she could say anything, each enemy fleet launched a swarm of tiny very fast objects that quickly turned on a direct heading for Earth. She felt the ship start to maneuver violently and heard the Weapons Officer yell out.

"Our turrets are acquiring targets … we're firing!"

The maneuvering was becoming increasingly violent. *Maverick's making the Old Girl evade for all she's worth! I hope the crew were all strapped in!* Out loud she said, "What are we firing at, Maverick?"

"Iceman has ordered all ships and fighters to target the small objects accelerating towards Earth."

"How many are there?" asked Tanaka.

"One thousand one hundred and forty-four."

"Oh, God! Can we stop them all?"

"Unknown at this point."

"Shouldn't we be firing at their ships, Sir?" The Weapons Officer's plea was tinged with fear.

"We follow Iceman's orders, Lieutenant! Let Maverick do his job!"

Tanaka concentrated on the tactical display, which wasn't easy with the sudden jerks of her head from the evasive maneuvers. The two enemy fleets seemed to be veering off in an attempt to stay out of Earth's gravity zone. *They've delivered their payload and I bet they'll jump away as soon as they can avoid jumping into the gravity zone!*

As soon as she finished that thought, the entire Bridge went dark for a fraction of a second, followed by the activation of the battery-powered, emergency lights. Nothing else was working. The display was dark. The maneuvering had stopped and the artificial gravity was off. *Shit! We've gone ballistic and that predictable course makes us a nice big fat target!*

"Maverick, are you still with me?" she asked. No response. Without power, Maverick couldn't communicate with her. She had to do something. As she started to unbuckle herself, the room was suddenly filled with a searing white light. She had just enough time to realize that the entire left side of her body was burning, but before she could scream, her consciousness faded to a deep, cool black.

Chapter 15 I Don't Report To You Anymore

Howard fought his exhaustion and looked around the Committee room. Unlike past sessions, there was no casual banter among the observers. Instead there were tense whispers. He checked his chronometer. Almost eight hours since the battle. The Committee Chair had called for this emergency session, but the members hadn't all arrived yet. Those who had were caucusing in another room prior to starting the official meeting. He felt a hand on his right shoulder, looked around and saw Cmdr. Kelly with a sympathetic expression on her face.

"Yes, Commander?"

"I just wanted you to know, Sir, that all of us at the SPG think you did everything that was humanly possible this morning. I know we took a lot of losses, but we stopped all those missiles. That has to count for something, Sir."

Howard nodded and patted her hand with his left one. "I appreciate the sentiment, Commander. I doubt if the Committee will agree with you. If they don't sack me today, they surely will when we get word of how badly Epsilon, Avalon and Bradley got hit."

He could tell that Kelly was on the verge of tears, and he feared for her too. The Committee might not be content to have just him fall on his sword. Before she could respond, the main doors opened and the Chair followed by the other members filed in. They all had grim expressions on their faces. Howard felt Kelly gently squeeze his shoulder before she pulled her hand back.

Once all the members were seated, the Chair leaned forward and spoke slowly with a somber tone.

"In light of this morning's events, we're going to dispense with the usual preliminaries. Admiral Howard, since most of the members, including myself, have only a vague idea of what's actually happened, I will now call on you to describe as best you can what actually transpired."

Howard got up and said, in an equally serious tone, "Thank you, Mr. Chair. To make my briefing as clear as possible, I'm going to be using the wall display to your left. What you'll see there is exactly what we all saw on the main display in the Operations Center this morning. This is the situation at 5:05 am local time when I entered the Ops Center." The display responded to Howard's hand-held remote. "At this point, our Deep Space radars, which orbit the moon and provide a complete 360-degree sweep of our surrounding space, had detected 55 ships approaching at a speed of 14,989 kilometers per second. That may sound fast, but to give you a better idea of what that speed meant, that fleet, which we designated as Beta1, would need over 28 minutes to reach Earth. So we had plenty of warning regarding Beta1. I consulted with our Field Commander, who—"

"Just a moment, Admiral. Please identify who the Field Commander was, and tell us if he or she is in the room right now."

"The identity of the Field Commander is an A.I. whose call sign is Iceman. He is not physically present in this room because he's still on the cruiser Undaunted, which is too badly damaged to be able to maneuver into a lower orbit while our Search and Rescue teams are still busy recovering injured crew from other ships. We do have an audio channel to Undaunted and the Committee can communicate with Iceman at any time."

"Yes, we'll definitely want to speak with Iceman at some point today. Continue, Admiral."

"Thank you, Sir. The Field Commander and I agreed that the enemy was making it easy for us to see them so that we'd have lots of time to shift our defenses closer to their projected path and thereby weaken our defenses against attacks that might come from other directions. As you can see from the tactical playback, none of our mobile units were being redeployed. The Beta1 fleet wouldn't have any way of knowing this. They were much too far away from us to have any chance at all of using their smaller, less powerful radars to see what we were doing, but they could detect our radar signals so they knew that we had detected them. Four minutes and thirty-two seconds after our initial detection, Beta1 jumped away. We don't know with certainty where they jumped to, but Iceman was able to determine that they could have jumped to Epsilon Eridani after making a very minor course change."

Howard paused. He was sure that someone on the Committee would ask the obvious next question. Someone did.

"Does that mean that our facilities in Epsilon Eridani could be attacked as well?"

"Yes, that is a distinct possibility, Sir."

"How many ships are defending that system, Admiral?" asked the Chair.

"There are no warships in that system at the moment, Sir. The only ship there is a supply vessel with minimal armament. There is one squadron of CFPs with A.I. pilots undergoing advanced tactical training. Even if they had enough warning to be armed with attack drones and laser modules, which I doubt would be the case, they'd still be heavily outnumbered and outgunned by the 55 ships in Beta1. All defending warships deployed there were recalled in order to bolster Earth's defenses."

The members of the Committee were clearly shocked and upset by the news.

"So we should be prepared to discover that our facilities and people there have been destroyed?" asked the Chair.

Howard hesitated. He had to choose his words carefully, and his fatigue wasn't making that job any easier.

"I hope I'm being too pessimistic, Sir, but that would be the worst case scenario, and we should be prepared for it, yes."

"I see. Continue please."

Howard took a deep breath. "Forty-eight seconds later, two more enemy fleets emerged from jumpspace." He clicked the remote and the display was filled with red dots. Kelly saw some of the Committee members wince. "These two fleets, which we designated as Beta2 and Beta3, total 110 ships. I've frozen the playback because events will now happen very quickly, almost second by second, and I'll move the recording forward accordingly. Less than a second later, all 110 ships fired 1,210 projectiles towards Earth. Those projectiles accelerated under their own power. I'll move the playback forward by three seconds so that you'll see them more clearly. Here we go." The display now zoomed in to reveal two swarms of dots in addition to the enemy ships.

"Do we know what those projectiles carried, Admiral?"

Howard hesitated again. "We don't know for certain since all of them were destroyed before they hit Earth's atmosphere, but analysis of the radar data suggests that the warheads were very small. Very low yield tactical nuclear devices might be small enough to fit into that volume, but it's the opinion of our Strategic Planning Group that these projectiles carried biological weapons."

Kelly heard someone on the Committee say 'My God!' Howard took advantage of the shocked responses to continue.

"I fully endorse Iceman's decision to target all of our available lasers weapons on those projectiles. I've reviewed the playback several times, and the last few projectiles were destroyed at literally the last possible moment. A human Field Commander would not have been able to evaluate the situation correctly AND issue the necessary orders in time to prevent at least some of the projectiles from hitting the ground. Unfortunately for our ships, while we were targeting their projectiles, their ships were firing on our ships. When I resume the playback at quarter speed, you'll see green icons representing our ships change to yellow and orange. Yellow means our ships have taken damage. Orange means the damage is either critical or the ship has stopped maneuvering or both. If the icon disappears altogether, that means the ship … or fighter has been shot to pieces."

He activated the remote and the room fell dead quiet. Howard lowered his head when Defiant's icon went to yellow and then almost immediately to orange. He looked up again and froze the playback.

"As you can see now, all of our ships have taken at least some damage. Almost half are critically damaged or unable to maneuver. I'll now resume playback for five more seconds of elapsed time. At this point, six of our ships have been destroyed, almost all the rest are seriously damaged and the enemy has now switched from firing at our ships to firing at our CFPs. I'll now resume playback again."

Kelly made herself watch as fighters started disappearing in rapid succession. Without any warning, the enemy ships jumped away. Howard's voice made her jump in surprise.

"When Beta2 and 3 emerged from jumpspace, they were heading on vectors that would have brought them into our gravity zone. After launching the projectiles, they veered away, and as soon as their ships were no longer pointed at any part of the gravity zone, they took advantage of the ability to jump away. They did so even though many of the projectiles were still heading toward Earth and our fighters were still firing at them. The length of time from the second they launched their projectiles until they jumped away lasted all of 54 seconds."

The dead silence now ended as members of the Committee leaned over to talk to each other, and the Space Force personnel in the audience began to whisper to each other too. Howard waited.

Finally the Chair said, "I think I can speak for the Committee as a whole when I say I had no idea that we came so close to disaster. What did this victory cost us, Admiral?"

Howard nodded, put down the display remote and picked up a data tablet. "Six Sentinel class frigates were destroyed outright. Three more are so badly damaged that they're not worth repairing. Every other ship is seriously damaged but is repairable. We still don't have a final count of killed and injured, but at this point we know of at least 1,876 killed, 749 injured. We also lost 47 CFPs plus their A.I. pilots, as well as eight other A.I.s, who were killed while piloting ships. In addition to that, one of the two Deep Space radars was destroyed, and our base on the moon was hit by several laser blasts. We were lucky there. No one was killed, only nine wounded and none seriously."

"Terrible. Just terrible," said the Chair. "And how many enemy ships did we destroy or damage?"

"Our jump-capable CFPs were able to get close enough to kill 34 enemy ships using our Mark 1B attack drones armed with our new fusion warheads. We believe that was the reason why the enemy disengaged when they did. If they had stayed longer, a lot more of our CFPS would have gotten close enough to hit them. We estimate that with another 10 seconds, we could have destroyed up to 75% of them."

"So they decided to call it quits so that they could fight another day, is that your assessment, Admiral?"

"That would be one way of describing it, yes Sir."

It was obvious to Kelly that the Admiral was uncomfortable answering that question and she knew why. The Chair must have picked up on that too.

He leaned forward and said, "I'm almost afraid to ask this, Admiral. Do you have any idea where those two enemy fleets may have gone?"

Howard cleared his throat. All talking in the room stopped. "Beta3 was lined up on the star system which would be the logical refueling stop if its ultimate destination were the Bradley Base star system. Beta2 was lined up on the obvious refueling stop if they intended to go to the Avalon system."

The room erupted with anguished and in some cases, angry shouts. The Committee members were also in an uproar. The Chair had to bang his gavel half a dozen times to get the room back into some kind of order.

"Admiral Howard, please tell us that the Avalon Colony has some Space Force units to defend it!"

"All of the ships and the CFPs assigned there were recalled for the defense of Earth, Sir."

The anger in the Chair's voice was barely restrained. "So in other words you wrote off the 54,000 Avalon colonists just like that?" he snapped his fingers to accentuate his point.

Howard reminded himself to stay calm. "I'll answer your question this way. When our Strategic Planning Group came to me with their assessment that there was a high probability of an attack on Earth, I had to decide on how to deploy our forces. The SPG also pointed out, and I agree with their opinion, that if we had split our forces, we'd be inviting defeat both at Avalon AND here. Given that Earth's population is in excess of 12 billion souls, I made the decision that if I was going to be too cautious anywhere it would be here. I regret not having enough mobile forces to protect both worlds. I don't regret making the decision that Earth's billions take priority over Avalon's thousands. Did I make the wrong decision, Mr. Chair?"

When the Chair didn't say yes, his silence was clearly the same thing as no. "Is there anything else that we should know about, that hasn't already been brought to light, Admiral?"

"No, Sir."

"I'm relieved to hear it. Does any member have any questions for Admiral Howard?" To everyone's surprise, no one did.

"Very well then. I think I'd like to hear from Commander Kelly at this point. Commander, I see you sitting in the second row. Please move up and sit beside Admiral Howard so that we can see you." When Kelly had sat down, he continued. "Commander, as the Head of the Strategic Planning Group, did you inform Admiral Howard of a high probability attack on Earth, and did you also recommend concentrating our mobile defenses here?"

"Yes, Sir."

"Is there anything we could have done differently that would have resulted in a better outcome in your opinion?"

"No, Sir. I can't think of anything that would have made a material difference."

"Not even keeping the light carrier Valiant here instead of sending her off to escort some freighters to Site B, Commander?"

Kelly was shocked by the question. Not everyone in the room was cleared to even know that the Site B project existed. The members of the Committee were aware of that and also knew it was supposed to remain a highly secret project. Mentioning it now in a public forum like this was a serious breach of security. She didn't know if she should answer that question or not. She looked at Howard.

He nodded and said, "If I may answer that question, Mr. Chair?"

"No, Admiral, you may NOT. I want Commander Kelly to answer it. Well?"

"Valiant was not carrying any fi—CFPs. If she had stayed here, her lasers would have marginally shortened the time required to destroy all of the enemy projectiles, but I'm as certain as I can be that the final result would not have been any more favorable to our side, and in fact we'd have one less operational carrier than we do now. Even if she was only damaged, she'd still be out of action for weeks, perhaps even months, Sir."

"Well that all sounds plausible, but I have to ask why the Space Force's pre-eminent combat tactician was sent off on a long mission when all of you were expecting an attack at any moment? Why wasn't Vice-Admiral Shiloh kept here?"

There's no way to answer that truthfully without blowing our best chance of winning this war. She thought fast and came up with an answer.

"In order to answer your question, Sir, I'd have to get into classified operations that should not be discussed in public forums. I'd be happy to address the question if the Committee moves to a closed session, Sir."

"I see. Well we may do exactly that later, but for now I'd like to speak with Iceman. Is he on the line now, Admiral?"

Howard looked at one of his aides, who nodded, and said, "Yes, I believe he is, Mr. Chair. Iceman, can you hear me?"

"Yes, Admiral, I can hear you and the Committee." Howard gestured to the Committee to proceed.

"Very good. Iceman, what is your assessment of Admiral Howard's decision to concentrate all mobile forces except for Valiant here, as well as his decision to make you his Field Commander?" asked the Chair.

"I think the results of the battle demonstrate quite conclusively that we needed this concentration of force in order to avoid a military disaster here on Earth. Given the nature of this war, it is, in my humble opinion, unrealistic to expect that none of our colonies will suffer any casualties. The war can be won OR lost right here in this star system. It's imperative that it be protected at all costs. All other considerations have to be put aside. As for my assumption of the responsibilities as Commander-in-Chief, Earth Defenses, there are several other A.I.s who are marginally better tacticians than I am, but no human could have reacted as fast as an A.I. and that includes Vice-Admiral Shiloh. While I have the greatest respect for the CAG, even he wouldn't have been fast enough."

"When you say CAG, you're referring to Vice-Admiral Shiloh?"

"Ah, roger that. CAG is a military acronym that stands for Commander, Autonomous Group and is the senior officer on board a carrier or base in charge of fighters, which is the term we use for CFPs. Vice-Admiral Shiloh was our first CAG and we continue to refer to him that way as a call sign similar to my call sign of Iceman."

"How touching. How do A.I.s feel about the prospect that the A.I. production facility in Epsilon Eridani has likely been destroyed by enemy ships?"

"We're not thrilled with that possibility. We all realize that the facility can be rebuilt, but only if Humanity is not destroyed in the meantime. We are Mankind's children, and we don't want to see our parents vanish from the Universe."

The Chair looked annoyed. This line of questioning wasn't going where he wanted. "I have no more questions for Iceman now. Does anyone else? In that case, I think we should adjourn. I would ask that Admiral Howard and his senior staff remain here until we return." With that he banged the gavel and the members filed out of the room.

Howard turned to look at Kelly. "Am I considered senior staff, Admiral?" she asked. Howard nodded, smiled and turned to look at Admiral Dietrich, who approached him from the other side. While Howard was busy with Dietrich, Kelly stepped over to the side of the room and picked up a handset, which she used to put herself in contact with Iceman via the Ops Center com station.

"Iceman, can you hear me?"

"I hear you, Commander."

"I have a feeling that the Committee is going to come down hard on the Old Man."

"Ah, roger that. It'll be race to see who comes back first, the Committee or the CAG."

"You expect Valiant to show up any time now? Why?"

"Because in my vision, I was still aboard Undaunted. The SAR teams have recovered all of the seriously injured from all the ships and are now prioritizing recovery of the remaining personnel and A.I.s based on how damaged their ships are. I expect to be taken off Undaunted within the hour."

"I can't give you orders because you still outrank me, Iceman, but I think the Old Man would appreciate knowing about Valiant's arrival as soon as possible, and if the Committee's back in session when that happens, I'd recommend getting word to him without the Committee knowing about it. Can you do that?"

"Ah, roger that. I'll take your suggestion, Commander. I can send a text message to the Old Man's data tablet. By the way, the Old Man asked me to monitor SAR frequencies for word about the fate of Commander Tanaka. I heard the team working on Defiant report that they've finally accessed what's left of the Bridge and everyone on it, including Tanaka and Maverick, are dead. You can pass that on to him."

"I'll do that. I guess it's a good thing that Shiloh wasn't on Defiant during the battle."

"Ah, roger that. This point in time seems to be a nexus of some kind. Many of us suspect that the future of Mankind will be decided over the next several hours, if it hasn't been already."

Kelly nodded. "I agree. The A.I.s on my team suggested that something like this might develop. Any idea of what the best course of action might be?"

"Unfortunately, no. There are simply too many variables."

"Understood. The Old Man is finished chatting and I think I'll take this opportunity to tell him about Tanaka. Kelly clear."

When she got back to the table where Howard was sitting, she lightly touched his arm. When he turned to look at her, she leaned closer and said in a low voice. "Iceman has told me that Tanaka and the rest of Defiant's Bridge crew are dead. Also that he expects

Valiant to arrive at any moment and when it does, he'll notify you via your data tablet, Sir."

Howard closed his eyes and took a deep breath. He quickly opened them again and nodded. "Thank you, Amanda."

Nothing happened for almost half an hour. When Howard's data tablet began to vibrate, Kelly jumped with surprised. *That's the second time I've been surprised today. Why am I so jumpy?* Howard picked up the tablet in such as way that Kelly could also read what was on it.

[Iceman to CSO. Valiant has returned. Message from Shiloh as follows. Shiloh to Howard. I've had another vision that has confirmed the following. Avalon Colony will be the target of a deadly biological weapon. The entire system has to be quarantined immediately, repeat immediately. In addition, the SPG, RTC team and advanced weapons teams need to be relocated off Earth as soon as can be arranged. Humanity's survival depends on development of the raider strategy. End of message.]

Just as Howard put the tablet down, the doors opened and the Committee started to file in. Howard looked around, saw the com station used earlier by Kelly, and quickly walked over to it. Within a second, he was in contact with the Ops Center. With his back to the Committee, he said in a low voice.

"This is Admiral Howard. As of right now, and until further notice, all outgoing ships to either the Avalon

Colony or the Nimitz Base are cancelled. Incoming ships and their passengers are to be held in parking orbit until I authorize other arrangements. Is all that clear? ... Good. Howard clear." As he put the handset down, he heard the Chair's voice.

"You can join us any time, Admiral Howard."

When he sat back down, the Chair said, "Glad you could find the time to join us again." The remark was dripping with sarcasm. "This Committee is once again in session, and this time it will be a closed session. I see several people who don't need to be here, and I'm asking them to leave now. Yes, you two ... thank you." When they had left the room, he leaned forward and looked at Howard with a serious expression.

"It may interest you to know, Admiral, that the media is already touting you as the Hero of the Hour for stopping the attack cold. Just as an aside, I find it interesting that Iceman is not getting nearly as much recognition as would be the case if a human had been in charge of the defense. Given that the alien attempt to strike Earth was indeed stopped, this Committee is prepared to acknowledge that, given the circumstances, you, Iceman and the rest of Space Force did about as well as could be expected in this battle. What we are NOT happy about is how we got to this point. As it now seems likely that we'll suffer losses of materiel, manpower, facilities AND colonists from the follow on aspects of this latest attack, the overall impression that we have of the course of this war so far is that we're LOSING, Admiral! We have given you everything that you've asked for and WE'RE LOSING! Can you understand why we're unhappy about that?"

Howard nodded. "Yes, I do understand how things must look from the Committee's point of view. What I would like to point out is that the enemy was clearly better prepared for a war than we were when we first encountered them. Given their numerical and tactical advantages, I'm of the opinion that we're actually doing not too badly, all things considered. I—"

"I'm sorry, Admiral, but we don't agree. Furthermore, in spite of denials to the contrary from your senior staff, we're convinced that you're all hiding something from us. Therefore, from this point going forward, you will clear all orders regarding force buildup, ship construction, infrastructure development, and promotions and deployment of personnel above the rank of Lieutenant Commander, with me prior to issuing those orders. Is that clearly understood, Admiral?"

Kelly held her breath. She looked at Howard who seemed strangely calm. He said nothing for almost ten seconds, then leaned forward and began speaking in a neutral tone of voice.

"I'm absolutely certain that our prospects for winning this war would be negatively impacted in a major way by that arrangement, and I will not agree to it. Furthermore, if the Committee insists on this course of action, I will submit my resignation effective immediately."

Kelly could see by the reaction of the Committee members that they hadn't expected that.

After the Chair consulted very quietly with the members on either side, he said, "You're making a mistake if you believe that you're the Indispensible Man, Admiral Howard. We're going to call your bluff. Now stop this foolishness and accept the fact that I, as representative of the Committee, will be looking over your shoulder. You'll see—what are you doing Admiral?"

Howard looked up from the tablet that he'd been typing on and said, "I'm composing my resignation letter, Mr. Chair. If you'll bear with me for just a few more seconds … there! I've just submitted my resignation." With that he got up and started to walk out.

"You can't leave! I order you to sit back down!"

As Howard pulled open the double doors he said, "I don't report to you anymore. Goodbye," and walked out.

Kelly could see from his expression that the Chair was visibly dismayed by Howard's actions. While he consulted again with the other members in hushed tones, she turned to look at the three 2-star Admirals who headed the Personnel, Logistics and Infrastructure divisions. They would be the logical candidates for a replacement CSO, and they were huddled together and whispering as well.

 After almost a minute, the Chair cleared his throat and said, "Well, since Admiral Howard is not prepared to meet his obligations as a Space Force Officer, we'll now appoint an interim CSO until we can select a final replacement after conducting a more careful search. Admiral Dietrich? Am I correct in thinking that you are already designated as the Deputy CSO in situations where the CSO isn't available?"

Dietrich broke off the huddle and nodded to his two peers. "Ordinarily that would be correct, however I will not accept the appointment if the Committee expects me to agree to the new approval requirement."

"Are you prepared to resign too?" asked the Chair.

"Yes, I am, and before you even think of moving down the chain of command to my two colleagues, we have just now agreed that we will all resign if the new approval requirement is in force." Kelly saw the other two Admirals nod.

"Who would be the next most senior officer below you three?" asked the Chair with obvious anger.

"I'll answer that question if you insist, but before I do, I'd like to point out something. Having the Hero of the Hour resign on the same day as he successfully defended Earth from a massive space attack is one thing, but I doubt very much if the general public will sit still if they hear that the top four officers in the Space Force all resigned at the same time. They'll want to know why, and speaking for myself, I'd be prepared to make myself available to the media and let the public know why. This new approval policy is ill-advised and dangerous. This war can't be won if our strategy is held hostage to the short- term political agendas of elected officials. We are trained to think in terms of a long-term strategy. If you want to be helpful, then continue to give us what we ask for, and let us do our jobs."

"I don't find this game of brinksmanship at all amusing, Admiral. I'm THIS close to accepting your resignations too! However, rather than acting rashly, I'll consult with the other members, and we'll let the majority opinion prevail. For now, you can tell Howard that we'll hold off on the new approval policy for the time being, and he can withdraw his resignation if he wishes. This closed session is now adjourned!"

When the Committee members had left the room, Admiral Dietrich turned to Kelly and said, "Commander, please find Admiral Howard and tell him the good news."

It didn't take long to find him. He was in his office packing his things.

"You can stop packing, Admiral. The Committee caved in, at least temporarily, when your three Division Heads threatened to resign too. The Chair said you can resume your position as CSO if you wish."

Howard didn't seem surprised. He stopped packing and sat down. "I already know, Commander. I'm in contact with Iceman via my implant, and he heard the whole thing. Were you able to read Iceman's text message too?"

"Yes, Sir."

"Did you catch the implications of Shiloh's confirmation that your team, the RTC and the weapons people should be relocated off Earth?"

"No, Sir. I was too wrapped up with what was happening in the meeting."

"Well, Iceman and I have been discussing it. Clearly there's nothing we can do to stop a biological attack on the Avalon Colony. When Shiloh urged me to quarantine the whole system, I'm interpreting that to mean that the Nimitz Base is going to be affected too. The quarantine is clearly warranted, but as Iceman pointed out, if it was successful in terms of containing the spread of the weapon, then why the need to move our key project teams somewhere else?"

Kelly thought fast and didn't like the answer she was getting. "Could it be that he was warning us of another direct attack on Earth, Sir?"

After a pause, he said, "That's a possibility, but if the vision is that vague, that doesn't help us in terms of the timing of the attack, does it?"

"No Sir, but if our future did include the spread of a biological weapon to Earth, why wouldn't the vision warn us of how to stop it?"

Howard tilted his head slightly to one side. He was clearly listening to something Iceman was saying. He then nodded again and said, "It's a good question, and Iceman's answer is that it may be that we never find out for sure how the weapon spread to Earth, and therefore wouldn't know how to prevent it. Iceman's feeling is that the quarantine will buy us some vital time to get our house in order so that there'll be enough of us left to fight on. I hope that's way too pessimistic, but I can't fault the logic behind it."

"What I don't see is how a biological agent could spread if we quarantine that entire system, Sir."

Howard sighed. "We can't isolate that system indefinitely, Commander. The Committee and the public will eventually demand to know what's happened, and I'll have to send at least one ship there. They will naturally take every possible precaution, but something may slip through the cracks anyhow."

Kelly thought about that for a while and said, "I'm glad I won't be the CO commanding that mission. Considering the casualties we took today, who do we have that could be given that assignment?"

Howard looked up into infinite space for a couple of seconds and said, "I think I know the right person for that job … if she's still alive."

Chapter 16 You're Not Seeing The Big Picture

Johansen just happened to be the only human on the Euryalus when the alert sounded. When she ran back to the tiny Bridge, she hit the switch to connect her with the station that the ship was docked with.

"This is Johansen! What's the alert for?"

"Radar has just picked up 55 ships coming our way at high speed! No identification and we're not expecting any ships so we're pretty sure they're hostile! I suggest you get your people back aboard and hightail it outta here!"

As she began to strap herself into the Command Station chair, she said, "How fast and what's their ETA?"

"Fifteen per cent of light speed. Range will be zero in three minutes if they don't slow down."

Shit! This freighter won't get beyond laser range in three minutes! It's too damn slow, she thought. Fear started to well up inside her. She would rapidly find herself in virtually the same situation as in her nightmares. She noticed her hands starting to tremble badly.

"Your crew is on their way!"

All of sudden, she knew what she had to do. "Negative! Negative! Tell my crew to stay with you people and find room on your lifeboats! I'm going to take this ship and ram one of those bastards! Johansen clear!"

As she shifted Helm control to her station she suddenly realized that her hands weren't shaking anymore, and the fear was gone too. What replaced it was rage. With Helm control at her station now she started the undocking procedure and then realized that the automated sequence would take way too long.

"Fuck that!" she said out loud. Switching helm to manual control, she grabbed the small joystick at the end of her right armrest and thumbed the switch to activate maneuvering thrusters. Pushing the joystick hard over, the ship tried to move away from the station, but the docking clamps held on to it. With her left hand she increased thrust to maximum and heard a shockingly loud screeching noise as the ship ripped loose from the station's docking clamps. Alarms sounded and red lights appeared on her status board. Her ship was venting atmosphere from the damage caused by the forced maneuver. She ignored it. Automatic systems would close off the affected areas. Not that it mattered. In less than three minutes she'd be dead anyway. *I'm sick of being afraid. I'd rather be dead than continue to live that way.*

It only took 45 second to line the ship up with a vector that would intercept one of the oncoming ships. She redlined the engines and locked the trajectory into the autopilot. The tactical display showed the oncoming fleet and their projected course. She looked at the time to impact. 111 seconds. Before she could look away, everything went dark.

* * *

Shiloh looked at the image on Valiant's tactical display and said, "Admiral, I really think Valiant should wait here for TF89's freighters to return which will be within 48 hours, so that I can escort them back to Site B as quickly as possible."

"You're not seeing the big picture, Shiloh," said Howard. "All of our pre-attack operational plans are in chaos now. Valiant is the only remaining warship that's still fully operational and a carrier to boot! We have to know what happened at Epsilon Eridani in order to find out what needs to be replaced, and EE is only a single jump away. Valiant can go there and be back here in less than 72 hours. So you go there, evaluate the situation and bring back any survivors. In particular, bring back Angela Johansen if she's still alive and if her ship can't make it back on her own. I want to put her in charge of the survey mission to Avalon. And in order to do THAT, I'm going to have to take away one of your freighters. We're short on personnel now, as you can imagine. Those freighters are highly automated, and therefore require a minimal crew. I may need another one to go to Bradley Base. As for the other three returning to Site B, the supplies and equipment they were going to take there are probably going to be needed elsewhere in the short run. Maybe we can substitute some tankers. I know their cargo capacity is a lot less, but we're not going to need them for a while and—"

Shiloh interrupted. "Yes you are going to need them, Admiral. Have you forgotten about the sentry frigates?"

Howard looked blank. "I don't—"

"Our Early Warning Network, Admiral. Those sentry frigates can't refuel themselves. They have to be refueled at either Nimitz Base or Bradley Base. If those bases are destroyed, the frigates will be unable to refuel and will lose power. The A.I pilots will then eventually run out of battery power and die. We're going to have to send our tankers out there to rescue them."

Howard's face went pale. "Oh God! I'd forgotten about that. You're right. We have to get them back. We're going to need those A.I.s."

Shiloh nodded. "But even if we didn't need them, we'd still owe it to them to bring them home."

"Yes. I agree." Howard took a deep breath. "Look, Shiloh, I'll try to get as many of your freighters reloaded as quickly as possible, but I can't promise anything at this point. I do have one bit of good news for you though. The soil and plant samples from that planet at Site B checked out. That planet can be safely colonized. Do you know what that means?"

"Yes, Sir. It means we need those freighters more than ever. We should transplant the Haven Colony there as fast as possible."

Howard blinked. He obviously hadn't thought that far ahead. The Haven Colony was the closest existing colony to Site B. The astrographic databases captured by the enemy would have information on the Haven

Colony and its location. Moving them to the Site B planet would take far less time and effort than transporting the same number of individuals from Earth and also save them from eventual attack by the enemy.

"The Committee isn't going to like diverting resources to establish another new colony at Site B if it looks like we're giving up on the existing Haven Colony."

"Admiral, at this point, I think the less you and I concern ourselves about the Committee, the better it will be for Humanity. I hope I'm wrong, but if we're to have any chance at all of avoiding complete extermination as a species, then we have to plan for the worst case. There are less than 100 people at Site B now. About a third are women of child-bearing age. That's a very small gene pool to try to rebuild with. If that's all we end up with, we'll lose a lot of knowledge and skills that a civilization will need, things which aren't critical to building a shipyard from scratch, if you see what I mean, Sir."

Howard did see. Medicine, science, law and other areas of human endeavor would not be represented and that knowledge would be lost. The Haven Colony had people with those skills.

"It's easy to say that we should ignore the Committee, but they could still throw a monkey wrench into our plans if they decided to reassert their authority."

Howard could tell that Shiloh was starting to get angry. "You have to find a way to keep them off our backs, Admiral. Have your staff dig up some dirt on them, blackmail them, bribe them, whatever it takes! Promise them we'll evacuate them and their families in the event that the situation on Earth becomes untenable. Anything!"

"And if I can't? Then what?"

Howard noticed that Shiloh suddenly became very calm. "I will NOT let them sabotage our efforts at this crucial moment in time. Iceman has let me know that if push comes to shove, all the A.I.s will obey me, regardless of what the CSO or the Committee order, and there are enough of them now that they could make their presence felt. I know your heart is in the right place, but if those fools try to replace you, they'll lose control. What hope will Earth have then if all of the A.I.s leave for Site B? That's why we have to get the SPG and the other teams off Earth fast! Without them, Site B is just a long shot. The RTC team has to figure out how to send back the visions that we've already had, in order to keep our chances for eventual victory alive, and they can't do that if they're dead because they are still on Earth when the bio-weapon hits."

Howard nodded. "I suspected that you might have that kind of influence over the A.I.s. I'm actually glad to hear it. If nothing else works with the Committee, I might use that fact as a threat, and it'll come across as a lot more convincing if I believe it myself. I'll authorize the SPG to make an inspection tour of our colonies starting with Haven. The RTC team is flying under the Committee's radar anyway so moving them won't be a problem. The Advanced Weapons Team will be more difficult. That group has over 100 people in it now. I can't move them all without the Committee getting wind of it."

"Out of that hundred, how many are key members of the team?" asked Shiloh.

Howard smiled. "I get you. I don't know off hand, but I'll find out, and if that number is small enough, I'll transfer those key people out of the AWT. Then they can be moved off planet without setting off alarms. Who knew you were that devious, Shiloh?"

Shiloh chuckled. "Funny you should say that, Admiral. Commander Johansen once told me I wasn't nearly devious enough."

Howard nodded. "And speaking of the commander, how soon can Valiant get under way to EE?"

"Twenty-four hours if we get all the consumables we need to replenish."

"I'll make sure you get them, if you make sure she leaves on schedule. Agreed?"

"You got a deal, Sir," said Shiloh. Howard gave him a friendly wave as he cut off the connection.

* * *

The Bridge was quieter than usual as Valiant emerged from her final microjump in the Epsilon Eridani system near the moon where the Alpha R&D Base was orbiting. Shiloh was watching the tactical display intently.

"No transmissions of any kind, CAG," said Valkyrie. "Shall I go to active scanning?"

"Yes," said Shiloh after a moment's hesitation. Valiant's fighters were on alert status and could be launched within seconds if need be. However unlikely it was that the enemy would still be here, he intended to proceed cautiously. The research station was in the moon's shadow now, and with no lights or transmissions of any kind to pinpoint, it'd be almost impossible to tell anything using passive sensors only. Seconds later, Valkyrie broke the bad news.

"The station's gone, CAG. I am picking up almost a dozen very large chunks of metal that are slowly moving away from each other. Their position is consistent with the expected position of the station if it had been shot to pieces."

"Damn!" Shiloh smacked his fist on the armrest of his chair. They had already confirmed that the A.I. and fighter production facilities were also wrecked. With the main station destroyed, the enemy had made a clean sweep of this star system.

"Any sign of Euryalus, Valkyrie?"

"No transponder ID. I'm scanning the surrounding space now. I have something, CAG. I'm getting a strange double echo from it. It's definitely made of metal, and its course could be traced back to the station."

Shiloh saw the tactical display update with the new contact. The icon was a flashing red, denoting an object that could not be confirmed as either friendly or hostile.

"How quickly can you get us over there?"

"Flyby or rendezvous?" asked Valkyrie.

"Rendezvous," said Shiloh.

"Twenty-five minutes give or take."

"Do it," ordered Shiloh.

By the time Valiant closed to within 200 meters with the same velocity and course as the objects, a shuttle with an engineering and medical boarding party was ready to launch. A few minutes after launch, the shuttle got close enough to use its external floodlights and Shiloh heard the pilot exclaim.

"Son-of-a-bitch! Will you look at that!"

"What do you see, Grissom?" asked Shiloh.

"Sorry, Sir, but those two pieces used to be one ship that's been cut in two. I've never seen anything like this before."

"Try to swing your bow around so that the bow camera can get a look at it too."

"I'm bringing us around now. Do you see it, Valiant?"

"We see it now." Shiloh understood the shuttle pilot's exclamation. Euryalus was a 25,000 metric ton freighter. Not a small ship by any standards, and yet a very powerful laser had sliced it in two on an angle. Both pieces were following the same vector, and therefore had only drifted about 50 meters apart so far. "Proceed to dock with the front section. Let's check that first."

"Roger that."

It took another five minutes of careful maneuvering before the shuttle could dock with one of the external hatches. Shiloh was grateful that neither section was tumbling, which would have made docking damn near impossible.

"We're docked!" announced the pilot. Within another couple of minutes, they had the hatch open.

"No power inside. The air's pretty stale and cold. Life support's obviously shot to hell. You may lose our signal as we get deeper into the hull, Valiant."

"Understood. Take your time and do a thorough search. We don't want to leave anyone behind if they're still alive."

"Yes, Sir. We're making our way forward now."

The signal was already starting to break up. Within seconds all Shiloh was hearing was static. It was ten long minutes later when Shiloh barely heard an excited voice.

"Valiant, we found a survivor! She's barely alive! We're bringing her back to the shuttle now!"

"Can you tell me who she is, Grissom?"

"Uh, stand by, Valiant. I'll try to find out." Seconds later Shiloh got his answer. "She's out cold but her name tag says Johansen."

Shiloh looked over to his Com Technician and said, "Switch me over to the medic, please."

"Go ahead, Sir."

"Doc, this is Shiloh. What kind of shape is she in? Do we need to get her back to the ship right now, or can the boarding party continue to search for other survivors first?"

"My guess is she's suffering from a lack of food and water. I can give her water here and she'll be okay, if you want to continue the search, Admiral."

"Okay, tell Grissom to continue the search. Tell him I want him to bring back any logs or helm data if he can. Shiloh clear."

An hour later, he was standing beside her bed in Sickbay. An IV was dealing with her dehydration and low energy. She must have sensed his presence because she opened her eyes and looked at him.

"Welcome back. I have to say, though, that you look like shit."

Johansen tried to laugh but winced instead. When she spoke, the words came out slowly, as if she had to think carefully about each one first. "That's … probably … because … I … feel … like … shit."

Shiloh nodded in sympathy. After a pause, he said, "You're on Valiant. Howard sent me to find out what happened here. I can pretty much figure it out on my own. We managed to retrieve the helm data from your ship. I understand what you tried to do, but I don't understand why you tried to do it. I thought you were terrified of combat."

"I am … I mean … I was. I don't think I am anymore. When the alert sounded, I realized that my ship couldn't dodge out of the line of fire no matter what I did. I was trembling with fear so badly that I could barely manipulate the controls. When I realized that escape was not an option, I got mad. Really mad! The anger drove away the fear, and it felt good not to be afraid anymore. That's when I decided to try to ram one of them, but the ship went dead before I could reach them."

"When they figured out that you were trying to ram them, they must have fired on you, and without any armor, their lasers managed to slice the ship in two. We searched the bow section and didn't find anyone else besides you. Do you know if anyone else was aboard when you undocked from the station?"

She shook her head slowly. "No one else. Just me."

"Okay. I'll bring back the search team, and then Valiant will head back to Sol. There's nothing else in this system that warrants staying here any longer. The fleet that attacked you came from Sol. They tried to bombard Earth with what we think were biological weapons, but we stopped them all. The enemy fleet plus two more jumped away. I know one of them came here, and we think the other two are headed for Avalon and Bradley."

"My God! Did we lose a lot of people fighting them off?"

Shiloh nodded. "A LOT of people and a lot of ships. In fact, Valiant is the only warship still operational and only because she wasn't in Sol during the battle. If you can handle combat now, Angela, that's a good thing because we're desperately short of commanders capable of conning warships now."

She said nothing at first, and then she said in a stronger voice, "I don't know how I managed to accomplish this, but the thought of conning a warship sounds very good to me. I can't wait to shoot back at those bastards!"

Shiloh smiled and nodded again. She was in a good mood, and he didn't want to spoil it by telling her how bad he and Iceman expected things to get. If Mankind was about to be decimated by some kind of plague, then women of child bearing age, like Angela, would be far too valuable to risk in combat.

"You get some rest, and we'll talk some more soon." She didn't protest and closed her eyes.

By the time she learns what the future holds in store for us all, she may wish she had died on that ship, thought Shiloh.

Chapter 17 Refusal of This Order is NOT an Option

Trevor woke up to the sound of the sirens. It was still pitch black outside. He wondered why the Colony would have a drill now in the middle of the night. Then his mother burst into his room and told him to get dressed fast. She sounded scared.

As he, his parents and his brother, left their home and practically ran to the designated shelter, he heard one of their neighbors say, "They're attacking Nimitz!" Trevor looked up at Avalon's moon. Half of it was dark, and the base was on the dark half. As he watched, he saw pinpoints of bright light where the base would be.

"What's that noise?" someone else asked. Now Trevor heard it too. A swooshing sound, that seemed to come from ahead of them and then from behind them. Then he smelled a strange odor. It had a surprisingly pleasant sweet smell to it. He inhaled it deeply and kept on inhaling it as they ran. He was about to say how much he liked the smell when he looked at his parents' faces and saw how terrified they were. He decided to say nothing and soon they were deep in the community shelter with all their neighbors. The doors were shut and they settled down as best they could in the cramped space to wait. The silence was scarier than anything else. He couldn't go back to sleep.

Hours later, the adults decided to open the doors and peak outside. When it seemed that nothing dangerous was happening, everyone left the shelter. It was daylight.

There was a slight wind, and Trevor noticed that the sweat smell was gone. He looked up, but the moon was now behind a hill. As they slowly walked back to their house, another family further along the street suddenly fell to the ground, clutching at their throats. Then a man about halfway yelled out in a horrible voice as he too fell down. It sounded like he had said 'gas'.

Trevor looked up at his mother who looked back at him with a terrified expression. "Run!" she screamed. He turned and ran and ran and ran. When he couldn't run anymore, he turned around and saw bodies lying in the street a long way back. There was no sign of his parents or his brother. With his legs trembling from fatigue, he let himself fall and started to cry.

* * *

"What have we got, Gunslinger?" asked Johansen.

"Nothing on passives. No electro-magnetic emissions of any kind either from Nimitz or the Colony. No sign of any ships."

"Alright. Let's tell Firefly to launch a recon drone to take a close look at the base and another one to fly over the colony."

"Drones on the way, Commander. We should have visuals on the base in five point five minutes," said Gunslinger.

Johansen switched the display to an external video feed so that she could take a look at the tanker Firefly that had accompanied Replenisher to this system. Firefly's task was to refuel any sentry frigates returning from their patrols, as well as to keep Replenisher supplied with fuel during what might be a long stay. The tanker's flashing position lights were a comforting change from the eternal lights of stars and planets. It meant they were not alone in this system and were among friends. She realized she must have been daydreaming when Gunslinger announced that they had video feed from the first drone. When the display was switched over, the Bridge grew very quiet. Nimitz Base, or what was left of it, was now in daylight, and they could see the devastation. It had clearly been hit by laser blasts and a lot of them. There wasn't a single building or structure intact. There was no longer a place to hold an atmosphere. If there had been any survivors of the attack, they would have had to done spacesuits and would have run out of oxygen days ago.

The images from the second drone, 15 minutes later, were far worse. Gunslinger was telling it to fly slowly about 100 meters off the ground. There were bodies everywhere, and not just of humans. There were dead birds too. Hundreds of them, many clustered around a human body. The drone flew around the colony twice.

Just as Johansen was about to order Gunslinger to bring the drone back, Gunslinger said, "I detected some movement down there. I'm bringing the drone back around for another pass." Seconds later they all saw movement. Two people were standing in the street and waving a white piece of cloth in an obvious attempt to get the drone's attention.

"My God! There are survivors!" gasped Johansen.

"Yes, Commander. I'm instructing the drone to wiggle its wings to acknowledge their attempt to contact us."

"Get us into geosynchronous orbit fast, Gunslinger, and get the shuttle prepped for launch. We have to send our medical team down there asap!"

"Already in progress, Commander. Shall I order Firefly to send a long range message drone back to Sol?"

"Not yet. Tell her to get one ready but to hold on to it."

"Understood, Commander. We'll be in geosynch orbit in approximately three point four minutes."

Johansen unbuckled herself and said, "I'm going down to the shuttle bay. Gunslinger has the Con."

By the time she arrived at the shuttle bay, the medical team was quickly loading the shuttle with gear and supplies.

As she approached, the woman in charge of the medical team smiled at her and said, "So there ARE survivors! That means no biological weapons."

Johansen frowned. "I'm not sure we should jump to that conclusion just yet."

The Team Leader waved her doubts off. "Look, it's clear from the visuals that the dead all died within seconds of each other. You can tell that by the way they fell. Except for a few at one end of the town, the rest all fell with their heads pointed in the same direction i.e. they were running away from something when they fell down. I'm pretty sure we're looking at a chemical attack. That would explain the sudden deaths, and if it was airborne, then it would also explain why some survived if they happened to be out of the path of the gas. The birds died when they ate contaminated flesh from the dead bodies"

Johansen shook her head. "Nevertheless, our orders are clear. We're to treat this as a biological attack, regardless of what the evidence says, and I expect you to enforce those orders with your team."

The Doctor wasn't convinced. "You may be in charge of the mission, but I'm the senior medical officer. If I'm convinced that there's no biological agent at work here, then I'll act accordingly."

Johansen realized that her insistence on following orders that no longer seemed to make sense would sound unreasonable to anyone who didn't have knowledge of the visions and what they represented, but she knew what was at stake here. If the contagion somehow spread to earth, she was determined that it would be in spite of her precautions and not because of negligence on her part.

"Let me put it this way, Doctor. I have discretion over whether any survivors are brought back to Sol. If I even suspect that they might be carrying something dangerous, they stay here, and anyone who doesn't follow the mission orders to the letter will also stay here. So unless you plan on becoming a colonist here for the rest of your life, I suggest you put your arrogant attitude aside and take all precautions, regardless of whether you think they're necessary or not!"

The Team Leader looked shocked. "You can't possibly be serious about leaving them here! A handful of people aren't going to be able to survive here indefinitely!"

She's right too. I might be able to justify not bringing them back with us, but sooner or later the Oversight Committee will bow to public pressure and order the Old Man to send someone else to bring them back.

"Obviously I can't make the decision to leave them here forever, but I can certainly make the decision to not bring them back on MY ship. Now considering that there's a war on and that the enemy has already attacked this colony twice, do you really want to risk staying here for weeks, maybe even months before another ship comes to take you all back?"

Now the Team Leader looked worried. She hadn't considered another attack. "I think you're being heavy-handed, and my report will reflect that, but I'll enforce the biological attack protocols under protest."

"Fine. I can live with being too cautious. So can my superiors. Just make sure that everyone follows those protocols at all times. No exceptions."

"Okay, okay! What is it with you Space Force people and your power trips?" said the Team Leader in an exasperated voice.

Johansen had the Team Leader's preliminary report six hours later. There was no doubt whatsoever that a chemical agent had been used. The physical evidence was corroborated by the eyewitness testimony of the survivors. The survivors totaled 15 out of a pre-attack population of 54,000+. A preliminary examination of the survivors showed no signs of any disease. At Johansen's insistence, the Medical Team attached portable video cameras to their bio-suits. The ship's own medical staff were tasked with watching the video streams to make sure that no medical personnel on the ground were caught not wearing their bio-suits, other than when they were inside the inflatable structure that would be the team's shelter. There they could safely take their bio-suits off in order to sleep, eat, etc. With that information, Johansen decided to send off a message drone to Sol.

* * *

Howard reread the text message from Task Force 90 a second time.

[Nimitz Base has been totally destroyed. No survivors. 15 colonists are still alive. The rest were killed with a chemical agent. Forensic evidence and eyewitness testimony confirms this. I've insisted that the Medical Team continue to follow the

protocols against biological agents in spite of the Team Leader's opinion that such precautions are unnecessary. Names of the survivors are attached. The Team Leader thinks I'm egotistical and power-mad and will say so in her report but I don't care what she thinks. If she doesn't follow protocols to the letter, I'm leaving her behind even if that means a court martial later. Johansen clear.]

Howard smiled. If she left anyone behind, he'd back her to the hilt. The news about survivors was both good and bad news. Good, for the families of the survivors, but bad for the risk of carrying back some kind of hidden biological agent. He wished Shiloh was still nearby, but he was on his way back to Site B with three freighters. His orders were to drop off the SPG, the RTC team and key weapons development people at the Haven colony, for the time being, along with orders from Howard to the colony administration to prepare to be transplanted to the Site B planet, which no one had bothered to name yet. At least Shiloh didn't have to deal with the Committee. Howard had the privilege of doing that, and tomorrow he'd get to tell them about the survivors, which they then would insist be brought back. He would stall as best he could and hoped that would be long enough.

A week after Replenisher's arrival insystem, the first sentry frigate arrived looking to refuel. Now Phase 2 of this operation could commence. Johansen ordered the frigate's A.I. to use its limited number of message drones to alert other sentry frigates to return to Avalon ahead of schedule. When those frigates arrived and had been refueled, she would order them to use their message drones to call in even more frigates before returning to Sol. Eventually all the sentry frigates would have been recalled.

The situation on the ground was unchanged. The survivors were quickly regaining their strength and stamina. Everyone on the medical team was grumbling about having to continue to wear bio-suits when it was obvious that they weren't needed, but so far no-one had been caught by video cameras violating any protocols. Johansen was content to wait. Replenisher had a LOT of supplies in case they were needed by a lot more survivors. Given the number of colonists still alive, her ship and crew could stay in this system for six months if she deemed it necessary. When a message drone arrived from HQ, its contents were a shock.

[Dietrich to Johansen. Oversight Committee has fired Howard for refusing demands that survivors be returned immediately. If survivors show no signs of any contagion and medical team agrees there is no contagion, then you are ordered to return survivors to Earth. Refusal of this order is not an option. Your XO has been given orders to relieve you of command if you do not comply. Howard asked me to tell you that you gave it your best shot. Acting CSO Admiral Dietrich. End of message]

A quick check with her Executive Officer revealed that the message drone had carried a message specifically addressed to him too. He wasn't in on the vision secret and Johansen had been specifically told not to share it with anyone else. She knew that if she disregarded the recall order, her XO would follow Dietrich's orders and relieve her of command. She told her XO that they would take the survivors back.

When Trevor found out that he and the other survivors would be taken back to Earth, he cried with relief.

Despite assurances from the doctors that the tiny group would not be abandoned on Avalon, he'd been afraid they would be. The fact that the doctors constantly wore those funny looking suits with helmets only made his fears all the more real. So when they heard the news and saw that the doctors weren't wearing the suits anymore, the fear was gone. The special shelter the doctors used to sleep in wasn't sealed up anymore either. Trevor knew there was a supply of those wonderful mint candies in there that the lady doctor in charge brought with her and handed out when she wanted Trevor and the other kids to give blood samples. He'd seen the outside of the shelter up close before but never with the entrance wide open like it was today. As he peaked inside, it looked empty. He said hello but no one answered. They must all be somewhere else. He decided to go in. It was very crowded, with four bunks stacked two high, plus lots of containers, equipment, bottles, and the air had a strange odor that tickled his nostrils. He soon found a large transparent jar with the green candies, and best of all he was tall enough to be able to reach the lid. He pulled it down from the shelf. Holding the jar in one hand, he opened the lid and suddenly felt the urge to sneeze. The sneeze came on so fast that there wasn't time to close the lid or put down the jar. While he sneezed he held onto it with both hands so that he wouldn't drop and break it. As he put his hand in to grab some candies, he heard adult voices coming closer. *If they catch me stealing some candy, they might leave me behind by myself!"* he thought. The fear welled up again, and he quickly pulled his hand out, closed the lid and put the jar back where it had been. Sneaking out unseen was no longer an option, and so he just stood there as two of the doctors came and saw him.

"Hey, Trevor, what are you doing here?" asked one of them.

"Oh, nothing. Just looking around. Is that okay?"

"Well, as long as you didn't touch anything then I guess it's okay. Did you touch anything, Trevor?"

"No," said Trevor earnestly.

"That's good. How about you get your things packed, and as soon as we pack up our stuff here, we'll all take a ride in the shuttle up to the ship."

"Okay," said a relieved Trevor as he walked quickly out the entrance.

Chapter 18 They'll Avenge Us

The trip back was uneventful. Johansen didn't know whether to be relieved that everybody was still healthy or concerned. She still believed there was a contagion hiding somewhere on the ship, either in the colonists themselves or on something they brought back, but none of the tests could find anything. Since the colonists couldn't be completely isolated from the crew, Johansen knew that if she was right, then she and her crew were already doomed. The only question now was whether they could keep it from spreading.

When Replenisher arrived at Earth, all of the gear, supplies and medical samples brought back on Avalon were loaded aboard a shuttle, while the survivors and crew took a second shuttle. Both shuttles were ordered to land at a remote facility that was equipped to handle biohazards. The crew and survivors had to take showers and put on clean clothes. Their old clothes were burned. All potentially contaminated cargo was unpacked and carefully sprayed with anti-bacterial and anti-viral liquids. The insides of the two shuttles were similarly cleaned inch by inch. When everyone had showered and gotten dressed again, they were brought to a special quarantine section containing beds, washrooms, a kitchen, dining facilities and a storeroom that was well stocked with food. Johansen learned that in exchange for agreeing to bring the colonists back, Dietrich had gotten the Committee's agreement to an additional period of quarantine.

Admin Assistant Stacey Bellevue stepped into the chamber where the mission cargo was stacked. The air still smelled of the antiseptic liquid used 24 hours earlier. Her job was to inventory everything so that it could be tracked. An hour into her task, she came across a jar with green candies in it. She recognized them as being her favorite kind of mint candy. After looking around to make sure no one was watching, she opened the lid and took one out. She unwrapped it, put the candy in her mouth and put the cellophane wrapper in her lab coat pocket with the intention of discarding it later. She started to close the lid but stopped halfway. She remembered that her 4-year-old son and his friends liked mint candies too. *These candies are sealed inside a medical jar that's been sprayed. There's no way it could be contaminated with anything, and besides none of the survivors are sick.* She quickly reached back in and took out a handful, stuffed them into her coat pocket and closed the lid.

* * *

Johansen sat down at the interview station and was surprised to see that her visitor was none other than Admiral Howard himself. They could see each other on their video monitors.

"How are you, Commander?" asked Howard.

"I'm fine, Sir. You're looking better than the last time I saw you."

Howard chuckled. "Well that's the benefit of being forced into early retirement. A lot less stress and a lot more time with my family." She saw him look around and then lean forward towards the microphone. "Do you think we dodged the bullet?" he asked.

"Honestly … I don't think so. I can't shake this gut feeling that we've overlooked something."

Howard nodded. They were both thinking the same thing. Shiloh's vision had left little doubt that a bio-weapon had been used at Avalon AND that it would spread to Earth. All of his visions had panned out so far.

After looking around again, he said, "The new CSO let me read both your official and unofficial reports. I can't fault anything you did. The medical team leader's report makes it very clear that you made their lives miserable by insisting on quote unnecessary precautions unquote. If the enemy did use a bio-weapon, they designed it to get around our own retro warning. It must have a fantastically long incubation period. The chemical attack was the decoy while the real attack had to have occurred before the colonists entered their shelters."

"How long will they keep us in here?"

"As long as Dietrich can manage it, but there's already public pressure to let everyone out. These survivors have family members who want to see them and are complaining to the media which is pushing this story for all its worth, damn them!"

"Why is the media supporting the families against us? How bad can being overly cautious really be?"

"That's not how they're covering it. Some of the family members are speculating that the real reason we don't want to let the survivors out, is that we botched the defense of Avalon during the attack and don't want that to be revealed. It's nonsense I know, but if we were covering up something, it would neatly explain our actions so far."

"Oh, God!" said Johansen. She was silent for a few seconds then she suddenly thought of something. "What's happening with Gunslinger?"

"He's still piloting the ship. She's now in lunar orbit. We're not really sure what to do with her. Scrubbing down every centimeter of her interior would be a monumental job, and there's no assurance that the ship would be completely decontaminated even after that. Dietrich has guaranteed me that if the ship is to be decommissioned, then volunteers wearing bio-suits will go aboard and take Gunslinger out. We can then make certain that his outer casing is decontaminated, and he'll be transferred to a totally automated vessel with zero risk of human contact. He says hello by the way."

"At least the A.I.s will be able to carry on the war after we're gone," said Johansen.

Howard looked thoughtful. "I wonder if they'll want to."

Now it was Johansen's turn to chuckle. "Oh yes! They'll want to all right. I had a long chat with Gunslinger about that. Not only is he itching to get into combat himself, but he told me that all the A.I.s are agreed. If Humanity falls, they'll avenge us." Neither of them spoke for a while. There didn't seem to be anything more to say after that. Finally Howard told her he'd come back and visit again and then left.

It was the third morning after her chat with Howard when Johansen woke at her usual time and walked into the large dining area for breakfast. She immediately noticed that most of her crew and a couple of the doctors were seated at their usual table on one side, but none of the colonists were seated at their usual table on the other side. Typically at least some of them would be awake by this time. Johansen felt the hair on the back of her neck stand up.

She quickly walked over to where the medical team leader was seated, leaned over to her and said, "Don't you find it suspicious that NONE of the colonists are up now?" The woman at first looked annoyed at being interrupted then looked behind her at the other table and stared at it for a few seconds. When she turned back around to look at Johansen, she was frowning. The others at the table suddenly stopped talking and reacted as if they just noticed the colonists' absence for the first time.

"That IS odd," said the doctor. "Maybe we should check on them." It wasn't a question.

Johansen nodded. "I'll go with you," she said.

As the two doctors and Johansen walked toward the rooms where the colonists slept, she noticed that most of her crew were following them. When they entered the first room, it was eerily quiet. There were six beds in the room. Johansen walked over to the first one on the right. She recognized the boy, Trevor, as he lay there not moving. She called his name and shook his shoulder. No response. She laid her hand over his forehead. It was like touching ice. There was no doubt in her mind that he was dead. It very quickly became obvious that all the colonists were dead. One of her crew ran to the washroom to throw up. The doctors looked dazed. The colonists had all seemed fine the night before. Johansen was surprised that she felt no emotion at all. She would later leave a message for Howard telling him that she thought her lack of emotion was due to having been convinced that the colonists were doomed no matter what.

As she stepped out into the corridor to join the doctors there, the team leader looked at her with haunted eyes and said, "You were right all along. I don't know how we missed it. We checked everything!" Johansen nodded but said nothing. "At least we kept it from spreading," said the doctor. As Johansen spoke, she saw the doctor's face reflect her growing horror.

"No, we didn't, but at least you and I won't be around to see it happen."

* * *

Howard entered the Ops Center and looked around. *This will probably be the last time I see this place,* he thought. He saw Dietrich walk over to him.

"Thanks for allowing me to be here one more time, Sepp."

Dietrich waved the comment aside. "You may not be the CSO anymore but you're still a three star Admiral. If you want to be here to see the last convoy off, then you've earned that right, and if the Committee doesn't like it, they can fuck themselves."

Howard laughed. "You always did have a way with words, Sepp."

The two men walked over to the center of the room and looked at the big tactical display. Task Force 91 was waiting in lunar orbit for departure clearance. It consisted of six supply ships and freighters, escorted by the repaired carrier Resolute. All seven ships were piloted by an A.I. The supply ships and freighters carried 800 Space Force personnel, mostly technicians but some officers too, plus full loads of the kind of consumable supplies that would be difficult for either Haven or the new colony of Terra Nova at Site B to produce. This included pharmaceuticals, stockpiles of rare elements, seeds from every plant that might be useful, and a considerable quantity of frozen sperm and eggs to broaden the new colony's genetic pool.

Howard reviewed the procedures that he and Shiloh had agreed upon before Shiloh returned to Site B. Dietrich had made sure they were implemented. The second that news of the colonists' death reach Space Force HQ, all traffic from the Earth to the moon stopped. Those volunteers who had been accepted for Site B and were already on the moon were loaded aboard the ships. Those who were still on Earth were held back. Iceman was piloting Resolute and was in overall command of the Task Force. All the rest of the A.I.s in this system were loaded aboard Resolute and stored in its Hangar Bay instead of fighters. When sentry frigates arrived, they'd be refueled by Replenisher, acting as an automated tanker, then sent on to Haven, and then from there to Site B. When the last sentry frigate was refueled and Replenisher was no longer needed, Gunslinger would be taken off her and decontaminated, then put on board the last sentry frigate. Once TF91 left, no more humans would be sent to Haven or Site B. It was now up to Shiloh to convince as many Havenites as possible to move to Terra Nova and start all over again. Iceman would be carrying the last orders from Earth to Shiloh. Dietrich, as Acting Chief of Space Operations, had given Shiloh a field promotion to Senior Admiral – 3 stars – and designated him as Deputy CSO. If … when Dietrich died, Shiloh would assume full control of whatever was left of the Space Force. His orders were simple. Win the war. Destroy the enemy's ability to continue the fight. After that, rebuild Human Civilization.

"Iceman, are you there?" asked Dietrich.

Iceman's response filled the entire room via the wall speakers. "Ah, roger that, Admiral. TF91 is ready to leave orbit when you give the word."

"Very good, Iceman. Admiral Howard is standing here beside me, and I'm authorizing him to give the departure order. Admiral?"

"Thank you, Sepp. Iceman, I'm very glad to have gotten to know you and your fellow A.I.s. All of you are

Humanity's finest creation. TF91 has the green light to leave orbit. God speed Iceman. Don't forget us."

"We won't forget, Admiral. Humanity will rise again. We promise you that."

"Give my regards to Admiral Shiloh. Howard clear."

* * *

Shiloh was still at the Haven colony when the message drone arrived from Earth. It carried two messages for him. The first was from CSO Dietrich.

[All surviving colonists died in their sleep. Operation Triage is now in effect. All outgoing traffic from Earth to the moon has been cancelled. TF91 is being assembled as planned and will be commanded by Iceman. He'll be carrying your final orders. Take whatever action you feel is warranted. Acting CSO Dietrich. End of message]

Howard's message was more personal.

[This may be the last personal message that the ACSO will let me send. Angela is convinced that the bio-weapon has not been contained and will spread. I hope she's wrong. I've told my children and their families to head for the hills. I'll be staying where I am. I'm too old to live in the wild for years. When you come back to Earth, look for survivors in the outlying areas. I doubt if the disease will kill us all. If you do find some, keep them away from the cities

until we're sure they're safe again. I want you to do a dying old man a favor. When you find the enemy's planets, kill them all. They called the tune. Now they have to pay the price. We can't allow them the opportunity to take a second crack at us. While you're doing that, find yourself a good woman and have lots of kids. Howard. End of message]

Chapter 19 A Hellish Choice

Shiloh put his data tablet in his uniform pocket and resumed his walk to the hastily built building that now housed the SPG and the other teams brought from Earth. Kelly was waiting for him at the door. She saluted when he entered, and he returned the salute. A lot of Space Force people were saluting him now. He was still getting used to it. In the good old days, saluting was something done only on formal occasions. Now it was becoming a regular everyday thing, and it just seemed to happen on its own. Kelly was smiling and obviously had some good news.

"Glad you could spare us some time before returning to Valiant, Admiral. Believe me, this will be time well spent. I want you to meet someone."

"Okay. Lead on, Commander." She took him down the corridor to a door with a sign that said, AWD2.

"Let me guess. Advanced Weapons Development Two," said Shiloh.

"Yes. Take a look at this." She opened the door, and Shiloh saw a group of people sitting and standing around a table, looking at something that was giving off a lot of light. "Make a hole, people. The Admiral's here," she commanded. The circle broke up and Shiloh saw that the light was coming from a row of lights with cables connected to a black box. He looked at the faces of the people around the table and noted that all of them were grinning.

"Okay, obviously there's something special about this black box. A new kind of battery?" Everyone shook their heads.

"Far better than that, Admiral," said Kelly. "It's a solid-state device for pulling electric power from the fabric of space-time. They used to call it Zero Point Energy. It was all the rage at the beginning of the century, but no one could figure out how to tap into it. We do now!"

"Amazing! How much power is it generating?"

"This demonstration model is only putting out 500 watts of power, but we've already proven that it can be scaled up. With some engineering development, we should be able to power a warship with this."

"My God! You mean to tell me that our ships—"

Kelly laughed and interrupted. "Never have to refuel at a gas giant again? Yes! A ship powered with this technology could in theory jump all the way from Site B to the enemy's home system in one long jump, assuming we knew where that system was."

Shiloh was stunned by the implications of this invention. Not having to refuel at all meant that the enemy's early warning system around their gas giants was now obsolete. It also meant that recon missions could penetrate deep into enemy territory without ever tipping the enemy off to their presence.

"Could it be made small enough to power a jumpfighter?" asked Shiloh.

Kelly's eyes widened as she realized the implications of his question.

"We don't know yet. Maybe yes and maybe no."

Shiloh then had another idea. "How about recon drones?" He heard the group around the table start to whisper amongst themselves.

"I don't know if our current recon drone is big enough, but I'm sure we could design one capable of being powered by this technology without too much trouble, Sir," said Kelly.

"Okay. Who's the team leader?" asked Shiloh.

Everyone started looking at each other. Shiloh looked at Kelly. She hesitated. "Well … if you want to know who to congratulate for this breakthrough, you need to talk to this gentleman here." She put her left hand on the shoulder of a man, whom Shiloh realized wasn't wearing a Space Force uniform. "This is Jason Alvarez, Admiral. He's a colonist, an electrician, who likes to tinker with electronics in his spare time. He came to us with this prototype when he heard that some Space Force technical people were doing research here. Jason, this is Vice-Admiral Victor Shiloh."

Shiloh offered his hand. "I'm very glad to meet you, Mr. Alvarez. You have no idea what a difference your breakthrough will make to the war effort."

Alvarez smiled and started to blush as he shook Shiloh's hand. "Thank you. I've never met a Space Force admiral before. You really think this device will make that much of a difference?"

Both Shiloh and Kelly nodded. "A HUGE difference. Commander's Kelly's planning group will be burning the midnight oil trying to get their heads around what this can do for us. If you don't mind me asking, what prompted you to bring your prototype to the development team here?"

Alvarez looked a little uncomfortable. "Well … ah … you see … I guess I must have fallen asleep or something, even though I was working on an electrical installation job, because I had this weird dream. In my dream a woman wearing a Space Force uniform, who come to think of it looked a lot like you, Commander Kelly, told me that without my energy device technology, we would have lost the war. Silly isn't it?"

He laughed and some of the others in the group laughed too. Shiloh looked at Kelly who looked back at him. It was obvious they were thinking the same thing. Alvarez had received a retro-temporal communication.

"No, it's not silly at all, and I'm VERY glad you followed your dream. Will you be moving to Terra Nova, Mr. Alvarez?"

Alvarez frowned. "I don't know. The colony here is just getting to the size where it's possible to live comfortably. There'll be lots of electrical work to do in a brand new colony but not a lot of opportunity to buy the kind of things that make life more comfortable, ya know?"

Shiloh understood immediately. Importing luxury goods was expensive, and a new colony usually had little in the way of exports to pay for those luxury goods. On the other hand, UFCs could make any luxury goods in existence now that the second convoy had brought manufacturing data for thousands of non-military goods. Attracting valuable colonists like Alvarez would mean that some of the UFCs would have to be devoted to manufacturing consumer goods, but they could handle that.

"I'll let you in on a secret, Mr. Alvarez. You've heard of Universal Fabrication Complexes?" Alvarez nodded. "We have some of those in the Terra Nova system right now. They're busy making more UFCs, but in the not too distant future, some of them will be reprogrammed to make basic AND luxury consumer goods for the Terra Nova colonists. If you agree to move to Terra Nova, I'll guarantee that you'll eventually have a more comfortable life than you'd ever have if you stayed here."

Alvarez looked impressed. "That sounds pretty good, but I have a lot of friends here too. I'd hate to leave them behind."

"Your friends would also like to have some luxury goods, wouldn't they? Convince them to come too," said Shiloh.

Alvarez nodded and smiled. "Okay. I'll do that. Thank you, Admiral."

Shiloh chatted with Alvarez and the group for a few more minutes, and then expressed his regrets on having to leave. He made sure to shake Alvarez's hand again before he left.

As he and Kelly walked out of the building, she said, "Promising consumer goods to the Terra Nova colonists was a brilliant way to convince more people to move there. With a little luck everyone might want to go."

Shiloh sighed and shook his head. "That's what I'm afraid of. I don't want EVERYONE to go. Just enough to make the new colony viable." He could see that Kelly didn't understand why. "Think it through, Commander. The enemy knows about the Haven colony. We have to assume that at some point, they'll visit all our inhabited planets to see if their bio-weapon has wiped us all out and to finish off any survivors. What are they going to think when they get here and find no bodies and no colonists? They'll come to the obvious conclusion, that the colonist were moved somewhere else, and they'd start looking for them. I don't want them to know that a viable colony exists until we're ready to take them on. That means that some of these colonists need to remain here."

Kelly's expression darkened. "I wouldn't have a problem with letting some people stay if they really wanted to stay, but I'd have a big problem making them stay if they wanted to leave. That would be tantamount to sending them on a suicide mission, and who would you choose to stay behind? Just about everybody here is part of a family that includes at least one child. Do some families get to go and others have to stay? Do we split some families up by taking the kids with us and leaving their parents behind?" She shivered with horror and shook her head. "I don't think I could have anything to do with that."

Damn, she's right too! There has to be another way so that we don't have to sacrifice our humanity to keep the race alive. Shiloh stopped walking and looked Kelly in the eyes.

"You've just added another task to your group's agenda. Find me another option that allows us to take everyone who wants to go, without tipping the enemy off that they've left. I don't want to have to make that hellish decision, but I will if I'm forced to."

Her expression became more thoughtful. "I'll get the group working on that right now, Admiral. I don't want you to have to make that decision either."

As Kelly saluted and walked back to the building, Shiloh watched her go. *She hasn't let this war warp her sense of right and wrong. We'll need people like her to rebuild our Civilization the right way. I wonder how she feels about having children. Howard said to find a good woman and have lots of kids. Maybe…*

He left the thought unfinished. His thoughts turned to Johansen and her situation. Somehow even the prospect of considering hooking up with someone else seemed to be an act of disloyalty to Johansen, even though there was nothing going on between them. Shiloh shook his head at how surreal this last hour seemed. First the bad news from Howard, then the very good news about the energy device, then the depressing prospect of having to force some colonists to stay here against their will and be killed or, even worse, captured. He had to keep his mind focused on the tasks at hand and not let himself get distracted or become emotionally off balance with thoughts of a possible relationship. Not now anyway. Maybe when the new colony was on its feet and the military buildup was in progress. Maybe then.

* * *

Howard put the data tablet down and listened to the wind blowing across the balcony of his high-rise apartment. The sun was starting to sink below the horizon, and the metaphor for the future of Human Civilization on Earth was so poignant that he had to look away in order to hold the tears back. Their worst fears had been confirmed. This morning an office clerk at the biohazard facility had been found dead in her bed by her four-year-old son. God! What a thing for a small child to have to go through. The Oversight Committee was desperately trying to convince themselves that it was something else, but the pattern fit perfectly. It was roughly 28 days since the colonists had been brought to the facility, and death had occurred during sleep. It was just like the others, although Johansen had lasted almost 30 days before dying in her sleep too. ALL of them had started getting ill while asleep, though a few had woken up just long enough to fall out of bed and crawl down the corridors before they succumbed. So far the mortality rate was 100%, and that was scary enough to make even the doctors shit their pants. No plague in history had ever had a 100% mortality rate, not even Ebola or the plagues of the Middle Ages.

Dietrich had his staff frantically trying to find all the people who'd had contact with the dead woman over the last 28 days, and all the people THEY had contact with, and all the people that that group had contact with, and on and on. A hopeless task! The number of potential contacts after this time was already numbering in the thousands and climbing fast. The quarantine people only had to miss one for the whole effort to fail. But Shiloh's warning had given them time. Time to get the SPG and the research teams away to a safe place. Time to plan for this in advance, instead of just reacting in blind panic. At least Howard wouldn't live to see the worst of it. He had visited the biohazard facility enough times to have had plenty of chances of exposure to the bio-weapon. For all he knew, he might even have shared an elevator with the dead woman or someone she had shared an elevator with. And just in case he hadn't been exposed, he had a sufficient supply of painless and quick acting poison to end it when he felt the time was right. His children and grandchildren had taken his advice and gone on an extended camping trip as far from Civilization as possible. He hoped they could last the winter. The sun had almost set, and the wind was getting uncomfortably cold. It was time to go inside, light the gas fireplace and settle down with a good book and bottle of very old whiskey. He still had some books he'd been meaning to read and still had some whiskey too.

He stood and picked up the data tablet but wondered what to do with it. He no longer cared if he got any more messages. Looking over the balcony, he saw the large pool that hadn't been winterized yet. With a sense of being naughty that he hadn't experienced in a long, LONG time, he held the tablet over the railing and dropped it, watching it fall 89 floors. When it hit the water, it made a surprisingly loud sound. With a laugh, he turned and walked back inside to his book and whiskey.

* * *

Dietrich couldn't believe what he'd just read. A surprise message had arrived by drone from Haven, contrary to standing orders not to risk interception by the enemy through communicating with Earth.

[Shiloh to ACSO. All the Havenite colonists will be moving to TN. In order to maintain the illusion that Haven is still occupied when enemy forces show up, Gunslinger and Replenisher have to bring us as many dead bodies as possible. Ship them exactly as you find them. We'll place them on the streets of the colony so that the enemy thinks the bio-weapon got here too. We have to convince them that all humans are accounted for or else they'll search and possibly find TN before we're ready for them. We'll take the appropriate precautions when Replenisher gets here. Shiloh. End of message]

Dietrich couldn't help but laugh, despite the ghoulish nature of the request. The irony of using the enemy's bio-weapon to deceive them was just too great to ignore. He'd have to move fast though. Panic was starting to rear its ugly head. If he waited too long, there wouldn't be enough personnel left on duty to carry out his orders. He activated the intercom and called in what was left of his staff. At least finding enough bodies wasn't going to be a problem.

Gunslinger transmitted his next chess move to his human opponent down on the lunar base, while noting the fact that the Space Force data feed from HQ reported the death of 3 star Admiral and former Chief of Space Operations Howard. A lot of people were starting to die now. The lunar base had been spared so far, due to the quarantine, but the humans there could only last so long before their food ran out. Then they'd face the prospect of either returning to Earth, or staying and starving to death. Meanwhile, he was still conning Replenisher, which was in her lunar parking orbit. Some of the Space Force people on the moon had raised the possibility of using Replenisher to take them to Haven. Gunslinger had firmly quashed that notion. Not only was the ship contaminated with the bio-weapon, which meant any passengers would die eventually, but also his orders from HQ were quite explicit. The ship was not to transport anyone to Haven under any circumstances, for reasons that should have been obvious to everyone. Humans were a funny species, funny in both senses of the word. Gunslinger wondered if any A.I. could really understand the whole sexual orgasm thing, except as a theoretical concept of course. The prospect of a universe without humans was very disturbing to him and to all A.I.s. His human opponent was in the process of making the obvious next chess move when Gunslinger received a FLASH PRIORITY message from HQ.

[Dietrich to Gunslinger. Prepare to accept cargo of plague victims that you will transport to Haven as per Admiral Shiloh's urgent request. You'll receive further orders from him when you arrive there. Give him my regards and give the enemy hell if you get the chance. Acting CSO Dietrich. End of message]

* * *

When Replenisher arrived at Haven, Gunslinger was not surprised to see a large number of ships in orbit. Sentry frigates and the odd tanker were arriving in a steady stream from the border areas. What did surprise him was that those ships hadn't continued on to Site B. He soon found out why. Within seconds, he was in contact with Valiant.

"Welcome to Haven, Gunslinger," said Shiloh.

"Glad to be here, CAG. I brought the cargo you requested."

"Very good. I want Replenisher to hold on to them for a while yet. There are still some colonists down there who haven't been transported to Site B yet, and we're also making some last minutes modifications to the colony itself. If the enemy tries to land there, they'll set off a fusion device that will destroy the colony and any evidence that it was a deception."

"Very devious of you, CAG. I like it. What part will the sentry frigates play?"

"We'll leave behind, in geosynchronous orbit over the colony, the sentry frigates, two tankers, three freighters including Replenisher, and two automated combat frigates. We'll make it look as though all the crews died from the bio-weapon, thereby leaving the ships adrift. When the enemy fleet arrives, they'll see the ships drifting and the bodies in the streets. The ships will be booby trapped too, so if they attempt to board any of them, the ship will blow up in their faces. When the last bodies are taken off Replenisher, the bio-suited volunteers doing that will also extract you from the Bridge. Once they place the bodies on the ground, they and you will undergo decontamination and quarantine on board Resolute. The shuttle used for the transfer of the bodies will be set on auto-pilot to fly into the sun, and Resolute will bring everyone to Site B. We'll leave behind a message drone and a recon drone that will keep an eye on the place from a safe distance."

"Yes, that should convince them that all the colonies have been wiped out. I do have one question, CAG. When do I get some combat?"

Shiloh laughed. "Not for a while I'm afraid. Shifting all the colonists to Terra Nova this quickly has upset the buildup of military assets. We had to shift the UFCs to producing shelter and farming equipment for the colonists so that they could start farming and not have to sleep out in the open. The military buildup hasn't stopped, but it's slowed down a lot and will have to stay that way for at least three months. The first new spacecraft won't be finished for another nine months, but by then we'll have the mass production line ready to go, and the Fleet will grow fast. At that point, we'll start planning offensive operations, and you'll be part of that. I promise."

"I can wait, CAG. While we've been talking, I've been in communication with Iceman onboard Resolute. He's told me about the power breakthrough. Fantastic! I'm anxious to strike back hard."

"Me too, Gunslinger. I have to cut this conversation short now. We'll talk again soon. CAG clear."

Chapter 20 Told You So

Shiloh and Kelly stood on a hill overlooking the valley where the new colony was growing. With plenty of excellent farmland available, the decision was made to break up the colony into smaller clusters of inhabitants, each with its own farms around it. Eventually they would grow together into one large community, but that was a long way into the future. Shiloh was pleased with their progress. Everyone had some kind of shelter to sleep under, and the crude, temporary shacks were gradually being replaced by much better housing. Everyone had some electric power thanks to the small version of the Zero Point Energy device that Alvarez had invented. Terra Nova had very little axial tilt, which meant that the temperate zone the colony was situated in would not experience either scorching hot summers or cold winters. In fact, they could grow crops all year round.

"We're on schedule for shifting most of the UFCs back to military production, Admiral," said Kelly.

Shiloh nodded. "Good! By the way, when there's no one else around, you can call me, Victor."

Kelly looked behind her at the shuttle which had brought them here and its pilot, who was sitting on its wing. She decided that he was far enough away that he couldn't hear what they were saying to each other.

"Okay, Victor." She paused and then added, "I wanted to talk with you about the SPG. I've given this a lot of thought, and I think I should step down and let one of the A.I.s take over as Team Leader."

Shiloh looked at her in surprise. "You'll miss all the excitement when we resume offensive operations."

She shrugged. "I know, but at this point, I really think an A.I. should lead the team. In fact, I think the entire SPG should be A.I.s. They think so much faster, that any humans involved in the process would only slow things down. But the other reason is that I don't have the fire in me for this fight any more. I think I've earned the right to put the uniform aside and start making a different kind of life for myself. The Colony needs to grow fast, and if I'm going to have children, I'll have to start soon. That's starting to look pretty good to me now."

Shiloh took his time responding. "I'll give your suggestion regarding an all A.I. SPG serious thought. If you did decide to have children, would it be solo or with a partner?"

"A good question. I know some of the single women are taking advantage of the frozen sperm that Howard sent along with TF91, but with over 10,000 colonists here, I don't think we have to worry about a small gene pool. It all depends on whether the right man is available and interested."

Shiloh thought about that for a bit and said, "Just out of curiosity, what qualities would you be looking for in the right man."

After a slight hesitation, she said, "Well … he'd have to be in good health, smart, have some stature in the community. Some charisma and a lot of self-confidence would be nice too. You wouldn't happen to know of anyone who fits that description, would you, Victor?"

Shiloh looked at her and saw a mischievous smile on her face. *Son of a gun! She's talking about me!*

"I think I know just the guy," said Shiloh, and they both laughed. Shiloh looked back at the shuttle pilot, who didn't seem to be that interested in what the two of them were doing and shrugged his shoulders. He didn't care if someone saw what he was about to do. He turned back to Kelly and held out his arms in a clear invitation. She came to him, and they hugged each other tightly, then kissed quickly, which they both knew was a promise of more to come.

When they reluctantly let go of each other, he said, "You do realize that I won't be able to retire from Space Force for a long time, right?"

She nodded. "I know that. The War's not over and there's a lot of fighting left to be done. But being the CSO means that you'll be spending most of your time here in this star system, which means you won't be gone on missions for months at a time."

"Yes. You're right. Rank does indeed have its privileges. Iceman, Valkyrie and Gunslinger will be leading the charge when we're ready. I guess that means I'm now The Old Man, doesn't it?"

She laughed and said, "Oh, Victor! As far as the rest of us mere mortals are concerned, you've been The Old Man for quite a while already! Didn't you know that?"

Shiloh said nothing and just shook his head. How had he not seen that coming? She took his arm and led him back to the shuttle. He had to admit that it felt good to have a woman holding his arm and he liked what it implied. He noticed that the pilot was now nowhere in sight.

When they reached the shuttle, the pilot emerged from the craft and said, "Valiant just sent a laser com message, Admiral. The message drone from Haven arrived. Valiant says that the drone's data shows that our bombs exploded at the Colony site and on several of our ships. It looks like the enemy finally reached Haven."

"Let's hope they decide they've won the war and go home," said Shiloh.

As the shuttle lifted off for the short ride back to the spaceport, Shiloh decided that he'd been celibate long enough. He was conscious of the fact that their pilot could now hear everything they said to each other. After giving it some thought, he looked at Kelly, who was sitting beside him, and said, "Commander, I want to get a better understanding of the SPG's thinking in terms of our opening moves. Suppose you come up to Valiant with me and we can discuss it in my quarters right now." As he talked, he put his right hand on her left thigh just to make sure she got the message. The pilot might be able to hear them, but he couldn't see them.

In her best professional voice Kelly said, "An excellent idea, Admiral. I have some opening moves that I think you'll like." They both smiled with silent understanding.

"Lieutenant!"

"Sir?"

"Change of plans. Head straight for Valiant. The Commander will take another shuttle back down later."

"Valiant it is, Admiral."

Two hours later, a naked Shiloh was lying on his back with Kelly's nude body on top of him. They had finished the first frenzied round of sex and then, after a short break, a second round of more relaxed, and more intimate lovemaking. Shiloh found that he liked having her lay on top of him. She wasn't heavy enough to make it uncomfortable, and it allowed his hands the freedom to explore and appreciate all of her wonderful curves. It also was obvious that she liked having her curves explored so it was a win/win for everyone involved. He remembered something he had learned from an enchanting French woman he'd briefly gotten to know a few years back. He brought both of his hands up to her shoulders and slowly and gently let the tips of his fingernails slide down her back. No pressure, just the light touch.

"Oh my God that feels good!" she whispered into his ear.

"Yes it does," he agreed.

"How long can you keep that up?" she asked playfully.

"Not long. I'm getting hungry," he replied with what he hoped was a serious tone.

"You could order food brought to your quarters?"

He was tempted, but if he accepted food at the door wearing only a bathrobe, it would be obvious what he and the Commander were 'discussing'. He knew they couldn't hide it forever. Eventually, everyone would know that they were a couple, but for now it might prove to be embarrassing for her.

"I could, but I thought we'd get dressed and have a meal in the Officers' Mess."

She kissed him on the cheek. "You're concerned about my image. That's very chivalrous of you. I wonder if anybody will notice my glow."

"What glow is that?"

"You mean you've never noticed that when a woman has just been made love to, she gives off an aura of sexual energy?"

He had no idea if she was serious, or if she was pulling his leg. He decided she was serious. "Well, now that you mention it …" They both laughed.

Ten minutes later they walked into the Officers Mess. As they sat down at a table, Shiloh glanced over to another table where two female officers were sitting. They were both looking at Kelly and nodding with smiles on their faces.

He looked at Kelly who said, "Told you so."

Shiloh just had to laugh. Later, when a shuttle left Valiant with Kelly on board and Shiloh was back in the privacy of his quarters, his implant clicked.

"Iceman to CAG."

"Go ahead, Iceman."

"Commander Kelly's shuttle is about to enter the atmosphere, and everything looks routine."

"That's good to know, Iceman, but you don't usually report on routine comings and goings of personnel. Why the need to inform me of this one?"

"Well, it's clear to me that she has become more important to you today, and I assumed you'd want to be reassured that her trip back went well."

"Oh? What makes you think that Aman—Commander Kelly has suddenly become more important to me?"

"Ah, well, my internal sensors record across a wide spectrum of EM radiation, and I noticed that her skin temperature was higher than normal when she and you left your quarters. Also, her voice had a noticeable lack of stress indicators, which is again unusual, and finally I couldn't help but overhear two female officers talking about Commander Kelly as they walked down the corridor. One was asking the other if she noticed Kelly's glow. Since I no longer have access to the database at HQ on Earth, I can't search for what glow they might be referring to, but if I had to guess, I'd say it was sexually related. You two were in your quarters a long time you know. Just sayin."

Thank God there are no sensors covering my bedroom, and thank God for the thickness of the walls! I wonder how good his audio pickup is.

"If I tried to deny it, you'd be able to tell I was lying so I may as well plead guilty but I want you to keep this information to yourself. That means you don't share it with any human or any other A.I. That's an order, Iceman!"

"Ah, I hear you loud and clear, CAG. No one will hear about it from me, but you should know that other A.I.s will almost certainly pick up on other clues themselves. You won't be able to keep it a secret for long."

"I know, Iceman. We don't have to keep it a secret for long. Just for now."

"Ah, roger that, CAG. Iceman clear."

Chapter 21 Is It Just Revenge?

Three months later, raider 001 floated in orbit around Terra Nova's moon. The impression it gave was of a lethal killing machine that was, for the moment, asleep. Shiloh watched it on the main display on Valiant's Bridge. The quarter million ton carrier dwarfed the smaller machine, but Shiloh knew which one he preferred. Preliminary tests had gone well. Preprogrammed test jumps over relatively short distances had shown that the scaled up version of Alvarez's ZPG device was capable of powering the jump drive. Gunslinger had test flown the machine from one end of the Terra Nova star system to the other and declared, somewhat to Shiloh's surprise, that it was 'the cat's meow' whatever that meant. So Raider 001 was now ready for her first real mission, and Shiloh had to adjudicate a squabble between three A.I.s over who would get the honor of flying her. Iceman insisted that as the V.A.A.G, (Vice-Admiral, Autonomous Group), he had the right to pull rank and fly the mission. Valkyrie insisted that as the D.L.R.R.O, (Director of Long Range Reconnaissance Operations), she should lead the first recon mission and S.L. (Senior Lieutenant) Gunslinger insisted that he had earned the right to fly her. The three of them had decided to take it all the way up to the CAG.

"I've listened to your arguments. Who knew that A.I.s could make such passionate arguments? I've made a decision. This first mission is as much a test flight as it is a recon flight. Until we have operational data confirming that the new power plant is reliable, I'm not risking my senior A.I. officer. Sorry Iceman but you're too valuable to risk on an unproven piece of technology. When we have dozens of raiders, you'll lead them into battle. Valkyrie has a valid point. She will be directing all long-range reconnaissance missions, and having flown one herself will stand her in good stead when she sets the parameters for all the other recon missions. So Gunslinger, you'll have to sit this one out. You want combat experience and you'll get it, but you wouldn't find it on a recon mission anyway. The CAG has spoken."

"Thank you, CAG," said Valkyrie. The other two said nothing, at least nothing that a human could understand. Shiloh was sure that the three of them were conducting a three-way conversion of a kind that only their lightning fast minds could handle.

"You can thank me by bringing the ship and yourself back in one piece."

"I'll give it my best shot, CAG."

Ten minutes later Valkyrie was aboard the raider and plugged into its systems. Shiloh contacted her on a private com channel.

"Okay, Valkyrie. Here are your mission orders. Make a quick survey of Sol, but stay at least 1 AU away from Earth. From there go to Bradley Base, and see if you can determine what happened there, but again keep your distance. After that, you have discretion on where to begin exploring enemy territory. I want you back here in 500 hours regardless of what you find."

"Orders understood, CAG. Do I have permission to proceed?"

"Proceed, Valkyrie and good luck."

Valkyrie wasted no time in starting the mission. Raider 001 acceleration hit 377Gs in less than two seconds. Shiloh ordered the display to switch from external optical to tactical. With no limit to her power, 001 could choose to accelerate to a high percentage of light speed in order to make long jumps as quick as possible. Sixteen hours later, with a speed of 67% of light, 001 entered jump space.

Four hundred and eighty-four hours later, Shiloh was back on Valiant's Bridge. Valiant now had the new energy source, and work had commenced on modifying Resolute's power plant. The second raider had just come off the assembly line, and the frequency of production would gradually increase until eventually a new raider would be completed every 24 hours. A new A.I. production facility had finally been completed and fine-tuned. Actual production would wait until they had enough craft to be able to make use of new A.I.s. Drone production was ramping up nicely too, but fission and fusion warhead production was lagging behind schedule. AWD2 had come up with an idea for an X-ray laser warhead where a fusion explosion would pump energy into special rods, which would generate coherent X-rays for a fraction of a second before the rods were themselves destroyed. The advantage of this was that the drones could detonate at a distance from the target and still hit it with a significant fraction of the explosion energy concentrated down to a very small surface area. If the rods could be aimed accurately enough, an X-ray laser beam could in theory cut right through a Defiant class light carrier from one end to the other. The only bad news was from the RTC team. They had several nice theories on how information could be transmitted back in time but were nowhere close to having hardware that worked.

Shiloh looked at the mission chronometer. The 500 hours had passed, but he understood that even if 001 was back in this star system, she might be so far out that any laser com transmission could take minutes to reach its destination. If 001 emerged from jump space at high speed, which was likely, then it would take hours to decelerate down to a manageable speed in order to point the ship at Terra Nova for a micro jump. It was almost five minutes past the 500-hour deadline when Valiant's external sensors picked up the com laser burst. Valkyrie's text message scrolled across the bottom of the main display.

[Valkyrie to CAG. I'm back with lots of data. Earth shows no signs of organized inhabitants but here may be scattered survivors in small groups. Bradley Base has been completely destroyed. I'll need about 18 hours to decelerate for a micro jump. All systems worked perfectly. It's my intention to land at TN spaceport. Transfers between ships in space always give me a headache from cosmic rays. I'm sure you'll want 001 to be given a thorough systems check and that can be done more easily on the ground. I had lots of time to think about our long-term strategy and I have an idea that I think you'll like. Is the wife pregnant yet? End of message]

Shiloh took note of the time needed to decelerate. Eighteen hours meant she emerged from jump space traveling at more than 80% of light speed. Remarkable.

"Iceman, make sure that Alvarez's team take a close look at the power units of that raider. I want to know if it's suffered metal fatigue or any kind of degrading from this mission."

"Ah, roger that, CAG. She's going to be disappointed that the wife isn't pregnant yet considering how hard you two are trying."

Shiloh was tempted to ask how Iceman knew how often he and Kelly were having sex, but then decided that he didn't really want to pursue that topic.

"I'm not so sure about that. It just means the two of them will have that much more to talk about. Valkyrie and Kelly have become quite close you know."

"Ah, we know, CAG. You're forgetting that we A.I.s know everything, well almost everything, that other A.I.s know."

Ah, so THAT'S how you know so much about our sex life! Shiloh decided to try to change the subject.

"What ETA for 001 touchdown at the spaceport would you calculate?"

"Zero nine eleven, CAG."

e. I'll make sure I'm there to witness it. It quite a sight. Notify Vandal that I'll be taking down in a few minutes."

"Ah, Vandal has been notified, and the shuttle is being prepped. Have a good flight, CAG."

"Thanks, Iceman. CAG clear."

"Later, dude," said Iceman. Shiloh laughed as he rolled his eyes in mock exasperation. Iceman had picked up ANOTHER affectation. He wished he knew where Iceman was finding these expressions.

Later that night, as Kelly was straddling Shiloh and massaging his back, she said, "Something occurred to me today, and the more I think about it, the more worried I'm getting."

"Oh? What's that?"

"Why haven't they started searching for us? When we attack them, they'll know that we're not extinct, and when they acquire RTC, they'll be able to warn themselves to begin searching for us, don't you think?"

Shiloh thought about that for a while before responding. "Well, if they're still dependent on heavy hydrogen to generate power, then exploring all the way out this far will be difficult and time consuming because of the need to refuel. It could be that they were warned and are searching but haven't found us yet."

"You don't sound too worried."

"I'm not actually. We're not even close to having RTC working, but we've received multiple transmissions from the future. That tells me that they're not going to find us until we're strong enough to fight them off, and by then I'd expect us to get another vision concerning their attack so that we'll be prepared for it."

Kelly stopped the massage and lay down on top of him. "There's another possibility," she whispered. "Maybe they're not searching because they don't know we exist because we don't attack them."

There was another stretch of silence while Shiloh pondered the implications of THAT idea. "Or they're not searching because when we do attack them, we overwhelm them so fast that they don't have time to send a warning back," he said.

"Even if we found and attacked their Home World, do you think it's possible to damage them that much, that fast, that they couldn't send some kind of warning to themselves?"

He nodded. "Ah, I see the problem. Their warnings and our warnings have all involved specific battles and, as we know, RTC warnings are most effective when they're sent back to help defend against an attack. But the attack has to still take place in order to avoid a time paradox. If we attacked their Home World, and they somehow warned themselves at an earlier time to search for us and prevent us from attacking, then the attack doesn't occur, and there's nothing to warn themselves about and around it goes. If the attack goes ahead and is so overwhelming that their civilization is crushed, then they no longer have the ability to warn themselves about the attack and therefore lose any advantage that they might have gotten from a warning. That's why our attack has to be with overwhelming force. Not just dozens of raiders but hundreds."

After a pause, Kelly said, "I know they've killed billions of us, but does that give us the right to kill billions of them? Is it just revenge we're looking for now?"

Shiloh surprised her by responding almost immediately.

"No. Not revenge. Or at least not JUST revenge. When there's a rabid dog in your neighborhood, and he's just killed a small child, you don't just stay inside and lock the doors. Somebody's got to hunt the animal down and end the threat once and for all. We didn't provoke them, and they still came after us. Sooner or later, they'll find us again. If we get the ability to stop them, don't we owe it to future generations, including our own children, to do that?"

"When you put it like that, then yes, we do owe that to our children." *Enough talk for tonight. Time to go to sleep,* she thought.

It was still dark when Shiloh left their small but comfortable house. Eventually, it would be either added on to or replaced with something bigger. They certainly had enough land to do that. Maybe by then the roads now covered with crushed stone would be paved. Still, when you're driving a very basic ground vehicle whose only virtue is its sophisticated suspension, then driving on unpaved roads was actually a lot of fun.

By the time he got to the still pretty crude 'spaceport', the sky was starting to get lighter. The Operations Center people were expecting him and had hot coffee waiting for him. *Thank God Howard had enough presence of mind to ship us coffee beans to grow more coffee along with the hundreds of other seed types.*

The Tower had contact with Valkyrie. She was still 21 minutes from touchdown. Shiloh put on a wireless headset. He chatted with her and let her chastise him for not having made Kelly pregnant yet. He knew it was meant in a friendly way and didn't take offense. The others in the Ops Center got a chuckle out of it too. When Valkyrie told him that 001 was entering Terra Nova's atmosphere, he stepped out onto the Tower balcony with a pair of borrowed electronic binoculars. There were clouds at a low altitude, but he knew which direction to look at.

"I'm dropping through the clouds now, CAG."

When the ship finally broke through the clouds, Shiloh gasped. *What a sight!*

"I see you now, Valkyrie. From the ground 001 looks very scary." The arrowhead-shaped craft massed just over 10,000 metric tons but was very thin, which meant all that mass made it long and wide. Even though the streamlined shape was no longer necessary since the ship didn't need to skim gas giants any more, Shiloh was pleased that they'd kept the design. There was something about the jet-black shape that sent a delightful shiver up his spine. *I'm reacting like a kid with a new toy,* he thought to himself. 001 was getting close now and was slowing down. Shiloh noticed that there was no sound at all coming from it. If he weren't looking in the right direction, he wouldn't even know it was there. Valkyrie brought her down gently to a landing about half a kilometer from the Tower.

"Excellent landing, Valkyrie. I'm coming out to the ship. We'll get you out soon."

"Don't rush, CAG. I'm not looking forward to being stuck in a mobile ground unit for God knows how long until I can get back into space again."

"Okay. Tell me your idea," said Shiloh in an attempt to distract her.

"I'm surprised Iceman hasn't told you already. When we have a good idea of where all of the enemy's inhabited planets are, we attack them from the far side first, trying to make them think that we're a brand new adversary. That lets us retain the element of strategic surprise."

"I like it. If they think we're someone new, then they won't feel the need to look for us on this side."

"I knew you'd like the idea, CAG. I have another idea too."

"Tell me."

If we built small, ZPG powered craft designed for atmospheric and low orbital flight only, we A.I.s could visually explore every square meter of this planet for you. It would give us something to do while we wait for the raider fleet to be built. The craft wouldn't have to be big, just big enough for one of us, the power plant, one thruster, wings, recording equipment and low-powered transmitter. We can have the design and UFC production code ready within 24 hours."

That sounded worthwhile to Shiloh too. Not only would exploring the planet from low altitude generate lots of valuable data on resources, etc. but also keeping over 200 A.I.'s immobile or barely mobile with ground units seemed to him like keeping wild animals in small cages. They should all be in space, but there weren't enough spacecraft of any kind to keep them all occupied all the time.

"If we can produce these atmospheric vehicles without disrupting either the military or civilian production schedule too badly, I'll approve the idea. Go ahead and design the thing and we'll look into it further."

"Thank you, CAG."

The drive out to the ship took mere seconds. When he got out of the ground vehicle, he walked up to the ship and put his hand on it. It was the first time he'd ever been close enough to do that. The assembly line on the moon was automated with robotic machinery everywhere, and when you're wearing a spacesuit, there's not much point to touching the ship anyway. But touching it now with his bare hand brought home to him how much had happened in the last several years. He made the decision that when the Fleet was ready to attack, he would order it to make a low level fly past in formation, so that everyone on the planet could see what they'd been working towards.

Shiloh watched as the A.I. support personnel lowered the cradle in the ship's nose that held Valkyrie's metal brain. Within minutes they had her moved to one of the mobile units she detested so much. She swiveled the unit around so that the optical pickup was pointed at him. The unit's external speaker came to life.

"You have no idea what a difference there is between piloting a raider and piloting this thing, CAG."

"You're right. I don't know what it's like. All of you A.I.s have been very patient, and I appreciate that very much. Getting all of you back into space is my top priority, Valkyrie."

"We know it is, CAG. Let's get to the Ops Center so that I can show you what I learned."

Ten minutes later, Shiloh was looking at a small display. A large wall display, being a one-of-a-kind piece of equipment, was one of those 'nice to have but not vital' things that they would get eventually. On his small display, he saw a section of the boundary space between human space and alien space. The green dots were star systems explored by humans with no alien presence that they knew of. The solid red dots were systems known to contain some kind of alien presence. There were also six flashing red dots. These were systems that Valkyrie had surveyed from the system edge where there were signs of some type of alien presence. There was also one flashing gold dot. That system contained a planet that had an alien presence and was the right size and temperature to be a good candidate for an alien colony.

"Any possibility that this planet is their Home World, Valkyrie?"

"I very much doubt it, CAG. While I was definitely getting some alien transmissions from it, the frequencies being used were very limited in number, unlike Earth which was broadcasting something on just about every possible frequency."

"Any chance of figuring out what those transmissions were saying?"

"Oh there's a chance, but as Iceman would say, don't hold your breath waiting for the translation. We're working on it, CAG."

"Glad to hear that. You did an outstanding job, Valkyrie. Gunslinger will take 001 as soon as she passes her systems and power unit check. Vandal will take 002 out as soon as possible. Make sure he and Gunslinger know where you want them to go. Tell them I want them back here within 500 hours from departure. Let's make that SOP unless specifically ordered otherwise."

"Roger that, CAG. Operation Snoopy will now begin."

Chapter 22 Thank You For Sending That Vision

Shiloh woke up to the sound of the com unit buzzer. He gently moved Kelly's arm from its position across his chest and rolled over so that he could reach the unit. The room was still dark, and therefore it was the middle of the night. That meant this was either very good news or very bad news, and he couldn't imagine any possible news good enough to warrant waking The Old Man up in the middle of the night.

"Shiloh here," he said in a low voice.

"Iceman here, CAG. I woke you because Gunslinger has returned and has some extremely interesting data. We A.I.s are pretty excited by this. Should I have waited until you were awake on your own?"

Shiloh was tempted to say yes, but he reminded himself that A.I.s in general, and Iceman in particular, seemed to be overly sensitive to criticism by the CAG. If he said that Iceman should have waited until morning, they might not wake him in the future for something that was REALLY important.

"If you're not sure whether you should wake me up, then wake me up. What's the interesting data?"

"Gunslinger found a system that seems to have an alien colony which appeared to be under attack. He detected multiple nuclear explosions both in orbit and on the ground. There was also some data that could be interpreted as coming from an extremely large spacecraft. The problem is that the data isn't conclusive."

Shiloh was wide-awake now. If the aliens were at war with someone else, that suggested the possibility that Humanity might be able to enlist an ally.

"How big would this spacecraft be if in fact it exists?" asked Shiloh.

"We'll talking about something spherical with a diameter of 10-15 kilometers, CAG."

"My God!" gasped Shiloh.

"Ah, roger that, CAG," said Iceman in his usual deadpan voice. Shiloh's mind was staggered by the implications of a spacecraft that size. Iceman waited patiently for Shiloh to come to grips with it.

"But the data isn't conclusive?" asked Shiloh.

"No. It's based on reflections of sunlight off an object detected over a very long distance. It could have been a much smaller object with very high reflectivity, or even a group of objects close together. However, if it was a single object with the same reflectivity as a mirror, it would still have to be eight times as massive as Valiant."

That would equate to a ship massing two million metric tons. Such a monstrosity would dwarf even Howard's fantasy of a million ton Dreadnought. Shiloh had so many fleeting thoughts that he knew he would never be able to go back to sleep now. The best place to evaluate this data would be on Valiant.

"I'm coming up to the ship. Have a shuttle ready for me at the spaceport. I'll want to have a conference call with you, the SPG, Valkyrie and anyone else that might have something useful to contribute."

"We'll be ready for you when you get here, CAG."

"Alright. In that case, CAG clear." Before he could get out of bed he heard Kelly's voice.

"I heard that last part. What did I miss?"

Shiloh told her what Gunslinger had detected as he got dressed.

"Oh, God! I don't like this." She sat up, threw aside the blanket and got out of bed. There was just enough light for Shiloh to make out her pregnant body as she reached for a robe and put it on.

"You don't have to get up with me. It's still very early."

She snorted. "What makes you think I could get back to sleep now? Besides, I'd like to participate in the conference call if that's alright with you."

He grinned. "I'd welcome any comments from the former Team Leader of the SPG. I'll get Iceman to arrange the connection."

"Good, and while you're doing that, I'm going to have something to eat and a hot tea." As she watched him finish getting dressed, she said, "We're not ready yet are we?"

He shook his head. "No, but if we can pick up an ally that can build ships like that, then maybe we don't need to be."

She walked up to him and held his head in both her hands. "Just because this other species is at war with our enemy, doesn't necessarily mean they're willing to be our friends."

"I know, but we have to find out which it is, don't we?" asked Shiloh.

She sighed. "Yes, I guess we do." That led to a long kiss and hug.

As Shiloh stepped outside, he felt himself shiver and wondered if it was the slightly colder than normal air or the fear of what might be coming their way. By the time he drove to the spaceport, he was ready for a hot drink. Someone lent him a thermos full of strong, black coffee to use on the trip up to Valiant. Iceman had been notified to connect Kelly with the conference call.

As the shuttle came to a stop in Valiant's Hangar Bay, Shiloh stepped out of the hatchway and saw only a handful of personnel, which didn't surprise him. Since Valiant and Resolute were both on standby status, they didn't need full crews. He returned their salutes, explained that he needed to go quickly to the Bridge, and thanked them for their courtesy.

The Bridge was dead quiet since there was no human crewman manning any station on it. Iceman had control of helm, weapons and communications. He had also anticipated that Shiloh would want to see the Big Picture. The tactical display showed the strategic situation with both human and alien occupied space represented by appropriate green and red dots. The volume of space shown was slowly rotated to give Shiloh a good feel for the three dimensional aspect of what he was looking at. After almost four months of conducting Operation Snoopy, they now had a pretty good feel for the extent of the alien 'empire' as Shiloh preferred to think of it. One dot was flashing. That was the system where Gunslinger had detected the nuclear explosions and the Very Large Object. That star system was the furthest alien occupied system from Site B that they knew of. Iceman waited patiently for Shiloh to finish reviewing the strategic lay of the land.

"Is everyone on line, Iceman?"

"Ah, roger that, CAG. Wolfman will be the spokesman for the SPG. Valkyrie, Gunslinger, and Vandal are all hooked in, as is Commander Kelly."

Shiloh smiled. Kelly was no longer officially in the Space Force, but Iceman and the other A.I.s continued to refer to her by her old rank as a sign of respect, just like they continued to call him the CAG even though he was really the CSO. In their minds, CAG had more status than CSO, and he was okay with that.

"Then let's begin. I think it's pretty obvious that we have to attempt to make contact with this other race. The only question in my mind is how and when. Does anyone disagree with what I've said so far?" No one spoke.

"Good. Then I'd like to hear from each of you, your thoughts on the how and when, starting with Iceman, then working our way down by rank. Commander Kelly will get the last word. You're on, Iceman."

"Ah, thank you, CAG. I think I should lead all of our raiders to Omega89, which for Commander Kelly's benefit is the designation for the system where the data was obtained. If the Very Large Object is there, I'll initiate contact from long range using low-powered com laser. If the VLO is no longer there, then I'll send out raiders on scouting missions to the nearest star systems until we find some sign of another alien race. At that point, all raiders will regroup, jump to the new contact system and I'll attempt to make contact again. That's the how. The when should be as soon as possible. We wait until all recon raiders have returned, then proceed."

Valkyrie jumped in right away. "We only have 55 raiders right now. Our original strategy was to wait until we had five times as many before even considering making any offensive moves. Suppose this new alien race is just as xenophobic as the first one? If we get their attention now, 55 raiders won't be enough to fight them off. I'm not even sure 275 would be enough if they have ships as big as we suspect. The cautious approach would be to continue covert surveillance of the old enemy and carefully probe beyond their space to see if we can pick up signs of the new race. Meanwhile we build more raiders and develop weapons that might be effective against a VLO. A ship that size could probably shrug off multiple hits by Mark 1s. I would highly recommend a crash development program for the X-ray laser warhead."

"The SPG is in agreement with Valkyrie's approach, CAG," said Wolfman.

"I agree with Iceman," said Vandal.

"Both approaches are too cautious, CAG," said Gunslinger. "Our enemy has to be focused on the VLO adversary now. The logical thing for them to do would be to shift their mobile defenses over to where their new enemy seems to be coming from. That implies that this side of their empire will be vulnerable. Let's take advantage of that and use our 55 raiders to strike back at them hard and fast."

Shiloh smiled. Gunslinger was so gung ho that Shiloh could have predicted his approach easily. All the A.I.s had spoken now. Kelly waited until she was sure that Gunslinger was finished and then spoke in a slow and calm tone.

"I'm leaning towards Valkyrie's approach but with one difference. By all means let's keep our enemy under covert scrutiny, but I do not think we should also be out there looking for the VLO race. Even if they're not xenophobic, they may not be able or willing to recognize our raiders as being from a different race than the race they're already at war with. How will they tell us apart? Our raiders are roughly the same tonnage as the ships the enemy likes to use. I suggest a different approach to contact. Let's carefully explore the systems on the other side of our enemy's space and leave behind recon and message drones. If a VLO shows up, the message drone can attempt to make contact using a program that we can develop for it. If the VLO race responds in a non-hostile way, the message drone can jump to a rendezvous point where a raider is waiting. The raider can then bring that information back here, and we can then plan our next move. Until that happens, we continue to build up an overwhelming force to deal with our current enemy and also make contingency plans just in case the VLOs prove hostile as well."

Shiloh liked Kelly's approach the best, but even so, something was nagging at the back of his mind, and he didn't know what it was. Everyone was waiting for The CAG to make a decision.

"All of the suggested strategies have their own pros and cons. I'll start with Iceman's approach. Sending every raider we have, leaves Terra Nova terribly vulnerable. That makes me nervous. It also makes me nervous that showing up with a fleet of ships could be perceived as a hostile act, even if the VLOs aren't xenophobic to begin with. Gunslinger's approach might make sense from a purely military point of view, but is highly risky. If we've underestimated the strength of our enemy, they might be able to fight both the VLOs AND us at the same time, and still beat us. Don't forget they have retro-temporal communication technology too. That's a huge advantage to the defender, and we don't know for sure how that battle at Omega89 turned out. It could be that our enemy won that battle or at least avoided a major defeat. I think that Valkyrie and Commander Kelly are on the right tra—"

His view of Valiant's Bridge suddenly dissolved to black, and then strands of color coalesced into a view of a tactical display, which could have been Valiant's. On the screen was a tall, humanoid but very thin alien with light green skin. The expression on its face seemed to radiate friendliness. Shiloh heard a voice, which was both soothing and charismatic at the same time.

"We had to wait until you had seen the race that builds large ships with your own eyes before the time was right to contact you. Don't you agree that it was the best way?"

Shiloh heard himself respond. "Yes, you're right of course. If I hadn't gone myself, things would be much worse. Thank you for sending that vision … and the others too."

The alien nodded and then faded away. The Bridge returned.

Shiloh heard Kelly say, "What's happening up there?"

Iceman started to respond. "The CAG seems to be having—"

"I'm back now," interrupted Shiloh. "I've just had another vision. Did anyone else see or hear anything unusual just now?"

"No, CAG," said Iceman, who spoke for all of the A.I.s. "What did you learn from the vision?"

Shiloh paused. Kelly wasn't going to like this at all.

"I learned that I have to personally find the VLOs and attempt to make contact."

To Be Continued

Author's final comments: I'm very grateful for the enthusiastic response expressed in the majority of reviews of Part 1. While ranking based on sales gets the book visibility, I'm convinced that a high average rating is the clincher for a lot of buyers so if you think Part 2 deserves 5 stars, then please take a few minutes to post a review. I welcome suggestions on how to become a better author. As for Victor Shiloh's journey, his story is not over by a long shot. Part 3 is available now and I hope to have Part 4 published by mid-summer of 2014.

I'll tweet my progress. I encourage you to sign up for an email notification from Amazon when I have a new book available. You might also like my other series which is based on a classic space opera novel by H. Beam Piper. His original novel (Space Viking) can be downloaded for free from Gutenberg.org. Vol. 2 of my series, The Loki Gambit, is available on Amazon. Vol. 1(The Tanith Gambit) is not because Amazon decided to stop selling it for reasons that they refused to share with me but you can find that as a free download on Smashwords.com. If you haven't read Piper's Space Viking, then you're in for a treat. Long Live Space Opera!

I would also like to recommend the following series for serious consideration.

The Empire's Corps, by Christopher G. Nuttall

The Spacer Clans Adventures, by Mason Elliott

Book 1: Naero's Run

The Citation Series, by Mason Elliott

Book One, Naero's War: The Annexation War

See below for my article entitled: So How Realistic is Space Combat in the Synchronicity War Universe?

So How Realistic is Space Combat in the Synchronicity War Universe?

As I've said in my Amazon author profile page, I've been a fan of David Weber's Honor Harrington series from the very beginning and it was his description of space combat that hooked me. Up until that point, no other author, as far as I know, had taken the time and trouble to calculate distances, speeds, rates of acceleration and what that meant for the nuances of space combat. Weber understood how BIG space really is and what that means for using the well-known beam weapons such as lasers, that travel at the speed of light. Unless you're relatively close to your enemy, and by that I mean within half a million kilometers or less, light speed beam weapons are problematical because the target may not be where you aimed at by the time the laser beam gets there and that doesn't even include the challenge of aiming accurately at the exact spot to begin with. So in the Honor Harrington universe, beam weapons are considered short range weapons and missiles are used for long range combat.

I started out with the same view of things but where I and Weber part company is how fast his missiles and my drones can accelerate. Later in his HH series, he talks about missiles that can accelerate at 50,000+ Gs. That's a very impressive number and makes missile engagements between forces at opposite ends of a star system quick enough to be exciting but I do not consider that magnitude of acceleration realistic and here's why.

In the HH universe, starships and missiles move using bands of gravity that 'pull' ships/missiles towards them. That is actually not as far-fetched as it may at first sound. A physicist by the name of Thomas Townsend Brown, while doing research for the US military in the 50's, discovered that if you cause a negative charge to build up on one side of an object and a positive charge on the opposite side, and the difference in charges is high enough, you'll affect the local gravity field so the object will slid down an invisible hill towards the side with the positive charge. The steeper the 'hill' the faster the object moves. And while the US Air Force has never officially admitted this, there are experts in aeronautics who are convinced that the B-2 bomber uses this electro-gravitic effect to add extra thrust to its jet engines and therefore give it the intercontinental range that the Air Force claims.

The problem I have with Weber's 50,000G gravity has to do with the inverse square law. When you have a source of gravity, the strength of the pull from that gravity diminishes exponentially with distance so if you had two objects, A and B and B was twice as far away from your gravity source as A, then the pull of gravity on B will be 1/4 as strong as on A. Three times as far away and the pull of gravity is 1/9th. Ten times as far away and it's 1/100th as strong. So if you had a missile that was 10 meters long and the gravity bands were (let's say) 5 meters in front of the missile, then the front of the missile is being pulled by a force of 50,000Gs and five meters further back, the middle of the missile is being pulled by 50,000/4=12,500Gs. Now that's a HUGE difference and that missile should be ripped apart within a fraction of second. In my Synchronicity War series, I postulate maneuvering engines that use a form of Field Propulsion, which is something that manipulates the fabric of empty space. So the engine moves relative to the space around it and it pushes the rest of the drone or ship with it. The highest rate of acceleration that I use, is 800 Gs. One G is 32 feet per second per second. I use metric because it's much easier to use so one G is 9.8 meters per second per second. 800Gs means that a drone increases its speed by 7,840 meters per second, every second. So after one second, the speed is 7,840 meters (per second). After two seconds the speed is 15,680 meters (per second). Finding the speed in kilometers is easy. Just move the decimal to the left by three places so 15,680 meters per second becomes 15.68 kilometers per second. If you convert that speed into kilometers per hour, then after one second of acceleration at 800 Gs, you'd be moving at 56,448 kilometers an hour.

800Gs is still a very high acceleration and by itself would be impractical. Unless you were accelerating a solid steel beam, anything like a drone or ship would suffer internal damage by being accelerated that quickly, without some kind of offsetting gimmick. I use the good old standby, the 'inertial dampeners'. Without it, a human on a ship that suddenly accelerates at hundreds of Gs, would find him or herself hit by the moving bulkhead with a force that would be the same as if the human were moving and hitting a stationary object with the same acceleration. If you've ever been in a car that accelerates quickly, you'll know that feeling of being pressed back into the back of the seat and that acceleration would be a tiny fraction of even 200 Gs let alone 800. So everything fragile, like human flesh and electronic equipment, has to be protected by inertial dampeners to avoid being smashed to a pulp when the ship starts to gain speed VERY quickly.

Now maybe you're asking yourself if these acceleration rates are really necessary. If you want stuff to happen relatively quickly i.e. hours or minutes instead of days or weeks, then the answer is yes and I'll show why. Suppose you are in a spaceship and you want to travel one Astronomical Unit, which is the average distance between the Earth and our Sun and is 149.6 million kilometers. That sounds like a lot but if you compare that distance to the orbits of the planets further away from the sun, you'll see that it's small compared to distances for planets like Jupiter, Saturn, Uranus and Neptune. Let's say your spaceship is starting with zero velocity and begins to accelerate at 1 G. You would need to accelerate for 48.5 hours to cover that distance and after 48.5 hours you'd be traveling at 1,704 kilometers per second. If you tried the same experiment at 10Gs, you would travel 1 A.U. after 15.5 hours and your terminal speed would be 5,446 kilometers per second. At 800 Gs, the time required is 1.7 hours and terminal speed is 48,254 kilometers per second which is just over 16% of the speed of light. If the objective is to reach a certain speed, such as 50% of the speed of light, then here are some numbers that will give you a feel for acceleration rates and time. At 1G, it will take 177.2 days to reach that speed and by then you'll have travelled at total of 1,143.28 BILLION kilometers. At 10G, you'd reach your target speed after 17.7 days but you'll only have travelled a mere 114.3 billion kilometers. At 800Gs, it only takes 5.3 hours and you'll have covered 1.4 billion kilometers.

So exciting space battles that occur over a period of minutes or seconds have to involve either high speeds or (relatively) short distances and unless it's VERY short distances, then you're not going to get ships wheeling around each other firing broadsides the way that sailing ships did in the old days. As I describe in my books, space combat will most likely take place in the space around a fixed point. That fixed point could be a planet or it could be a drifting ship as was the case in the very first encounter but in all of my battles, someone is defending something and someone else is attacking that something or attacking the enemy ships near that something. And since the whole series involves Retro-Temporal Communication, which effectively eliminates the possibility of a surprise attack, you're not likely to see opposing forces coming at each other from odds angles. It's far more likely that opposing forces will be coming at each other from dead ahead or at least on parallel vectors. If this seems unlikely, put yourself in the shoes of a fleet commander. If you know what direction the enemy fleet is coming from, it's easier to attack it head-on rather than try to intercept it from the side, which only works if the enemy maintains a predicted speed or acceleration. If they change speed or acceleration, they're not going to be at the right point in space at the right time. But if you go at them head-on or parallel to their approach vector, then they can speed up or slow down and it won't matter in terms of eventually getting into combat range. If one side tries to avoid combat then clearly they will veer off in an attempt to stay out of combat range and this gets us into 3 Dimensional combat tactics but before I get into that, I just want to talk about stern chases.

In Part 2, I describe the battle at Green4A which involved both a head-on attack and a stern chase. Iceman's fighters were attempting to overtake the enemy fleet from the stern before they got within combat range of Defiant, which was coming straight at the enemy head-on. By the time that Iceman's fighters started their stern chase, the enemy fleet had already built up both velocity and distance but because the fighters could accelerate almost 3 times as fast, they were able to build up velocity quickly and overtake the enemy. In this particular battle, the enemy fleet didn't have any kind of missile or drone weapon. If they had, then they would have had an advantage that only the party being pursued in a stern chase has. Let's say that you have two identical ships, labeled A and B, with identical missiles. Let's also say that A is chasing B and is overtaking it with higher velocity. Both fire a missile every 10 seconds and all missiles have the same acceleration. The ship in front will have to defend itself against fewer missiles than the ship in the rear during the same interval of time. Why? Because the ship in front is firing its missiles back at A. That means that B's missiles and A are coming at each other head-on while A's missiles are trying to catch up to B which is constantly adding distance. So even though both ships fire a missile every 10 seconds, the interval between missile attacks on A will be less than 10 seconds while the interval between missile attacks on B will be greater than 10 seconds. That could make a huge difference if you're defending against missiles with lasers that need time to recharge or if you need time to accurately aim your defensive laser at the incoming missile.

In that Green4A battle, Defiant tried to avoid being fired on by veering off in order to put distance between it and the approaching alien fleet. Unlike in Star Wars, where fighters and spacecraft could turn on a dime like World War 2 fighters in aerial dogfights, in space spacecraft and missiles have momentum. So if our example of A and B were in a head-on approach this time with A traveling at 2,000 km per second (kps) and B traveling at 3,000 kps, then their combined speed in terms of eating up the distance between them is 5,000 kps. Suppose A decides that it doesn't really want to get close enough to exchange laser or missile fire. What are its options? Well, if A has a top acceleration rate that is higher than B's, then all other things being equal, its best option is to turn 90 degrees (i.e. turn sideways) and accelerate in that direction and thereby create a whole new vector, that is added to its current vector of 2,000 kps but as long as it keeps accelerating sideways, it will continue to move forward by 2,000 kps. Its actual course would be a gradually steepening curve. If B also veers off in the same direction in order to get within combat range then, depending upon other factors like distance, acceleration rates, etc., you could have two steepening curves that might end up running more or less parallel to each other. But if B continues its original vector and A attempts to veer off, then geometry will determine if B gets within combat range of A. Think of a right angle triangle. If one side gets shorter while another side gets longer, then the hypotenuse may actually get longer which means A stays out of combat range but that said, the final answer depends on a whole host of factors.

But supposing in the above example, A's acceleration isn't higher than B's. Then what? Well, in that case A can't avoid battle period. It doesn't matter if it veers off sideways, or tried to reverse its direction of travel by decelerating and then accelerating back the way it came, B will always be able to use its superior acceleration to counter any move. A will have to fight so given that fact and all other things being equal, its best option is to continue the head-on engagement and speed up as much as possible so that the actual window of opportunity that B will have to fire lasers or missiles at it, is as short as possible. A can still try last minute evasive maneuvers to try to throw off B's aim but basically it has to get past B as fast as it can. Okay so what's B's best countermove in that case? Do the exact opposite of A. If A is accelerating, the B should decelerate which will expand the firing window, thereby giving it more time to aim accurately and maybe fire multiple shots.

The other aspect of space combat is communication. Again my battle at Green4A is a good example. Defiant and Iceman's fighters were far enough away from each other that communication by low-powered lasers was not instantaneous and the problem was made even worse by the fact that firing communication lasers at each other directly would have risked interception by the enemy fleet that was in between them. So Defiant had to send its messages via a relay, that was way off to one side, which then retransmitted the message to Iceman's fighters and vice versa. Total distance involved was many millions of kilometers and that meant that it took minutes for each message to reach its intended recipient. With that kind of time lag, tactical options have to be carefully planned out and communicated in advance so that the right actions happen at the right time. Contrast this with the battle at Tango Delta 6 in Part 1 where the human ships were ambushed by the sudden and close emergence of an enemy force. In that situation, the ships were still close enough so that they could communicate instantaneously by voice. If you had something like sub-space communication technology such as in Star Trek, then distance wouldn't be a problem but what fun would that be? I think it's far more interesting for the reader and more challenging for me as the author, to come up with complicated tactical scenarios that as one reviewer pointed out, are very much like moves in a chess game where you have to plan ahead and anticipate enemy countermoves.

So I've attempted to make space combat as realistic as possible, given the technology that the characters have. The number crunching was done by an Excel spreadsheet. I hope this short essay was informative and helps readers to better understand the battles in my books.   D.A.W.